J U D I T H

C R Y B A B Y   B U T C H

a novel

Portions of this work previously appeared in The Massachusetts Review and the Harrington Lesbian Fiction Quarterly.

Firebrand Books gratefully acknowledges the following:

Epigraph from *Native Speaker* by Chang-Rae Lee, copyright (c) 1995 by Chang-Rae Lee. Used by permission of Riverhead Books, an imprint of Penguin Group (USA) Inc.

Passages from *Stone Butch Blues* reprinted by permission of SLL/Sterling Lord Literistic, Inc. Copyright by Leslie Feinberg.

Passage from "The Joys of Butch," by Susie Bright and Shar Rednour as published by Cleis Press in *Dagger: On Butch Women,* ed. Lily Burana, Roxxie, Linnea Due.

Epigraph lyrics from "World Falls" courtesy of the Indigo Girls.

Passages from *Bastard out of Carolina* courtesy of Dorothy Allison.

Cover Design by Jonathan Bruns
Book design by Jonathan Bruns

Printed in the United States

10 9 8 7 6 5 4 3 2 1

An application for cataloging has been filed with the Library of Congress.
Frank, Judith

Crybaby Butch by Judith Frank p.cm.
ISBN 1-56341-143-1

For Liz

I remember how Mitt liked to have the same book read to him each night for two or three weeks, how he would sit rapt with the tale and eventually murmur the words along with me, though on the first reading he would hardly listen and climb all over the bed and my shoulders and laugh frantically at the suspenseful moments, which for him began with the first *Once, long ago.* There is something universally chilling about a new plot.

    Chang-Rae Lee, *Native Speaker*

I'm looking for a sacred hand
To carve into my stone.

    Amy Ray, "World Falls"

PART ONE

CHAPTER ONE

Not a Harley butch, not a working-class he-she with a D-A; a soft-cheeked Kevin Costner butch, a Paul Mitchell hair products butch. Not a breast-binding butch, not a cigarette-pack-in-the sleeve butch, not a square-jawed butch with callused hands, not a handy butch; neither shattered nor wired: a glad-handing butch. Not off-kilter, not maddening, not hard to see: a sight-for-sore-eyes butch. But God help you: a cat under a human's touch butch, tail flickering. A guiding hand at the small of the back butch. A here, let me take that butch. A sleight-of-hand butch, between her thighs. A baby don't leave me butch.

After dinner, shuffling by in your slippers, you glance in and stop on a dime. Transfixed: she is crying. Alarm wails in you, then subsides; ah, she's watching *Rescue 911*. She's sitting cross-legged on the couch in pajama bottoms and a t-shirt, with the tissue box by her side. Dabbing at her eyes, with an elaborate self-mocking clown-grimace, she gestures at the television and says, "It's so sad." Some ordinary citizens have been roused from the torpor of the everyday. At first they thought the cry was children at play; at first they were annoyed by the ruckus; at first they explained away the strange apparition. But now they have pulled a woman from a burning car, wrested a child from a flash flood, risked life and limb for a panicked puppy, fashioned makeshift ropes, harnesses, tourniquets, and slings out of their clothes. You sit down next to her and put your hand on her leg, because your femme in tears is cause for interruption of your work, your rest, or your prayer. She didn't ask you to.

What kind of hurt is this welling up in her eyes? What kind of girl is this, easily crying? You run your hand over her flanneled thigh, pressing at the knee, imagining touching her warm wet core, imagining some final perfect gallantry. An unkind person — such as the femme herself in certain moods — might say you are pawing your femme as she tries to watch television. It's a fact that at any moment you could turn into an oaf.

Later, there is always a reunion. The rescued person does not have brain damage, and the spinal cord was spared. Since his rescue, his relatives tell us from their fishing boat or their backyard barbecue, he is more sober, more happy-go-lucky, more appreciative, more careful. The rescuers couldn't look more homely, with their white freckled balloon faces and their babies crawling everywhere. The two of you sit there quietly, scrutinizing, marveling. She pulls her hand away gently. They're speaking in code, a language you could easily repeat by rote but can't quite crawl inside of. Those set-piece speeches can't answer the things you need to know. How saving a life made a difference. What life was like after being saved. Whether there will be a reunion.

You were never like the rest of the girls, you beat the boys at all their games. You fled when ordered to wear a dress, brooded in your private hiding place, played the husband when you played house, skinned your knees, kissed the pretty girl next door, were looked at askance. You wish that at sixteen, holding your breath, you'd walked into your first gay bar and seen women like yourself. That you'd been astounded, sized-up, mentored. For lack of imagination, or audacity, it didn't happen that way. It took another ten years for a femme to take you home, to teach you that you'd always known what to do.

The butch you jokingly call your sponsor is a slim blue-jeaned butch with a ponytail and a baseball cap. When she leans against a fence, legs crossed at the ankle, hands shoved in her pockets, your adolescence wafts back to you, warmer, like Indian summer. She gives you things to read about butches, which your eyes gallop over so madly that you dizzy yourself. She says slyly, "If you weren't a butch I would have snapped you up long ago," and you snort "Oho! You would, would you!" She says "Wear it like this"; she says "Face it girl, you were born to serve." She slides her wallet out of her back pocket and peels off bills with the unconscious charisma of a young dad. When her lover wants her to play yet another sexual role, she consolidates instead, putting Eddie the male hooker and Howard the suburban husband in the same men's group. She says "If you wear it around all the time it will come to feel like a part of your body." She calls you "my best butch buddy," and just once — heartbreakingly — "doll." She's a rude butch, who thinks her dick is bigger than everyone else's; over time, you learn that you can parlay your own hesitancy in this regard into what looks like a quiet self-assurance.

You have to be at the restaurant in fifteen minutes to meet a friend, but my, your femme looks luscious as she folds laundry on the bed. It is still early in your affair, when love has made her radiantly beautiful, and you gaze at her in astonishment.

You come up behind her and throw her on the bed, landing hard beside her, and reach for the button on the fly of her jeans; you unbutton and unzip them quickly and slide your hand in, down her smooth round belly and under the elastic of her underwear. Her head lifts tensely out of a pile of unfolded whites. She clutches at your hand in alarm and says What are you doing? You whisper It's okay, let me, it's okay, I am here with you. Come, you think, on this carnival ride with me.

You push your hand firmly down her jeans, knuckles scraping the hard seam at the crotch. Then reach in with two fingers, stroking, burrowing into her, feeling for moist spots. Your fingers sting where you have chewed the skin.

She still has that worried look, as she moves and adjusts to your hand. She closes her eyes as if against the sight of a misery and clutches at your shirt. All the while you're whispering, coaxing. Her thighs start to grip your wrist, and your hand starts to cramp as it moves inside and around her. *Now?* Now. *Now?* You tell her when, and she comes. Your heart freefalls, wings at full expanse.

You lie there, breathing hard. She sighs as you ease your cramped fingers out of her, and grins, her eyes still closed. You laugh, and flex your sore sticky hand. A few minutes later you gently kiss her once more and leave for the restaurant with her smell still on you.

So you know what she wants, alright. You are a cocky butch with the smell of cunt on your hands. But you can't help but wonder, backing out of the driveway: What if it hadn't worked? What if she had thrown you off her — as later, she will — with real fury? Well then you would have stopped. But without the final resounding okay, what would you have been to her? You might have had to throw your hands up in surrender. You might have had to go limp all over. You're like a ghetto kid who has made it to the NBA: if you weren't an awfully lucky butch you might be a criminal.

What did you do before you knew what to wear? It takes some courage to conjure that girl in peasant skirts, high-waisted slacks, blouses with shoulder pads, pumps, a pocketbook. Better to think you were always like this. A friend of yours once spoke derisively about a woman she knew who had learned to tie a scarf by reading fashion magazines. Better to have always known, to have fingers genetically predispositioned to scarf-tying, to not have to face your own gross hapless self. It was only years later, thoughtfully fingering your first necktie, that you realized your fingers had their own disposition and their own memories. Tying a necktie you know from your father, who died eighteen years before you had occasion to tie your own necktie. He must have let you tie his ties, you realized, your heart stopping just for a moment: you must have stood between his legs as he sat, working with clumsy kid's fingers, breathing through your mouth.

What did you do before you knew what to wear? Before you discovered with such pleasure your own fine appraising eye? It seems like such a small thing, to know what to lay against your breathing flesh. But you've learned that when you greet the question of what to wear with thoughtful pleasure, your life has changed forever. With most things you've had to acquire your taste; in this, you discovered a taste that seemed already formed and waiting, and looked over new expanses of cut and fabric with a wild surmise. It feels as though you never even had to practice, although in truth you have made some mistakes over time.

Some days you want your shirt open wide at the neck, to look like a smooth-chested teenaged boy. Some days you won't wear a necktie, only a bolo tie; some days you will wear a necktie, but only loosely, with the top button of your shirt unbuttoned. Some days you go softer butch, because you feel so square cut and buttoned up inside that the actual items of clothing make you look as though you're trying too hard, as though you're trying, and failing, to look like a man. But some days you are not wearing three items of women's clothing. Some days you wear men's jockey shorts, but never on the days you have a chiropractor appointment. Some days you're sauntering down the street in a three-piece suit, a fine figure of a butch; but you're crampy from your period, and your pants are a tiny bit tight in the thigh.

You learn to accommodate to small humiliations. Just because you're a butch doesn't mean you can open every jar. You learn to be modest, not to say, "Why just give that here, little lady," but to wait till it's offered to you. So if you fail, it looks truly impossible, and if you succeed, it looks like *voilà*! a butch to the rescue! Men must know this trick, at least the men you like: carelessly letting their authority spin to the floor, then snapping it back into their hand. At ease, hands not in fists but cupped and open and held aloft, doves fluttering out of them and up to the rafters.

She knows the infield fly rule. And she knows why it's good if a runner gets on first with less than two out and the pitcher coming up (you are National League girls; you have taught her to scorn the designated hitter). "Because then he can bunt," she once said, "right?" "Right," you answered, "but say it this way: 'because then he comes up in a bunting situation.'"

She laughed: "A bunting situation," she said, with relish. And then later, at various moments during the summer, glancing at the TV, "Look honey, a bunting situation!"

But her favorite thing about sports is when they fall down; this makes her shriek with delight.

One day, before you were living together, you came over and flipped on the TV to the first round of the NCAA basketball tournament. It was Princeton and Georgetown, and you blinked incredulously when you saw the score: improbably low, and tied, with five minutes to play. What? Your perception was screwed up; maybe you were in a dream. But no: those Princeton boys were playing an ornate passing game, and the Georgetown players — disoriented or just hugely bored — were flailing at them with helpless grace. She came into the room as you were standing close to the TV, and stood next to you. You explained the significance of this moment, what a huge upset it would be. She nodded, impressed, and the two of you sat down on the edge of the bed to watch it play out.

When Georgetown pulled it out in the final minutes, she hit you on the arm and burst into tears. "Why did you get me so involved?" she cried. You laughed, bewildered; it was just a basketball game. The thing is, when she gets involved, she can't detach, even for a moment. You put your arm around her and with the other hand you snapped your fingers, showing the proper amount of time it should take to detach after your team loses.

One morning the four-year-old son of a good friend asks you which one of you is the mommy and which is the daddy. You had spent the night there; you were leaning against the kitchen counter and drinking coffee with your hair sticking straight up, while she was still sleeping. You started in on some rigmarole about how sometimes you're the mommy and sometimes you're the daddy and sometimes you switch off and it's very fluid, when she walked sleepily into the room in her pajamas and asked "What's the question?" You told her. She waved her hand and said breezily, "Oh that's easy, she's the daddy," and walked into the bathroom. You hit yourself on the forehead with the heel of your hand. Duh. What had you been thinking?

She's the one who fixes things, the one with special competencies. So people say, Oh, but you guys also swap roles. But at those moments you couldn't be farther from feeling as though you're swapping roles. The femme sitting cross-legged on the floor with a slight sweat mustache, screwing furniture together: the more butch she looks, the more transcendently femme she looks. You can only see one way. Sometimes your friends recoil from you as from a fanatic; and indeed, you have been soaked in a vision. She's standing there in sneakers and her jean jacket, impatiently jingling the car keys. Hey girl, she's saying in the quick tilt of her head, c'mon, let's hit the road. And here's what you see:

> a woman who's going to take you for a ride
> dark curls against a smooth white neck
> a woman you would like to delay, insolently
> yourself leaning back in the passenger seat and sighing
> your legs easing open
> her fingers unfurling around the keys
> your face smothered in denim

You don't see her as a femme right away, maybe. You feel out in your head how you could be a butch to her, your fingers running expertly over the braille of your own hunger.

"No," you say firmly, moving her hand away, "not like that." Haven't you said this a million times before? Why can't you get the touch you want?

Her wrist stiffens and she pulls away, ostentatiously reaching for her book on the night table. You blow dust off an ancient shard: way back in the archeological layers of your time together, she touched you with a doubting hand, and when you pulled away in disappointment, your hearts sank and you entered a stone age. You are in a stone cycle, and it is vicious indeed.

She's so different, easily offering herself to you, turning rosy and convulsing as you whisper in her ear; and often, your hands and mouth glistening and the petals of your heart unfurling, you are glad and satisfied. But sometimes there's a rebellious murmur inside you, and you wonder what it would take to get *you* to that place. You've tried. Touched by her, you've gripped her hair and started flipping through the Rolodex of your fantasies — the ones with the shuddering femme; with the handcuffed football players, horny and grass-stained; with the astonished teenager, ass clenching as an older woman unzips his chinos; with Batman bound and watching Robin get violated by the Joker's henchmen; with the women forced to their knees; with everything in them but yourself. You've lain there anxiously flipping from one to the other, listening for that fine high note in the distance, not yet audible, trying to imagine it forcefully into existence. But it's no use; you trust only your own practiced hand.

You try not to believe it's because you're the better lover, so much more attuned to her, but secretly you do believe that. You lie under her hands staring at the bugs in the bowl of the halogen lamp, imagining her to be bored or faintly disgusted or maybe just selfish. You hate her for the diffidence of her hands.

She is back from Christmas with her family, overfed and under-recognized, her face a little greasy. She has a slightly marionettish quality; she walks off the plane, her jaw moving on its hinges, saying things like *alrightee then* and *okee-dokee.* They spent the whole time telling stories about some make-believe daughter, and changing the subject when she alluded to her actual life. They're not so happy with the queer she has become. You know that when they think of you, they think: *bulldagger.* At home you put her in a hot tub with a magazine and a glass of ice water, and wait for her to quake back to life. When she does, she'll cry out and clutch you, and her tears will soak the neck of your grateful shirt. You'll recognize each other again. Till then, you patrol the place like a sentinel.

When she towels off, you peek in and see a gleam of something like affection, or maybe hostility, in her face. You follow her into the bedroom — you can't help yourself — get into bed with her and, feeling the chill of the sheets on your bare legs, take her hand. You offer her a neat breakdown of the problem into component parts, capping it off with six or seven solutions. If only she'll make her needs known; if only she'll take the bull by the horns. She regards you thoughtfully, and says she'd like to write a sitcom about you, in which every episode is about someone you know having a problem, and your coming in and fixing it. It would be called by your name, and have a theme song about how you can solve every problem in a minute.

One day she takes you with a cold fury. Ties you up and fucks you with a vibrator, at the same time that, with a gloved and lubricated finger, she fucks you for the first time in the ass. This gets your attention. You are riveted in place and also going through the roof. It takes a little while for you to come down and get organized enough to come. Afterward you turn on your stomach, your fists balled under you, slathered with your own excitement. You turn your face to her — oh, she's so smug, holstering her pistols after she blows at their smoking tips — and ask with your eyes stinging and a laugh burbling up from your throat, "What was *that?*"

She never does it to you again, even though you ask her to.

When you cry, you hear yourself crying in her voice. You feel your face crumple like hers, feel as though you're looking out through her streaming eyes. Crying is a language whose grammar you're only just learning, so for now you're imitating your best teacher. So much crying! You're a crybaby butch, giddy from crying. You learn to be seen crying, caught just as the tears swoop into your throat; you learn to breathe evenly, skimming atop the huge racking surf inside you. After a few weeks the skin under your eyes starts to burn. A recently-divorced friend recommends Puffs Plus, because, she says, they have lotion in them and though that makes them a little gross, they're easy on the skin. She takes you aside and says confidentially, "Hon, this is not the time for recycled products."

They can overcome you at any time, these tears. They're having their way with you.

Your face is so blotchy and sore you go to the linen closet and pick up the blue corn facial mask. "What would you like to dress up as?" she asked you one night, holding it in one hand, and parsley mint facial mask in the other: "A tortilla chip or a leg of lamb?" You were in trouble, in your last months together, and you were about to go away for a week, to get a life, as she had requested. And what she taught you was how to put on a facial mask. She joshed you into repeating the steps aloud: steam, apply, rinse, moisturize. You sat on the bed in your underwear with your faces immobile watching *Nick at Night,* wisecracking out of the sides of your mouths. She wore a towel as a turban, and you wore a headband she fashioned for you out of an old pair of nylons, to push back your short hair.

You repeat the steps aloud. You feel the good cold burn of the mask. What would you like to dress up as? You sit down on the bed, acclimating to the pungent smell of cosmetics as the mask hardens and hardens. You put your hand tentatively to your cheek, and a little bit of it crumbles in your hand.

C H A P T E R   T W O

Her Legacy speeding westbound over the Indiana Tollroad, Anna's stomach came up and crowded around her heart, and she inhaled sharply to get herself breathing again. It was Labor Day, a hot summer afternoon; she was driving through farmland and sand dunes, eyeing the smoke mushrooming in the pale sky ahead of her, readying herself for the plunge into the filthy haze of Gary. From two stacks in the distance, flames spurted into the sky. When she was little, her family sang "Gary Indiana" from *The Music Man* whenever they drove through Gary, the showy swing of "my home sweet home!" broken by an incredulous "Eeeeww!" from her and her brother as the stench enveloped them. She passed three huge billboards, each one blank. Then, although the windows were rolled up and the air conditioner on, the smell started seeping through. The mill was gargantuan and chaotic, a rusted-out erector-set city. It was clearly working, but there was a demolished look to it; in places, it appeared to be on fire. It scared and amazed her. She was on her way home to Chicago, driving through desolation and dragon-fire; she could only breathe through her mouth and hit the gas.

How could people stand to live here? Passing Gary always infuriated her, the rank fact of social immobility pressed up against her prickling nose. Just as she was starting to snuff at the air like those wet dogs on Foster Beach, a mere forty miles away. At this moment Anna herself was shiny-coated and bright-eyed, a little prone to drool. The world through her windshield was as vivid and unreal as a movie set. She was mourning her girlfriend, Patricia, who had left her three weeks ago. She had bowed her head and committed herself to time; she had let grief fill her till she quivered.

She turned to the R&B station, and heard the silky bass voice of the DJ. Once she had driven past Gary and it had smelled like french fries. Once she had seen, a little past the city in gray stagnant pools, a flock of wild swans, and at the sight of nature her heart had swelled right up. Down to her right, boys were playing on a weedy and unkempt baseball diamond. How did they stand at the plate peering undemoralized through the haze at the ball coming toward them? Tomorrow she'd force herself to take a run along the lake, and it would be a heaving slate against a blue sky, or maybe glassy and even lighter than the pale lowering sky, almost milky. And gulls would be grouped on the shore, their white breasts flashing against the water, or they'd be cawing and beating against the wind at eye level, almost at a standstill as it gusted against them.

And not far from the lake, her apartment, which she dreaded entering. What would be gone? Would the stereo be there? Patricia had bought it by strong-arming her usually-neglectful parents into giving her money for her birthday. The kitchen table? Anna's throat ached from scared speculation. When Patricia made it clear that the breakup was final, which took her a few days to assimilate – they'd had so many fights, and there was still so much love, and she was working so hard to be a person Patricia would want to stay with – Anna had fled. Huddling with her best friend Scott in upstate New York, she took several baths a day, choked down milkshakes with vitamin supplements in them, and was trundled by him to his health club, where she moved her legs on the treadmill, her mind a terrible blank. When their friend Terry heard about it, she yelled at Scott for letting Anna run on a treadmill, feeling that it was bad symbolism.

She was approaching the exits for Hammond. Right around here: she scanned the streets below, past the row houses to the main strip, looking for a Holiday Inn she was pretty sure she wouldn't find. In the distance, small wisps of white smoke ribboned into the sky from the mills along the lake. About ten years ago, she had been driving on this

19

road and when she saw the Holiday Inn she had thought: *Oh!* She wasn't sure how she knew that that's where her father had killed himself, having been just twelve when he died, and fending off the details the best she could. Maybe it was simply in the family memory. She wondered what advantage, fiscal or legal, he had gained from committing suicide out of state. Since that time, she had never been able to find the hotel again. Either it had been demolished, or her memory was mistaken. She thought of David Lambeau's father, who had asked to have his ashes scattered at an old vacation house in the Adirondacks — and how when David got there with the surprisingly heavy urn in his trunk he realized that his father had designated as his final resting place, the place of his eternal dreams, the wrong house.

Men were fishing in the little lakes, on man-made piers. In the distance she saw the girders and the arc of the long steel bridge, the Skyway looping into Chicago. Without Patricia, what would her life be like? Over time, so much had happened. Sickness, debt, the death of their beloved cat George, learning literary theory, non-monogamy, couples therapy, the job market. "Remember when...?" she would ask Patricia, and "Remember that time?" She was like a child asking for the story of the day she was born. One night during a downpour they were sitting together in southbound traffic on Lake Shore Drive, inching forward and squinting at the road through the streaming windshield, and Patricia turned a blank face toward her and said, "Remember everything that's ever happened to us?"

Anna sped up the bridge's incline. To her left church steeples speared the sky, mills and factories clustered behind them, and on the other side, down in the distance and glittering along the lake, the Chicago skyline. She was atop this whole city topography in her cool throbbing car, its churning gut behind her, its scrubbed face down below. Then she was dumped onto the Dan Ryan, passed rows of tenements and shiny, empty Comiskey Park. A billboard read *Who's the father? 1-800-DNA-TYPE,* its print decorated by white sperm. She bore all the way to the right, shot onto the Stevenson, then, her neck craned and her heart racing, immediately cut to the leftmost lane across three lanes of traffic to get onto Lake Shore Drive. She passed the stately institutions of tourist Chicago. Past them, on her left, parks and shimmering skyscrapers, and a few minutes ahead, traffic starting to thin, ornate brick highrises, slightly darkened by car exhaust. On her right rollerbladers, bikers, runners, sunglasses and Walkmen, dogs loping on leashes. An armada of sailboats, white against a white sky. The lake pale, lapping mildly against the shore.

Exiting from the Drive, Anna drove past her one-way street and looped around. She nosed the car down Wayne Ave., looking for parking and watching for children darting into the street; she had a horror of her white lesbian self running over a child of color, the collision witnessed by the entire neighborhood association. It had been a good era of apartment building: the three-story brick buildings had apartments with big rooms and porches, formal dining rooms, bay windows, and off the ends of the courtyard buildings, glassed-in sunrooms.

Kids were sitting on stoops; clusters of men stood around the raised hoods of cars with their hands in their pockets, consulting. The block looked shabby, wilted by late summer; the lawns were littered by popsicle wrappers, husks of discarded *elotes*, beer bottles. She had come to love her street in both its shabbiness and its occasional glory, when the setting sun glowed on red and yellow brick, or when the late-afternoon sky darkened, wind and thunder whipped and rumbled, and the trees lit up like neon. Sometimes, lying on the couch in their apartment on winter afternoons, she looked out the window at the lacy arc of tree branches patterned against the sky. The neighborhood was in a state of early gentrification; it had a mix of Mexican families and young professionals of different races, and rainbow stickers dotted car bumpers and apartment windows. In the apartment building closest to Ridge, where black families still lived, a police cruiser was often observed driving slowly up the street and around the alley. On the other side of her building, down the next block, which was lined by large brick and stucco single-family houses, nice weather brought roofing and landscaping trucks, and parking was made difficult by large temporary dumpsters loaded with tiles, shingles, empty paint cans, large branches.

There was a space right in front of her building. They had always thought Patricia had a parking angel, but after three weeks of outstanding parking in Ithaca, Anna was beginning to suspect that the angel was hers. She would wait to judge, though: it was still untested by city streets. She popped the trunk, took out her bag, and, slinging it over her shoulder, walked up the walk trying not to think of anything. Her mail had been held. She went upstairs and opened the door.

The apartment was warm and close. There were two notes by the phone. She grabbed the one in Patricia's handwriting first.

Hi —

Here's a check for my half of next month's rent. You can bill me for my share of last month's phone and utilities, c/o Tracy.

P.

Anna put the note down, her eyes stinging. There was absolutely nothing in it, no matter how hard she marshaled her considerable close-reading skills, to suggest that Patricia was sorry or uncertain about leaving. Or even cared about her at all. And she knew that Patricia had purposely crafted it that way. Her hurt was laced with indignation. It was so typical of Patricia to act curt and severe, when it was Anna whose heart had been broken.

The other note was from Janice:

Hi hon! So glad you're back safe and sound. Everything seems fine here, and I watered the plants this morning. Come over for dinner tonight, okay?

She went into the living room. Patricia had left the couch, but had taken the coffee table; Anna looked miserably at the pressed squares in the carpet where its legs had stood. The TV was still there but the TV cart wasn't, so the TV sat on the rug. The stereo was gone, and so were Patricia's books from the built-in shelves. Anna's own books had toppled into the emptied spaces. She had a thought, and went quickly into the bedroom. The bed was gone. In its place was the air mattress, which Patricia had taken out from their storage space, inflated, and made up. Conjuring that — some moment of Patricia's bustling around imagining herself to be considerate – made Anna so faint with defeat that she had to sit down, right where she had been standing, on the floor. She wondered if she would find dishes and silverware in the kitchen, and started to cry. Where would she get the money to replace all these things? Technically, the missing things were, it was true, Patricia's, furnishings she had brought with her into the relationship. And yet, Patricia was beginning a new job at the University of Wisconsin for over $45,000 a year, while Anna would be making less than half that much. Patricia could have cut her some slack; how much did she have to take away from her?

She had to get out of the house. Anna lurched to her feet. She yanked the dresser drawers open and found half of them empty. She peeled off her t-shirt and wiped her face with it. She had lost weight; her shorts slipped off as soon as she unzipped them, and she kicked them off her ankles. She ran the shower and got in, put her head under and ran her hands over her hair. Normally buzzed on the back and sides, it was shaggy and ragged. She would get it cut at the end of the week. She liked looking a little like a marine, but didn't want to walk into her first classes like that.

Warm and moist from cooking, in shorts and a tank top, Janice greeted her at the door with a bear hug, and for a moment Anna pulled up anchor, releasing herself into firm human touch, tears pressing hard at her face. "We are so glad to see you," Janice murmured into her ear. Anna smelled garlic and cumin, and the mysterious product that produced the Janice-smell she loved so much. Just minutes after Patricia walked out, Janice had come to pick her up for a movie and found her in her bathrobe, sobbing; she had sat with her on the couch holding her hand, asking in bewilderment, "Are you sure this is for good?" She had been stalling, holding out for a misunderstanding, or a technicality. She was completely unprepared for the tornado of grief that had met her at the door. As Anna sat there bawling, her eyes and nose streaming, she knew that she had already left Janice way behind, and it made her feel hard. She was crossing into new terrain, into alpine tundra, where the only growing things were scrubby, shrinking from the wide wide sky.

"Sorry, hot peppers," Terry greeted her in the kitchen, holding up her latex-gloved hands, which were glistening and dotted with seeds. "We're having Indian food." She offered Anna a kiss on the cheek, and momentarily rested her face against hers. Anna, who would have preferred a more meaningful greeting, felt a little wounded. Terry was a person with pointy edges: vivid dark eyebrows, hair slanting sharply down over her forehead, a decisive opinion the moment she walked out of a movie theater. Anna helped herself to a can of Diet Coke from the refrigerator, standing for a moment in its cool air staring at the organized abundance inside. She closed it and slid down the wall, seating herself on the linoleum and popping open the can. The ceiling fan was whirring, and from the window opening onto the alley came the noise of salsa music and engines.

"How was your time in Ithaca? Did that skinny homosexual take good care of you, or was he too busy writing some important, cutting-edge article?" Terry didn't like Scott. She disliked his glinting intelligence, and how he liked ideas to be as complicated as possible. Once they had gotten high together and he had spent the whole time quoting *Paradise Lost* at her from memory, at very close range, meaning and pathos suffusing his face, while she tried to swat him away and enjoy her buzz. And once when they were at his apartment, Janice had spent half an hour talking him down from an anxiety attack — using every resource of empathy and cunning she possessed — and he had promptly picked up the phone, called someone else, and started the whole thing over in the exact same way. Scott was half-Japanese; Terry called him "Pearl Harbor."

"It was sort of like that movie *Weekend at Bernie's*," Anna said; "I feel like he lugged me places and set me down and arranged all my limbs in the proper position." She mimed him standing back and appraising her with his hands held up, ready to catch her if she keeled over.

Terry snorted, and rubbed her nose with her forearm. "How's he doing in Ithaca?" Janice asked. "What can I do, honey?" she asked Terry.

"He likes the job a lot, but he feels isolated from gay folks."

"Here, stir," Terry said, handing Janice a wooden spoon. "Why? There are gay folks in Ithaca, aren't there? I thought it was a progressive town."

"It is, but it's still a little town. Not a scene like here." Anna found herself working up a head of explanatory steam on Scott's behalf, but then stopped. What was she doing trying to convince Terry of his need for sympathy, when she herself had trouble sympathizing with the man who had gotten the best job that year?

Terry scraped the peppers into the sizzling pan, peeled off the gloves with her thumb and forefinger, and tossed them into the garbage while Janice moved in to stir. "Whew, sweaty," she said, rinsing her hands in cold water. "We're almost ready."

"So we promised that if we were still alone at 50, we'd sleep together."

"Oh, yuck," Terry said.

Anna looked up at the back of Janice's neck as she stirred and the smoke of garlic and hot peppers started to permeate the kitchen. Janice's brown hair was gathered up and loosely pinned, a few moist strands sticking to her neck. Femme heaven, the back of the neck — the first place she had kissed Patricia, feeling the tiny soft hairs against her lips. Terry added a bowl of sliced cabbage, which hit the pan with a hiss. Anna breathed in, felt her sinuses start and prickle. The pop and sizzle of the cooking, a horn honking outside, her underarms starting to stick, her friends' voices murmuring instructions and advice. They weren't listening to her yet, but she knew that later they would.

A few minutes later Terry was holding out a plate for her. "Here, take this," she said, "and help yourself." Anna hauled herself to her feet. "Here's the rice, and this is cauliflower and potato curry, and this is the cabbage."

The dining room was cooler. Anna chewed the curry thoughtfully, as though having been asked to taste squid, or iguana, for the first time. It ran races over her palate. Over the past few weeks, she had wondered what it was she liked to eat. She felt sure only about food familiar from her childhood, so Scott had strapped her into the front seat of the car and taken her to the supermarket, where they stocked up on peanut butter and jelly, Jell-O, boxes of macaroni and cheese. She had stood in the cereal aisle staring at the breakfast foods. When she was little, she remembered, she had loved Pop-Tarts. It had always been hard to decide whether to toast them or eat them untoasted, both ways being equally delicious. Recently she and Patricia had seen a commercial for a Pop-Tart-like product, which distinguished itself by claiming that unlike the other nearly-identical products, its fruit was not exposed. Patricia had hooted: "Now *there's* a problem we hadn't considered: exposed fruit!"

The sautéed cabbage made her sputter. "Oh man," she laughed, tears streaming down her face, which already felt rubbed and raw. "Are you okay?" Janice asked, handing her water.

"I think my face just exploded." She drained the glass and sat back, panting.

"When do you get back to work?" Terry asked.

Anna swallowed and cleared her throat. "Pathways starts tomorrow."

"And how're you feeling about that?" Janice asked carefully. They knew Anna was crushed that she hadn't gotten a university job, and was chafing at the idea of herself as an adult basic education teacher. Terry didn't get it, or more likely, Anna thought, refused to get it. "Oh I know it's not what you were trained for," she'd say, "but it's such good work, what could be more important?" For her part, Anna believed that Terry, who was a caseworker at an AIDS clinic, just disliked academics; she often mocked Janice and her friends about the words they used. "What can I say?" Anna had once said irately, last May, when she was deciding whether to take the job at Pathways. Her last academic chance, a job at the University of Tennessee that she didn't want anyway, had fallen through in April. "That I want the perks and prestige of an academic job? That all my friends got jobs and I'm the only shmuck who didn't? That I want educated and challenging students? That I never imagined myself being paid by the hour?"

Terry had called her an elitist. "No shit," Anna had snapped.

"I'll tell you," Anna said, "at the moment I can't imagine dragging

26

myself into a classroom."

"You'll do it," Janice said, nodding her head encouragingly. "You'll do it because you're really good at it and it'll make you feel better."

Anna sighed. "Okay, let's change the subject," she said.

"Oh!" Terry brightened. "Janice, you have to show Anna the present your mother got you. Oh, go on," she scolded, as Janice's shoulders crumpled. Janice's mother Phyllis was an anthropologist at the University of Maryland, who had recently decided to study the practice of fisting among dykes in San Francisco. This had stunned Janice and her friends. No one in their cohort had ever had such an experience with a parent, unless you counted Mike Ferguson, whose mother was the head of PFLAG Ohio.

Janice got up and left the room, returning with a book in her hand, which she handed to Anna with a stoic expression. "Hey!" Anna cried as laughter broke across her face, "*Her Tongue on My Theory*, by Kiss and Tell!"

Janice gave her a look. "It was my birthday present. Can you believe her?"

Still laughing, Anna scooted back her chair and crossed her legs at the ankle. She thumbed through the glossy book, looking at the pictures of naked body parts and women doing it to each other. She began to read aloud, a passage with a lot of fucking and screaming in it.

"Shut up," Janice said.

"Shouldn't you have a little talk with your mom?" Anna asked, peeking at Terry. Terry gave her a resigned look. Janice hated conflict. Her stories about her life always had a tightly-woven plot about all the minute yet viciously-inevitable circumstances that made it absolutely impossible for her to do otherwise than the grotesque thing she was being asked to do: sleep on the couch for two weeks while her visiting parents slept in her bedroom, ferry other people's badly-behaved children all over town during rush hour; go to a church service where the sermon was against homosexuality, and where she couldn't get up and walk out because there was a man in a wheelchair blocking the end of her pew. And not just do those things, but receive no credit or recognition for them. She hadn't ever gone through the to-hell-with-them phase of family relations, that cold ardent pulling back that Anna and Terry considered vital to any healthy functioning in the future.

But then again, Anna and Terry had both been braced by plenty of parental homophobia. Terry, whose mother refused to acknowledge any of her lovers, loved to riff on their telephone conversations to her friends:

"How are you?"

"Janice and I are fine, we're doing really well."

A long pause; Terry would mime looking into the phone receiver.

"How's work?" her mother would finally ask.

"Pretty good, although Janice just started *her* new job, so things are a little crazy around here."

"And Jake?"

"Fat: Janice has put him on a diet."

Then her mother would chatter about the dogs and the progress of the tomatoes in the garden, and complain fondly about her husband Frank, who was procrastinating about cleaning out the garage, tuning her out as he watched his football games, making a mess with his new power tools, unable to boil water, acting just like a man. Terry would perform for her friends the mighty clenching of her teeth those stories provoked. Her friends would call out: "Janice had a garden in her last house!" "Janice bought me a drill for Christmas!" "Janice hates it when I act just like a man!"

Later, Anna lay on their couch with her head bolstered by pillows and her feet in Janice's lap. Their cat Jake lay on her stomach. Janice and Terry had names for all of his various positions, which Anna found a little cloying: this one they called "meatloaf."

"Okay you guys," Anna said, "tell me, has Patricia left yet?"

Janice and Terry exchanged glances. "She just left yesterday," Janice said. She hesitated. "If it's any comfort, honey, she's devastated too."

"It's not any comfort," Anna said. They sat silently, Terry sipping her wine and Anna feeling the weight of Jake on her stomach as she breathed. "She took the bed, for Christ's sake."

There was another pause, and Anna's eyes filled at the thought that Patricia had no doubt consulted with Janice and Terry, given them her side of the story; she could see her nervous, expressive face as she spoke, disarming them with pained spurts of hilarity. Maybe they had even told her that it was her right to take the bed; maybe they had even helped her *move* it.

Finally, Janice offered, "You have a lot of friends who love you."

"I know," Anna wavered, letting her change the subject. Friends, these days their colors were pushing through like hologram pictures, making her ashamed at how she had let them recede. "Remember Scott's goodbye song when he moved to Ithaca?" She sang, "Make new friends, and dump the old; One is silver and the other mold."

They laughed. "That's the same guy, though," Anna said, "who crawled into bed with me one morning and kissed me on the mouth and said 'Lovers come and go, but friends are always there.'"

Terry made a face, pretending to be grossed out. "When I used to go to those international AIDS conferences," she said, "someone would get up and begin by announcing that 200 of their friends had died of AIDS. And you knew those were the Americans, because only Americans could imagine they had 200 friends."

Anna laughed. "You know," she mused, "this feeling is so intense, I really can't describe it. I've never cried like this." She choked up and paused to regain control of her throat. "I've been paralyzed with depression before — for twelve fucking years. And this isn't that. It really isn't! And because it isn't that, it's almost, you know, like joy." She looked at them shyly. "You don't think my being such a crybaby makes me any less of a butch, do you?"

"Of course not, honey," Janice smiled, patting her foot with that sexy maternal attitude that, if she had been capable of arousal at the moment, would have turned Anna on. "It just shows that you're secure in your masculinity."

"You do look..." Terry said, scrutinizing her shiny face and puffy

eyes. "You know what you look like? Janice and I were just saying
before, when you were in the bathroom. You're like a city street after
rain. All washed." Anna twisted her head and looked at her with interest. Terry hesitated and blushed; it was an uncharacteristic flight of
fancy for her. "And you know how you have to look away sometimes
because the light from the puddles is so sharp?"

In Ithaca, a few nights earlier, Anna had sat outside a café with
Mark Swan. He was an old college friend who was running a restaurant
in Ithaca, and he too was recently divorced. Mark was kind of a jerk, the
kind of straight guy who thought he was so cool he could say *queer* and
dyke and not sound homophobic. But they had a lot of friendship time
under their belts, and Anna was stuck with him just as surely as she was
stuck with her family. And she had gravitated to him that humid August
night: he was handsome and solid, with a very good haircut and a hangdog smile that knew exactly how charming it was. Sitting there next to
her with his big Birkenstocked feet up on a chair, taking up a lot of
space, he had spoken about his two-year-old daughter Michelle. He
said it was so hard to contemplate her leaving town with her mother,
and seeing her only one weekend a month, that he could understand
how some divorced men became deadbeat dads.

A woman had sauntered by in a tight black mini-skirt, and simul-
taneously, their heads had slowly turned to watch. Mark turned to
Anna, the beginnings of a laugh making his eyes gleam, and said, "Life
is a very big fishbowl." A look of confusion passed over both of their
faces. We live in a fishbowl? There are lots of fish in the sea? So he
added, with a wise look, "Just don't forget to change the filter."

Anna slid between the sheets. She had turned the air conditioner
on, and they were cold. She buried her face in the pillows, trying to
discern Patricia's smell. She reached for the remote control and turned
on the TV, flipping past the toupéed millionaire dispensing advice on
a Florida hotel deck; an infomercial about working every one of your
abs — every one of them!; monsters, explosions, screaming women. A
man attempting to outrun a fireball: to her and Patricia's delight,

Roger Ebert had once called "the practice of outrunning fireballs" one of his pet peeves in movies. Then a cooking show, the only unterrifying thing on late-night television. Two women were making *empiñatas*.

She tossed on the air mattress, thinking that it would do for a while, till she had the time and money to buy a new bed. She didn't have anyone to tell about this day, its grief and its blessings; she covered her face against the beating wings of Patricia's absence. She thought about Mark. She wouldn't forget to change the filter, she thought, and laughed to herself, and then started, suddenly, to cry. *Oh wow,* she thought, her eyes opening in the dark. *Oh wow.* She was crying for her dad. She lay there for a while, communing quietly with her own surprise. Her hand rose and fell on her bare stomach. She couldn't even imagine him; it had been so long, his image in pictures had become an abstraction. She was crying because she was small and sad. She imagined what she knew how to see: a man in his thirties, just like her and the men she knew, hair curling from his arms, wiping his glasses, bravado in his smile, his chest gently swelling as he breathed. She cried for about an hour, till her face was swollen and pounding, curled up on her side, rocking herself and whispering *Shh, it's okay.*

CHAPTER THREE

The next morning, Anna carried her backpack in her hand through the bare halls of Pathways, Inc., past opaque glass doors with schedules and announcements and lists of names Scotch-taped to them. She was heavy-headed from sleep, and her face was greasy from the smells of marijuana and fried chicken in the thick air outside. She walked down the corridor trying to move from grief's dreamy sluggish element into the bright, brisk light of real time. The El roared by at eye-level, and she felt the noise rip through every molecule of space around her. She was looking for Renée, who wasn't in her office. The learning center looked dishearteningly grubby to her, even though it had been spruced up for the beginning of classes, the floors freshly mopped and construction-paper welcome signs posted on the bulletin board and Renée's office door.

She poked her head into the teachers' lounge, and shyly greeted Mavis and Joyce, two of the GED class teachers, who were working, with torn wrappers and an open box of breakfast bars between them. "You're a regular now," Mavis called. "Welcome, you poor sap!" The room smelled of coffee and microwave food.

Anna smiled. "Thanks. Just no hazing rituals, okay?"

They laughed. "Honey," Mavis drawled, "just walkin' through that door is a hazing ritual."

Anna went back to Renée's office and waited. Her eyes felt grainy; she took off her glasses and rubbed her face. Sometimes she wasn't so pleased with her attitude. She came from a cultural place that valued irony and wit — she had just spent three weeks with the wittiest gay man alive — but in a place like this, where people of different races, cultures and classes mingled precariously, there seemed to be a million ways of being misunderstood, and you couldn't afford ambiguity. One woman, Selma Watson, thought to this day that Anna was her angel because she had somehow mistaken an offer Anna had made to drop her off at family court for an offer to represent her there. In the official language here, the language of empowerment and self-esteem (*"Sometimes, if you go the wrong way, God lets you make a U-turn"*), the kind of laughter that predominated was hearty, sedate, common-denominator laughter. *We've all been there!* It made Anna gleeful when harder, edgier laughter made its way into the lesson, like the time she had pressed Yvonne Gittings, who was almost getting it, to do example after example of a word-pattern exercise, until Yvonne had finally looked up with irritation and just a hint of amusement and sputtered, "You know, slavery is abolished in this country now!"

She heard the brisk clack of Renée's heels approaching, stood and peeked out of the office. Renée's face lit up. "Hey girl!" she shouted, and gave Anna a hug. Anna fought back tears; it seemed as though she would burst from loneliness and gratitude anytime someone touched her. Holding her by the shoulders, Renée said gravely, "I must say, Anna, the university's loss is my gain." Renée was the director of the school, a crisp slight African-American woman with a gap between her front teeth that Anna adored. They had met two years earlier when Anna had first come to Pathways as a volunteer, looking for something besides writing her dissertation to structure her time; finding her a gifted tutor, Renée had cultivated her, giving her material to read and taking her to conferences. Renée wasn't really severe, but she was contained; some of the students, Anna knew, found her snooty. Anna felt she lived to make Renée laugh, to shatter her composure and make her eyes glisten.

"How're you doing?" Renée asked. She sat down behind her desk and adjusted the skirt of her peach-colored linen suit. Anna, in chinos and a black button-down shirt, felt, for a fleeting second, inadequate-

ly feminine. An old and anachronistic reflex: its residue puffed delicately, like powder off skin.

"I have major butterflies."

"No, I mean about your friend."

"Patricia?" *Girlfriend,* Anna thought: *lover.* "It's been awful. How do
people get through divorces?" She said *divorces* tendentiously. Renée
wasn't homophobic, but she said things like "What you do in the privacy of your home is your own business," and called Anna's life a
lifestyle. Around her Anna expended a lot of mental energy excusing
the tiny inflections that made her cringe. She admired Renée and
wanted badly to be close to her.

A student poked her head in, and Renée raised her eyebrows.

"I hear Johnny P. ain't coming back," the student said.

"Yes," Renée said, as Anna craned around to take a look. The student, a Hispanic woman in a jean jacket, was leaning on the metal door
handle, weighing this information with a judicious expression.

"Here's where you made your first mistake," she said.

"Isabel, let's talk about it later, alright?" Renée said. "I need to
finish up with Anna."

After she left, Anna mused, "Do you think there's such a thing as
empowering them too much?"

Renée put her head back and laughed. *Score.* Her bared throat was
nice against the white shell she wore under her jacket. "Okay," she said,
reaching for a pile of folders, "let's see if there are some things you
should know about these students."

"But not too much, okay?" Anna preferred not to have precon-
ceptions.

"Right. Just a few things to watch for." Anna listened closely, not taking notes. "There are six students. Don't expect to hold on to all of them."
She looked up, her eyebrows raised, waiting for Anna's consent.

"Okay," Anna said. But she knew already that it would wound her
pride when students dropped out.

"Cheryl Dupree is seventeen, and was brought in by her parents,
who felt she'd be better off here than in a high school. She spent four

years living with her junkie boyfriend. Recently he OD'd and died, and she went home. She's very sharp, a tactile learner, restless. She might disrupt class, so try to keep her stimulated and don't take any nonsense from her.

"Vanessa Harris is a very nice lady in her late twenties with three kids, and she has a learning disability. When she took the SORT placement test, she leaned her head so far back and narrowed her eyes into such tiny slits I thought we were both going to throw up."

Anna nodded anxiously. She wasn't very practiced with learning disabilities.

"She's got a tutor who's been trained by Eileen Corrigan, who seems to be working out pretty well. And if you'd like, I'll fix you up with someone at the Corrigan Center for a consultation." She glanced up at Anna, who nodded. She flipped through the files. "Oh yes, Brandy Edell is in your class."

Anna moaned. She had tutored Brandy before. Brandy had dropped out of school at thirteen to take care of her seven brothers and sisters after her mother died, supporting them with the money she got from an uncle for having sex with him. She was a white student with a watery compliant smile that drove Anna crazy. She consistently went to class, though, and she did some things well: she was, for example, a precision punctuator, and Anna was told she was good at math. But from lesson to lesson, little else seemed to take. Her home life — she was raising her youngest brother and three kids of her own now on public aid — was chaotic, so she didn't do her homework; and she seemed to Anna to have huge chunks missing from her memory. Thinking about her, her stomach churning, Anna thought: this is my job now, teaching people like Brandy.

"Again. You'll just have to do your best with her," Renée said. She briefly described the other students: a man in his fifties who had served in Vietnam and struggled with heroin addiction, a plumber, and a young man named Antwan who Renée thought was primed to invest and achieve in school. Then she placed both palms on the stack of folders before her, and looked up brightly at Anna. "I think that's about it," she said. "Welcome, and good luck!"

Anna sat still, refusing to be moved by her perkiness. "That's all you have to say to me? I'll bet you're the kind of mom who flung your babies into the swimming pool the minute they turned three months old."
Renée laughed. "Sink or swim, baby, that's right."

Brandy was frazzled. She was biting her lip and thumbing through the crumpled papers in her bag, looking for an exercise she had done on past tense with her tutor. She must have left it at home, or Charisse must have taken it out of her bag; she was always grabbing at loose pieces of paper to draw on, even though Brandy had smacked her hand the last time she drew on her homework. Brandy's blond hair was pulled back in a ponytail, and strands of loose hair hung around her worn face. On her desk was a deluxe multi-compartmented organizer with a bright red canvas and velcro cover, which her kids had bought her for Christmas last year, and which was still empty.

Slumped in her chair and twirling one of the rings on her manicured hands, Cheryl looked on with amused contempt. That cow was having some trouble getting it together. She suffered from too-many-kids disease, Cheryl thought, just like that sister over there with the purple lipstick. She herself was seventeen, sleek and quick. She looked at these women and thought, *Hello, anybody here heard of birth control?*

They were in room 205, where a government class was held in the summers and on alternate afternoons. A construction-paper timeline covered one wall, with historical events from antiquity to the present written in colored markers. The most recently added entries were for 1991 – "George Bush bombs Iraq" – and 1996: "Tupac Shakur murdered in Las Vegas, on September 13." On the opposite wall Antwan Johnson tried to tilt his chair back against a taped-up essay question written in large letters: "Describe an experience that you or someone close to you had that involved an interaction with one or more of the government agencies listed. Give who? what? where? when? And tell us how you felt about it." Antwan ran his hand over his hair, his eyes taking in the other students, a look of practiced and genial impartiality on his handsome, light-skinned face. He was here because his girlfriend Sheila had finally worn him down about it. Last night he had been hanging with Patrick and them outside J.J. Peppers, listening to them brag about money and women. Now he was crammed into a little chair, his knees knocking against the desk, the back of the chair cutting into his shoulder blades.

John McCaskey sat stonily next to him, his thick hands on his new notebook. He had noticed that other than Brandy, he was the only white student. He was a plumber, and had moved well in the world, always made decent money. He didn't belong in a classroom of gang-bangers and welfare cases. Panic surged through him: if not in this class, where would he learn to read? Paula had left him, and he had no one to help him anymore. Paula had left him: pain stalled over him like a cold front.

Outside the door, Anna paused, quickly touched the zipper of her fly to make sure it was closed, and walked in.

For the first few moments she felt sealed off, a fright reflex, and sensed only smell, heat, the extent of space and light. She took what she needed out of her book bag, shuffled through attendance sheets and notes, turned her back to the group to print her name on the board. Yet even while her back was turned to them, she was starting to blend into the field, conscious of the heat of their gaze on her clothes, her hair, her butt. Then, when she turned to them, she met somebody's curious eye, and smiled.

She leaned against the desk with her palms. How were adults supposed to act on the first day of school? Hair pulled back, braided, shaved up the neck; stubble, full cheeks and the glisten of makeup. Aftershave and perspiration. Hands folded on desks, the curl of fingers around pens. Her own smooth pale face, blinking, the set of her hips against the desk. "My name is Anna Singer. You can call me Ms. Singer or Anna, either one." The older white man and some of the women were looking her over with doubtful expressions; she imagined them to be taking in her youth, wondering if they could count on her to handle the class, or maybe disapproving of her boyish clothes.

"I don't know most of you yet," she said, "but one thing I do know is that you have courage. If you didn't, you wouldn't be here." She looked at Antwan, and wondered how she would capture the imagination of this handsome man, with fill-in and prediction and word-pattern exercises. And that older black man in the corner, with the bloodshot eyes and the battered blue jacket: who was he, and had Renée said anything about him? What would she have to say to him? His hands were set on his desk; his nails were long and yellow.

"There are a few things I want you to bring to every class. First, notebook and pen. Even more important, your energy and your glasses. If you wear glasses, please don't forget them. I won't take that as an excuse when it's your turn to read."

There was a rustle; unease was shimmying through them. Anna felt a ghost waft through the classroom just as the El stormed by on the other side of the building, making the windows shudder — the ghost, she guessed, of forgotten books and homework, of sudden diversionary tactics and emergency trips to the bathroom. "Your secret is out, at least in this room. You don't know how to read." It was a harsh thing to say, she knew. It was a risk she took, thinking that if they heard it loud and clear, they might let themselves drop the burden of constant lying, of conning each other, and would thereby give themselves an extra small reserve of energy to use to learn instead. "Each one of you is going through this, each one of you has your own struggle. So I expect you to respect each other in this classroom. You've been disrespected enough in school."

Cheryl thought: I bet she love that movie *Stand and Deliver.* Next to her, Robert was thinking about his dream of Reggie Jr. In the dream he was in the jungle, heaving in the rotten liquid air, when Junior appeared out of nowhere without a combat helmet, his face caked with dirt, his Afro crazy. *I thought you was killed,* Robert wondered, reaching out a hand, his heart silver and leaping from the river inside him. Junior smiled and handed him his lucky baseball. Robert closed his fingers around it, and awoke unhinged.

They had to go around the class and say why they were there. The girl before Robert sassed "Because my parents made me." When it was his turn, he said his name, and then, "The Dream of the Lucky Ball." Anna leaned in, questioning.

"The dream of the lucky what?"

"Ball," he said.

She considered. "That must have been some dream."

"Yes I reckon it was."

His skin had goosebumps from talking to the whole class. The next man said he was there because of reading instructions for fixing engines. And the woman after that said she wanted to be able to help her kids with their homework, and set an example. By then Robert's heart had skidded to its normal rhythm.

When they had gone all the way around, Anna hitched herself on the desk, leaned forward confidentially, and asked, "How many of you told your family or friends or boss that you were going someplace else today?"

There was silence, and then laughter, and five hands.

"How many of you told yourselves you're just coming for one day, and it probably won't work out?"

They were quiet, their eyes evasive, and then Cheryl raised her hand.

"Come back," Anna said. "How many of you feel like you're about to throw up?"

She was making them laugh at the crazy teacher, and they did, except for John and Cheryl, who looked at her with varying shades of shrewdness and resentment. All right, she thought. She asked them to come to the board together and write their names, and they rose with a great scraping of chairs and came to the front, where they huddled uncertainly and fumbled for chalk. "Where should we write it?" Vanessa asked.

"Anywhere you'd like," Anna said.

There wasn't enough chalk to go around, so some of them had to wait as others wrote. Writing her name in rolling cursive in the middle of the board, Cheryl paused and glowered over her shoulder, and Brandy took a step back, her hands held up placatingly. When they were finished and seated, Anna had them raise their hands as she read the names aloud. "Good!" she said. "Welcome, everybody." Then she asked, "Does anybody know what the word *context* means?"

Brandy looked around and then raised her hand, an old pro. "It means what comes before and after," she said.

"Good," Anna said. "As Brandy says, you can sometimes make a very good guess at what a word is by looking at what comes before and after it." She turned to the board and wrote:

After work she was exhausted. So she went to bed.

She read the sentence aloud, drawing a line in the air at *exhausted.* "From the context," she asked, "what could that long word beginning with *ex* be? You know the words that come before and after. What are some words that make sense there, in context?"

There was silence. "Look at the board," Anna said. "There are lots of words that could go here and make sense. Don't worry about getting the exact right one." John raised a tentative hand, feeling like an idiot — were they supposed to raise their hands? A flash of understanding for his wife tore through him; he was too ugly to stay with.

"Good," Anna said, as words began sounding hollowly, as though from a creek bed. "What's that? Good. *Tired, upset, exhausted.*" She printed the words over the word *exhausted,* and told them to copy down the sentence and the words. "So even if you didn't recognize this word," she said, pointing backward over her shoulder to the board, "you could figure out what the sentence means."

During the break, Anna took her wallet out of her backpack and slid it into her back pocket, then left the room to be by herself for a minute. Standing in the hall she felt a sudden surge in her chest — a fist, a knot, a fall; she recognized it from depression. Oh God. She was so committed to feeling this grief as different from depression, and it was, it really was, as different as an aria was from a foghorn. She was teaching, it was okay; no one seemed disruptive or completely out of it. She was backing into them on the dribble, feeling out the defense and the quickness of her own moves. But she was alone here in this bare unlovely place. She stood outside the door and stuffed her hands in her pockets.

Depression had settled over her at sixteen, and numbed her for twelve years. She had it before the emergence of psychotropic drugs, just as her father had had a drug addiction before the emergence of the detox clinic and the twelve-step program. He had gotten it while treating a beloved aunt for lung cancer, shooting them both up with Demerol, staggering blankly around the house, once crashing the car. Patricia said, hearing her talk about it much later: He was treating himself for someone else's pain.

She stepped back quickly as Antwan rushed from the classroom; he smiled shyly and excused himself, then trotted down the stairs fishing a cigarette from the crumpled pack in his hand. Depression's landscape was a wasteland; nothing could make her feel deader than that flatness and dust. And when she got involved with Patricia, and came out, and began to understand herself as a butch, the depression miraculously went away. She herself wouldn't have believed anyone who told her that the moment they came out, their depression disappeared, but it had really happened. She had become happy; her present began feeling vivid and dimensional to her, sometimes filling her so completely she cried.

Cheryl came out of the bathroom daintily patting her hair, which was straightened and swooped up on her head, and gave Anna an appraising stare on her way back to class. Anna tried to ignore the challenge to her presentability, and checked her watch. Almost everyone was back in the room. She looked up and noticed, down the hall, a figure coming toward her, carrying a newspaper and peering at each door. The image wavered in her sight undefined for a moment. It is a weird slice into vision's fabric, the he-she, no matter how accommodating that vision is. Looking at this one, Anna felt herself hovering just above gender's runway, feeling an exquisite irritability as she waited for the wheels to touch down, bouncing and giving off sparks.

The butch also wavered; she had just taken in Anna's short hair when her vision slackened and split. She was trying not to panic. She had been told to meet somebody called Renée in the library, and all the doors on the third floor looked alike; her back was killing her, and she could feel the prickle of sweat under her arms as she told herself it would be a door with writing on it, not just a number, and that she could recognize the word *library*. Maybe this was a big mistake. She had already missed one appointment, and they had wrangled tediously over the time for this one. She was about a week late. The El passed; she took a huge breath and let it shatter her.

Wow, an old-time butch, Anna was thinking. Now that her eye knew how to account for the details, it unfurled with generosity, taking in the dark hair, swept-back and gelled, the muscle underneath the slightly-aging flesh of her arms, the gut pushing out from jeans slung low on her hips, the keys hanging from her belt-loop.

"Are you looking for someone?" Anna asked.

"Yes, for Renée."

"Oh, are you here for an intake test?" Anna asked, pointing to the library door across the hall.

It was a mistake to ask that, she knew the minute she said it; you didn't let fly the word *test* the minute you met a new student, who was probably there because of a lifetime of pathologizing experiences with tests in the first place. What an asshole, she thought, trying to be friendly, trying to ingratiate herself. With her $40 haircut and her interest and her courtesy.

The butch gave her a look and stalked into the library. Antwan was bounding up the stairs. Anna stepped back to let him into class, then followed him, her face burning. The thing about depression, she thought, is that it presents itself as the truth: it tells you that whatever joy or peace you've felt is nothing more than a moment of mystification. That now, in its grasp, you're no longer a naive idiot; you are finally seeing clearly.

Alarm was flapping through the classroom: there had been an angry blast of horn and a screeching of tires outside, which had sent several of them rushing to the window. No collision this time, although

Brandy said that since she'd been coming to Pathways, there had been five accidents at that corner. Plus, Anna had come back in and asked them to write. "I know you're not gonna believe this," she said, raising her voice above the commotion of fumbling for pens, tearing off sheets of paper, sudden explosive chatter, "but writing is scary for every single person in the world, including professional writers. Really." A few of them nodded, but she knew they were humoring her.

She wrote on the board,

In my life, I want _____.

She read it aloud; the words were all sight words they could recognize. "Just one sentence, okay? Fill it in, tell me what you want. And you know what? Are you listening? I don't care at all about spelling. If you don't know how to spell it, just write the first letter and then a line." She was talking very loudly and plunging into the middle of the desks, feeling herself lose their attention.

"Just that?" Cheryl called derisively.

Anna could see John's face go splotchy with irritation, and shoulders deflating around her. She turned to Cheryl with an icy smile, a soft pin, a knee gently prodding at the small of her back. "Maybe you could write two sentences, Cheryl."

Cheryl gave her a cool, calculating look and Anna stared her down, her face hot. Cheryl was going to say something humiliating to her, she thought, it was only a question of time. It would be something that made Cheryl feel very triumphant even though it was too boorish to touch Anna; but her triumph was going to be so gaudy and scalding that Anna would be humiliated anyway. She walked over to Vanessa, who wasn't writing anything, and crouched by her desk. "Tell me what you want, Vanessa," she said.

Vanessa smiled uncertainly, a dimpled hand touching her cheek. "I want my kids to be healthy and not in trouble and not on drugs," she sighed. "I want God to bless us and keep us safe."

Anna nodded, taken aback at her candor. Vanessa looked away, peeking anxiously over at John's paper. Without seeming to notice her, he drew it toward himself and leaned over it. She turned back to Anna.

"I don't know what to write," she said.

Anna laughed. "Write *that*," she said; "write what you just said!"

Vanessa looked at her, incredulous. "I can write that?"

"Yes! What do you *think* you're supposed to write?"

Vanessa looked at her, sighed, and took the plunge, writing *I want my* quickly and faintly, as though tiptoeing in dirty boots over a new carpet.

Antwan was sitting glumly, tapping his pencil on the paper in front of him. "Antwan, right?" Anna said. She stood beside him with her hands in her pockets. "Why don't you start by writing the first three words." He gripped the pencil and ground it into the paper, writing in a shaky and ornate script, then brushed off the little shavings, *tsking* irritably as they smudged the paper. Anna remembered her Literacy Volunteers of America training session, some years ago, when the teacher had opened by asking the volunteers to write a paragraph about themselves with their non-dominant hand. He wanted to show them how awkward and painful writing is for an unpracticed hand. "So what do you want?"

"Lots of things," he said. He turned on the politeness. "A good job in auto mechanics." He paused. "To take care of my family." To take this pencil my hand is sweating all over and shove it up somebody's ass, he thought. He looked at Anna, her baggy pants, light slouch and impassive chest. "What should I write?"

"Write what you just said," she said.

With fifteen minutes remaining, Anna had them put away their notebooks and pens. "Clear your desks," she said, noticing Cheryl plunk her bag on her desk and hold onto the handle, ready to spring out of her chair the moment class was over. Anna was going to read to them, and she wanted their desks free of chaos.

It took a few minutes for Brandy to get her things packed away. "Sorry," she giggled as she scooped her pens together and one fell to the floor. She bent to pick it up, groaning. Anna hopped up on the desk and waited quietly, holding a book. When they were settled, she held it up and showed them the front cover. "This is a novel, which means it's fiction, a made-up story. It's by a writer named Dorothy Allison, and it's called *Bastard out of Carolina*."

Vanessa frowned, jarred by the cuss word in the title. But when Anna began to read about a little girl named Bone, born following a car accident where her uncle was driving drunk and her mama was thrown from the car, she came to attention. The mama still asleep while the baby got named, and the relations' foolish nonsense and how they couldn't write the names right: Vanessa moved into the story and made herself at home.

The room was quiet except for Anna's smooth, animated voice and the occasional laugh or "Ha!" She peeked up a few times and saw Antwan at rigid and wary attention and Cheryl either listening or sleeping, her head down on her desk. She read through the passage where Bone's mother tries repeatedly and unsuccessfully to have the word *illegitimate* expunged from her birth certificate, and up to the words of Uncle Earle: "'The law never done us no good. Might as well get on without it.'"

Then she stopped and smiled. "See you tomorrow," she said.

As she gathered her papers, John approached, clutching his brief-case in both hands. "Hi," she smiled.

"Hi," he said faintly. "Look, I'm sure that was an excellent class, but I don't think this is going to work out for me."

Anna tried not to look stricken. "Why not?" She didn't know whether to press him or not. Some of them really needed to be pressed to persevere; Renée once called Brandy and told her that if she didn't show up for class in fifteen minutes, she was going to come over and break down her door, and Brandy had been a steady student ever since. But you couldn't do that with everyone. They were adults, and presumably knew what they wanted.

He looked at her uneasily and pushed back his shoulders. Anna could see he was working himself into a state of indignation with her, to make this easier for himself. "I have a tutor, and it's just that I think I'll be better off in a one-on-one type of situation," he said.

"Okay," Anna said. "Best of luck to you. I hope you find what you need." She dropped her attention back down to the desk, gathering loose papers into a stack.

John hesitated. He thought that was a nice thing to say, and a nice way to put it. He turned with a mixture of resolve and regret, and left the room.

On her way out, Anna bumped into Renée, and told her that John McCaskey was dropping her class. "I'm really bummed about it," she said. "He seemed really present during class."

Renée pressed her forearm and leaned in, as though talking to someone who was hard of hearing. "Anna, he's not the only one who's going to drop out. I'd suggest you not get hung up on him, and focus on the students you have."

Anna looked at her irritated face, absorbed the surprise of her sharp tone, which Anna had never been the target of before. Shit, Renée probably thought she was invested in him because he was white. Her shoulders deflated and she looked up at the ceiling, willing herself to be patient. This school could be a fucking minefield.

"Besides which," Renée said, "you've got a new student."

Then Anna remembered. "Oh!" she said; "you mean, that" — she paused for a fraction of a second — "woman who came in before?"

"Yes," Renée said. "Her name is Chris Rinaldi. She tested at third grade. She's in your class."

CHAPTER FOUR

It's the same old same old, walking down the crummy hallway of that school. Everybody turning their eyes away, trying not to look scared or embarrassed or disgusted. Admit it: some secrets you just can't keep. The way you look, you can be scoped out in a second by the biggest jackass. Talk about wearing a sign advertising what you are! A sign that everybody but you can read. Is it just you, or is God fucking with you in a big way?

Sometimes you go looking for trouble, craving hatred as clear as crystal, as plain as day. Once — it's a long story — you creamed a punk with a dictionary. If there would've been a femme involved, it would have combined all your interests.

Your femme figures it out within three months. She's cooking veal parmesan from a *Tribune* recipe one hot evening back in the day, and you're sitting at the table holding the sports section. You picked it up to look at a photo of a play at the plate. What is wrong with you? You've always said, there's no such thing as an accident. But now, you forget to have a headache; you forget to forget your glasses; you forget to say, I gotta go. Rolling and unrolling the paper in your hands, you're thinking how you're supposed to be used to the idea that a beautiful woman would fix you a meal, but you're not. You stretch out your legs with lazy pleasure, forgetting that her hands are wet and greasy, and that you're sitting right beside the recipe. So that when she says,

How much oregano, honey? Read that to me, will you?

When she says that, you can only look up stupid and pop-eyed, like a cartoon character bonked on the head with a frying pan. *What? Huh?* Adrenaline rushing through you like a brushfire, newsprint bleeding all over your sweating hands.

She is very still. Then she backs away from the pot, takes off her apron, and carefully wipes her hands on it. Her cheeks are very red and her eyes very shiny, and for an awful moment you think she might start crying. She takes the newspaper from your hands, hikes up her skirt and straddles your lap, facing you. Rubs her face against yours like a blind person, and kisses your neck. You close your eyes. You worry that you'll ruin her dress, so your ink-stained hands hang awkwardly at your sides, like giant dirty paws. She stands for a second and quickly removes her panties, then settles back down and takes your hand, rubbing it up her thigh, guiding it into her. Surprise licks and rattles you. She's sighing, her arms tightening around your neck. She rocks on your hand and cries *Oh!* And when you remove your fingers, they are wet and fragrant, and clean.

You were never like the rest of the kids; you were always between radio stations, trying to tune out the crackle and get a blade of sound. You forgot your glasses, made wisecracks, knocked over the stuff on your desk, punched the kid sitting next to you. You calculated which line was yours and practiced — heart pounding, lips sputtering — before your turn. You were put into a special ed class, and made D's simply by showing up. You bluffed and cheated and procrastinated, got the instructions wet and had to call the manufacturer, carried around a newspaper and a roll of cash. You were a model worker and a genius with your hands. You stared blurrily, counting to twenty, at every form or petition handed to you, and then signed, a compliant motherfucker. You wormed yourself out of things so often you felt like an actual worm. You were such a liar you had to carry around a special fire extinguisher for your pants.

You always check the exits, and not just because of raids. You devise twenty appropriate things to order at restaurants, twenty ways to avoid this and that, twenty ways of not saying *I can't.* After a while it's such a habit your mind is on permanent speed-up. Whenever you drive somewhere you budget an extra twenty minutes for traffic, and run through alternate routes in your head. You're as bad as an old Italian grandmother, righteously certain that somebody's going to lose an eye, that roughhousing will end in tears. You can't do laundry without worrying that all the machines will be taken. Or tell a lie without fretting about its consistency with all your other lies. Or sit on a pier without worrying that your keys will fall into the lake.

Can it be so many years — decades! — since you first arrived? How you got there: by hook and by crook, that's how. You soon find out that this is the crummiest of the syndicate bars, with the filthiest johns, the most watered-down drinks, the nastiest manager. But for now, some big old raucous butches are crowded at the bar, leaning on their elbows and laughing and talking. One of them notices you and elbows her neighbor, and the next thing you know they're all squawking like chickens. They're busting your chops. You think, *Okay now.* Then one of them sends you a drink, something fluffy and *green,* for God's sake. You leave it right there on the table, march up to the bar in your sneakers and order a beer. You can see that some of the butches are surprised, and some are grinning. They make the bartender serve you; they shout, For Pete's sake, can't you see she's at least twenty-seven?

And then suddenly one night you're the toughest craziest butch around. You didn't set out to be. Your ambitions were modest: don't piss anyone off, maybe make a friend or two. But one night a fat man with a gold bracelet puts the moves on your date, and you whirl around and deck him, without even thinking. By now you're wearing boots; and when he pulls out a knife you kick it out of his hand.

What drama! Your buddies and the bouncer throw you out on the street. What were you thinking? They're looking at you with amazement as you stand up and wipe dirt off your new dress pants. Apparently you just decked the owner's cousin. You say: *oops.* You can never go back in there, or they'll kill you. You laugh thinking about it now: here you were clobbering a mob guy, when you should have been in algebra class.

One of the toughest butches has just moved away, and another is shacking up with her new girlfriend. So there is a vacancy at the cat's meow position. The older butches start coming up to you and roughing up your hair, the younger ones mimic your clothes and gestures, and suddenly you have only the most beautiful girlfriends. You walk into bars and turn heads. People buy you drinks all the time. You can go out on a Saturday night with a dollar in your pocket, and come back with the same dollar. You are the high school quarterback of the perverts' team.

You feel funny about it then; but later, how you'll miss it! Especially after women's lib. You don't know if it's good or bad; all you know is that before it you were hot stuff, and afterward, you had to stand on your head to impress a woman. You're older now, and sometimes you throw out your back; you spend way more time on it than any butch should. On your feet, you feel like Lurch on *The Addams Family.* Put it this way: you haven't been assaulted for a long time, because you're no longer pissing people off by appearing to like the way you look. But you haven't been flirted with either.

You're attracted to your first real girlfriend because she's trouble; there's something about her that says *I'm wise to you, buddy.* You're living a little over your head, with a reputation as a rough stud and an expert lover. But sexually speaking, you're really just cutting your grown-up teeth. At most, you have one, maybe two tricks up your sleeve. This girl you like boycotts grapes and listens to the Rolling Stones. She talks so smart and dirty she makes you duck your face and reach for a cigarette to keep your cool. Your pals look her over and shake their heads. *Killer pussy,* is what they call her. It shocks you a little.

Those are the crowded carnival days at the women's bar. You're all working in card shops and printing presses, hanging out at the drive-ins and the roller derby, throwing unemployment parties where the working people bring food and pay for drinks. The bar is fielding six sports teams. People drop in while doing their laundry; the girls on the street come in to get into the air conditioning. Femmes in big chunky heels brush their bare arms against your jacket as they pass by. The drinks are short and strong; the pool balls drop at noon, crashing like thunder. There are raids on Fridays. The girls give a lot of lip. They don't mind lockup too much except for the strip searches and the bedbugs; they like the slices of baloney, the coffee and fresh doughnuts. You gauge when to haul off and when to go limp. You hold on for dear life.

You let this girl make you blush and make fun of you, you even let her make scenes at the bar, laughing like she's a character. But you never let her touch you. You pin her down, you make marks on her wrists, and when you feel her legs ease open you laugh at her. When she asks you put your head down there, you call her nasty. The truth is, it's very complicated down there, and you're afraid you'll fumble or hurt her or make her laugh. But it's also your first taste of butch power, of how to punish a femme. One night when you're messing with her head, she turns away and gives herself a lonely climax. You watch her naked back arch and her long hair sliding over her shoulder blades; it mortifies you so much you have to leave the room.

Can you be crazy about someone you don't even like? Once you smack her for being smart. It's like smoking, you say later: back then nobody knew any better. And she stuns you with a pop in the jaw, telling you to mind your manners. It doesn't hurt, but you sure are getting an education.

You smacked her because she called you stupid. Because of your opinion about something, which was, it's true, stupid.

Finally, you say it's just not working out for you. You say it in the bar, because you are a chickenshit and a coward. She tosses back some whiskey and gives you a smile. You think: if she found out, you'd have to kill her. It's kind of funny, feeling like a gangster in a movie, the phrase *rub her out* coming out of nowhere into your nutty head.

She has a fight with her boss when he tries to feel her up, and gets fired. She says she doesn't want to stay forever in this pit anyway. That's what she calls it, a pit. It hurts your feelings, but to be perfectly honest, you're also relieved. Her sister comes to pick her up in a station wagon on a cool October day, when the wind is carrying the pungent sulphurous air north over the lake. You watch them drive off with your hands in your pockets. Your hair is perfect, your head as messed up as it's ever been.

So almost ten years later, when your femme finds out, there's a letting go. It's like exhaling your first drag on a cigarette, like pancakes and syrup, like the time at the beach you lay on the warm sand in your shorts and t-shirt, looking through your shades into the blue blue sky. You wake in the early hours, a baby mammal, pink and hairless, eyes bunched shut; you burrow into her and sink back into sleep.

Your femme was married! — That poor sap lets her go to the bar with a friend because he trusts she'll be safe there. It's hard to believe, but they do that back then.

When she first comes in, she has her long hair pinned up in a leather barrette with a stick through it. When she fishes change out of her little change purse for a drink, she reminds you of a mom on a black-and-white TV show. You and your friends laugh at her and call her The Little Wife. You glide up behind her and growl, *Watch out darling.* Then one day she comes in with a tight-fitting blouse and her hair down around her shoulders, and you almost fall off your bar stool. You ask one of the femmes, who teaches you about the color auburn, and while she's at it, laughingly teaches you the word *luster.* It's like *shine,* she says, only somehow deeper and thicker.

You help her out of a jam you guess, but you use a little too much force. What can you say?: she finds what she wants with you. Her climaxes are like pictures you've seen of river beds swelling and spilling over. When you try to draw them out, show her a good time the way you've become expert at over the years, she half-laughs, half-pants, *Oh honey, don't get fancy!* You yourself could explode with pleasure, a millrat's wife coming all over herself beneath you, calling your name.

You try to hide the meanness of it from her. But you can't help it, you hate those guys. They cruise by you in their Chevys, taunting and throwing things. A guy throws a used rubber at you one night, and it splatters against your shoes. You take them off, pick them up with two fingers, and throw them right in the dumpster, walking home in your socks. Later, when the mills start closing, things get even worse. Once you get your shoulder dislocated. You hear the neighbors saying on the news, If someone was hurt or out of work, we brought them noodles, or strudel, or cash, or casseroles. You don't remember anybody ever bringing you noodles. There's a lot of stuff on Channel 7 about how they're losing their way of life. To be honest, you don't give a damn.

A cool summer night, another decade later: you're back from softball, after a quick beer with your team at the bar. You're still playing, but with taped knees now, like a lot of your teammates; you'll retire when you can no longer give one hundred percent to the game. Right now you may be slow, but you can still scald the ball. She's sitting in an armchair, her feet up, reading a magazine about show business. *Listen to this, honey,* she says, and *Imagine!*

Ooh! you tease her in falsetto, holding your hands up to your cheeks in mock marvel. You're on your back stretching, feeling huge and tired and muscular, contemplating the picture of Elizabeth Taylor in a tiara on the magazine's cover, and your femme's nice thigh where it disappears into her shorts. You have very satisfying grass stains all over your pants, and your team is in first place after winning tonight. You know that they're all busy bragging, and clapping each other on the back, and tormenting your right fielder, who's always shaky out there and who let an important fly ball get by her. They're calling her a weenie and a sieve, and comparing her handiwork in right field to how she must be in the sack. You clasp your bent knee closer to your chest. Her voice is grainy, like brown sugar mixed into oatmeal, or sand on a slick road, providing good tread. You'd kind of like to be at the bar, but you'd kind of rather be here, near the sound of her voice as she reads aloud about movie stars, near her beautiful lips moving.

The contract is a swirl of gray, like the PC boards you screw onto computers these days, with their inscrutable circuits and prongs and tiny teeth. You bend your heads and sign your names. She's in a nice dress with her hair drawn back in a bun, you're in dress pants and a jacket. It's the closing for your house, and you're surrounded by people in suits, only a few that you recognize. You follow your lawyer's guiding finger, huddling down in the penciled X's as though they're bunkers. You think, signing is like dreaming; it's not real but it is.

Your real estate agent is a gay guy with a slightly-receding hairline. Every estimate he gives you about what it'll cost to repair something in a house you look at is ridiculously low. Yeah right, it'll only cost five dollars to get the moisture out of that finished basement where the file cabinets are rusted from water! Your lawyer is a fat, clownish, badly-dressed lesbian. Your femme found them in the *Pink Pages*. The lawyer buddies up to you with long stories about her life with her girlfriend — as though you want to hear that boring crap, as though she doesn't have to act like a professional just because you're all lesbians.

Your back is killing you; this morning you wrenched it at work, bringing in some boxes of parts. The thought of needing workers' comp scares the daylights out of you, especially because you have a preexisting condition, and you've heard stories about that. You can't back out now; it's too late. So even as you sign the papers, you're doing frantic calculations, guessing what you would get on workers' comp, say you could even get it, adding it to your femme's check, deducting mortgage payments and food.

Your femme reaches into her purse and pulls out the certified check, hands it over to you to give to the bank person. You remember it later without any sound, like a pantomime. Most of it is not money you made; it's money she got from her aunt who died. Her aunt was a schoolteacher who lived for forty years in a little house in Gary, with her best friend.

Your new house is a tiny yellow brick house on a dead-end street on the North Side, around the corner from the Y. It has a fenced-in yard the size of a matchbook, and no garage. It makes you think of the houses you and your parents used to pass on the drive from the suburbs to visit your grandparents. It's the smallest house on the block, in a neighborhood they call up-and-coming; your realtor praises your far-sightedness, but frankly, it's just what you could afford in a white neighborhood in the city. The whine of construction becomes your life's background noise, and as you walk down the street, fine dust chalks your lips. You're not the only ones who have decided to move into the city.

You drive there following your real estate guy in his aging Honda. You park at the curb and walk together in your nice shoes up the stairs onto the porch, your back twinging with every step. It's the only thing you can feel; otherwise it's like when you've stubbed your toe, and you're waiting for your brain to get the message. There's some leftover adhesive where the previous owners peeled their name off the mailbox. The real estate guy stands back as you fumble with the keys and unlock the door, then grins: *Wanna carry her over the threshold?*

She's sitting at the kitchen table in her housedress, paying the bills. Your back is better. You've handed over your check from the plant, and the smaller one from helping out weekend nights at the bar. Her glasses are low on her nose, and her hand scuttles along the check she's writing, staccato and fussy. The skin on the top knuckle of her third finger is pressed flat and shiny from the pressure of the pen.

You lost part of your pinky finger about five years ago, right at that knuckle on your right hand. Good thing you're ambidextrous where it counts! you wink at your friends. Everybody thinks you lost it in a fight, or at the rendering plant, or in a motorcycle accident. The truth is you got a weird infection when you fell on the nailboards for carpeting you were putting in for a landlord over on Paxton St., and then delayed too long going to the doctor.

You ask her how you're doing this month; she says pretty good except for that new crown she needs. You pick up the mortgage payment booklet and flip through it with wonder and a little dread, feeling the tiny breeze spit at your chin. Thirty years worth of slips! You can't imagine even living that long, but the booklet seems to say with authority that you will.

She cranes her head up at you, and says *I'll do this, honey, why don't you go watch TV.* A spasm of irritation makes you turn away and go into the living room, where you sit in front of a stupid sitcom, useless and brooding.

How you got this way: it's a question you refuse to entertain on any level. To you, it's like the black people crying about slavery: milk so spilt it'd take a thousand overtimes to mop it all up. The question is: where do you go from here? With this body, this face, this so-called mind of yours with its evasions, its wasted energies, its hatred, its gaping holes?

One day you and your femme are sitting on your front porch when a Toyota hatchback drives up, and two very young dykes with pierced noses and eyebrows and God knows what else get out to ask directions. They get one look at you and their faces start to glow. Your femme turns toward you with a groan: Oh for God's sake, we're *foremothers*.

Suddenly, she's looking a little fat. She was always a big girl, a farm girl from a place in Indiana where nobody looks at you twice — where your codes get whacked out by the stocky and coarse-cheeked farming women you see in town, who aren't butches at all, but rather straight women buying Pepsi and diapers at Greene's store.

She was always a big girl, ample, with a hospitable face that blushed easily. You liked that she had a big appetite. Your mother, trying to look like an elegant wife in front of your father's friends, was always on a diet, and okay, you admit you have a mother problem. Once she put a padlock on the kitchen door and handed the combination to you, making you swear not to tell it to her no matter how hard she begged. Then she woke you up in the middle of the night. You could smell her and see her nipples through her nightgown. She said, *C'mon sweetie, please,* and *Indulge your old mother.* She wanted to get at those Sara Lee cakes in the freezer, shaving away with her knife one almost translucent sliver at a time, her bare feet cold on the linoleum, her throat warm and sweet. You felt sorry for her and also despised her; you knew the next day she'd be on you to dress nice and sit still, and here she was, loose and gross and cunning and hungry.

So when your femme starts looking fat, you wonder. Maybe she hasn't even gained weight, maybe it's just you. But suddenly you can't stand to watch her chew. And you think: *something's up.*

Who would have thought a car accident would come as a mercy? A guy in a suit, driving back from lunch, gets into an argument on his cell phone and clips you with his car as you're crossing Ashland Avenue, then veers into a light pole. You beg the bystanders not to call an ambulance, but they do anyway, and the fact is you can't get up, your leg is broken. You keep your mouth shut in the ambulance as they refer to you as "he," focus on planning when and how to present yourself as a female before they can take your clothes off and notice themselves. Once inside, you lay rigid on a hospital gurney, your pants off and your BVDs out there flapping in the breeze, wondering how many martinis that guy knocked back, getting a knowing look from the doctor, feeling the slap of wet plaster. The next day, your femme comes in with swollen eyes to tell you that the owner of the bar has dropped dead of a stroke. After the first shock it's hard to remember the news from one minute to the next, because whatever it is you're taking for the pain is giving you amnesia. Your boss comes to visit, bringing you a card signed by everybody at work. On the front there's a picture of a puppy with its paw in a splint. He sits, embarrassed, in a chair by your bed, and you hope to God nothing is showing through your hospital gown. He would put you on light duty at work, he says, doing filing and helping track orders, but he just doesn't have a vacancy there.

You lie in bed for weeks, for longer than they say you should, even after the cast comes off. Your femme is gathering the documents on your condition and taking in extra freelance work now. Before the accident you took up the old bathroom floor, but you're too crippled to lay the new tile. When you hobble out of the bathroom your feet carry grit all over the floors.

The bar is up for sale, you hear. You sleep twelve hours a night; when you wake up your head feels like someone poured concrete into it. Old hurt moves silently to the surface and breathes, sending up a towering jet of spray. During the afternoons, with the ball game on, you tilt your calculator toward the light and try to figure out how much you'll get per month for a year if you get the settlement your femme thinks you'll get. Then you calculate again, estimating the amount more conservatively. With the two months wages your boss is paying you, and the advance you're going to try to get on the settlement, you could probably make it for about a year without working. It's dawning on you that you've taken one for the team. A new thought pokes out its head comically, like a salamander. You lie there with your eyes closed, woozy on painkillers, fingering the calculator.

CHAPTER FIVE

She could smell bacon cooking. Chris stooped over the small bathroom faucet, her hand cupped, the Advils on the back of her tongue tickling her gag reflex. She slurped water from her hand and swallowed, shuddering. Straightening carefully and wiping her mouth with the back of her hand, she caught a glimpse of her face in the mirror, and looked away. She hadn't slept well, and she looked as puffy and tiny-eyed as a bully. What a piece of work she was! Unable to lie down comfortably since the leg injury had aggravated her back, and hardly able to stand for more than ten minutes. Floor tiles she had bought before the accident were stacked under the window, in the corner near the bathtub. Her heart had been in her mouth as she paid for them, splurging on tile rather than vinyl, but they had been irresistible. They were off-white and a color the guy called charcoal, and if she was ever able to get on all fours and lay them, she had in mind a pattern whose subtlety delighted her. At the moment, though, the unrepaired wood subfloor was a damned eyesore, and it was making the whole house dirty.

Leaving the bathroom, she let the bedroom carpet wipe the grit off the soles of her feet, reluctant to disturb her back by bending to clean them off with her hands. She put on some jeans and slipped into her flip-flops. Down the hall, the kitchen was light and smoky; the fan on the stove's hood was broken, so Kathleen had set up a window fan, which was humming and stirring the curtains. They were still shopping for a kitchen table, in the meantime using an old card table of

Kathleen's with a tablecloth over it. On it sat a large shiny present with a red bow, looking incongruously like nighttime and champagne. Chris stared at the glittery silver wrap. "What's this?" Kathleen turned from the stove, raising her eyebrows and opening her mouth as if to say: Surprise! She was dressed for work, in a skirt and blouse, sneakers over her nylons. Her hair was pulled back; wisps of it clung to her face. She shook the skillet lightly to loosen fried eggs from its bottom. Their dog Rufus was on the prowl around the stove, and Kathleen nudged him away with her foot.

"It's a present, what do you think it is? For your first day at school."

Chris rolled her eyes, pleasure and annoyance roughing each other up inside her. "You'd think I was six years old," she said. She eased herself into a chair with a stiff arm and set the package on her lap. She peeled off the ribbon, then started working fastidiously on the Scotch tape, trying not to take the shiny part of the paper off with it. Kathleen flipped the eggs and tried to be patient. They didn't even save used wrapping paper.

"A book bag!" Chris sat back and put her hands on her thighs. She looked at it painfully and scratched her jaw. Kathleen was peeling an oil-soaked paper towel off the bacon, snatching toast from the toaster with quick fingers. "Honey, I already took care of it."

"What?" Kathleen stopped, the full plate in her hands. "When?"

But she probably shouldn't have been surprised. Chris had spent the last few weeks — ever since she heaved herself out of her long sulk in bed and decided to go back to school — in sporadic and secretive activity. Most of the time Kathleen saw her she was lying on the floor with her eyes closed and her knees clenched in her arms, but then she'd come home and suddenly Chris had gotten a haircut, or, just a few days ago, had pushed all the living room furniture to the middle of the room and covered it in plastic, in preparation for a wallpaper-removal and paint job that Kathleen just didn't see happening anytime soon. Last night when she got home, she saw that Chris had been to the grocery and bought canned goods and frozen dinners. Condensed milk: had they ever even used that? Sardines? Kathleen didn't like it. Her philosophy was that as long as Chris was injured, they should be realistic, and focus on the little things that would make the house warm, make it theirs. Chris, meanwhile, seemed to be preparing for a nuclear attack.

She set the plate in front of Chris. She knew she should be kind; this was so much better than the three weeks Chris had spent in bed, glazed with painkillers, her hair greasy and her eyes yellow and bruised. Kathleen had never seen her like that before, and she knew it wasn't just her back. She had never seen Chris look so *old;* sometimes she imagined she could see exactly what her skull would look like as the flesh melted off it.

Chris salted her eggs. "Last week," she said belligerently. Rufus was eyeing her, his tail waving gently, and she ordered him to lie down, then regretted her sharp tone. She put the shaker down and ran her fingers thoughtfully over the canvas of the bag on her lap. It was beautiful. A deep green with black trim, a handle that felt good when she grasped it; it also had a shoulder strap that was cushioned where it would rest on her shoulder. She focused on it severely, picking it off her lap and joggling it in her hand for a second; it was substantial but light, weight that felt nice. And there were pockets.

It hadn't taken Kathleen long to lose patience. She would come in from work with her jacket open, the grime of the summer workday layered upon her, exhaustion rimming her eyes. Taking off her sneakers and peeling off her nylons, she'd look at Chris staring slackly at a ball game, and angry virtue would puff her up. She came from a farming family, and one thing she and Chris had always shared was their work ethic. "At least change your t-shirt; you stink," she'd snap, and stalk into the bathroom to wash her face. *I'm too old for this!* — the words pounded in her ears as she held her cold wet hands to her face. She had nursed two teenage siblings through their moods and tantrums after their mother died, when she herself was still a teenager, and damn if she was going to do it again.

"Where's the one you bought?" she asked, her hands on her hips. She was furious, and felt a little foolish about her own contrariness.

First she was mad that Chris had taken to her bed, and now she was mad that Chris had gotten up and done things without telling her.

"In the bedroom closet, in a plastic bag."

Kathleen left the kitchen, her sneakers squeaking on the linoleum. Chris put the bag on the table in front of her plate and bent over her food. She had taken the bus to Target and bought the first black bag she found. Kathleen's was much nicer. Kathleen's bag looked — it wasn't that it looked expensive, it was that it looked like a gift. She felt something sweet and awful pushing at her face and throat. It hadn't occurred to her to buy herself something really nice.

Chris's bag was shoved in the back of the closet. Kathleen brought it out to the rustle of clothes and hangers. She took off the Target bag and let it fall to the floor, turned the book bag right side up. It was one of those computer cases. She stood in the quiet of the bedroom, her throat hurting as she looked at it. What was the difference, really, between this and a book bag? It wasn't as though you couldn't carry books and supplies in it.

When she came back into the kitchen, the computer case in her hand, Chris was hunched over her plate, mopping up the rest of her yolk with a piece of toast. "So what did you think," Chris asked with a funny smile: "that I wouldn't know I needed a bag to carry books and notebooks and things like that?"

Kathleen flushed. "I'm sorry I tried to do something nice for you."

"It's okay, I'll just take mine back, it's no big deal." Chris wiped her mouth and set her napkin down, thinking, Why am I such a huge pain in the ass?

Kathleen saw her sag, sat down on the edge of a chair and sighed. "I have to go soon," she said.

"Okay," Chris said. Kathleen would be staying late at the hospital to freelance on the office computer. Chris looked down at her useless hands.

"I shopped for a week," Kathleen said. Chris's face struggled, then lightened a shade with indulgence. "I found it at a camping store downtown, and then went to Penney's and found it for eight dollars cheaper. I wanted to get something light, that wouldn't hurt your back to carry."

"Well thanks."

"Don't you want to look in the pockets?"

Chris picked it up and fished inside, pulling out a notebook, some pens and pencils in a tin case, a sharpener with a plastic bubble around it. She set them down on the table and reached in again, canvas scraping her knuckles. A big pink eraser. She held it up with a comical look. "What, no mittens with clips on them? No Flintstones lunchbox?" Oh God, memories swam at her, mouths gaping. A peanut butter sandwich, Fritos, an apple, Oreos. Her mother's kiss, hurried and choked. The yank away, away from that passion, to catch the bus. Breathing hard, the gates of her face closing as she hauled herself up the big steps.

"Don't be fresh," Kathleen said. This butch, with her precise hands and her knowingness about the world; you'd nestle in her toughness and let yourself be little, and then you'd realize that she didn't know about the time zones, or what continent they lived on, and your heart would just break. She prayed that the world wouldn't eat Chris alive.

Chris shifted and winced. "Back?" Kathleen asked.

"Yes."

"Did you take something?"

"Yes."

They sat together for a moment. Kathleen noticed that Chris's upper lip looked blotchy from shaving. "What're you going to wear?" she asked.

Anna sat on the edge of her mattress in her underpants, hugging herself as irritation and loneliness thrilled through her. Her bare feet were chilly on the tiny bedroom's carpet. She was having trouble picking something to wear. Patricia would have marched her into the light, given her outfits the once-over with a connoisseur's narrowed eyes, opined. *You've got a David Niven thing going.* Or *Wanna hop into the back seat of the Chevy?*

Since she awoke something nervous-making had been slipping away from her mind's edges, showing her only its shadow, and when she rousted it out of hiding, it had that butch's face as Anna remembered it, haughty, all jaw. Her name was Chris, and this was the day she was supposed to start. Anna's impulse was to get butched-up to the skies for this first class with Chris in it, wear jeans and a t-shirt and her black motorcycle boots. To slick back her hair, though that desire always made her think of Terry's account of using Brylcreem for a while back in the late '70s, till a woman told her that the smell reminded her of the uncle who used to molest her. She reached for the phone on the night table, wanting to call Janice, or Monica, and then remembered that Janice had a meeting and Monica was at her new girlfriend's. A muggy breeze came in from the window; she heard children's voices and the quick beep of a car nosing its way out of the alley. There was no one to call. Her arms and chest at once clammy and covered with goosebumps, she stared unhappily at the blank space on the wall where Patricia once hung a poster she'd stolen from a hallway during Black History Month at DePaul and had framed, a schedule of events printed over a vivid sexy sketch of Billie Holliday. Man, did she not want to go to work this morning; the thought of trying to connect with strangers frightened her. Her class had shrunk to five people, six including Chris. The hook was still hanging over the blank space, and she stood up and removed it, causing tiny bits of plaster to trickle down the wall.

She turned toward the closet. She couldn't butch herself up entirely; there were other codes to consider. The African-American women were good dressers in bright colors, and they made her feel grubby and drab. Plus, she was still closeted to this class, which irked her. Not that she thought they didn't know, or even that she didn't want them to know: it had just not been said yet, she was waiting for her opportunity. She didn't want to blunder in, look like a big old homosexual *schlemiel* by one day teaching them how to spell *suitcase* and then blurting, Speaking of which, I'm gay.

Her clothes were still bunched on the right side of the closet, into about a third of the space, sleeves cuffed and the collars of the rayon shirts flared and flattened; the other two-thirds of the closet were entirely taken up by empty plastic hangers. She reached in bravely and began spacing her shirts till they were occupying the whole closet. With most of the people she taught, it was enough that Anna was white: she worried that being a dyke would completely strain her credibility, the way she worried that if she ever had to, say, testify before a Senate subcommittee, she would be viewed by the television audience as the lunatic fringe. She wanted to approach her students with food in an outstretched hand till they would approach, and agree to learn from her.

She'd come out often to her college classes, and even though it had seemed to cause greater astonishment when in one class, she'd compared something they were learning to Donna's passing out on prom night on *Beverly Hills 90210,* it always got a reaction. Often the students, one by one, reported that they already knew, and told her how they had come to know. Scott called this testifying. They were testifying, he said, that they were, and always had been, in control of the information. His own mother, struggling to deal with his coming out, had written him a letter saying that she wouldn't have been so devastated if he hadn't actually *told* her — if he'd just let her slowly figure it out and then approach him about it. "So it's okay for me to be gay," Scott figured, "as long as I'm not in charge of my own self-definition."

The thing was, until she came out, they held a lot of the cards, thinking they knew something she didn't know they knew, even possibly, God forbid, that they knew something about her that she herself didn't know. It was convoluted, knowledge going off like rogue fire-crackers, illuminating the classroom in intermittent startling flashes; their minds were always a split-second behind their vision. She worried sometimes that because she was closeted, they took her masculinity to be unwitting, mistaking it for fashion cluelessness.

After careful consideration, she chose black jeans, a maroon cotton button-down shirt, and a bolo tie. She hiked the jeans over her thighs with her thumbs, feeling their tug and scrape, and the quick apprehension before she could wrestle the button closed and crouch and bounce, reconciling flesh and denim to one another. But they fit easily this morning, because she was still having trouble choking down food, and she tugged up the zipper with a satisfied flourish. Studying herself in the mirror behind the bedroom door, she tucked the shirt in evenly all around. When she looked like a man, she looked like a young husband, fresh from a shower, checking what's left in the refrigerator and compiling a shopping list so that after work he can bring home the groceries. A kind and helpful bourgeois man whose wife dressed him nicely. She raised her arms above her head, bringing up the shirt, then lowered them and let the shirt drape over the jeans. Last summer, in a swanky men's store, buying her first men's suit — a $300 cream-colored tencel suit that made her feel like Mr. Giorgio Armani himself — she had done that in front of the mirror, and the languid ponytailed proprietor had flattered her by saying approvingly, "A lot of guys don't know how to do that." She left the top button of her shirt unbuttoned. Because she wore mens'-sized shirts, the sleeves were always too long, so she had to roll them to midway up her forearm, creating the perpetual impression of being ready to get to work. She brought the knot of the tie up to the top, then pulled lightly to loosen it. She wanted the tie's effect to be understated. *I know I'm a butch, and it's a thing I am without even trying.* She put on black shoes instead of boots, because she didn't want to go to the adult learning center as Willie Nelson. The knot of the tie was metal, a tiny folded silver oxford shirt, with an olive-green tie knotted over it. She loved the wit of the tie.

Chris squeezed into a desk at the back of the classroom, in front of the windows' white light and the dry spidery plants in hanging pots set on the long ledge. She planted her feet to take weight off her back, and brushed her fingertips over the top of Kathleen's bag. She felt the bounce and ring of the other students' vision. She looked up at the walls, the first hit like a cannonball dive, her vision spraying and making a great blur of the blackboard and the posters with their vivid script and bold drawings, their photographs of people in beaded hats and Indian headdresses. She tried to focus, to swim in the writing. *The, stop, she, danger.* Words she knew how to reach up and grab onto. Here she couldn't, though; she couldn't muster the quiet. She let her eyes go slack and her vision splay. There were shouts and a yelp of laughter from the hall. She could hear the two black women whispering, saw the hulk of their bodies leaned in together. That younger one, she'd keep an eye on her. She had taken in the long painted nails and the gum in Cheryl's mouth, and was reminded of every saleswoman who had ever given her a hard time.

When Anna walked in, tossing her book bag onto the front desk, it took Chris a second to register. This baby dyke, the one from the hall the other day, was her teacher! The little flame of faith she kept her hands cupped around flickered at the sight of Anna's face. You could knock this person over with a feather! Plus, a teacher wearing a tie like that? *Howdy cowpoke, I'd love to mount your... bronco.* Chris remembered a butch from the old days named Dana who had worn one of those ties a few times, until one day she walked into the bar wearing one and someone had called out that fatal line, which had them falling off their stools with glee.

Anna was breaking a belated sweat from the stairs, and her forehead gleamed. After a whole summer in nothing but sandals, she felt her feet prickling in her socks. Antwan, she noticed, was absent. She wrote on the board: *Chris Rinaldi.* Then turned, and said, pointing to each word, "Chris, Rinaldi. She's a new student, and I want to welcome her. Did I spell that right, Chris?" Anna forced herself to look at her. It was hard to do, she was such a complicated sight; it was like peeking at the sun during an eclipse, wondering if it would really burn your retinas.

Chris was electrified, seeing her name go up there. Heat seeped up her neck. "I forgot my glasses," she said, her voice splintering and burying itself in air.

"I'm sorry, I didn't hear you?"

Chris cleared her throat and pushed the sentence out of her mouth again. It seemed to require a huge effort of breath. She was already disgusted with herself. "I forgot my glasses." Hell, it was automatic. She knew how to spell her own name!

Cheryl snorted. Anna shot her a look, walked over to her desk, stepping delicately over Brandy's many bags. "Okay, let's get Chris caught up, since it's her first time. Our policy in this class is that the most important things you can bring are? Besides paper and a pen?"

Cheryl and Vanessa and Brandy rolled their eyes, reciting in a schoolroom singsong, "Your energy and your glasses."

"Your energy and your glasses," Robert pitched in, a millisecond later.

"That's right," Anna said. She stood very close to Cheryl, crowding her, her hip almost touching one of her big hoop earrings, as she introduced herself and had them each say their names. Cheryl craned her head away, her restless hands becoming still. Looking down at the page, Anna saw cube and pinwheel doodles, and a quick accurate sketch of her bolo tie. "Okay, let's pair up and write what's on our minds. Two sentences. Chris, you pair up with me; Cheryl, you pair up with Robert, and Vanessa and Brandy together. Ten minutes of writing."

Okay, Cheryl thought, so that's how it is. Robert gave her an apologetic look as she grimly scooted her desk closer to his, making it screech on the floor.

"Those of you who need a jump start can complete this sentence," Anna said, writing on the board: "I came to school today, but _____ ."

She beckoned to Chris, who got up stiffly and walked to the front of the room, yanking down her jacket, which had bunched up on her waist. Her name blazed up there on the blackboard. They neared, eyes averted, heads ducked, sniffing. Anna was still holding the chalk; she tossed it to the blackboard ledge, where it clanked and bounced to the floor, and smacked her dusty hand against her thigh. She pulled up a chair for Chris and tore a piece of notebook paper off her pad to set between them. Chris sat; she smelled of cigarette smoke and something else, it was the aftershave of Anna's eleventh grade English teacher, Mr. Reque, whom she'd adored. *Oh man,* Anna thought. She looked at Chris. Her face was broad, blunt at the nose and heavy at the chin; as she aged she was getting jowly. She had bright and haggard blue eyes, aging downwards in pouches; the contrast between her eyes and her dark hair — sprinkled now with the slightest hint of silver — was arresting, and must have been, Anna thought, her claim to handsomeness when she was younger. Her gender was dull and heavy, like tarnished metal. "Let's think," Anna said, "what's the thing that's most on your mind right now? I'm going to write it down."

She was going to write it down, thank God. Yes, Chris was sure she was not expected to write. She folded her hands in her lap. "It's a thing we're going to be doing at the beginning of class," Anna said. "I think of it as burning off the fog."

She looked at Chris expectantly, and Chris felt her heart start to pound. She didn't know what was on her mind, except getting through this first class without passing out or her head splitting wide open. How was she going to make it, coming five times a week for so many weeks, maybe years, when it was such an effort to come even once? And was this the person she was going to have to count on to teach her to read? This queer with the stupid tie and her naive face, as eager as a puppy. Who could barely look her in the eye. She didn't even look like a teacher.

"I don't know," she said. She rubbed her temple with her thumb.

Anna waited, quieted herself down. It was a delicate moment, the initial part of Language Experience Approach, eliciting what was thought of as "their own story." You'd be sitting there, pen in a practiced hand, trying to introduce them to the things they cared about, as though they didn't know they burned with rage and hope and deeply-held opinions. Because the thing was, in a way they didn't know: they were in a classroom, where every one of their ideas had always failed to count as an idea. And God knows what she looked like to Chris, probably like some caseworker, some idiot sent to help. She tried to look at Chris's tight uninviting face without staring. She thought that eye-contact was way overrated, that sometimes the last thing you needed was someone boring into your eyes. "What kinds of work have you had?"

"All kinds," Chris said.

Anna nodded and considered, then ventured softly, "It must be pretty hard coming back to school."

Chris blinked rapidly, and for one disarming second looked to

69

Anna like a little boy with a new haircut. "That's for sure," she said. "Okay, I know. I watched the Cubs game last night."

Anna paused. Then she nodded and wrote it down. She kept the page turned so Chris could watch her write. Because she was left-handed, she gripped higher up on the pen than normal and held it at a sharp angle, to keep her hand from covering each word as she wrote the next. "Okay, good, you can tell me about it, because I missed it."

Chris dictated, peeking at the words Anna was writing down in neat print letters, as though she'd been told she wasn't allowed to look. When she was finished dictating, Anna asked, "You a Harry Caray fan?"

"Can't stand him," Chris said.

Anna grinned, gave her the thumbs up. From here on she had a script, and that relaxed her. "Okay, here's what you said. Watch and listen while I read it to you. Is this the way you wanted it written?" She pointed to each word as she read it:

I watched the Cubs game last night. It was incredible. The Cubbies snatched defeat from the jaws of victory. They went into the ninth inning with a 4-run lead and the wind blowing in, and then the bullpen blew it. They definitely need a closer.

"How's that?"

"Pretty good," Chris laughed. *Defeat from the jaws of victory,* that was a good one.

"Okay, now read the first sentence along with me. You already know what the sentence says because it's your words." She prompted, "I watched…"

Vanessa's head jerked up and she called, "How you spell *groceries?*"

"Don't worry about spelling," Anna said. "Just write *gr* and then a line for now, and keep going." She turned back to Chris, who was furiously scanning the page. "I watched…"

"The Cubs game last night," Chris whispered. They read each sentence like that, then the whole passage, Chris's voice wind-drafting on Anna's.

"Good," Anna said. "Okay, now pick three words from the story that you want to learn."

Chris studied the page. Her head was pulsing. She ran the sentences through in her head again, from memory. "Game," she said. "Defeat. Wind." The truth was, the whole time she had been watching baseball in bed, she had barely recognized it, what with realignment and interleague play and the live ball and whatnot, with those 18-15 scores that made you lose track of anybody who'd done something small and amazing. She hadn't mentioned in this writing that the Cubs had been playing the *Brewers,* which had made the game seem unreal, like a spring training game, or a charity game.

Anna fished in the side pocket of her bag and took out some word cards. She would remember *blow* and *blew* for later. She wrote down the three words, one on each card, then asked Chris to place each word under its duplicate in the story. Chris put down *game,* and Anna saw that the pinky finger on her right hand was missing at the bottom joint. "What's the word?" she asked.

"Game."

"Good." After Chris put down all three words, Anna had her take up the cards and shuffle them, then read each word again.

Wind. Game. Defeat.

"Good job," Anna said. "Here, you keep these cards."

Robert pushed his paper over to Cheryl. In smudged pencil, it read:

The Ax____

By Robert Day

"I didn't get very far," he said. He had been trying to write *accident.*

"No shit," Cheryl agreed. What a loser. She turned her paper toward him. It opened, "I came to school today, but ____," and was followed by a list of numbers, up to 10, to mark grievances. She read aloud the only one she had actually written, making just the barest pretense of showing Robert the words: "She pick on me all the time."

"She don't pick on you," Robert said.

"She put me with you, didn't she?" Cheryl snapped.

Brandy was struggling to read Vanessa's sentences, but was stuck at the very first word. Vanessa swiveled the page with her fingertips and read them to her, pressing her thumbnail on each word. She read,

"Desirée baugt gr____. She baugt soda." She looked up, added, "I don't let the kids have soda."

Brandy considered. "Why not?" she asked.

"It's bad for their teeth," Vanessa said. "But she have to go buy it anyway, so they think she special." Her lips were tight. She had told Brandy about Desirée's surprising arrival on her doorstep, this young woman from her father's other family. They had never even met — Vanessa hadn't seen her father since she was four — and suddenly, here she was, light-skinned and speaking all proper, and Vanessa couldn't fathom what she wanted from her. She hadn't told Brandy that Tisha, her littlest girl, thought Desirée was as pretty as Pocahontas, or that she herself was trying these days not to eat any food till noon, because she was sick and tired of looking at her fat self in the mirror.

Brandy wondered if it was right to say *kids* or if you were supposed to write *children*. She thought she remembered some tutor having told her that once. On her page she had written, "I came to school today, but _____ ." The rest of it was a furious mess of scrawls in red pen, every word crossed out with an urgent obscuring zigzag.

Chris returned to her seat, the back of her shirt soaked with sweat, the glare of the day slicing at her temple.

Anna too was sweating. "How'd we do?" she asked. She bent and picked up Robert's paper, which had swirled to the floor, glanced at the dirty page. "Wow, sounds like a spooky story," she smiled, handing it back to him. He took it and looked searchingly at his half-written word. Spooky? Anna erased Chris's name and wrote on the board: *groceries,* and *grocery store.* She showed them how the plural of words that end in *y* are spelled *ies.* "What other words are like that?" she asked, writing *city* on the board. Then, as they called out, *family,* and *cherry.* Anna walked around the room with her hands in her pockets, looking at the words as they wrote them down. Chris copied the letters painstakingly from the board, stopping to flex her hand as the old ache radiated through her little finger. It wasn't sulking. That's what Kathleen called it, but it wasn't. It was backaches, and painkillers, and not being able to do anything. And that house! How could that house, which they had been so hot to buy, feel so much like those rooms where whole families are buried in vaults, her voice seeming inside its walls to sob and echo? What was the matter with her? She wasn't the first person in the world to buy a house.

Now that she had settled down, the shirt plastered to her back was ice cold. That teacher had made her feel like she could read. But to be honest, if someone had given her those words to read and she'd never heard them before, she wouldn't have been able to read most of them. It wasn't really reading. Not when you thought about it.

CHAPTER SIX

Summer was hanging on, thin and bleached, like clothing it was high time to throw out. Anna had taught six classes and overdressed for five of them; she just couldn't get it in her head that it was still short-sleeves and sandals weather. On her block people walked their satchel-laden children home from school, their dark hair whipped by the wind, a sweaty shine on their faces. Anna came home from work stinking, her socks drenched. She ached to be released from this summer — if nothing else, to wear different clothes than she had when Patricia left her. On Monday afternoon she got in the mail from her best butch buddy Monica a copy of Emerson's "Give All To Love," with a yellow post-it on it saying "Thinking of you — Love, M." She stood on the tile floor of the little foyer, her book bag on the floor between her feet, scanning the poem quickly and curiously, until she came to the last lines:

> *Though thou loved her as thyself,*
> *As a self of purer clay,*
> *Though her parting dims the day,*
> *Stealing grace from all alive;*
> *Heartily know,*
> *When half-gods go,*
> *The gods arrive.*

She shut the mailbox, and fumbled for the tiny key to lock it. On her way up the stairs the tears rushed into her eyes with a fury so efficient it made her marvel. She crawled into bed, and guessing that

Monica would be in class, called Scott. "Of course," he said when she asked if he knew the poem, and then, more helpfully, after she read him the last stanza: "Oh honey." She wept the entire day. When she was able to think about it, she knew that "a self of purer clay" was a bullshit way to describe Patricia — a bullshit way to describe *any* woman. But the rhyme entering at *day* just broke her heart. And the final promise: how did Monica know that was true? Because on occasion, she sensed the same thing, and when she did, it made her feel like a small bright kite taken by a gust of wind.

And still, each day when she awoke, she groaned as memory broke over her: Patricia was gone. She heaved herself out of bed wondering how she would make it into the classroom, and what she would do without a witness to her day. Scott called it the ontological echo: the person who mirrors back your day on earth. For the first time in many years, she bought a Yartzeit candle and lit it on the anniversary of her father's death. She wrapped her tongue around the impossible sounds of the Kaddish, and sat at the kitchen table watching the little flame. It would be Rosh HaShana soon; she listened anxiously for the sound of the new year's cold thunderous hooves. The Jewish new year suited Anna as a new beginning more than the secular new year, for she was one of those achieving children whose year had always burst open like a pod in September, when school started. At school they were a delight — excelling for parents whose attention was riveted by their disappointing or disturbed or dying siblings, or slipping from cold homes, and tottering with matted wings under other adults' warm and brooding eyes. In high school Anna had fled in early-morning darkness, before she could hear the quick footsteps of her mother's baffling rage and wonder *What did I do?* She sat with her algebra teacher Mr. Legleiter in his office, a cubicle enclosed on two sides by glass. He marked papers, stroking his long beard and drinking coffee from a thermos, while she sat cross-legged on the floor, in blue jeans, getting ahead in her homework. He wore flannel shirts, and had the smart-ass sense of humor of the counterculture. Recently she had remembered something: that he had approached her one day — was it in his own basement? what was she doing there? could she have been babysitting for him and his wife? — with a look on his face so still and blind it had made her whirl and run up the basement stairs, and after that cut him dead whenever she saw him. When she thought about it now, she wondered: what was he seeing when he looked at her? And what kind of need had driven him toward her in that only half-remembered dark place?

On Tuesday, dragging herself reluctantly out of the car and locking the door, Anna was arrested by the sight of Chris above on the El platform, cupping her hands to light a cigarette. She had returned! Chris disappeared and reappeared trotting down the steps, exhaling through her nose. She wore her book bag slung over her head, with her arm covering the bag's openings. She sure had a way of making a cigarette look delicious, Anna thought, with an ex-smoker pang. Crossing the street briskly and at a diagonal to avoid a group of men arguing outside a bodega, she watched Chris approach with a slow roll in her walk that she knew must come from her injuries — she had looked through Chris's file yesterday after class — but that looked as though it came from attitude. Chris's face was slack, her mouth slightly open; she was stupid with absorption, as though her plan was to ward off street danger by simply refusing to notice it. She didn't seem to notice that she and Anna were approaching the door at the same time. Anna looked at her, then down, then peeked again, trying to time it so they'd recognize each other at the same time, so that she wouldn't be caught looking more interested than Chris. But she kept missing, until they got to the door, as unwarmed by recognition as rocks unwarmed by sun, chilling you, when you sit on them, at the seat of your pants.

"Hey Chris," she said. She was sure she had seen her.

Chris blew smoke out of the corner of her mouth away from Anna, and flicked the cigarette butt into the gutter. "Oh hi." When her eyes finally did rest on Anna, they came down with a thud. She was almost half a foot taller than Anna. They stood awkwardly at the door till Chris reached forward and grabbed the metal bar, and pushed. She crooked her body around so that Anna would slip in before her. Anna's heart made a little yelp, and then she scooted on in. The right thing for

Chris to have done would have been to push it open and then go through first, keeping a hand on it so it wouldn't slam in Anna's face. Anna ran up the stairs, taking two at a time, feeling foolish and rude, hoping that Chris had opened the door for her out of respect rather than chivalry.

Chris watched her go, thinking: *Okay.* She trudged up the stairs, her back stabbing at her and dread worming its way into her throat. Returning home yesterday, she had worked herself into a full-fledged panic by the time she walked through her door and kicked off her shoes. By the time Kathleen got home, around 5:45, Chris had drunk three beers and was brooding over all those rules in the world she couldn't read — *hey buddy, can't you read?!* She and Kathleen called them imaginary rules. Once, in a pharmaceutical plant she'd worked at for a few months, she had been laid off for placing her lunch on a certain counter.

Kathleen looked at her, and at the TV; Chris was watching *Full House.* Through the woolen tingle of her buzz, Chris could see her thinking: *uh oh.* "How did it go?" Kathleen asked, very still, her purse still slung over her shoulder.

"It was okay," she said.

"Really?" She sat down on the couch next to Chris. "So I don't need to kick anybody's ass?"

That surprised Chris into a wet and teary laugh. "I learned three words," she said.

"Well that's good, isn't it?"

Chris looked at her. "Do you know how many words there are in the English language?"

Kathleen sighed and patted her knee. "Rome wasn't built in a day, honey."

Chris returned to the same seat she had sat in the day before, and sat down without taking off her jean jacket.

"Okay," Anna said, and asked them to write what was on their minds. She wrote on the board, for those who needed a jump-start: "I get scared when I think about _____." She had once attended a workshop on teaching creative writing in adult basic education, where the teacher had said that that assigning scary or exciting stories worked well for adult new writers, since they could create something compelling with short sentences.

The students sighed and shifted and stared at the board, and the wind jarred the windows. Anna sat quietly at the front of the class. She was trying to listen, in accordance with the most important principle of adult basic education: the material emerges from the needs and interests of the students. She listened as well as she knew how, blocking out her expectations of them, just as she'd learned to block out her expectations of a piece of literature, to bend a quiet ear to it, let it teach itself to her. She did individual LEA's with them, had them write something immediately in the morning, in that vulnerable space between the roar and strife of getting their days started and the stillness of blank paper. She grasped onto the hand of their life-concerns and tried to let them pull her out of herself, to the brisk air where they stirred and shook her. Robert looked to her like a street person who'd come in for a moment to get warm; his long thick fingernails made her recoil. She had taken that recoil home with her every day last week and worked it over and over, trying to extrude the racism from it. Brandy, who labored over her notebook among an explosion of bags and papers, had disconcerting bruises on her face and arms; it was hard to tell if she was being beaten, since she seemed to be the kind of person who really did fall down flights of stairs and walk into doors. Since both she and Vanessa were raising children alone, they didn't have the time or space to do homework; they did homework only once a week, when they saw their tutors. And Brandy wasn't even doing that now, since the state had cut the subsidy for her eleven-year-old son Watson's after-school program, and he came home earlier. There always seemed to be at least one person absent, and it felt to Anna as though effort was seeping out of the gaps where the empty chairs were, like heat through badly-insulated windows. She looked at Chris sitting rigidly over her paper and wondered about her; with no children and a good work history, implying discipline and coherence, she had a solid foundation to progress quickly. The main thing that could set her back was landing a well-paying job. Or freaking out. Anna looked at the cloze exercise she would do with them later that morning, a passage about nutrition in which they had to figure out from the context the missing words. She was trying to settle into the mood that suited her best, a kind of relaxed readiness. It was a balancing act: she would try, for her own protection, not to expect steady progress from her students, yet at the same time to cultivate a readiness to see achievement, and at that moment both celebrate and push.

Vanessa shook out her writing hand. She kept a word card with *Desirée* on it propped on an eraser on her desk, for easy reference; her half-sister's interest as a writing topic seemed inexhaustible. "My daddy lef when I was 4," she wrote. "He did not leave Desirée." Yesterday Anna had written the word *leave* on the board and drawn a circle with spokes around it, and had the whole class do a semantic mapping exercise with it: who leaves, who you leave, by which form of transportation you leave, why you leave (you are angry, you are in trouble, you just can't anymore!), *left, leaving,* and in a corner of the board, *leaves* and *leaf.*

Cheryl was writing copiously and noisily; then she stopped, flung her pen down on her notebook and left the classroom. She worked part-time at a beauty salon, shampooing and sweeping floors. Last week when Anna did her first LEA with her, asking her to describe how to put in a weave, Cheryl had thrown back her head and cackled, then mocked: "How y'all do dat wit' yo hair?" Anna had laughed — she couldn't help it — but her face had grown hot and stayed that way for days, it seemed. In a way the sting of that response was better than the geological time between her and Robert, eons of calcified insult and response. Anna knew Robert lived with his mother, who was losing her eyesight, and that he had been in Vietnam. But generating vocabulary that would be close to his heart felt difficult and presumptuous; for all she knew, if she asked about either of those things she might be asking him to visit his biggest traumas. He worked afternoons in the pharmacy on the first floor of a high rise assisted-living facility on Sheridan Rd.,

delivering prescriptions to Jewish widows. She asked him about that.
"They call me Bobby there," he said.

"What do you think about that?"

He laughed and shrugged, a complicated amusement playing
across his bloodshot eyes. Anna imagined the pharmacist with his
smooth brown hair and wire-rimmed glasses and cartoons taped on the
walls about men loving golf more than their wives, explaining slowly
with his hand on Robert's shoulder. And the old ladies — *oy vey!* the
caressing voices, the brownies and sandwiches, the way they'd latch
onto the fact that he lived with his mother, and report it approvingly to
their families, and ask him how she was each time they saw him.

Now she sat for one more second, then rose and went over to Chris,
pulling up a chair to sit next to her. Chris could smell her, she was sitting
so close; it was a fruity smell, maybe her shampoo. Anna had light skin,
hair shaved above the ears, and brown eyes with serious lashes. When she
spoke to Chris her eyes looked so moist and shiny it was embarrassing to
look at her, it was like seeing her crying, or naked. She reminded Chris of
Angel from the bar days. Angel ran with the butches, but would get the rest
of them in trouble by taking just a little too long, being a little too slow.
Once they were leaving Ray's Canteen after having burgers, and a bunch
of guys in letter jackets strutted in; and while everyone sliced neatly and
distractedly past them, not looking or touching, wouldn't you know that
Angel would drop her change, and have to bend to pick it up, and running to catch up with them, not only bump into one of those boys, but also
look confusedly into his beefy face. You just couldn't let things like that
happen. In the end, somebody had ended up in the hospital with a frac-
tured hand, and it wasn't Angel.

Chris had printed her full name in the center of the top line, and
copied the sentence from the board. She had thought of a lot of ways
to complete that sentence, each one a spelling minefield, each one
opening onto a hurricane of other fears. She had finally written over
the blank, in pencil fainter than the rest, "the stares."

When Anna saw it, she thought: Now we're getting somewhere.
"Whose stares?" she asked.

Chris hesitated. Whose stares?

"People stare at you?"

She turned and looked blankly at Anna's face. "No, why would people stare at me?" she asked. Then she looked back down at the paper, and embarrassment started seeping over her. It made her think of the lava she'd seen in a nature show. "I meant the stairs that you walk up," she muttered.

It took Anna a second to register; then her heart started to pound. Oh Jesus. "Oh," she said, a tiny tremor in her voice. "That's spelled S-T-A-I-R-S."

Chris erased the word with such disgust she ripped the paper. "Hey, take it easy," Anna said; "you're gonna make mistakes, that's natural."

Chris looked up quickly, and then around, her face red, checking to see if the other students had heard. "Everybody does," Anna said, trying to contain her irritation; that was not another faux pas!

Chris was writing *stairs* in dark letters over the angry mess she'd made. "Because of my back," she snapped. "It hurts to go up them."

It was one of those things you can never take back, or pretend you never said. Anna turned left onto Sheridan Rd., on her way to Northwestern to have lunch with Monica, then teach her afternoon class. Her neck ached from the rigidity of her jaw, and a full fury of self-loathing was coursing over her. Had there ever been a bigger asshole? She was the least discreet person she knew. She thought of Patricia, who had been unnaturally discreet, shushing Anna in restaurants and public places. You could be an hour into a conversation with Patricia, well on your way into the minutiae of your day, before she'd tell you that she had won a big award, or that her mother had broken her hip. To Anna that had always felt downright hostile, designed to trap her into looking like a blabber-mouth oblivious to the concerns of others. Anna drove along the street shadowed by high-rises, trying to stay in sync with the lights. God, Chris. Thinking of her made heat come roaring back into Anna's face. That arrogant stoicism. The way she looked at Anna, like a mechanic looking doubtfully at her car's engine, declaring that he can't promise anything, he's not a magician, making her feel morally small for having such a lame and ruined car. Tears pushed at the hollows of her eyes, and she felt faint with defeat.

By the time she reached Monica's office, her mood had swung extravagantly, and she was feeling awful for Chris, who had made the courageous effort to come back to school, only to be insulted by her teacher. Monica came from around her desk and hugged her. They hugged like men, thumping each others' backs with their paws. On the wall above the filing cabinets was a framed picture of James Baldwin, Monica's muse. Of all his writing, Monica said, she loved most his account of the first time he saw Bette Davis on screen. He had been astonished; her pop-eyes were popping just like his own, he wrote, and she "moved like a nigger." She loved that, she said — not only because it was true that Baldwin looked like Bette Davis, but also because of the ardent ingenuity that found a way, across so many barriers, to thrill to their likeness. Just as she herself thrilled to Baldwin, Anna thought, which must have had to do, at least in part, with the fact that like him, Monica had been a queer child from a poor family with an enraged and terrifying father.

She held Monica away from her and thanked her for the poem she'd sent. "You're such a geek, sending me Emerson as a cure for heartache!" she teased, and Monica laughed her small laugh, through her nose. She was looking prosperous and buttoned up, a little pale, her hair hippyish in a frizzy ponytail. Monica had gotten tenure last year on the strength of a book too good and influential to allow her department to debate whether queer studies was the sort of thing they wanted around. It had been on sexuality and the formation of the American literary canon; but she felt that the book she was working on now, on Baldwin and Henry James, was her real love. She was very prolific, and like many prolific academics, had serious sleep problems. She also had weird compulsive rituals; when Anna went running with her on city streets, they were never allowed to cut across the grass when turning corners, but had to run the precise right angle of the block. At the same time, she was really fun, and constantly amazed Anna with expertise as random as it was abundant. She knew all the British kings, and loved tiny gadgets; she was trained as an EMT and as a volunteer firefighter.

"Do you mind if we eat here?" Monica asked.

"Nope, I brought my lunch with me."

Monica closed the door, and settled into one of the easy chairs in the corner of the office. As Anna took a tuna sandwich in a Ziploc out of her bag, she sat back and sighed and rubbed her face. It was narrow and pock-marked, tired now but normally arresting; she had a penetrating look that made Anna feel profoundly seen by her. Monica's mother had been a huge reader of detective novels, and so was she. She said that when she got to Harvard — from a tiny town in the mountains of North Carolina — it had stood her in good stead. "It helped me nose around for clues about how to be," she said.

Monica had helped get her this adjunct job, teaching one freshman composition course each semester. Now that Anna had defended her dissertation, teaching these courses for about as much money as she could make babysitting was her only contact with an academic institution. This fall was her third consecutive year on the job market. She had spent the last year revising her dissertation, which was about the portrayal of the poor in the Victorian novel, into a book; and after sending out several unsuccessful queries to presses who were apparently no longer doing period studies, she had sent the introduction and a prospectus to a slightly less prestigious press with a good Victorian line. She had also applied for about thirty jobs, only six of them tenure track and in her field, the rest part-time and adjunct positions, mostly in composition. She couldn't bear to hear stories about people with more than one book who couldn't get work, and still less could she bear to hear about the isolated successes of people like Patricia and Scott. Scott had once referred to the arbitrariness of his getting a job "while perfectly smart people don't get jobs," and occasionally Anna remembered that remark and it rankled her all over again.

"Boy am I glad you're here," Monica said.

"How come?" In a crestfallen split second, Anna prepared to put the incident with Chris on the back burner.

"I had a really bad night with Martha," Monica said. "Really bad."

Martha was a woman Monica had started seeing just as Anna

returned from Ithaca; Anna hadn't met her yet.

They had had their first fight: Monica offered to buy for Martha a jacket she couldn't afford on her own, and Martha was deeply offended. "She called me Lady Bountiful," Monica said, with a pained laugh. "Can you imagine?" It had turned into a ravaging fight that lasted all night, and plunged them into their darkest places.

She'd made a mistake, she knew that now, Monica said, offering something like that so early in the relationship. Was it was some kind of unconscious hostility, or insecurity, that had made her need to display her financial superiority? As she spoke, analyzing her own motives with pitiless rigor, and enumerating the painful circumstances of Martha's childhood, Anna liked Martha less and less. She seemed to have quite the mean streak. She'd accused Monica of being spoiled by tenure, out of touch with the reality of most working people; she clearly already knew that was a sore spot for Monica, who, having risen above her family's social class, believed on some level that she'd undeservedly landed in the catbird seat. Anna thought nostalgically of Monica's previous girlfriend, who had since moved to Namibia to work for a non-profit. Their sex had been rough and fantasy-filled, and they had a series of witty monogamy agreements that Anna had loved: initially they were allowed to kiss other people but only if they made loud smacking noises, and then, when Monica started sleeping on and off with one particular woman, they agreed that she was allowed, but only if she paid Robin a substantial fee each time she did. Their relationship had given Monica an aura of cockiness that Anna had enjoyed and studied.

Monica was quiet. Then she looked at Anna and smiled faintly. "Women," she said. It was a routine they had.

Anna smiled and shook her head. "So what's going to happen?"

"I don't know," Monica said. "She's not picking up the phone."

"Monica," Anna said gently, "what do you like about this woman?"

Monica thought for a second. "She's really pretty," she offered. "And the sex is sweet."

Anna had never heard Monica describe sex as sweet before, and she didn't like the sound of it. She looked at her watch. "Whoops, only 15 minutes." She wouldn't have time to tell Monica about her own day. To tell her about, for example, having humiliated an illiterate he-she.

Monica sighed and turned her attention to her sandwich. "What's on the docket for class today?"

"A paragraphing exercise," Anna said. She was a little pissed off at Monica, who was clearly feeling rejuvenated from having hogged the entire conversation, and then she felt selfish. She had flung herself upon her friends, in a hailstorm of need. And Monica had treated her tenderly. Anna thought of the day Monica urged her to come over and help her paint her apartment, then came back to Anna's to sleep over; she'd stripped down to her underwear and climbed into bed with Anna, throwing an arm over her body. Maybe Monica was letting her know now that her convalescence period was passing, and it was time to rejoin the other troops at the front. Anna tried not to let herself think about all the need she'd put out into the world. She lifted her bag onto her lap. Monica took a long swig of water from the bottle, then carefully screwed the top back on. There was something glittery in her eyes; she seemed to be humming with crisis. To her surprise, Anna found Monica's eagerness to latch onto this woman's pain a little grotesque. She suddenly remembered last summer, when she had thought Patricia might break up with her. She had been electrified with dread. Could you feel yourself changing as a person? Because she had; it was like a ship groaning among ice floes — sound so thick it sounded like sighing. She had submitted to Patricia's otherness. She had agreed to her sleeping with someone else, and groping for a way to think about it that was less deadly than the age-old narrative of betrayal, had found herself surprisingly buoyed and even a little turned on. She began walking away when Patricia was crying. She practiced, in the face of a woman in distress, taking a deep breath and letting her be.

She didn't get the payoff she'd hoped for. Patricia had not rewarded her for being so fabulous and creative, so much what Patricia needed. But now, watching her exhausted friend, Anna couldn't say she regretted that time. It had felt good for a moment to offer her lover something simpler than help, or healing. To offer witness. A gaze, she thought, that's unafraid.

CHAPTER SEVEN

But for now, provided with blank placards and crayons, your task is to exhort. *What should we write?* your little brother asks, sitting cross-legged on the rug of your parents' bedroom, bewildered. At eight, he is still chunky, and still whispers his passionate secrets to his stuffed Snoopy. The two of you stare at your mother with open mouths.

To tell the truth, you don't even remember this. You were only twelve. All you have is the official memory, the part you might as well be reading out of a junior high school history textbook: that one time, after he ran his Mustang into a tree, your mother kicked your father out of the house. And you and your brother were supposed to write supportive signs for him to take with him, with messages like *We love you, daddy!* Your mother wanted you to, and she presented it to you as a thing that you yourselves had thought of. The idea was that he would hang them around his hotel room and derive strength and comfort from them.

What you actually remember is nothing that could make this a good story, nothing with flavor or detail. Your memory is terrible. Your femme used to ask, How could you not remember? Sometimes she joked, taking your chin in her hand and turning your face toward her, applying blazing eye contact: *Do you remember who I am?*

Just dread, cracked as a dry riverbed; just a weary and ancient groan. And then doing what your mother told you, being supportive of your father. Writing: *We love you, daddy!*

There are some memories, but they no longer have images attached to them, the way you imagine retinas detaching from the eye. All that's left are the words for the memories. Your mother telling you, her voice elevated with significance, so he can hear: Your father can empty his mind so completely that he is thinking absolutely nothing. You sense vaguely that she's trying to shame him. Later, in bed, you try to completely empty your own mind, and find that it's possible for a very brief moment, like wobbling on a bike before falling down, when you don't yet know how to ride. You remember saying once, pointing, as he teased you: *Look daddy, your eyes are smiling but not your face.* He tells you that that's what's meant by "twinkling eyes," and for a bookish child such as yourself that comes as a tremendous revelation. You remember climbing out your bedroom window onto the garage roof and sitting up there during one afternoon of the five days that the detective searched for him, while your mother and uncle sat with blank faces at the kitchen table. You pretended the roof was a horse, and the elm trees tossed and rustled around you, making you feel little but regal, perched on a wild horse that only you knew how to control.

The loose v-necked undershirts he wore, the shadow of his chest hair underneath. His staggering past you in the downstairs hall, your calling him, his annihilating oblivion. That's the core memory, the one that must have happened, the one that's like the flank of a deer vanishing into the forest alongside the highway you're driving on, which you think you see but wonder if you only imagined.

Twenty years have passed, and you remember so little of substance. It's like a foreign language you once spoke fluently, where what remains is *God bless you,* and *Ouch!* Except in therapy, where once in a blue moon the past blows up through you like strange unseasonable weather, and you hear the words it speaks through your mouth. *You don't see me, why won't you see me?* One day your therapist loses a contact lens, which gives you grim satisfaction: a truth revealed.

You do remember respite. When you were eight, he was in the army, in Germany, off drugs, in a rage. You look back years later at the letters of your father's that your grandparents have saved; they're full of hatred for the army and the fat, red-cheeked, anti-Semitic Germans, anxiety about money, bluster about a threat to send him to Vietnam, about how he's the only doctor who knows what he's doing on the whole goddamn base. Apparently, he was something of a ranter. You remember one day when you were locked out of the house, and he tried to get in from the balcony: he leaped up and caught a rail, and when it broke off in his hand, he crashed into the bushes, shouting curses. You remember captain's bars, and the order of the military ranks. You remember that one day your parents fought and when your mother shoved him, he slapped her and stormed out of the house while she howled and gathered the two of you around her.

And meanwhile, you and your brother were flourishing at the army school, annoying your parents by goofing around in the back seat as they tried to navigate a new European city, relishing *schnitzel* and *escargots* and *croque monsieurs,* living in anger's element, which is like the first smell of burning leaves in the fall.

One day you and your femme are looking through old boxes of papers that you took out of your mother's basement, and you find a poem you wrote in junior high. It's called "Sonnet #1."

> *The winter moon is showing in the sky,*
> *Though only afternoon, it's getting dark,*
> *I'm feeling kind of sad but don't know why,*
> *As I walk home from school through Estes Park.*
>
> *When I come in you scramble up and stretch,*
> *Your joints they pop like popcorn and your tongue*
> *Shows when you yawn. You sit, lie down and fetch,*
> *You lick my face and I feel like I'm young.*
>
> *I tell you everything that's on my mind,*
> *You always listen but you never tell.*
> *You let me be the child I've left behind,*

You help me find the innocence that fell.
O Frisky, when you die I'll feel a pall,
And bury you with biscuits and your ball.

You remember a lot about this. Your teacher and your mother were deeply moved, and their moist tender looks embarrassed you. You were particularly fond of the popcorn metaphor, which seemed to you *exactly* what Frisky's joints sounded like when he stretched, and of the run-on in line 6, which in poetry, you learned, is called enjambment, and which you found extremely sophisticated. Now, looking at it, you cringe at the combination of cuteness and pathos that reminds you of an egregious foul in basketball: flagrant pathos. Your femme's favorite thing about it is the title.

It makes you think: how hard it is to mourn! When the dog dies, it's the cleanest grief in the world. You think how blessed you were to have this doggie in your life for fourteen years; laughing and crying, you tell stories about the time he was such a bad dog, and the time he was such a good dog; you close your eyes and whisper to him, thanking him for coming to live with you, wishing him safe passage. How unlike this other grief, which can't even be called grief, which expresses itself in your sight-lines gone flat and your face wooden, your being ruled by a puppet government that's severed ties with all the neighboring countries.

When your mother comes home from identifying the body, she says Kids, there's one piece of good news. You know exactly what's coming, and you help her the way parents mouth the words their children are reading for the first time. You say, It wasn't suicide. Right, she replies; he died of a heart attack. Two years later, she gathers you and your brother for a talk, her manner suspiciously ceremonial. You say, It was suicide. She gives you a look. Right, she replies. Your father's brother has told his kids the truth, and your mother is furious with him because he's forced her hand; she doesn't want you to hear it from your cousins.

And yet it remains a secret for years. It turns out that it was a big mystery to your high school friends. It remains a secret until you grow up and start having an autonomous medical history, and don't want your future doctors to think you're at risk for whatever disease you say your father had. Until you're smoking pot by candlelight with your roommate late one night, and whisper the truth, feeling not exactly shamed, not exactly sad — feeling foolishly melodramatic, like a Tennessee Williams character. It takes a while, but over time you develop the art of saying that your father committed suicide. Your timing between question and answer becomes suave: you don't gallop in, the big news streaming behind you, but neither do you wait so long you create a hush of anticipation. You become deft at saying it right: not matter-of-factly, but not dramatically either. You develop a look of understanding that it might be hard for your interlocutor to hear. Until, beginning to grasp the thing about secrets, that their potency is often vastly disproportionate to the power of the actual information, it's hard to go back and remember why you kept this secret in the first place.

Your brother is a Jewish boy, his mother's child. Their hearts pound wildly when they're upset; they huff and puff. As a child you lose every single fight with him, no match for his fury. He's a brooding, high-maintenance child with strong opinions about the outfits of Olympic ice skaters and the voices of R&B singers; his taste is unerring and relentlessly pounded home. He throws up sometimes before going to school; he cracks you up by imitating his fourth-grade girl classmates, their pouty slang, the way they flip their hair. When your father dies, the boy who used to lock himself in the closet talking to the vacuum cleaner gets released from potentially feminizing chores. And the ensuing years of taking out the garbage and mowing the lawn apparently pay off. When he gets old enough, he starts speaking in platitudes, like a rabbi. He says things like: *My father was the most giving person I've ever known,* and *If there's one thing that gave my father a sense of satisfaction, it was his children.* He calls people "individuals"; he says things like: *There's no call for that kind of behavior.* He's like those guys in college who made out with you and then got mad if you told anybody. He's become as thin as a rail.

Your mother's family is an immigrant family, in its third American generation, affluent and accentless. You live in a large dark brick house in the suburbs, with a den where you watch TV and bring your messy snacks, and a living room with fussy furniture and shiny silver ashtrays. Your neighbors across the street, first meeting your parents, ask what church they go to, and your parents take silent umbrage. Your grandparents have a lot of stories about your grandmother's sister, the only woman of that generation to go to college; they imitate the English accent she affects, and laugh over stories in which your grandfather's mother, Grandma Bessie, triumphs over her with peasant witticisms in a heavy Yiddish accent. At the same time, there are also stories about serving shrimp at big dinner parties and cleverly preventing Grandma from getting a whiff of the *treyf* circulating in the house. Even as a child you wonder why they had to serve shrimp.

Your grandmother's most indelible memory from her youth concerns the time the two lawyers she worked for as a secretary took her out to a swanky restaurant, and when the waiter passed around a salad dressing tray, she almost put thousand island dressing on her meat. She maintains the belief that it's watching pennies that has made her and your grandfather wealthy. Over dinner she tells you how much the brisket cost. Hey Ma, how much did this bite cost? — your uncle wisecracks as he lifts it to his mouth. He and your mother belong to the generation of Jewish children who find *Portnoy's Complaint* hysterical; your grandmother shakes her head and mourns for Philip Roth's poor mother.

Your mother claims that her father, a CPA, used to consistently underestimate your father's income at tax time, making him have to pay back taxes and penalties.

Everybody in your family always wants to know how you're planning on getting where you're about to go. Don't take the Drive, that's crazy! they cry; the Expressway is much faster. And they're huge teasers, negotiating affection and aggression with varying degrees of finesse. *Oh come on, I was just teasing, where's your sense of humor!* — is a thing that's said a lot to crying children.

You're fourteen, and your mother is bleeding. You were doing your homework in your room when you were alarmed by her cry. In the breakfast room, the phone cradled between her ear and shoulder, she pulls down her slacks and pushes a bath towel between her legs, revealing the bloodied splotch on her flesh-colored underwear, which bulges over a soaked sanitary pad. Your uncle is on his way to take her to the emergency room. Three heavy crimson drops have widened raggedly on the white linoleum. She pulls her sweater up to the waistline with her other hand so it won't get bloody.

Not again! Your sullen adolescent heart sinks like a stone. It seems as though there's a kind of warfare between you now: as though every time you or your brother gets sick, she gets sicker the next day. And your mother, who wonders aloud, when you spill sugar all over the counter because you weren't holding the container over the sink, how such a smart girl can be so stupid, has been having huge ludicrous accidents. During parents' night at school she gets an allergic reaction to some snack she eats that closes her throat and makes her face balloon to twice its size. Your handsome English teacher is racing for the phone and she's doubled over and heaving, right there in your homeroom; the father of a boy you like plunges a needle into her thigh from his own epinephrine-loaded syringe while you look on, mortified. And last Thanksgiving — when for the first time there were enough relatives around the table to hide your immediate family's sickening lack of numbers — she threw flour down the incinerator, not realizing it was lit, and it burst up and burnt off her eyebrows and lashes, and you and your grandmother had to get the food on the table while the kitchen stank of burnt hair and your brother brought cold wet towels to press against her face.

You give her another towel, visualizing the blood pouring from her womb and out her vagina, and she hands you the one she's been using, thick and heavy with blood. You hold it away from you at its clean corner, horrified. *Oh stop being a baby!* she snaps: *Just throw it in the garbage.* Your mother is a powerhouse. She refuses to call herself a feminist; because her mother and grandmother were so domineering, she believes that women really run the show. She's a vice principal at a junior high school, and by all accounts an intimidating disciplinarian. And yet, she has a relish for the ridiculous, and will be the first to laugh, in later years, about her accidents. *The bleeding! the bloating! the facial burns!* she cracks, throwing up her hands. *Oy vey!* Both you and your brother can make her face stream with laughter, and when that happens, her surrender to hilarity feels to you like an act of great love and generosity.

This bleeding undoes her. Her face starts working violently. You push against the cool pitiless feeling in your chest, and approach her. After your father died she used to invite you into her arms to cry, but you wanted her out of your face. You felt as though it was for her, not for you, as though you were supposed to be reassuring her that it wasn't her fault. Now you put your face on her neck and your arm around her shoulder but hold the rest of your body carefully away from her. You can smell the sweetness of the blood, the way you can smell her underwear when you do the laundry. You hate her for this display. And at the same time, a driving pity drenches you to the bone.

When you're in high school, your mother begins running away from home, for hours at a time, and once for the whole night. What had you done? Who knows: you were stubborn, you were fresh. Something apparently so terrible that she had to storm out of the house. You remember the slam of the car door and the grind of the electric garage door closing when she drove off. She refused to tell you when she'd be coming home. You'd come into the quiet living room and see your brother standing in front of the window, staring out onto the dark street, holding onto the drape.

Meanwhile, you're a great student, cruising along the Advanced Placement track in your vast, integrated, teeming public high school in the suburb that jars right up alongside the city. You talk your head off in English class. In theater, knowing that you can't aspire to be one of the glamorous actors who awe you into tears, you target small parts to try out for — old people and sidekicks. In choir you sing with full-throated ease, not needing to sing the melody, because you love the way the alto part brings out the flavor of the soprano, like salt on food.

Your choir leader is mild-mannered and perfectionistic, and this is the only time in your life you'll encounter this peculiar and divine combination. It's not *wha-chyew*, he cries, it's *what you*, giving the *t* a smart tap on his palate. He nods, eyes wide, when you get it right. His jaw and mouth are big as a bullfrog's, and out of them comes the sweetest baritone you ever heard.

These days, when you encounter your old high school friends your body sidles up for warmth, remembering the intimacy, as though you'd been puppies in the same litter. Meeting your best friend ten years later, you remember vividly hanging out in her room; once she was changing her jeans and you noticed she wasn't wearing underwear, which made a big impression on you. But you can't remember what you actually used to talk about. When you ask her, she laughs and says, Oh, you know, how shallow everyone else was.

You're the valedictorian of your class. And yet, you're never good at facts; in fact, you're afraid of them. You manage math and history and science as though carefully stepping over live electrical wires. As a student you often feel like high quality laminate on particle board, a pretty good imitation of real oak. Even years later, as you're working on your doctorate, you're so afraid to learn! You read books as though you're parrying blows; you leap up from your computer whenever you're on the verge of an insight. And you wonder if for you, learning about his death is the figure for all knowledge: your arms thrown up in front of your face, your mind gone as blank as a Demerol addict's, before it comes.

She's been having searing headaches, and fighting with you, and the day before you're supposed to leave for college, your mother has a headache so severe you call an ambulance. At the hospital she's rushed into MRI, and then into surgery. She has a brain aneurysm.

In the waiting room you and your brother exchange haggard looks. You finally pipe up. *What a coup!* you say. You open your arms and enlarge on your theme. Why, it's not a tactic to get love; it's not a threat to die, like Dad, if we misbehave, or grow up, or don't love her enough.

It's a brain aneurysm! You mime doffing your hat to her and say: *Touché*.

He laughs miserably and tells you to shut up.

She's in a coma for four days. A week later you leave home for the first time on your own steam, borrowing one of your uncle's cars and driving it through miles and miles of farmland. You've missed orientation, and your heart thuds with dread. The late-summer corn fields are cut to stubble.

And then, in college, something in you groans to a halt. You don't know how to remember, so for many nights you lie in bed giving yourself chills by imagining the silent spin of the planets, and yourself dead and unremembered. As if to blackmail yourself, saying, how would *you* like it, total oblivion? It seems that, memory forsaking you — for who can bear to remember being too puny, or unremarkable, or unloved, to tie her father to this earth? — you are staying faithful to his memory by enacting his stupor. In between going to classes, writing papers, talking with friends, you lie in bed stunned, as though you've gotten a hammer to the head before being slaughtered. A different world has pushed its way through the canvas of the old, and now fills your sight with dust, up to the heavens and to the furthest horizon.

Your mother surprises you by getting a job as a middle-school principal in Boston, and taking your brother and moving there. You understand later how good the promotion was for her, and how much she needed to get away from her own parents. But now you believe that she's punishing you for leaving home by snatching your home away altogether, like an angry mom stuffing the vegetables you won't eat into the garbage. In your sophomore year, you start taking Valium, skimming it off of your roommate's supply. Over holidays you fly to this strange friendless place, yell hello to your brother through his closed bedroom door; you fall into bed in your new room, smelling the walls' fresh paint and feeling the Valium seep like syrup down your face, your mind entirely empty. How you love it! Valium brings moisture into the flat dead landscape of your depression: it makes it sensuous, it makes you swoon. And it makes your mother frantic to see you this way; she screams at you that you'd better get your ass into therapy. It gives you a mean, hollow, satisfied feeling.

Now, when you look back at pictures of yourself in sundresses and blouses, you let out all that loathing: what a freak! And yet, maybe you weren't, maybe at times you were presentable enough, and your recoil comes from the accumulated weight of years of not recoiling, of trying so very hard. Your femme comes across a picture of you in a junior high school yearbook, a round face smiling apprehensively through drapery of long straight hair parted in the middle, and she grins and gives you a kiss, claiming that you pulled that look off much better than most white girls in the 70s.

You're short, and you've been on a diet since you were thirteen. You never choose a handsome man to desire; you strategically aim for mid-level looks, adapting to your status on the food chain. You seem to attract young men who begin their sentences with "I'm the kind of person who....," who claim that they're a giver, not a taker. You remember first seeing an erect penis, bobbing at you like a clown balloon on a parade float – the skin, surprisingly, soft as a tulip. The sex you have is hasty and anxious, the two of you worrying about getting it right, about getting it in the way you're supposed to. It's only later that you realize that you're not deformed; it's just that the men you choose are as inexperienced as you are, and need to slink away after not performing very well. Your femme interrogates you closely about this, and concludes from the evidence that all protestations to the contrary, several of these guys were in love with you.

And in between those brief relationships, you think: boy, it sure would be nice if I could be a lesbian. Later, it gives you a new respect for repression. It's not either *Yes* or *No way!* It's not like pregnancy: you can be, it turns out, a little bit repressed.

And you can enter therapy explaining, "I'm like this because my father committed suicide," knowing everything you need right there at the beginning. But years later, after dozens of squirrely exchanges around lateness, payment, your therapist's vacations, his strange visible injuries, something flippant – and when you think about it, really really mean — that he said, you bury your head in your hands and begin to wail. You're like this because your father committed suicide! You know it in a totally different way. It's like stepping into the frame of a movie that has the same plot, but in a different genre. You have no patience for your snooty academic friends who think they're too smart for therapy. Where's the smartness there? You got on transference's train and it took you for a ride.

One day in grad school, before you meet your femme, a lesbian friend of yours backs you up playfully against the department mailboxes, and for the rest of the day you walk around with a goofy look on your face. It's not the first time something like this has happened.

You didn't choose women, they chose you. The second time they met you, they recognized you from the time before. Your mother thinks you've taken the easy way out. Anyone, she says, can have an intimate connection with a woman: it's men who are the challenge.

You know you're breaking a kind of pact. It's just that you're no longer sure that rigor is a feature you require in your romantic life. You prefer backfloating off the island resort of lesbianism, where women surface beside you without your even having asked them to, hair slicked back, eyelashes pearled with water drops, faces lighting up at the sight of you.

It's an outlandish transformation, the kind only fairy tales, or American movies, can express. Your deep deep loneliness and need: left in a dank basement for years, when your femme comes along they sputter and flare into desire, and you come running out of the house, alarmed, glowing, with time to throw on only boxers and an undershirt.

Here's how you come to think of it: when you become a butch, the paralyzed part of yourself suddenly, somehow, becomes erotic. It's as though your woundedness becomes an electric stillness; when she comes to you, it makes her fly into a million pieces, and cling to you for dear life. You've felt desire before, but it was a bashful thing, and needed to be coaxed. Now you're constantly wet down there; when you wipe yourself after peeing, the toilet paper comes away slick and shiny. Now you know exactly what a hard-on feels like.

After your first days in bed together, your pecs are killing you, and she laughs and says that's where butches hurt after sex. It's from holding yourself over her, whispering encouragement and commands. Her pecs are fine, she says, but she has yet to fully master the movement of her legs.

Is it a second-tier beauty, a runner-up kind of beauty? How much should you care, if you might count as a very sexy lesbian? You have found your niche, like in advertising: you have found the demographic that will buy your product.

You're figuring out a way to be.

She says that butches are very gratifying to love, because they never in a million years dreamed that they would be loved, so they greet it with perpetual wonder and thanksgiving. And it's true: you're not religious, but you have suddenly remembered, from your childhood, the words for the *Shehechianu.* You think of it now as the Jewish prayer for coming out of depression, and you love each phrase it uses to describe God's gifts. Who gave us life, and sustained us, and brought us to this day.

CHAPTER EIGHT

When Chris loomed at the classroom door the next day, twenty minutes late, her face hectic and ruddy, glad surprise welled up in Anna. Apparently, even her finest efforts at insensitivity had failed to daunt the old warrior. Chris limped in, wearing a faded brown sports jacket, her shirt disheveled around the belt. Cheryl stared at her thoughtfully, and Antwan looked up from his paper. Chris set her bag under the desk behind Cheryl's, where she was sitting every day now. She carefully eased her jacket over her gut and her shoulders. She fumbled in the inside pocket for a handkerchief, then draped the jacket over the back of her chair and sat down and studied the board. Anna had written: *My favorite meal is ____.*

Anna passed Chris without looking at her. She'd been sitting with Brandy, and had learned that the toaster was broken, that Brandy was on the waiting list at the survival center for a new one, and was having to make her oldest boy Watson's toast in the oven. Anna and Brandy had come away with four cards: *oven, toast, toaster, fruit.*

Chris put that second perplexing word, the one after *my,* on ice for a second and thought: she's giving me the cold shoulder. As long as she had been under the kitchen sink taking care of the clog she'd felt fine, but now her back was acting up, festooned with pain. She blew her nose with a discreet honk. *Favorite,* she realized as she patted it dry, it was *favorite.* Its spelling shocked and aggrieved her.

She knew that Kathleen hadn't wanted her to come back to school, that she'd hoped the plumbing emergency would keep her at home.

"She said *what?!*" Kathleen had said last night, fluffing up.

"She said, *People stare at you?*" Chris had paused to see if she got it.

"She got that off of how I tried to write *stairs,* like the steps you walk up." She hadn't really meant to tell Kathleen about it, but when Kathleen had come in around nine and found her sitting at the kitchen table with homework, she had suddenly felt self-conscious. And then Kathleen was leaning over her touching her shoulder, poking her nose in to see what she was doing, and Chris had found herself creeping her crooked arm over the paper she was writing on, like a goody two-shoes trying to prevent the bad kid from copying from her. So she had said, "Hey, get this," and told her about Anna's comment.

She shifted at her desk, trying to distribute the weight evenly along her lower back, and thought about how Kathleen had sat down next to her with a big huff, her cheeks brightening, and started taking pins out of her hair. "I can't believe she said that," Kathleen said. "What kind of idiot says that to another person?"

And later, when they were in bed, Kathleen had reached over and touched her back. "Here?" she asked, pressing into the flesh.

Chris closed her eyes and groaned. "Oh God, not too hard." And then Kathleen rubbed it for a while, while Chris tried to lean into it and relax even as her conscience told her that Kathleen was expending muscle after having worked all day. "I should be giving *you* a massage," she murmured.

"You know, honey," Kathleen had said quietly, her warm breath lapping at Chris's ear, "It would be understandable if you didn't want to go back, after a comment like that."

The thing was, Chris thought, you could use anything as an excuse. She looked at the board. It was steak, of course, her favorite meal: cooked rare, with a twice-baked potato. The people in the class always had some problem with their check, or some office they had to go to because their electricity or phone were about to be cut off. They seemed shocked every single time it happened, which amused Chris. Brandy was always negotiating with social workers and Children and Family Services. The fact that she and Vanessa even came back to class at all seemed to Chris to come from the inertia of habit rather than from inner strength or discipline. She watched their gaits, the way their shoulders were pulled back and settled in alignment with their big butts, and thought: those ladies are in no hurry.

Well, she had fixed the sink, saved a fortune in plumber's bills. Still good for something.

Next to her Robert was writing with unusual abandon. He liked an old-fashioned southern meal: fried chicken, cornbread, greens, potato salad, pie. Was *greens* spelled like the color, he wondered? — and because he knew spelling to be so perverse, he second guessed it, writing: *greans*.

Anna stopped by and pointed at it. "It's just like the color, Robert," she said. "Robert, why don't you read this aloud?"

He read it, and glanced around sheepishly, knowing they all thought him country.

And then the others read: spaghetti and meatballs; Chinese food — garlic shrimp and pork dumplings; the macaroni and cheese they made in a certain West-side courthouse cafeteria, which Brandy claimed was so good it made her wish someone in her family would get arrested. Anna wrote every word on the board, and made sure they copied them down. There was a brief debate on the relative merit of regular and deep-dish pizza; Brandy liked deep-dish, but Anna argued that it was overrated, hyped for tourists to Chicago, and Vanessa exclaimed amazed assent, as though Anna was finally, after a thousand inchoate years, giving voice to her most vital opinion. Anna was enjoying the exercise; it had them all laughing and chatting. She looked at their faces and thought about how other than the potato chips or the Popeyes chicken and biscuits some of them occasionally brought in, she didn't have the foggiest idea how they ate, whether they or their kids ever went to school hungry, what was going to happen to their food stamps when their benefits got cut, what a conversation about favorite foods even meant to them. She asked what kinds of packaged and canned foods they bought, and wrote a list of those words: *tomato sauce, sugar, flour, chicken, margarine*. Then after the break she shifted gears and did an exercise on the word *because*. At the end of class, Anna pulled out *Bastard out of*

Carolina. She had arrived at the scene where Glen Waddell, who will turn out to be Bone's abuser, proposes to Bone's mother. Anna read Bone's account of how Glen, dripping with sweat and moaning with emotion, reaches into the old Pontiac and gathers the whole family into a fierce embrace. "His face slid past Mama's hair, pressed into mine, his mouth and teeth touched my cheek." And when Mama consents to marry him, he jumps back. "He slammed his hands down on the car top, once twice, three times. The echoes were like shots."

Anna read to the end of the scene, then peeked up. Vanessa was sitting with her hands around her notebook, her face rigid. "Vanessa?" she said.

"That ain't right," Vanessa said.

"What's not?"

"They supposed to be all happy, but it's scary." Brandy was nodding, looking back and forth from Vanessa to Anna for guidance.

"It's true, it is scary," Anna said. "What's scary about it?"

"He violent. It's like he shooting a gun."

"Yeah," Anna said, smiling, thrilled by Vanessa's sensitive ear. "He is violent. I think you're hearing exactly what we're supposed to be hearing."

She was still smiling at the end of class, as Chris got up and pulled her jacket on, reaching for a cigarette from the inside pocket.

"Chris," Anna called, "Hang on a second."

Chris rolled her waiting cigarette in her fingers and waited for Anna to approach. "Sorry I was late," she said.

"What? Oh, that's okay. Listen."

Anna was wearing belted jeans, an oxford shirt, that haircut, and a significant look on her face. What could she want from her? Chris wondered — she'd already apologized for being late.

"Listen," Anna said. She stood with her weight back on her heels and her hands in her pockets, as if to say that even though she was asking Chris to wait, she wasn't going to beg her to. "I feel we got off on the wrong foot."

"I'm sorry, I had a household emergency," Chris said.

Anna shook her head. "No, I mean in general." She paused, embarrassed, and sucked her upper lip between her teeth. "You know, that thing I said yesterday."

Chris looked past her at the board, and then back at her.

Oh for God's sake, Anna thought. What's she going to do, make me say it again? "Anyway, it was a stupid thing to say, and I'm sorry."

"Okay," Chris shrugged.

Anna considered, then plunged ahead recklessly. "It's not as if I don't get my own fair share of staring, in bathrooms and stuff like that. I think I was just identifying with you."

Whoa, Chris thought. "Okay," she said.

"I'm glad you came back."

"Why wouldn't I come back?" Chris asked.

Okay, fine, Anna thought.

"Okay," she said.

A few days later, Chris was summoned to Ms. Wallace's office after class. She wondered what she'd done to be called to the principal's office, and prepared to be furious if it turned out to be about being late that one time. Renée's small office had recently been repainted; the walls were pale yellow, and Renée had hung framed photographs from a trip to Greece and Italy, pictures of houses and ruins and sand. Taking in the smell of fresh paint, and noticing Renée's bright lipstick and big hoop earrings, Chris was warmed and disarmed by aesthetic pleasure.

"Hey there," she said.

"Hello Chris," Renée smiled. "Have a seat."

Chris sat and crossed her legs at the ankle.

"How're things going for you?" Renée asked.

"Not bad," Chris said, struggling for the right level of conversation, and suddenly aware of her grammar. "To be honest, I suppose I'm still getting used to it."

"It takes a little time, I know," Renée said. "But I know Ms. Singer has high hopes for you."

High hopes for her! Chris swallowed her surprise, and then thought: that was a line Ms. Wallace probably gave all the students. She'd noticed that everybody in adult education was always trying to be very encouraging.

As it turned out, what Ms. Wallace wanted was to assign her a tutor. Chris was taken aback; she'd heard some of the others refer to their tutors, but she'd thought that was a social services requirement, like a social worker, or a parole officer. Ms. Wallace assigned her a retired lady named Mrs. Barry. "She's very experienced," she told her, and she could meet Chris after class, several times a week. And she did this all as a volunteer, for free. Chris thanked Renée and left her office nonplussed, wondering what the catch was. It was only later that evening, washing up her dinner dishes and waiting for Kathleen to get home, that she finally let the thought come home to roost: it was just a nice perk they gave you.

But when Chris met Mrs. Barry a few days later, she discovered what the catch was. Mrs. Barry was an older lady with a plaid skirt and a cashmere sweater, and eyebrows that had been plucked out and penciled-on. She visibly recoiled when Chris walked into the little classroom they'd been scheduled to meet in, and Chris spent most of her energy during that hour trying not to make any big or sudden movements. It made her appreciate, she thought later, how Anna brought up a chair and plopped down right next to you, sometimes putting her arm around the back of your chair, a thing that up to this point, Chris had found obnoxious and unnerving. She and Mrs. Barry went over her vocabulary homework together, but she made Chris a nervous wreck; when she waited for Chris to write down an answer, the silence made Chris's mind spin like tires in mud, and her praise made Chris feel like a dog about to be given a treat. One time Mrs. Barry's husband came to pick her up, and the old guy had such a grim and resolute air about him, Chris could swear he'd come to protect her. How the hell was she going to get out of this? Chris wondered. She brooded about it at home, and when Kathleen suggested she talk to Ms. Wallace, she said heatedly, "I can't just turn down free help learning to read and write!"

Then one day, during Chris's third lesson with Mrs. Barry, Anna popped her head in the door. "Oops, sorry," she said, and withdrew, but a second later peered in again. Chris was sagging in her chair, her legs open, and Mrs. Barry's mouth was so tight it had almost disappeared altogether. The next day Anna was waiting for Chris at the classroom door. "Chris!" Anna said. "I was wondering: is that really the best time for you to see a tutor? Right after class, when you're tired? Because I know a tutor, a really nice guy, who might have time a little later on in the day."

Chris looked at her earnest face. Was she really tired after class? "Frankly," she said, "I haven't thought about that. Can I think about it?"

"Sure," Anna said. "Talk to your partner."

Chris blinked. "My what?"

Anna froze: Christ, had she blown it again? "Your partner," she repeated, steadfastly.

During class Chris wondered how Anna knew she had a partner, then remembered her file. Still, where did she come off? Then she suddenly had an idea: that saying it was the wrong time would be the perfect way out of her sessions with Mrs. Barry. It would be a shame to lose that time right after class; if she went later in the afternoon, she had no idea what she'd do in the hours between class and tutoring. But she had to extricate herself from working with Mrs. Barry before the strain of tolerating each other gave one of them a hernia.

What had Renée been thinking? Anna wondered later that afternoon, sitting at home grading homework. At her right elbow were piled maps, menus, schedules, job applications, prescription labels, the Bible, issues of *Streetwise,* and clippings from various papers about different city neighborhoods, about social services, about poverty and achievement. Anna found Mrs. Barry an utter tight-ass, and it was hard not to see assigning Chris to her as a hostile act on Renée's part. And man, she herself had almost blown it again with Chris, assuming things about her. During the break she'd raced to Renée's office, fumbled through the file cabinet for Chris's file, and looked it up, her hands trembling. Yes, there it was, under emergency contact, a woman's name, Kathleen Petty, listed at the same address. The rest of the day she started to get really burned up, that Chris was always making her out to be an indiscreet and presumptuous asshole.

Anna looked out into the little courtyard tended by the people in the neighboring building, at the Japanese maple arching over a stone fountain, the lilac tree against the chain link fence, and the small flower bed below it. It was a lovely verdant patch right off the alley, and on summer nights the companionable smell of barbecue smoke and the murmur of adult voices came up through the heavy open windows in the formal dining room she used as a study, and pleased and soothed her. Soon the grill would be taken inside, though, and right now she was lonely as hell, and depressed by her students' homework. She was learning some things: that if she gave adult basic ed learners *macaroni and cheese* to use in a sentence, every one of them would write, "I like macaroni and cheese," which served her right. And Anna was totally confounded by Vanessa's incomprehensible errors: she had written "No kind" instead of "no one liked," and "Tisha called the time" for, Anna suspected, "Tisha cried all the time." Vanessa had a great tutor, who lately had been printing out lines of print with a label-maker, and laying those strips under lines in books, to see if it would help Vanessa to touch the letters. But Vanessa hadn't seen Grace in weeks, what with one appointment or another, and she had missed class twice this week because her son had missed the school bus, and she had to take an El ride with a transfer to get him there, then come all the way back.

Anna picked up the copy of *Streetwise* next to her and glanced over the cover story, which was about community policing. Each time she cut out an article for her students, she felt like a grandmother clipping articles and mailing them to her grandchildren, making them puzzle: Let's see, I'm a psychologist, she's sending me articles about cults, so does she imagine that I deprogram teenagers, or that I'm the one brainwashing them in the first place? Her mind flickered back to last week, when she had read the class an article about Ebonics, and was surprised to hear Vanessa and Cheryl treat it with derision. "They just

wanna keep us talkin' like niggers," Cheryl argued, and Vanessa nodded, lips pursed. Anna thought that was a spectacular misunderstanding. She had sat on her desk and stared at the two adamant women. "It's
not like these kids wouldn't also be taught standard English," she said.
But she saw their conviction and grew uncertain, and she took that back
to her cave and fussed over it. It was like spelling, Renée had said later;
unlike many adult basic ed teachers, she believed you shouldn't tell
them spelling wasn't important when they were writing, because sometimes they just couldn't go on if they thought something was incorrect.
"Think about it, Anna," Renée said to her. "Spelling is a very puzzling
thing, both unimportant and important. You know that some brilliant
educated writers are bad spellers, and their spelling problem has
absolutely no bearing on their brilliance, right? But at the same time,
if you got a business letter from someone with misspellings in it, what
would you think of the writer?"

Anna gripped her pen and tried to sit quietly as loneliness pressed
at her. Sometimes, when she was grading, its ache tipped off desire,
and she lay down on her bed and took up the vibrator and let it yank an
orgasm out of her. Sometimes she perused her address book, wondering *Who are my friends? How many do I have?* — and picked up the phone and
left messages on the machines of every friend she could think of, and
even her mother's. Sometimes she walked over to Clark St., and grad-
ed or read in the hippie café, trying, among the familiar faces of regu-
lars and wait-people, to draw sustenance from the mild and unde-
manding intimacy of the neighborhood, like a plant in winter light.
Lately she'd been lucky; they'd been showing playoff games on TV in
the afternoons, and she settled happily into the sociable chatter of
baseball play-by-play.

She sat there by herself and breathed, feeling that old broken feeling of before-Patricia, of those years she had been so stunned and paralyzed. But she was starting to sense it differently, as a dry husk falling
away. Now, sometimes, if she just sat quietly, and leaned into it, she got
a brief whiff of what it would be like to be still and vibrant, so vivid in
her own loneliness that it was like watching a movie about a beautiful

alone person. She lay her hand over the messy scrawl of Cheryl's home-work, touched another person's furious mark, saw the blood bridle in her hand. She was glad she'd figured out a way to help Chris end her relationship with Mrs. Barry, and hoped she'd take the hint.

And indeed, the next day Chris went back to Renée, having craft-ed a careful lie about convenient times, and mentioned that Anna knew a tutor, a man, who tutored later in the afternoon. His name was Dennis Oliphant, and he was a big man in his forties with ears that stuck out and the shadow of a heavy beard on his pale, shaved face. He gripped Chris's hand hard, and when he laughed he cracked up like a fool. He called her "pal," and when she did well, yelped "Bull's-eye, my good friend!" He talked volubly about his wife, but she didn't get the sense he was trying to prove anything by it. He was a social studies teacher who had been teaching at Francis Parker for fifteen years; he told her that when he turned forty, he'd decided he didn't want to spend his whole life teaching only the children of the wealthy. Chris won-dered how many ways the children of the wealthy found to torment him. The first time Dennis called her at home to change a meeting time, Kathleen answered, and Chris laughed watching her pull the receiver away from her ear, her eyes widening with alarm as his loud bray came trum-peting through. She thought of him fondly as a big old doofus, and Doofus Oliphant is what she and Kathleen privately came to call him.

A week passed, and she realized that with a tutor, she was learning twice as fast. Without the hostility she felt coming off of Cheryl and Antwan and Brandy, and without that loose cannon Anna Singer, who might at any moment either insult you or cry or God knows what. Try to bond with you.

It was the second Monday in October, and Anna was pointing over her shoulder at the words she'd written on the board in large clear let-ters. She read loudly, "I'm daydreaming about _____."

It was 8:40 and dark outside; Anna could hear the hiss of city traf-fic through rain. The room had the righteous smell of cleaning chem-icals, and the brittle leaves that had fallen from the plants had been swept off the window ledge.

Vanessa was squeezed into her desk, her heart still rushing in her ears from the stairs, her face greasy from sweat and the rain. She had left Tisha at home with Desirée. She freed her jacket, draped it over the back of her seat, and took out her notebook. Desirée didn't seem to be going nowhere soon. The boys sidled up and whispered *Mama, she live here now?* She walked like she was on the moon, like she was slow, or spoilt; or she sat at the kitchen table writing in her journal. She said she was writing down her thoughts and feelings, and something about that made Vanessa want to smack her little behind. But this morning, Tisha had awoken with a cold, and Vanessa was grateful not to have to send her to Smith House. Something was not right with Tisha's teacher. She let the kids play unsupervised; last week Tisha had come home with a bruise on her nose, and Lisa said she fell from a swing but one of the kids said another little boy pushed Tisha. Sometimes Lisa was nice and sometimes she was real cold and mean; yesterday when Vanessa had arrived to pick Tisha up, Lisa's boyfriend was there. That had shocked Vanessa.

She could hear rain outside, and a ripple of thunder. The fluorescent lights were humming, and one in the front was flickering and making a tinging sound. She looked at the words she'd written down, *Smith House*. She thought Tisha's teacher might be on drugs. When she came into Pathways this morning she had stopped to talk about it with Rosie, who worked at the front desk and whose little boy was also at Smith House. Rosie said it was true that Lisa acted strange, and that she heard she took the kids to her apartment once, and it was nasty. Thank God Desirée was there to stay home with Tisha, so she could continue trying to get her education. Because if it wasn't one thing, it was another.

She had to write something; she was paired with Cheryl, and that always scared her and made her feel stupid.

Next to Vanessa, Antwan was writing with a little stub of pencil, his legs stretched out and crossed at the ankle, the tendons working in his hand. His thoughts crisscrossed in his mind like traffic with no rules. He had sighed when Anna asked them to write, feeling as he often did that she was failing to live up to her responsibility to teach them, sitting there not doing anything while they wrote some misspelled non-sense on a piece of paper. He recalled Gerald's stash, which he had got rid of one hour before Lamar came looking for it. He was lucky; he had a knack for staying out of trouble. That's because all his life women came and dragged him out of trouble by the ear. A year ago Sheila had taken him and his little brother in to live with her. Now Marcus was going to high school and it was almost like when they were little and living with their mother, and Antwan had been a first grader at the magnet school.

He wrote, *Magnet Scool.* There was a disturbance in his peripheral vision; he looked up and saw Anna swing a desk in his direction and then sit down next to him. "Not to sound like an old lady or anything," she said, "but it's easier to write if you sit up straight." She sat down and looked at his paper, then leaned over and wrote with her blue pen, "What about the magnet school?"

Antwan heaved himself up straight, a yawn glittering through his whole body. She was leaning in close because she wrote with her left hand, and he could see the blue vein that ran under the skin at the base of her pointer finger. "I used to go there," he said, looking straight ahead, "when I was a little kid." Before their mother passed and he and Marcus had to move in with his auntie and her four kids in the projects, and he had to go to a new school.

She wrote, "Really? Which one?" And then said, "Write it down, okay?"

Antwan waited till her hand left the paper. He wrote, "Thurgood Marshall," the spelling coming right back to him with a little smack of satisfaction.

Anna looked up from the paper. "I have a friend who went there," she said. She looked down and wrote: "Did you ever have Mrs. Sharp?"

Antwan peered down at the paper, and started to pick his languid and conscientious way through the sight words, when he was dumbstruck. He sat back, and the look of wonder on his normally impassive face made Anna laugh. She could never tell what was going on there: sometimes she thought she repulsed him, sometimes that he was fending off feeling ignorant, sometimes that he might be high, and once she had wondered if what she was seeing was depression.

"Did I have Mrs. Sharp?" he asked uncertainly. "I sure did have Mrs. Sharp. For first grade."

"My friend thought she was the bomb," Anna said.

"She was!" He was stunned that Anna knew about Mrs. Sharp; it felt as though she was peeking through a window onto his life. He sneaked a look at her and noticed the light freckles at the corners of her eyes. Mrs. Sharp was a real strict lady. He remembered how startled he had been when she came to his mother's funeral to pay her respects, how during the service he'd found himself craning around to see how a teacher acted in the outside world. Afterward Mrs. Sharp had knelt down to speak to him. She took his hands and said, "Now Antwan, don't you lose your shine, you hear?" *Lose your shine,* he had never forgotten the way she put that. But right after that, after he was taken out of Thurgood Marshall and placed at Harper, he started losing things — his mittens, his lunch box, his homework — and it seemed like every day he unlearned just a little bit, like a spool of thread being unwound. Harper was like ghetto schools he'd seen in the movies. He was scared a lot, and tried not to show it. *Dang,* he thought: someone else that Ms. Singer knew, another kid in Chicago, had had Mrs. Sharp! It made him feel as though a long long time ago, he had been a real first grader.

"Who Lisa?" Anna heard Cheryl ask Vanessa exasperatedly behind her. "And who Rosey? How you expect me to know what you talking about if you don't explain who these people is?"

"I'll tell you what," Anna said to Antwan, "Write down *Mrs. Sharp*" — she watched him do it, reminded him of the period after *Mrs.* — "and now a sentence about her."

Antwan looked at her; she was sitting so close it was hard to think, it was a thing she did, getting into their face. It was as close as he'd ever gotten to a white person who wasn't a cop, and it made his skin prickle and his mind shrink back. "Mrs. Sharp was my teacher," he wrote in print.

Anna shrugged. "That's correct, but not so interesting," she said. "Try one more sentence, one that says something interesting."

Something interesting! He looked at her, his eye twitching at the corner. She backed off, got up; but before she left she tapped his notebook with her pen, looked at him meaningfully and said, "One more."

Anna went to the board and wrote the words *fact* and *opinion*. A Post-it over her desk at home, intended to remind her of the reading goals for her students, read: "Literal comprehension comprises recognizing facts; identifying main ideas and supporting ones; categorizing; summarizing; following specific directions; following a sequence; understanding cause and effect; using context clues to supply meaning." Today, after three lessons on fact and opinion, she had an ad she wanted to work on with them. She worried that it was too hard, but she wanted to use a print ad, and this was the easiest one she'd found. After their freewrite she had them pull their desks a little closer so she could get them all into her vision. She could hear the whoosh of rain from the wheels of passing cars. "Brandy?" she said; "Robert?" They were both staring off into space. "You with me?"

She started with a vocabulary exercise with the words in the ad. *Luxurious, world-class, elegant, facilities, quality, services. World-class* was easy, from the world of sports: world-class athlete. And they quickly let her know that they knew *services* from the world of social services. They talked about how *elegant* was different from *beautiful*. "It's classy," Brandy said, in some approximation of an English accent. "Thank you for a most elegant dinner," she said, with an airy wave of the hand.

After the break, Anna said, "Okay. Now: remind me what a fact is." She tapped her chalk stub on the words over her shoulder.

"What?" Brandy asked.

"What is a fact? Antwan, what is a fact?"

Antwan was slumped in his chair, the taste of Cheetos and cigarettes still in his mouth. He straightened. "It's something that's true." He'd written *Mrs. Sharp came to my moms fu----*. That was pretty interesting, he thought, amusing himself. And below that, the new vocabulary, a list in snazzy slanted print.

"Give me an example," Anna pressed.

Antwan looked up and saw, regretfully, that she was still looking at him. "Reading is hard," he said, resorting to an idea there was always consensus about in the class. But the minute he said it he knew it was wrong, even though it sounded right.

Vanessa said, "That's just his opinion. For someone who reads real good, it's not hard, it's easy."

"Well," Anna said, "What if Antwan said, 'Reading is hard for beginners, especially if they're adults'?"

"Now that's a fact," Vanessa laughed.

Anna presented some of the incontestable facts they'd gone over. Chicago is in the state of Illinois, we live on the planet Earth, the El costs $1.50 without a transfer, there are seven people in the room. Then she ventured, "What if I say that somebody's fat? Say Oprah? Is that a fact?"

The women looked astonished. "Oprah ain't fat," Vanessa said, mildly correcting her, "not no more."

"Oprah *was* fat," Brandy said, as though working with her on a tense exercise.

"That's right," Cheryl said, in rare agreement.

"So you all agree that she was fat," Anna said. They murmured assent. "So it's a fact that Oprah was fat."

"Yes," Cheryl and Vanessa said.

"It's not just your opinion that she was fat? She really was?"

"Yes!" Cheryl said.

Anna could see she'd picked an uncontroversial example, that when it came to Oprah, size wasn't relative, or culturally variable, or debatable in any way whatsoever. "Okay," she said, giving it one more try, trying to evoke the fragile line between fat and not-fat, "At what point did Oprah stop being fat?"

Vanessa and Brandy looked at each other as though deciding who should explain. "Well," Vanessa said. "First she lost all that weight. Then she gained it back, and then she lost it again. So it was the second time that she stopped being fat."

They looked at her expectantly; they were trying to be helpful. "Maybe," Vanessa offered, "you should talk about that Selena in the movie. She had a behind like a sister!" she said appreciatively, making everyone laugh. "But she wasn't fat."

Anna had just rented *Selena,* and agreed completely with Vanessa's assessment of Jennifer Lopez's behind, which had captured her imagination too.

"That's right," Cheryl murmured.

"So is that a fact or an opinion?"

They hesitated. "She sure was pretty," Vanessa mused.

Anna nodded, and considered that it seemed acceptable for a woman to say she was pretty, and thought about Vanessa's own behind, and decided to be supportive of her embrace of alternative body images. "She sure was," she said.

Suddenly silence was rocketing off the walls, and six pairs of eyes were on her, a few mouths actually hanging open. She stared back. "What!" she demanded, making Brandy cover her face, and Cheryl giggle and look sneakily over at Antwan, who was wearing an unsuccessful poker face. Oh Christ, they thought they'd outed her! It didn't matter how low-key she was, they believed their moment had arrived. *Okay,* she thought, *here goes.* "Oh come on," she scolded, "Vanessa's been admiring Jennifer Lopez's butt for the last five minutes, but when I *agree with Vanessa,* that means I'm gay."

A gale of laughter passed over the class. Anna thought Shit, I missed it, I have to say I *am* gay. She was annoyed that they felt they'd caught her, annoyed mostly at herself; this is what happened when you waited too long. Brandy was bright red; Cheryl was sitting erect, her hair as festive and delectable as a wedding confection; and Chris over there, what was she going to do about her? — she had gone perfectly still.

"You think I'm gay — fact or opinion?" she asked. Good God, why was it so hard not to be coy? Anna backed up and hiked herself onto the desk, and looked at each of them as fully as she could. "Well, it's a fact, I am gay," she said: "and that seems to be very exciting to a lot of you." There! It was never pretty, coming out to a class — she'd never done it gracefully in her life — because it seemed at once the most relevant and the most gaudily irrelevant information you could give them.

Cheryl and Vanessa and Brandy and Antwan thought: *I knew it!* Chris thought: *Well if it walks like a duck and talks like a duck, it doesn't have to wear a big fat sign saying I'M A DUCK!* Jesus Christ, she'd had it. You bust your ass, she thought, you come to this loony bin to try to get an education, and now this. She took a deep breath against the panic straining in her chest.

"Tell me," Anna said, her palms on the desk beside her, hoping she was projecting an aura of relaxed interest. "What difference does that make to you?"

Cheryl paused, then blew air out of her cheeks defeatedly: the wind out of her sails, Anna thought. The rest of the class she seemed to have suddenly embarrassed, or bored, into assiduous doodling. Robert was examining one of his jacket cuffs with fierce interest. "What are some of your stereotypes of a lesbian teacher?"

Chris blushed fiercely at the word *lesbian;* it was all she could do not to moan and bury her face in her hands. "Do you know what a stereotype is?" Anna asked, and got faint nods. She waited. Finally, Vanessa raised her hand. "I got something to say," she said. "My cousin Jerome got AIDS and died, and he was the sweetest person in my whole family, always good with the kids, and always helped you out when you needed something. He didn't do some of the bad things the other mens did." Her face ripened with emotion. "So I ain't judging nobody."

Anna smiled faintly and looked at Vanessa's dear brimming face, at her hair only half-braided because she was letting Tisha help her. She wanted to thank Vanessa for her words, but she didn't want to seem dependent upon their good graces. "I'm sorry about your cousin," she said.

And that was that. Vanessa had put an authoritative end to the conversation; suddenly it seemed to Anna like an indulgence to elicit more discussion about herself. She was a little disappointed; she'd wanted more time to air out the knowledge in the breeze of conversation. But she didn't imagine they were through, and besides, she reminded herself, teaching is like baseball: we play every day.

Chris looked down at her balled fists. She wondered if she could get into a classroom where everything wasn't gay this and gay that. But even if there was another class at this level, which she didn't think there was, she'd probably be hounded by Anna anyway, who would want to know about her feelings and why she left.

Anna got up and asked Antwan to turn off the lights, then went to the back of the class and turned on the overhead projector. She sent a picture with words on it skidding onto the wall beside the blackboard upside down, and then inside out.

Ms. Singer, Cheryl thought: she knew she was gay! — because she didn't look like a real teacher who could give you knowledge. Wanted to talk about Oprah! Slumped in her chair looking at the dim and vacant front of the room, Cheryl felt suddenly drained. Why didn't they ever put her in a real school? Thunder broke outside and a driver angrily leaned on his horn. She looked at Brandy's puffy arms and the scrawled mess in her notebook, and at Robert, who was scratching his ear with one slow finger. They reminded her of two girls in that Special Needs class they'd put her in, who wore bibs and had to be led to the sink every morning to brush their teeth. She looked at the handwritten entries on the history time line, faint in the dim light, and thought that if this was a classroom for white people, they'd have typed them neatly, on the computer.

Where you stay says a lot about where you're going. That was the caption on the ad Anna put up on the overhead. It had a drawing of an atrium, and a short text:

> *The Park Plaza has 420 luxurious guest rooms, a world-class restaurant, elegant meeting facilities for groups up to 1200, indoor pool, complete 24-hour fitness center, and the quality of service you deserve. Just 10 minutes east of O'Hare at Rt. 72 in Park Ridge.*

Anna read it aloud slowly, and then started calling on them, to review the vocabulary and keep them alert. "Brandy, what's this word?" she asked, pointing to *elegant;* "Cheryl?" — pointing to *luxurious.* She stood at the back of the classroom because she knew it unnerved them. "Hello!" she called. "Who can read the whole thing?"

There was a long silence, which she let settle. "You already know what it says," she said finally. "I'll read it with you."

"It's hard," Brandy complained.

"I know it's hard," Anna said.

Cheryl raised her hand and read it with her, tonelessly, disregarding the punctuation. When she finished, Anna read it aloud again, the way it was supposed to sound.

"Okay," she said, "tell me what the facts are in this ad."

After a rocky twenty minutes in which Anna did everything she could to steer them away from choosing the vocabulary words, she had marked up the overhead:

> The Park Plaza has 420 luxurious guest rooms, a world-class restaurant, elegant meeting facilities for groups up to 1200, indoor pool, complete 24-hour fitness center, and the quality of service you deserve. Just 10 minutes east of O'Hare at Rt. 72 in Park Ridge.

Anna stood still and let it sink in. She had done most of the underlining herself. Then Cheryl whirled around and objected. "How we know it's 10 minutes east of O'Hare? What if there's traffic? What if they just saying that?"

Chris perked up and nodded; she'd been staring glumly at the text on the wall wondering whether to believe that its meeting facilities could fit 1200. She had been in one of those big hotels once, when Kathleen was taking a seminar on being a Coalesce salesperson. They were big on having a positive attitude. She remembered how those women had been crammed in there like sardines, their faces shiny and their make-up clotting.

Anna caught her nodding. "Chris?" she said.

Chris cleared her throat with a little groan. She hadn't wanted to call attention to herself, and she definitely didn't want to be agreeing with Cheryl, although to Cheryl's credit, she seemed at least to have something going on upstairs. "When they say they can fit 1200 people into their meeting facilities, that's definitely their opinion, because frankly, they'll say anything to get you to stay there."

"Ah, my skeptics," Anna laughed, amused at their meeting of the minds, and glad this disaster of an exercise was provoking a little conversation. She laughed again as Cheryl and Chris craned around and looked at her suspiciously. "You're right to suspect that maybe they're just lying," she said, "but there are laws about that in advertising. Plus, if they are lying, that doesn't make these things their opinion, it makes them lies."

"They all liars," Cheryl said. "Or they trying to trick you."

"That's right," Antwan spoke up. "They all the time saying on those car commercials that they give a cash rebate. But what's that? So they just add that money to the price they selling you the car for."

He'd never said so much at one time; Anna put her hand on her chest and staggered backward with playful surprise. "Yes! I've always wondered about that myself. But tell me this: does that mean that advertising never works on you?" She had moved to the front of the class and turned on the lights; she put her hands on her hips and looked toward Brandy and Vanessa.

Works on you? Brandy thought.

"No," Cheryl said.

Anna turned toward her with an incredulous look. "Never?"

"Never," Cheryl said.

Here's a person who likes things to be unambiguous, Anna thought. Someday soon she'd teach Cheryl "on the one hand" and "on the other hand." She leaned in and said, "Let me get this straight. There's never been one commercial you kind of liked, or took notice of."

Get this straight? Cheryl thought merrily. "No," she insisted, although she felt a grin press in at her eyes.

"I like them commercials with the frogs that say Budweiser," Brandy volunteered.

Oh Lord, Chris thought.

"And what about this ad," Anna asked, gesturing toward the wall. "Do you like this one?" She wanted to start a conversation about its audience, and its tactics.

"Not really," Brandy said.

"Anybody like it?"

No, they murmured.

"Why not?"

They were quiet. "Robert, do you like it?"

"Not much," he said.

"Why not?" Anna asked.

He knew why, he just couldn't express it. It was too hard. And it gave him a coldness. Could he say that? A lot of things he read gave him a coldness, but he didn't think it was polite to say. He stared at the text on the wall till it blurred in his sight.

Cheryl thought: it makes you feel small, like you not going anywhere. It was 12:26, almost time to go. She heard Chris shifting in the chair behind her, making the legs of the desk screech against the floor, and closed up her notebook. "Ms. Singer," she singsonged, pointing with her thumb over her shoulder: "your girlfriend knows the answer."

It took Anna a second to digest. Whenever she was walking down the street, and boys yelled obscenities from a passing car, she invariably turned to her companion in befuddlement. She was sure that if she understood them, she'd feel very bad indeed; but as it was, she was protected by paying attention too late, by her own cluelessness.

And this wasn't even an obscenity; it was just, she finally registered, a stupid junior high school insult.

But Chris always understood every word yelled from cars. She stood up and yanked her jacket off the back of her chair, glaring at Anna, thinking: *Are you happy now?* "Chris," Anna said. Chris put her things in her book bag and without zipping it shut, stalked toward the door holding it by the handle, blazing with embarrassment and rage. She turned and pointed at Cheryl. "You watch your mouth, you piece of crap," she said, and left the room.

Cheryl rose, amazed, and there was an anxious rustle for jackets, a loud "Whoa!" from Brandy. "Sit still, everybody!" Anna barked.

Cheryl barged for the door, and Anna raced over and blocked it. "You're not dismissed," she said, as Cheryl stopped an inch away, so close Anna could see her nostrils work and feel her hot breath on her face. "You're not dismissed," she said again, crossing her arms in front of her chest to make herself bigger and more unmoveable. To her great relief, Cheryl took a step back.

"Don't *nobody* call me a piece of crap," she seethed.

"I know," Anna said, "That was uncalled for. But you're not going after her."

She would have to walk her to Renée's office and have somebody escort her to her transportation source. "You're not dismissed," she said, to a glowering Cheryl and to the rest of them. She watched Robert sigh and run his fingers over the spine of his workbook, and Antwan lean back watchfully with his arms crossed. "This is not going to happen again in this classroom," she said. "Are you listening to me, Cheryl? I don't care how you feel about each other, in this classroom you will treat each other with respect."

She had wanted to talk about audience, about who the ad was addressing, about how advertising tries to prod its audience into feeling incomplete and inadequate without the product. Now she'd never get to that. And that stuff about respect: how many times had they heard words like those? "Why do you want to torment each other?" she cried. "It's not hard enough as it is?"

CHAPTER NINE

Anna sat across from Renée, her back hunched and her elbows propped on her knees, the lower part of her face in her hands. Cheryl had been escorted to the bus by one of the security guards, who waited impassively as she gathered her coat around her, smiling in amused disgust, and now Anna was trying to beat back the defensiveness flapping stiffly inside her, as she explained that she had come out to her students. She looked hard at Renée; she said, "I felt it was important to come out."

"Why?" Renée asked. "I'm not saying you shouldn't have, I'm just trying to follow your reasoning."

"Because until I did, they would think I was afraid to be myself around them," Anna said. She knew there were other, better answers, a lot of them, but her thoughts were skittering anxiously around her. Renée was quiet, her arms folded across her chest, her chin between the thumb and forefinger of one hand. *What's on my mind?* Anna asked herself mockingly. Wasn't there this whole list of reasons for teachers to come out? Finally one came into view. "Also," she said, "I don't want to be too cowardly to take the kinds of risks *they've* taken. Coming out of their literacy closet, I mean." She paused. "Do you get what I mean?"

"I think so," said Renée, "I'm just trying to imagine." She was sinking into slow deliberation, as Anna sat coiled across from her, her forehead gleaming and her hair reared stiffly back.

"I trust you," Renée finally said. "I trust that you weren't being self-indulgent."

Anna sat back and sighed. She knew that if Renée said she trusted her, she really did, and that Anna should be proud to be worthy of that trust. She also knew that Renée was just voicing Anna's own anxiety: that she had been somehow, or would be thought to have been, inappropriate or self-indulgent. But having that confirmed by Renée's speaking it aloud, even in denial, was bruising.

"Renée," she said, "Coming out in class is not only not a bad thing."

"Yes," Renée said, "I see what you're saying. You're saying that it establishes the teacher as a strong and proud individual, someone at ease in her identity."

"Right!" Anna said, her face quickening with gratitude.

Renée laughed at her evident surprise. "Anna, you underestimate me. Don't be sitting there acting as though Suzie Straight Girl here has never had to establish her own identity in the classroom as strong and proud!"

Anna laughed sheepishly. "Okay," she said.

They sat back as Renée shook her head at her, at what she had to put up with sometimes. Then Renée ventured: "One thing I don't understand, though, is the vehemence of Chris's response to Cheryl's comment. If you're both out of the closet, is implying that you're girlfriends considered an insult?"

Anna looked at her blankly, then wanted to laugh, it was so complicated to explain, and so stupid. "Well that's just the thing," she said, "Chris is not out to the class, so she felt that her privacy was being violated."

Renée frowned; Anna thought she was probably wondering how a person so flagrantly deviant could think of herself as not out of the closet. And the rest! — what a can of homosexual worms, explaining how being thought of as each others' girlfriend, even as a joke, made them both feel grossed out and humiliated. How insulting it felt, the idea of these two butches together, the implication that Anna couldn't get a more beautiful girlfriend, that Chris was what she wanted!

"That's just the thing," Anna said. "Just because I came out doesn't mean that Chris should have to. You're not out till you come out, Renée; somebody assuming you're queer doesn't count."

"Do you think there's something you could have done about that? — perhaps letting her know in advance that you were preparing to come out?"

"I don't know," Anna said. She tried to imagine consulting with Chris about coming out, her blunt hostile attention, her beginning each cutting sentence with "Frankly," or "To be perfectly honest," implying that Anna was unused to having people be forthcoming with her, that Chris alone dared to speak hard truths in her presence.

Renée reached for her Rolodex, and flipped till she found the number she wanted. "At any rate," she said, "both Chris and Cheryl will have to undergo a week's suspension and one day of anger-management counseling, before being permitted back in the classroom." She picked up the phone and cradled the receiver between her chin and her shoulder.

Anna nodded faintly; she knew the rules. But it made her wince. She wouldn't be surprised if at some point in her youth, Chris had been institutionalized for some kind of gender-management counseling. And Cheryl: she knew she had been ground up by the mill of psychiatric evaluation, defined her whole childhood as a behavioral problem.

"These are not people who have reason to trust the idea of counseling," she said.

"No, they're not," Renée said, pressing down on the hang-up button and giving Anna a hollow-eyed look, as though she was exhausted by her but was still trying to be courteous and pedagogically effective. "Four years ago, when the policy was made, I sat through numerous meetings debating exactly that. We had to weigh the disadvantages of pathologizing our learners against the advantages of offering them help channeling their anger in a more productive way. The latter won out." She pressed her lips together and cocked her head to the side, in an efficient and mechanical rueful look. "It's a valid position, even if you disagree."

"What if they refuse to go?" Anna asked, sensing that she had used up Renée's time and patience, but suddenly panicky about losing Chris, and wondering, to her surprise, what on earth she'd do without Cheryl. What if the class sank into a bog of incompetence and inertia?

Renée consulted the card in front of her and dialed. "I think they'll go," she said.

She was being tested, Chris knew; it was a test of her resolve. It was a few days later, and the message from Renée was still on her machine at home, and Chris was down on one knee laying out two-by-four sole plates on top of a deck in the backyard of a big gabled house in Andersonville. Right after Renée's message had come a message from Keith, Kathleen's ex, saying that two of his guys had bailed on him, and asking if Chris wanted to help out on a job framing a hot tub into the backyard deck of two yuppies. He'd hoped that with Chris's help, he'd be able to swing the whole thing in one Saturday, and cover the repairs he needed on his truck. He'd cut her $250, in cash. Kathleen hadn't liked the idea; Chris was in no shape to be doing all that bending and squatting, she insisted, and if anyone connected to the settlement heard she was doing physical labor, they'd be in big trouble. But Chris's heart had jumped right up at the sound of Keith's voice, at the thought of making some money, helping out a friend, being herself, Chris Rinaldi! — not a school kid who needed to be disciplined. She picked up the phone to call him despite Kathleen's protests. Holding the receiver up high, out of Kathleen's exasperated reach, she ticked off on her fingers: it was only one day, nobody from State Farm was going to find her in the back yard of a house in Andersonville, and they needed the money.

It seemed as though every house on that block had a truck or a dumpster parked in front of it, or scaffolding set up against its side, and the sounds of grinding and hammering rang out through the cold air. Chris's nose was cold and her body warm from layers of sweats. Keith Serynek was measuring a two-by-four laid onto sawhorses, his goggles on the top of his head and his work gloves stuffed into his back pocket, and singing along in falsetto with an old disco hit coming from the radio propped against the deck railing. Over the past few days, he had taken up a portion of the deck, reinforced it with extra beams and posts, and reinstalled the decking boards after the plumbing and elec-

trical lines had been put in; now he was cutting the joists for the platform that would support the tub. He wore a faded baseball cap over his
thinning brown hair; he drew a quick line in pencil with a freckled
hand. He was in his early fifties now, long divorced from Kathleen and
remarried, expecting a grandchild in February; and with the building
boom on the North Side, he had more business than he could handle.

Chris heard him singing and laughed, tickled out of her brooding
about school, about whether if she quit, it would mean she was standing up for herself or caving. She was enjoying being nose-to-nose with
freshly-cut wood, drinking in the smell, the palms of her hands pocked
from pressing into shavings. She heard the rush of the El way over on
the other side of Broadway. It seemed to be disco hour on that radio
station; it swung into "I Will Survive," and Chris groaned audibly as
Keith joined in with a high dramatic flourish. "Keith," she hollered,
"I had no idea you'd just been fixed!"

"Screw you, buster!" he yelled cheerfully, as he put on his gloves
and picked up the circular saw. One thing about Keith, you just could-
n't get him mad. Talk about anger management! They should make her
hang out with Keith for a few hours every day. Back in the old neighborhood, when Keith was still in the mills and Chris had just stolen his
wife, she had expected out-and-out war with him and his mill buddies.
She knew those guys and their ways of being together – the lunch-time
swapping of sandwiches, picrogies, tamales, meat cooked on steam
pipes or radiators; the pranks, many of them involving grease or con-
doms or rats; the nicknames. Keith's nickname in the mill was Egg,
because he was a good egg. Sometimes they called him Soft-Boiled,
because he was afraid of grease fires, and because one day when a but-
terfly, of all things, had floated through the machinery, he had said
dreamily to the guys around him, "It's like God." Later he claimed he'd
been stoned. And sometimes they called him Hard-Boiled, mostly sar-
castically, for the same reasons they called him Soft-Boiled, but also
when he worked straight midnights, or stood toe-to-toe with a foreman who was getting in the way just to hear himself talk.

She also remembered years of taunts from some of the guys he hung out with, and the feel of their fists on her face, and how one night two of the butches had wrapped their thick arms around her and held her still while Jo Vieceli popped her shoulder back in place. So the first time Keith appeared at Chris and Kathleen's doorstep after Kathleen left him, he had caused a ruckus inside, surreptitious scurrying to the windows to peek at him, a chaotic and inconclusive consultation about whether to open the door, whether there were other guys lying in wait. Finally, Kathleen said, "For heaven sakes, we're like Abbott and Costello in here," and opened the door a crack, peering out and saying, "Hi Keith, what do you want?"

He stood there alone, his hands in his jeans pockets, his hair brushed back into a ponytail, his beard freshly trimmed. He was wan, and almost inert with patience. Kathleen took his sleeve, pulled him inside, and locked the door behind him. She plopped him in front of the television, and went into the kitchen to get him some iced tea. Chris was in there behind the door, flattened against the wall with a steak knife in her hand, feeling like an idiot. She whispered fiercely, "What's he doing here?" Kathleen shrugged and said, "Maybe he needs to get out of his parents' house." He had moved back there when Kathleen left, taking solace in the home cooking of his bewildered mother, who thought, when she heard that Kathleen had deserted her beloved son for a pervert: How did that make sense in the scheme of things? How could it be that God had spared him, sending him to Cuba instead of to Vietnam after his brother Hank was wounded, only to let happen a thing so ludicrous and baffling it left her speechless?

Keith poked his head into the kitchen, saying, "Can I come in?" Seeing his freckled face, the way his worn red-and-blue flannel shirt made him look like a kid in pajamas, Chris slipped the knife onto the counter, thinking that attacking him would be like knifing Opie. Had they seen, Keith wondered, the latest U.S. Steel newsletter? His crew had worked a record shift and gotten their picture taken for the newsletter. "And it came out doctored," he said, "so my hair looks short!" He unfolded the picture and showed it to them and said "How do you like that!" like a senile person.

"Yup," Chris said, "sure looks doctored."

Later, as Kathleen was putting cold cream on her face before bed, she murmured to Chris, "I think he's in shock."

He was a marvel to Chris, his manliness quiet but imperturbable. Over the years they had become good friends; Kathleen and Chris had been at the christenings of his kids, and the four of them had spent many hours together drinking beer and doing jigsaw puzzles or playing poker or Parcheesi. One Thanksgiving, as Kathleen and Keith's wife Margaret were in the kitchen and Chris and Keith stretched out with beers in front of the game, Chris, at the threshold of the confiding stage of her drunkenness, had come right out and asked him about it. "Frankly," she said, "If you took a woman from me, man, I'd never let you forget it." Her voice was huffy from the mere thought.

Keith shrugged. "What's the point?" he said. "It wouldn't have gotten Kathleen back for me, would it?"

He was a third-generation steel worker, and worked at U.S. Steel for thirteen years before he finally quit and started his carpentry business. He had grown tired, he said, of having his kids field phone calls at night so that he wouldn't have to go in for overtime, tired of the speed-up wars and the danger and the petty sabotages, and not having had a raise since the contract of 1974. Also, the hearing in his left ear had deteriorated from the noise.

By 12:30 they had cut all the studs for the supporting walls. Huddling over the plans with Chris, Keith showed her how they would put the whole thing together. "Where's the tub?" Chris asked.

"In the garage. It's a heavy son of a gun," he said.

"How're we gonna lift it, just two of us?"

He laughed. "I thought we'd cross that bridge when we came to it. You want to cut the decking boards while I get some pizza?"

"Sure."

"What do you want on it?"

"Pepperoni," Chris said.

She calculated the time as he got into his truck and the engine coughed and then blasted. She wasn't sure they'd get the wall done before dark. She lifted the circular saw and put her goggles down; Keith had already measured and marked the decking. As she sawed, she thought how good it felt to work on somebody else's goddamn house. This one would be a doozy to take care of; it was probably at least fifty years old, a lot to handle. Her own small house seemed uncontrollable enough. With $250, she thought, she and Kathleen could buy a new dryer before the old one, which was running on low heat only, broke completely, or buy a new kitchen table, or do the electrical work they needed so they'd be able to use the coffeepot and the microwave at the same time. In her head she spent the money five times. Her hands began to shake as the saw bucked over a knot in the wood. She stopped the saw, then ran it again, powering cleanly through the knot, impatient with herself imagining all of those things taken care of, when she could only take care of one.

Keith tooted the horn when he returned, and got out balancing two cans of Pepsi on top of a pizza carton. They ate on top of a tarp spread on the front lawn. Chris sat down with a groan and Keith asked, "Your leg?"

"More my back," she said. "It's like I'm moving wrong because of the weakness in my leg, and the pain is crawling up my back." She reached for a piece of pizza, folded it lengthwise and bit off half of it, pepperoni and cheese scalding her palate.

Keith grunted and stretched his legs out. "We ain't the men we used to be, buddy," he grinned. He pulled up his layers of sweats and showed her his white belly bulging over his pants. Chris made a disgusted face and growled "Put that away." But he actually looked pretty good, she thought; he had a lot of life and some prosperity under that belt, and she respected that.

"You should go to a chiropractor," he said, wiping his mouth with his sleeve. "I have a real good one."

"No way," Chris said.

"No really," Keith said. "You don't even know what a chiropractor is, and you're already saying no way."

She gave him a look. "I know what it is."

"What is it?" He looked at her with amusement.

"Fuck off, Egg," she said.

He leaned forward slowly, in comic and gracious concession. And trying to let her off the hook, he changed the subject. "How's the financial planning business?" he asked.

Chris tipped her can of Pepsi and took a long swig. He thought the classes she was taking were on managing your finances, which was what she and Kathleen had agreed to tell him.

"It's good," she said. "Not that we have any finances to plan about at the moment."

"Until the settlement comes, anyway," he said. "Then you can invest and retire."

"Yeah right," Chris smiled.

"Any tips on hot stocks?" He lightly kicked her boot, joshing.

She laughed. "Starbucks," she said. "You can't lose on Starbucks."

They worked till late afternoon, managing to drag the tub out over the grass, hoist it onto the deck, and build a wall around the exposed side. But there were still stairs to do, and by this point it had grown so dark they had to squint to see the bubble in the level, so they called it a day. "Thanks, buddy," Keith said, taking a wad of cash out of his tool belt and peeling off worn twenties. As he drove her home, Chris shifted on the seat, trying to ease the stitch in her back, thinking it had been stupid to try to pull up that tub, and Kathleen would say she'd told her so.

The tips of Anna's fingers were freezing and sore; it was late Sunday morning and she was kneeling on top of her desk, putting the screens up and the storm windows down as she waited for her blind date to show up for brunch. She was squeezing the little switches at the bottom of the screen, trying to get them to uncatch; she couldn't release the one on the right side. She sat back on her haunches as cold air streamed into the study and up her shirt, stiffening her nipples, flexed her fingers, and said, "Fuck."

She had been fixed up with this woman by her chiropractor, Ruthie Shapiro. Anna loved Ruthie because while she had New Age things to say about Anna's condition, she came from Brooklyn and therefore said them in a loud Brooklyn accent, and the effect was tremendously therapeutic. She was also very pretty, a warm and dramatic straight woman with big curly dark hair. Sometimes when she leaned over Anna, gathering her thigh and knee and side to be adjusted, and her hair brushed Anna's face, Anna's eyes closed with arousal. And she knew Ruthie probably knew that, and didn't mind; Ruthie had her number, and knew how to work her. She had a wide arsenal of tactics designed to coax or trick Anna into relaxing for adjustment, or letting her touch certain parts of her body that she hated having touched, like her toes.

In the days following her break-up with Patricia, Anna had lain on her stomach on Ruthie's table getting her back rubbed, weeping and weeping, undone by the touch of a murmuring woman. And now Ruthie wanted her to meet a woman named Sharon, who was a therapist, and, she said, one of the nicest, most grown-up people she knew.

The right switch finally popped, and Anna pushed the screen up in its track, leaning out a little, getting a cold blast of air in her face, and finally getting it to settle. Then she brought down the storm window and shuffled over to the next window. She pushed in the switches of the screen, and suddenly the propped-up storm window came hurtling down and smashed onto the fingers of her freezing right hand. Shock and nausea roared into her head. Stupefied, she extricated her hand; the skin of the knuckles was torn and bloody. She could flex it; it wasn't broken. She slid off the desk and holding onto the wall, let herself down to the floor, and sat there, hunched over and holding her hand, the room raging around her. Her hand expanded and ignited and pounded; she felt it till it became abstract. She relaxed her cramped and panicked muscles, let go of her hand, felt the crackle of air on the torn bleeding skin; she lay her head back against the wall and closed her eyes.

Later that afternoon, running with her along the lake, Monica laughed when Anna told her about mangling her hand right before the arrival of her first date since Patricia. "It's the lesbian version of Ahab's wooden leg," Monica shouted, against the stiff northerly wind. And laughed again and shouted "Oops!" when Anna told her that Ruthie, whom she had thought really *got* her, had sent her a butch about ten years older than herself. Anna knew the moment she opened the door that this wouldn't work. "I was so totally positive I couldn't get it up for her," she panted, feeling the blood glow in her bandaged hand, "that I might as well have been a gay man." Sharon Macalroy was stocky and broad-faced; with her shaggy hair and downy older-people's skin, she reminded Anna of a pony with its winter coat. She worked with gay runaways, but as though she willfully refused to be interesting, or interest simply refused to accrue to her, her job was to keep statistics on the kinds of social services they used. As far as Anna could tell, Sharon rarely met any actual gay runaways.

Anna and Monica ran on the shoulder of the bike path that ran along the high-rises off of Hollywood, touched the water fountain that marked the end of their run, a ritual Monica insisted on, and stood heaving, their hands on their hips. "So what did you do?" Monica asked, fumbling for Kleenex in the pocket of her windbreaker, and wiping her nose.

"I talked incessantly about Patricia," Anna said.

Monica smiled. "Good one."

"You'd think Ruthie would have gotten it about me," Anna said. As far as she was concerned, Ruthie had lost some of her allure. It was disappointing, like seeing a person's face light up as she comes toward you, and then realizing she's not recognizing you, but the person behind you.

Monica was subdued. As they stretched on the floor of Anna's living room, she had told Anna that she had gone into couples therapy with Martha. Anna frowned, and considered, and then offered, "I don't know, Monica. Tell me if I'm out of line. But don't you think that if you have to go into couples therapy with someone after being with them for three weeks, maybe the relationship is not meant to be?"

Monica, extending her leg and reaching for her ankle, had laughed. It was more complicated than that, she said.

God knows, Anna thought now, looking at her wintry red-faced friend, she knew just what it was like when it was clear to everybody else that these two people should not be together. Her friends had thought Patricia was a selfish prima donna, and sometimes she saw it that simply now, in retrospect. But it didn't feel that way when you were locked in struggle, when she goaded your most sensitive places till you burst with cold and revelatory pain.

Steam puffing from their noses, their sweat starting to encase them in cold, they pulled their sleeves over their knuckles and walked up Bryn Mawr. They stiffened at the wind tunnel on the corner, turning their faces and fighting for breath, and emerged into the windless cold, whooping, their eyes streaming.

She was right: without Cheryl and Chris the class sagged like an old mattress. The good news was that they had appointments for a counseling session; the bad news was that they'd still be out a week. Meanwhile Anna tried to regroup her straggly band of remaining students. She would do an LEA with one student, and call out vocabulary words to the others. She did more drills on fact and opinion, having them number their papers 1-10, beginning with "Ice cream is delicious" and "It snowed outside today," and building up to "Chicago is a segregated city" and "Chicago is a racist city." Vanessa wrote *onion* every single time, but at least she got them all right. The last two propositions didn't elicit the conversation Anna had hoped for. With Chris or Cheryl there, she might have gotten somebody to say "Depends what you mean by segregated," or "Depends what part of the city you're talking about," or "White people don't think it's racist." Somebody's mind clambering over those ideas, figuring out the angles. As it was, everybody wrote *fact*, and that was that.

On Friday Brandy peeked her head in the door and said in a stage whisper, "I'll be right back, I have to meet somebody," and then vanished. Anna handed Antwan a cloze exercise she'd written that used vocabulary from the past few weeks, and drew her chair up to Robert's desk. "What's on your mind today, Robert?" she asked.

Robert blinked. "That's a hard question to answer," he said.

"Yeah," Anna said, making a face, "I'd have a lot of trouble answering it too."

"Either so much on my mind," Robert said, "or nothing at all, or it just freezes up when you ask the question."

"Right," Anna said. "Well let's see."

They sat quietly together for a while, till it started feeling companionable. Robert thought about the way to school today, where nothing out of the ordinary had happened. Then he thought about work, where it was always the same, an apartment number and the elevator, and a knock at the door, and a shaky gray head peeking out. That elevator drove him crazy, it was so slow. And the old people were so slow. A querulous voice calling out *hold it, hold it!* from the back of the elevator as it eased to a stop and the old person tried to maneuver out with her walker. The stocky and round-faced Phillipines women with ID cards on chains around their necks, backing against the open doors and saying "Okay, okay!"

He thought so much about it he realized that that was what was on his mind. "The elevator," he said to Anna, with an air of mild surprise.

"The elevator?" she asked. "Tell me about it."

"Well," he said, sitting back in his chair, "It's very slow."

Anna started writing. "Is this the elevator at your building, or the one you work at?"

"The one I work at," Robert said.

"Okay."

"The people are very old," Robert said, "and they worry they won't get off on time. And they tell the same jokes again and again. When it just goes right up to the top, without stopping at a lot of floors, they say, 'This must be the express.'"

Anna laughed, writing what he said, and then looking at him again. "In my grandparents' building, they get very cranky. Do they get cranky in your building too?"

"Oh yes," Robert smiled. "They cranky. Or maybe it just sounds that way because they talk so loud, cause they can't hear so good."

It was the longest narrative Robert had produced with her, and she was pleased with it. She had him read it aloud, first together with her and then by himself, reminding him that he already knew what it said, since it was his own words. She had him pick three words: he picked *elevator, express,* and *floors.* She wrote them on note cards, and asked him to put each card under the corresponding word in the paragraph. After she did that, she shuffled them, and presenting them to him one by one, asked him what they said.

"Good, Robert," she said. "Now you know how to write about the elevator."

He laughed. "Won't make it come any faster," he joked. And then felt a small hollow ache, about his days going up and down, nauseated, with the old people.

That night, Anna sat with Janice at a new restaurant in Wicker Park, eating pork chops with fancy chutney, and worrying about the prices. Now that she was paying the entire rent by herself, she couldn't afford restaurants like this one; but she hadn't figured out how to tell her friends, and at the same time she was furious at them for failing to realize it on their own. Janice was drinking a micro beer, and Anna's mind flew ahead to the arrival of the check. She hated calculating what each person had eaten instead of just splitting the bill; it made her feel small and cheap. But here she was drinking a glass of water. She looked at the soft mauve-painted walls, and the oddly-shaped gourds set up high on abutments from the wall. The space was small for a Chicago space, unlike those restaurants with great prairie-like expanses, the defining movement of what they called Chicagoland. It seemed unfair, she thought with a rush of indignation, to be denied small pleasures like these when she was so lonely, and when she was paid so little for a job that demanded so much.

Terry was working, and Anna had been glad to get Janice to herself. At the moment, though, Janice was a handful. She was pale in a black sweater, and with her hair grown long she looked a little pinched around the nostrils, a wife at a cocktail party, the kind of girl who's always been watching her weight and her moods, but who has sucked it up uncomplainingly, as an inevitable burden of womanhood. Anna listened and nodded, thinking of Fran Leibowitz's joke that the opposite of talking is not listening, it's waiting to talk.

Janice opened her hands and gestured bleakly. In her third year teaching at the University of Chicago, she was not only swamped with students wanting to work with her, but was serving on two university-wide committees. She had no time to work on her book, had two conference papers to write within ten days, and hadn't been to the gym in months. She explained the crucial political good for curriculum reform and minority hiring that would be done by each of the committees, and why the success of each was contingent upon the other. Anna took a long drink of water, thinking: *blah blah blah*. She knew that committee work was not what Janice was going to be rewarded for in the end: that what she needed to do was teach reasonably well, and write her brains out. And Janice was also cagily trying to forestall Anna's criticism by complaining about Terry, who had no patience for Janice in this regard.

Savoring the garlic mashed potatoes, Anna thought of how to formulate a more nuanced and powerful argument than Terry apparently had for why Janice should try to maneuver herself off of at least one committee. But she was tired of helping Janice strategize about how to manage her well-paying job. Man, that excessiveness! Janice often operated on three hours' sleep, and relished doing things in mammoth hunks of time, grading for twelve hours straight, pulling all-nighters like a college student. She wrote way too many comments on her students' papers, composing warm and lengthy praise and fleshing out in full paragraphs the ideas that appeared in crude and rudimentary form, in a tiny cramped hand; she had carpal tunnel syndrome. When she exercised, she overdid it, and then had to take weeks off to nurse shin splints and aching knees. It annoyed Anna that she had so little self-protective common sense. But thinking of harnessing all that crazy misdirected energy gave Anna a little frisson, and that was, for her, the joy of Janice. There was also her neck, delectable with its three delicate defining rings, the graceful strength of the bones moving down to the hollow below. Janice's femininity was conventional, with little camp or exaggeration. She wore flats. She shook her head at the way Anna treated Terry and her as butch and femme. But she also preened shyly, a little guiltily even, under Anna's occasional gallantry.

They sparred for a while over the way to best effect Janice's release from a tiny piece of her burdens, Anna trying not to get strident, Janice putting final stitches into her tightly-woven case against her own well-being. "Anyway," Janice finally said, putting down her silverware and wiping her mouth. "Enough about me. How are you?"

Anna rested her fork on her plate and organized her thoughts. The waiter came and they gestured that they were done, and said the food was delicious, and Anna recklessly ordered an espresso. She told Janice briefly about her date, but found herself mostly talking about coming out to her class, how she and the class had struggled to wrest control of that information, about Cheryl's comment and Chris's response, and then, with a game attempt at self-mockery, about her embarrassment when Cheryl implied that she was a butch's girlfriend. Janice listened, her face gratifying in its series of strong reactions. "It sounds stupid," Anna said, "but it had a big impact."

"Of course it did," Janice said. "Poor Chris."

"I know," Anna said, although it rankled a little for Janice to be feeling for Chris. "I come out of the closet, and now she has to see a therapist." She thought about it and it grew big and scary. "I have so many protections she doesn't have. I take the risk of speaking my full self, and it's Chris who's pathologized."

"Wow," Janice said.

"No kidding."

"That thing about your feeling embarrassed, though, at the idea of being Chris's girlfriend. What's up with that?"

Anna grimaced. "It's a stupid butch thing."

"Whenever you talk about her," Janice said, "It sounds like she makes you feel like you're not a real butch."

"Man!" Anna snorted and shook her head. "We're hardly the same species: compared to her, I'm a little mosquito butch whining around somebody's ear. She doesn't treat me as a butch, either."

Her voice had gotten petulant. Janice studied her. "What would that look like?" she asked.

Anna paused, then laughed, thinking of one her male colleagues at Northwestern. "You know, clapping me on the back."

"Calling you *sport*," Janice said, deadpan.

"Exactly," Anna said.

"Well," Janice said, "You can worry about not being an authentic butch, darling, but just think of all those West Coast butches who are turning into men these days. Sometimes I worry that all the butches will disappear."

Something about her look made Anna blush. "You worry about that?"

"Oh my God, are you kidding? Who would kill all the spiders? Who would come flying to our rescue?" She laughed a throaty laugh that made Anna think of her childhood crush on Vanessa Redgrave in *Camelot,* Gueniviere covered in white fur, laughing deliciously.

Enjoying her flustered reaction, Janice leaned forward and rested her hand on Anna's arm. "Look at you," she teased. "You're great, you're firing on all cylinders. Grief becomes you."

"I feel like crap a lot of the time," Anna grumbled, her arm aglow, suddenly on the verge of tears, because Janice had seen her grief.

"I know you do, honey, but it does the heart good to see you like this. You're an emotional world cruise. You are the Norwegian Line of emotions."

That cracked them both up. Anna stopped, then was overcome by laughter again. "And my class," she said, shaking her head. "Sheesh."

"You're in the trenches, is all."

Anna finished her espresso and ran her tongue over the tiny grains on her palate. The waiter brought the check and put it in front of Anna. "My treat," Janice said, reaching out to grab it, and after a courtesy protest, Anna thanked her, hiding her tremendous relief. They walked out to Anna's car, and Anna unlocked and opened the passenger door for Janice. Inside, they huddled in their coats, their breath filling the car. Anna started the engine and sat back letting it warm. The garlic and espresso on her breath were walking the line between tasting pleasantly like strong food she'd eaten and occupying her mouth as a hostile alien force. She looked at Janice, who was staring straight ahead with a strange expression on her face, as though she might be about to cry. And suddenly, Janice leaned over and kissed her. Not a hesitant or exploratory kiss at the corner of her mouth, but a full warm open-mouthed kiss, a kiss like a glowing hearth. Anna shrank with embarrassment for a fraction of a second, thinking her breath must be awful, but in a moment she felt their breath and saliva blend, and then it was simply the flavor this kiss was. She scooted toward Janice and took her by the back of the neck, felt her head lean back, and took her in her arms. She could feel Janice wanting that, succumbing to her. Desire leapt in her like a stag after a rifle shot, spraying snow.

They were swathed in Polartec and down; Anna took off her gloves and let them fall to the dirty floor mat. The only skin she could feel was Janice's cold face and neck. She kissed her on the eyes and all around her mouth; she brushed back her hair and kissed the part of her neck behind her ear lobe. Janice was moaning and clutching her; it shocked Anna to be wanted like that, embarrassed her to see her friend so quickly become a moaning woman. And then, kissing Janice's mouth again, she too passed over, stunned, a new dimension tearing open. Time spun furiously outside. It was like the still strange space of mourning, or the first week of having a new infant, like leaving the hospital after surgery, people seeming to rush by, the revolving door dizzying with its spin.

She grabbed Janice's hair and tilted her head back and kissed her deeply, brushed her lips against the corner of her mouth, ran the tip of her tongue along Janice's lower lip, bit it. She was telling Janice: *here, feel this, and now feel this.* Janice's eyes were closed in deep concentration. Emotion surged into Anna's throat. She rested her face against Janice's, and whispered in her ear. "Come home with me."

Janice made a noise, part laugh, part groan. "Oh God," she said, "You know I can't."

Anna kissed her again and murmured smiling against her mouth, "C'mon."

Janice sighed and put a hand to her heart, laughed and hiccupped and then grew serious. Anna hesitated, then pulled away, letting Janice feel the cold surround her. She waited for a minute, then shifted into reverse and eased out of the parking space. They drove home down a dingy and deserted Ashland Ave. After a few minutes Janice put her hand on her knee, which made her want to cry. It was okay if Janice didn't sleep with her — that would get too ugly with Terry — but it was hard not to want to persuade her.

When they arrived at Janice and Terry's, Anna pulled up next to a parked car, shifted into park and sat back. Janice reached over and took her face in both her hands, and looked at her searchingly, her eyes glistening. "I loved that," she said. "Do you have any idea what a great kisser you are?"

Anna was already pulling back into real time, back into irony. She took one of Janice's hands and kissed it on the palm, returned it to Janice's lap. "Terry's gonna kick my ass," she said.

Chris's therapy session was in Lincoln Park, on Armitage and Halsted, and afterward, she moseyed down Armitage, where yuppies in spandex, as toned and muscled as whippets, ran and rollerbladed through the lit streets, and young men in suits cut around her with briefcases and dry cleaning. Her back was better after days of ibuprofen, just a mild background stiffness as she walked; she'd really caught a break there, she thought. Dragging a hot tub! — what had she been thinking?

She stopped at the Old Town School and looked in the shop window. Suddenly she heard a rumble from inside. It was guitars, she realized, fifty or a hundred of them, all playing at the same rhythm, switching chords. She peeked into the doorway. There were a few hippies sitting and drinking sodas at a desk with stacks of paper on it in an open, brightly-lit hallway. She hesitated, then walked inside toward the thunder of the music. Nobody stopped her. There was a big open door, and

inside an auditorium, where everybody in the audience was looking at
a piece of music on a stand in front of them and playing the guitar and
tapping their foot. It was deafening in there! Well I'll be damned,
Chris thought, laughing to herself. She slipped in and eased herself
into a folding chair. They finished their song and whistled and
stamped and swigged sodas and beers. They seemed like a truckload of
folks from a different neighborhood, dumped here; they wore flannel
shirts and had gone too long without haircuts.

A bearded man jumped onto the stage, cupped the microphone
and moved his mouth close, and said in a suave voice, Give it up for
Guitar 1! They were having some sort of a show. The audience burst
into applause as nine or ten people shuffled up onto the stage and sat
down with a great clanging of music stands and the hollow sound of
guitars being whacked. They looked to Chris as though they were in
their thirties and forties, a few of them even her age. A man perched
on a chair at the end, who, she realized, must be their teacher, said
One Two Three, and they started playing what turned out to be, after
a few minutes, "Brown-Eyed Girl." They were flushed and sweating
under the stage lights, intent upon their fingers; for some of them,
every chord change was an adventure. And then the sound of voices
rose around her, as the audience joined in for moral support.

And then applause; they yelled "whoo-HOO!" The performers
grinned sheepishly and jumped off the stage. Then the audience was
asked to give it up for Guitar 2, who got up and played "Dock of the
Bay," and Guitar 3, who played a picking song without words. Each
performance was a little better than the last. And then four red-faced
middle-aged folks got up and performed an awkward clog-dance. That
was too much for Chris. It was one thing to get lost among ten guitars,
but quite another to make a spectacle of yourself, your chunky thighs
working and your chest bouncing like that.

She thought: she liked the therapist. Who'd of thunk it? She was a
tiny bustling straight woman in a suit and lipstick, but she looked at
Chris with calm frankness, and cut through the bullshit, and didn't ask
her about her childhood or say *How does that make you feel?* And she didn't

think Chris's comment to Cheryl was that out of line; she called that whole business nonsense, a distraction. She said matter-of-factly, "Of course you're angry, you're learning to read." Chris had stared at her and felt a tiny ripple in her throat, and the therapist stared right back at her.

Women's Acoustic Country was called up onto the stage. They were all women; as they settled in, wisecracking and anxiously adjusting their music, Chris's expert eye searched out the dykes, finding one definite and two probables. Their song was called "Lying to the Moon." The guitar was simple, but after singing a stanza in unison, they broke into startling harmony. Those gals had some sets of pipes on them, she thought. She closed her eyes and felt the harmonies arch open. The song ended, and she opened her eyes, a strange feeling pushing in her throat and head, surrounded by the sound of hooting and applause.

CHAPTER TEN

How did you get this way? Boo-hoo, your parents didn't understand you. Isn't that how you're supposed to tell the story?

You could say aha! she was seven when they moved away from their house to the suburbs, aha! just when she started reading, they started taking away their love, aha! one day she brought her notebook to her teacher to show her some words she'd written, and the teacher said, If you keep acting like a boy you're not going to be very popular. Just when you were getting the pleasure of tracing roundness and stems, of the smell of eraser crumbs on your paper. You could say that it was at the time you started learning to read that you started getting punished. The sudden headaches, your face in flames.

You could say that you were the wrong child for your parents. That here was this angry classy man and his beautiful wife, and to them was born Fred Flintstone, jowly and bellowing, a club in his ham fists.

You could look for all kinds of reasons from your childhood. But what good would that do? Let you say it was somebody else's fault? Those people who cry about childhood sexual abuse, and verbal abuse (*yelling!*) – you want to smack their whiny faces. If you can't rise above what happened to you forty years ago, what does that mean about your fortitude and strength of mind?

They fed and clothed you, they put a roof over your head. Plenty of people, like the people in Africa, don't even have that. They even loved you, at least for a while.

On Juniper St., there are tons of cousins, first and second, once and twice removed. You go up the hill to your cousins' house, scrabbling on hands and knees through the dry brush that grows on the hillside, instead of taking the stairs. You take baths with the other kids, and on weekend nights you sleep in the same bed with them, cigarette smoke snaking into your nostrils and legs twitching against yours, listening to the voices of the grownups, the flap of cards being shuffled, Sinatra on the phonograph having a very good year.

There's lying and tattling and squabbling, the swap of nickels and dimes for candy or marbles or favors. You have the run of this neighborhood of row houses and scrubby grass and Kick the Can and laundry flapping on lines. *Yuns get in here! — In a minute, Ma!* — that's your neighborhood's summertime song. The gang of you are like thunderclouds rushing across the sky. You look out for each other. Once in a softball game you hit a home run, and the opposing catcher tackles you at home plate and flips you over, knocking the wind out of you. He didn't even have the ball. And the next thing you know two of your cousins are rushing him and holding his arms, egging you on to let him have it. You punch him right in the gut and he falls to his knees and gags. That's your best memory from being a kid, your cousins rushing to your defense.

Not that life with them is a bowl of cherries! One of the boys — Bobby or Christopher or Frank — bloodies your lip and then starts bawling, and it's you who gets punished. Frank's ice cream falls onto the sidewalk and you have to give him yours because he's a big baby. You love Bobby with a passion; he's always looking at you with a quirk in his face, like there's a funny secret between you. And yet he torments you. He does your homework for you and then keeps threatening to tell, so you have to give him money or be his slave for the day, which means doing his shoeshine job at Ira's shoe repair and giving him all the money you make, and in the winter shoveling the walk in front of his parents' house. Once he makes you kiss his shoes and call him *Mighty King*, and when you do, the other kids laugh at you. That hurts. You thought a deal is a deal: you were keeping your end of the bargain.

You remember things about play: the intricate highways you patted and molded into the dirt of the vacant lot at the corner, the pleasant small weight of the cars, their chipped paint. And marbles! You had a stretch as schoolyard marbles champ. You sat on the ground, your red Keds splayed behind you, thumbnail pressing against the cloudy glass. The bell ringing you back into class came like a mortal wound.

And you remember a pair of cowboy boots they indulged you with when you were seven, making your heart cram itself into your throat with shock and gratitude. (Seven is the turning point for butches: after that, just looking at you seems to ruin everybody's day.) Their black shininess and the firm clump of the heels — had anything ever felt so right? They made your heart thrill like a trumpet. Walking down movie theater aisles in those boots, you invented your first swagger, a string of licorice dangling from your mouth.

After that, well. Being sent to your room, insulted, beat up, suspended, committed, drugged, yack yack yack, what's there to talk about? Sometimes when you think about it, it doesn't even seem like your life.

What makes him look so different from the rest of them?

Your father definitely has the looks in the family, his face heart-shaped, his skin pale, his eyes blue and piercing. But it's not just that he's the most handsome. His sisters have that same shaped face. But the skin is looser and stupider on them. In his wedding pictures, their hair is piled up and wisping down over their temples. They want to look elegant, but it makes them look hassled. And his brother too, with his bug-eyes and his hair brushed down in bangs.

It's the Navy, you decide. The Navy showed him how to hold his face right.

At college your father roomed with Uncle Vincent. They were on the GI Bill. They learned to cook sauce on a hot plate in their dorm. They'd practice the same one over and over, for weeks, till it was perfect, then start learning another one, and make that one perfect too. Your father leans over your mother as she makes sauce; he sips from a stirring spoon, licks his shining lips, and recommends a little more this, a little more that.

Your father is not a foreman or a skilled technician or a craftsman. He is an engineer. Those things might seem the same, but they're really as far apart as the earth is from the moon. He goes to work in a white shirt and tie. He is helping to rebuild Pittsburgh; his expertise is flood control. He takes you and your mother for a picnic on the edge of a big empty crater that used to be a slum and is going to become the Civic Arena. You sit on a blanket and he points toward the swarming cranes and backhoes, describing, as your mother exclaims and feeds you bites of hard-boiled egg. A guy in a suit comes over and shakes his hand, messes your hair and plunks his hard hat on your head. When your mother wonders where all the poor Negroes are going to live now, that does it. You're both dragged to your feet and clapped in the car, and outside, your father shakes out the blanket, cursing as the wind twists it and the crumbs blow all over him. He gets in the car and the engine starts with a roar. In the back seat you try to make yourself very small, knowing it's you he's really mad at, because the guy thought you were a boy. *I was just asking,* your mother says. He says, *You try to have a good time...* and shakes his head because it's impossible, it's impossible to have a good time with the likes of you.

And yet, the truth? You love him as hungrily as a dog. The feel of his fingertips on your head makes you quiver.

Your mother loves your father's family; she says they have a great love of life, which makes your father roll his eyes. He calls it slumming, her love for them. They don't love her back. You overhear them bad-mouthing her parents, who own a five-and-dime store; once they hired your cousin Frank, and they wouldn't let him take off for his sister's christening. Your mother had only one sibling, a sister who died of polio. So you think of her family as weaklings, like watery tea, while your father's family is loud and proud as espresso.

Your father's mother prays over you. *It's easy to be a boy, it's being a girl that's hard,* she tells you, smoothing back your hair, or wetting her finger in her mouth and scrubbing at some dirty spot on your cheek. *What am*

I gonna do with this child? she cries with great drama, pulling you roughly toward her and smashing your cheek with a kiss. She treats you like you're as worthy to be mauled as anybody else. She makes salami sandwiches with spicy mustard and cuts them on the diagonal, your favorite way. She brags about how you like jalapeños from the jar, and likes to tell people how when you were a baby, you preferred a hot pepper over your pacifier, a story your father calls a myth. She gives you a chunky little St. Jude medal on a silver chain for your tenth birthday that you love and wear for years; when you lose it later in a scuffle on the El tracks, that undoes you in a way leaving home never did.

She takes you to confession, where the old priest smells of cheese, and where you confess your little lies. Church never does much for you. Honestly, it would've done better if you were a little boy fag, so you could love all the frills and doodads, the sad punished Jesus reminding you of yourself. To you it just smells bad, like the phony sweet smell coming out of those bath or candle shops they have now in malls. Your father calls the Catholic faith a lot of mumbo-jumbo, and after you move away, you stop going altogether.

At first, though, your parents can't even find a house. The real estate agents don't want to sell to Italians. They're scared they'll move the whole family in and start yelling out the windows and cooking huge pots of smelly food and hanging their underwear out to dry in the front yard and letting their dirty kids crawl all over the neighbors' property. But then your father proves that they have the money, and convinces them, you hear him telling your mother, that you're quiet, respectable people. You don't know how he did that, but it scares the crap out of you, because by now you're pretty sure you're not respectable, not at all.

When your parents move out to Friendship, they might as well have moved to China. Your grandmother says, her voice high and tight: *Well, he has his own life now.* In his family they all work construction, for Equitable Gas and the City and the like. Your uncle and aunts mimic the way he talks, in a hurt sarcastic way, so it doesn't even sound like him. If he uses a word that's even a little big, they take it and toss it around, like bullies with a

146

runty kid's cap, even though they know perfectly well what it means, even *you* know. They call the friends your parents play bridge and tennis with "strangers." Your father buys your grandparents a color TV, and that turns out to be a big production; he learns a lesson: It Obviously Doesn't Pay To Be Nice. He starts complaining about having to go there on Sundays, about the smell of garlic and onions on his clothes and hair when he leaves. Now when he yanks their chains, instead of laughing they get real quiet. Your grandfather doesn't talk to him for a whole year after he calls the row houses they live in an eyesore. Who does he think he is? your grandfather wants to know.

You never thought of yourself as dark till now, at your new school. Once you overhear a teacher calling you a gypsy child, and you smile at her, thinking that she's referring to how wild and free you are. But when the other teacher she's talking to laughs, you realize with a jolt that she's insulting you. What a moron you are! You make friends with an Arab kid named Abdul. He's weird and has an accent and flinches at the slightest twitch of your hand, which arouses a strange sadism in you. But he lets you copy off his paper, and he has sticky sweets with pistachios in them for lunch, which he gives to you in exchange for your HoHos.

When you get put in special ed your parents are furious; your father thinks it's because you're Italian. They never find out that you can't read; they don't believe what the teachers tell them. Every morning before school there's a huge fight about what you're going to wear. *You're not leaving the house like that,* your mother announces, but she doesn't really have a leg to stand on, because staying home suits you just fine. On the days you come home from school with a bloodied face or torn clothes, she sets her mouth. She says: *that's the price you pay.*

The whole nine years you live there, you think of it as the new house. The pictures on the walls are in black and white, because your parents don't want to seem too loud or enthusiastic. Your mother keeps the house spotless; her whole life is a war against your dirty dishes and toys and muddy shoes. You can't eat ice cream without standing over the sink with it, or paint by numbers without a big sheet of plastic spread under you. You get so nervous that you spill your milk at the table more often than not, and when you do, they send you to your room without dinner, because they think you're doing it to spite them.

The house is spotless except for the guest room, which your mother has to herself, and which is an explosion of magazines, bottles of pills and lotion, loose papers, knickknacks, scattered earrings and perfume.

The basement is taken over by your father's train set. You're not allowed to touch his trains. As he lays the tracks and places the stations and scenery and miniature people, you sit cross-legged on the basement carpet, which is damp to the touch or maybe just cool, watching the bulge of the veins in his hands and the tiny criss-crossing lines at his knuckles. Two trains run on tracks that never cross or collide; each time the trains approach each other you hold your breath, but they swerve and run side by side, separated by the tiniest sliver of space, and veer away again. They whiz through tunnels and snake around curves. They are perfect. You sit absolutely still, entranced by motion separate from you and your will.

Would you look at that! your father marvels, making the skin on your arms prickle. He didn't praise you, but you were next to the thing he praised.

Your mother is begging you to come downstairs in a dress, to meet the guests. She is dressed nice and her breath smells of gin, and even as she is forcing you, she is crying for you. *Please*, she says: *for your father.*

When you come down the stairs, they tell you to sit on the boss's lap. You walk numbly toward him and lower your rear end over his bony knee like a baboon in heat presenting herself, your face burning, smelling his old man smell. You are blind; you can't see a godforsaken thing, but you can feel everyone around you red-faced and stiff. Finally you feel a hand clasping your wrist; your father is yanking you to your feet. You remember the panic: maybe you didn't understand what you were supposed to do, maybe what you did was terrible and dirty.

The truth is, you still don't know what it is you did, except be disgusting to the core. They never make you come downstairs again.

You're just not who they want to see, coming into the room in your pj's, when their friends come over for bridge.

You have a picture of yourself from this time, one of the few pictures of you as a kid. You're wearing your dad's hat from the Navy, and one arm is in a sling. It has not been hurt; it's just a way you play dress-up.

Who could have taken this picture? Who wanted to remember you this way? Your other hand is on the doorknob. Already as a kid, you're on your way out the door.

Your father has a youngest sister, your Aunt Gloria, who's only six or seven years older than you. You remember the first time you take notice of each other: you come across her loitering in front of the drugstore with a friend. She has dark eyebrows and a beauty mark under her eye. They're smoking Virginia Slims, sending up lazy rings. The friend wants to know if that's a boy or a girl. Gloria tells her to shut up and stop being rude. You tell her she's not supposed to smoke, and she says *Yeah, who's gonna tell?* You give her a kick, an experimental tap on the shin with your sneaker. Next thing you know you're flat on your back with your shoulder blades pressing into the pavement, and God knows what chewed-up bubble gum and spit and cigarette butts, and Gloria and her friend are sitting on top of you and you're yelling that you can't breathe.

Come to think of it, all of your games with Gloria seem to end up with her sitting on top of you, tickling you or pulling up your shirt. And she bites. Once she breaks the skin on your hand and you have to get a tetanus shot.

One Christmas, when you've wormed out of wearing a dress but the compromise is a hideous sweater with a reindeer on it, you leave your grandparents' hot, sweet-smelling house, where the women are clearing plates and the men are sprawled and sighing from food and booze, and go out to sneak a smoke. She's standing out in the alley without a coat, next to a couple of old bikes leaning on a peeling gate, her arms crossed across her chest, shivering and sucking on a butt. She gives you a light, and as you exhale, she says, *Nice sweater.* Then she asks you, real light and curious, what it was like in the loony bin.

You spit a bit of tobacco off the tip of your tongue. Is she scared of you now, you ask, the way your cousins are?

She'd better be! You're crazy, loony, a fruitcake. For emphasis you snarl, holding up your hands like claws.

Then you drop the act. It was boring, you say. You had to take pills that made you nauseous and groggy, and the food was nasty, and people peed themselves like babies, and they made you talk to a head shrinker every day about why you didn't like being a girl.

The sounds of "Ave Maria" start to roll sweetly out into the alley from the neighbors' phonograph, and you both look up toward their window, which has been cracked open a few inches, and a pie set to cool on the sill. The song makes you sad. She asks if they ever gave you the electroshock. She says she read about it in *Life* magazine.

You grind the cigarette butt under your heel, shame seeping up in you like black water. You're terrified that those shocks burned to a crisp the little knowledge or intelligence you had before.

You ask: *so how come you're not married yet?*

Ol' Aunt Gloria: in the end, she's the straw that breaks the camel's back. One fine night when you're fifteen, she comes over for dinner with your grandparents; they must have been on speaking terms with your father at that point. While they're all downstairs, she tiptoes into your bedroom. You watch her take off her dress; she gently pulls back the covers and climbs on in, twining her bare legs around you. *Don't tell,* she murmurs, taking your hand and putting it on the moist crotch of her panties, her breath hot on your ear. *Aren't you lonely here all by yourself?* You close your eyes, lust gulping you down its gigantic throat. *Yes,* you whisper.

You honestly believe they won't catch you. She's older, almost a grown-up – she must know what she's doing.

But she doesn't. They walk right in – all of them – as you're having a field day between her legs and she's just about strangling you.

And then it's like a cartoon: screaming, fainting, grabbing for clothes, ear-pulling, and mayhem. It's actually pretty funny until your father breaks your nose. He punches you in the face and then looks with horror at his bloody hand, and your mother falls all over him with sobs and caresses, comforting him, because it makes him feel so terrible to lose his temper like that. To act like his father, right in front of his parents, when he's supposed to be so much better than they are.

You get a lot of mileage out of this story later, in the bars, when the bulls are swapping tall tales about how daring and perverted they are. You say: she wasn't even that pretty, Gloria, with her little tits and her too-close-together eyes. You say: How come there's no Hallmark card for this kind of thing? But even now, when you conjure her whisper, you feel a glow down there, and it makes you wonder whatever happened to her, if she has a husband now, and if he's a decent guy.

You leave that night, with $70 in your pocket — your money and the money you steal from your parents' wallets. As far as you know, nobody ever tries to find you.

You take the train to Chicago, your forehead pressed against the cloudy dirty glass. You're like every little squirt in a new city. You work in a rendering plant where it's 100 degrees and the stink hammers you like a fist, and then on the loading dock of a Jewel. Nobody pays for the first two weeks, so you go from diner to diner all night long, nursing a cup of coffee and nodding off till someone chases you away. You spend one night in a porno theater, slipping in and out of sleep to the sound of fake moaning, and grim jaunty music that torments your ears for days. You awake with a neck spasm and an old faggot's hand on your knee, and beat it out of there. The next night you try to go to a shelter, but after a conversation in loud whispers, they tell you they won't put you with the women, so you hit the streets again. You eat dry cereal, and Fritos, and from time to time, diner meatloaf. You move to Cal City on a hunch, after hearing somebody at work say it's a town full of Mafia and queers. You can bet they don't mean it as a compliment! — but you pack up that very night, and within a few days you have a job in the stock room at Sears in downtown Hammond.

Cal City, now there's a town. Flat and stocky with a huge dull

Midwestern sky. Parking problems and floods, a field day for an engineer. People want the bar traffic the fuck off their streets, the pissing drunks off their lawns. Meanwhile, every time there's a storm, cars cut water like wings.

It's just like you: everyone keeps trying to reform it. The mayors and the police chiefs and the vice squad guys — Linkiewicz, Nowak (the White Knight), Rybarski, Stefniak — they're like good guys and bad guys in a Polack fairy tale. You like how their names feel in your mouth; you like how talking feels now in general, now that you're freed from your mother's fussy ear: your mouth thrust out with your chin, your tongue full, your teeth biting down on your lower lip or your throat closing and then sound exploding out. Sometimes you even spit when you talk. Who's gonna stop you?

And that's the story, the traumas and the foolishness that led you to be the big illiterate bulldagger you are today. See? You're not stupid, you know these things. You can do this song and dance for all the curious people who wonder how such a sad thing happened, such a sad and fascinating thing, how such a freaky thing happened to a freak like you.

How you got this way: ask it about your own damn self.

CHAPTER ELEVEN

It was early on a Saturday morning in December, and the radiators were knocking on. Anna lay in bed fantasizing about Janice. It was the weekend, and she was lonely, and she couldn't call their house! Janice had called and left a tense message on Thursday, saying that she'd told Terry and that they'd better not be in touch till things cooled off a little. Everything was suddenly a big drama. Anna was glad Janice had told Terry, but here she was, the girl who'd never gotten to be wild as a teenager, suddenly a sexual outlaw. It tickled her, but it also embittered her. Terry and Janice would now retreat to recover from the threat she posed to them, while Anna — open, inflamed, her heart raging — was all dressed up with no place to go.

Her mind drifted and puzzled over yesterday, when one of the Mexican-American girls who hung out on the neighboring stoop had run up to her, come to an abrupt halt, and reported, "Marcela's sister really likes you." Marcela? Marcela's sister? She must be the little girl who lived next door, about thirteen or fourteen years old, who said a shy hello whenever Anna passed her. Anna had stared at the messenger, who had rings on every finger and a cigarette in her hands, wondering whether she was being taunted. The girl's face was earnest — at least as far as Anna could tell from its unsettling blend of childishness and shrewdness. "Okay," Anna had said, and turned up her walk, thinking that she was either the neighborhood heartthrob or the neighborhood laughingstock. *Here too*, she thought, *here too!* — how did Anna look in the story Janice was telling Terry? Was Janice downplaying her own role in their kiss even at this very moment, making Anna look needy and pathetic, herself hapless and kind?

Distress whirred in Anna like a flag in a bicycle wheel. The job market was going badly again; she'd been asked for seven writing samples, but couldn't imagine wanting any of those jobs. Places like Ole Miss, Florida International, Texas Christian: most of them were one- or two-year replacement jobs with huge teaching loads, hurricanes, and fraternities, where she'd be forever teaching the nineteenth-century survey course some old geezer had invented thirty years ago. She almost didn't feel inferior about her lack of success anymore, knowing from Janice and Monica's reports that there were up to 700 applicants for each position. She'd revised her job letters from last year, making bigger claims about what fields she could teach in, sent offprints of her published dissertation chapters, and left the rest to fate. The good news was that her book was being considered by the press she'd sent the prospectus to. But sometimes she felt a sneaking shame, and wondered: what did her friends have that she lacked? She was as pedigreed as they were, as well trained. She was pretty sure she was as smart as they were, and she knew she was a beautiful writer. But lurking unpleasantly in Anna was the suspicion that she lacked a certain intellectual courage, that her book centered around ingenious and ornate close reading because she didn't dare make bolder claims.

She closed her eyes and ran her fingers down her stomach to the crease of her thigh, her knuckles brushing over her pubic hair, imagined Janice on her knees, on her stomach. Was Janice a harbinger of future erotic windfalls? Caressing herself with her fingertips, Anna fretted about money, and about whether she should draw on the small inheritance her grandparents had left her, which she had been holding in a money market account for the day she would need a new car. She wished there was a mental health provision in her health insurance because she could really use some therapy; she worked herself into a state of outrage on behalf of the poor and mentally ill, the people who *really* needed health insurance. Then she imagined Janice on her back, coming, eyes fluttering upward, unseeing, mouth rigid, thighs clamped around Anna's hand. It was arousing and hard to look at, the image of her friend's face in orgasm.

She turned the TV on to ESPN. Once, Patricia had been lying in her arms while she was watching *Sportscenter*, turned her face up to her and said gratefully, out of the blue, "I'm so glad you're not a man." Anna had turned absently toward her and muttered "Huh?" There was a split second, then Patricia had cackled with delight.

Anna closed her eyes, felt the tears come, felt herself cracked open like an egg by grief's tapping fingers.

A few miles away, Chris too was lying in bed, hearing the crinkle around the baseboards that sounded when the heat came on. Kathleen was up and talking on the phone in the kitchen, so she stretched out into the rumpled spot, grabbed an extra pillow and folded herself around it, bringing her knees up high to stretch her back.

She didn't have to get up if she didn't want to. She didn't have to go back on Monday if she didn't want to. But God help her, she knew she would. With all the things she'd been through, if she couldn't stick to school, she'd really be a loser. And there was always Dennis. He'd come over to her house during her suspension, for a tutoring session on the sly. They'd sat at the kitchen table drinking cup after cup of coffee, and she served him pie she'd bought at the supermarket and heated in the oven. Later, after he left and she was clearing the dishes, she saw that he'd left behind a mess of crumbs and blueberry smears on the table, and laughed to herself over what a big slob he was. No wonder Rufus had set up camp under his chair!

Kathleen was roaming with the cordless phone. Her voice rose and punctuated; there was a string of 'right's, then, in an ominously can-do tone of voice, "Just get a cab," then "Okay, bye." A few minutes later she came in the bedroom with a cup of coffee for Chris. She placed it on a coaster on the bedside table and sat at the edge of the bed, contemplating her.

"That was Dell," she said.

Chris stretched and groaned. "I should have known, calling so early."

Dell always called at the worst moments: when they were fighting, or having sex, or running out of the house late for something. She was an old friend of Kathleen's from the bar days, the first lesbian Kathleen had ever met. When pressed, Kathleen had to admit that she didn't even like her very much any more – she found her bossy and a little phony – but Dell was extremely loyal, and considered Kathleen her best friend, and the weight of all that history lay on Kathleen like a brick. Dell lived in Omaha now with her girlfriend, and was selling real estate.

Kathleen looked nervously at Chris, who was piling up pillows and sitting up. "She's coming on Monday," she said.

Chris froze. "Here? To this house?"

"Where else do you expect her to go when she's in Chicago?" Kathleen asked. "She's got some kind of work thing, and decided to come at the last moment."

"Sonofabitch," Chris muttered. "How long?"

"Four days."

Chris's mind blanked for a second with panic, then she looked at Kathleen coldly. "What time is she coming on Monday?"

"Not till the afternoon," Kathleen said.

Chris's mind raced: that meant she would only have to prepare some lie for Tuesday, Wednesday, and Thursday. "And what exactly am I supposed to do about going back to school?"

Kathleen's mouth tightened defensively; why was Chris always acting like Kathleen was trying to keep her from going to school? "Make up some lie," she shrugged. "What's the big deal?" She started taking off her bathrobe and headed toward the bathroom.

Chris sat up in bed, her mind working furiously. If she left a few hours before school every day, she could pretend she was going to work. What work, what job? She heard Kathleen flush the toilet, then turn on the shower. Dell of all people! she thought. She'd slept with Dell for a while, shortly before she'd gotten involved with Kathleen. Dell was a brassy, opinionated femme. She thought Chris was the roughest toughest butch around; she'd tell Chris that such-and-such butch was giving her a hard time, or saying things about Chris behind her back, and urge Chris to fight her. Or Chris would lift a hand to scratch her face or smooth back her hair, and she'd flinch excitedly. Her current lover, Jan, didn't know they'd ever slept together, because Dell claimed it would make her insecure. "It would just kill her to have to compete with you," she'd said to Chris, when she'd first begged her not to tell Jan.

At first it was nice to be treated like such a hot shot by someone so aggressive and sure of herself, but eventually it drove Chris crazy, as though Dell was making up a whole imaginary lover. She knew she filled some strange need in Dell, and she was terrified Dell would find out she couldn't read. She stuck with the affair for a while because Dell came on so strong, and because it felt good to be wanted so badly.

Kathleen came marching back into the bedroom with her hair wet and a brush in her hand, and gave Chris a lecture on the importance of hospitality to her, especially now that they had their own home. *Home,* Chris thought bitingly; since they'd started looking to buy, she'd noticed how people always said *home* instead of *house,* and she hated it. It was too much pressure; it was like they were trying to force something on you, something more than it was.

"You don't even like Dell," she said.

Kathleen put on underwear and took off her robe, opened a drawer on the old oak dresser with the brass handles that somebody had left on the curb when they still lived in Cal City, which Chris had stripped and refinished. She pulled out a bra and put it on, her back turned to Chris from long habits of modesty. "That's not the point," she said, "She's still our guest, and we should make the best of it." To her own surprise, Kathleen was actually glad Dell was coming. The thought of an old friend made her feel keenly her loneliness, how her life tunneled from work to Chris. She hooked her bra, lifted the underwire and resettled it more comfortably.

"You could consult with me, Kath."

Kathleen whirled on her. "What was I going to say," she demanded: "hold on, I have to consult with Chris? How would that look?"

"Who gives a damn how it looks? You don't even like her!"

Kathleen pulled on a sweater. "This is my house too," she said.

"Just take a look at the mortgage payments and refresh your memory."

There was silence. Then Kathleen left the room. Chris got out of bed and pulled on a pair of jeans, sat there feeling her gut moving against the buttoned waist. She took a sip of coffee and contemplated throwing the mug against the wall. But the walls were freshly painted; she didn't like it if anyone even touched them. She set the mug down on the bedside table and looked at it miserably. "Fuck you," she said.

Anna sank into a doze, and the phone rang. She picked it up and said hello, her hair smashed and one side of her face red and creased. It was Dan Irwin, an administrator at Literacy Volunteers of Illinois. Anna picked herself up alertly and leaned on her elbow. Dan had been her teacher when she was trained as an LVA volunteer. He was a plump middle-aged white man with a Burl Ives beard and tremendous charisma. He had been functionally illiterate himself till his thirties, although he had managed to get a high school degree; he didn't think too highly of high school degrees as an index of literacy. Now he taught adults in prison. He gave off the beauty of a man who had blended with his vocation, like a piece of music resolving on a beautiful chord.

Now apparently he had moved up the hierarchy, and was organizing teachers for the training sessions. The teacher for the two Saturday sessions in December had had to cancel because her father had had a stroke. "And for a variety of reasons I won't bore you with," he said, "others can't take it either. Including myself," he said, "although I'd certainly like to. So I ran into Renée Wallace the other day, and she recommended you very highly."

"Oh, that's nice," Anna said, "I'm flattered." She was surprised to be treated as someone experienced enough to teach Adult Basic Education, and happy to do it. She had loved her own training sessions, had felt plummeted by them into the heart of Chicago life. And she had loved learning a new vocabulary, which had felt like a foreign language, but an intuitive and logical one.

"Great," Dan said. He arranged to FedEx her the teaching materials, and they set up a phone date to talk about a lesson plan.

"It's pretty fresh in my mind," Anna said. "It shouldn't be a problem."

"You're really helping us out of a jam," Dan said.

"Oh it's my pleasure," Anna said, then added bashfully, "You know, Dan, you were my teacher."

"Is that right! When was that?"

"Oh," Anna hastened to say, "That was a few years ago, you wouldn't remember me." There was a pause, and then she said, "But anyway, you were great, and it meant a lot to me."

Two days later, looking at Dell across the kitchen table, Chris thought that at fifty, she was looking a little stringy. Her hair was the same blond, dyed now, and she had definitely kept her figure. But she was too made-up, and there was something ravenous-looking about her. Maybe, Chris thought, it came from years of selling real estate. The moment she arrived, bringing in a cloud of her strong distinctive perfume, which Chris knew would linger in the house for weeks after she left, Dell had said, "Oh, what a cute property!" — making Chris feel like she was implying it was tiny. Looking at her now, Chris couldn't imagine having been attracted to her. Next to her, Kathleen looked very pretty, and Chris regarded her with a thump of approval.

And she had forgotten the whole food thing. Dell was peering suspiciously under her hamburger bun, checking for God knows what. She came off like a big sport, but you'd be in a deli with her and she'd make a big production of asking to have her food heated in a toaster oven rather than a microwave, or look at her sandwich and slap her thigh with exasperation, and say "I *specifically* told them I wanted a poppy roll, not a kaiser roll." And then Chris and Kathleen, already licking the crumbs and mustard from the sides of their mouths, were supposed to encourage her to stand up for herself and take it back.

Kathleen had put a burger on each plate and set a bowl of potato chips and a bowl of salad on the table, which had been cleared of Chris's books and notebooks; Chris had stuffed everything in the bedroom closet before Dell arrived. For good measure, she'd picked up the *Tribune* on the way home, unfolded the sections, folded some pages back, and tossed the paper on the living room table. Spearing salad with her fork, Chris noticed that Kathleen hadn't dressed it, but had put two bottled dressings on the table so that Dell could choose.

"What are you looking for?" Kathleen asked Dell, setting her glass on the table and wiping beer foam from her top lip.

"Oh nothing," Dell said. "I just wanted to make sure there was no horseradish."

Chris and Kathleen looked at each other. "Horseradish?" Chris laughed. "Just eat it, Dell. I promise, it won't bite you back."

Dell cast a sardonic glance at Chris, who had a mouthful of hamburger and a spot of ketchup at the corner of her lips. "You should talk," she said, "You're the most cautious person I've ever known, peeking under every rock." She laughed. "Everyone thought you were this big stud, and I have to admit, you did come off that way."

Chris looked at her with surprise. The aggression was familiar, but the content a new development. She swallowed. "I seem to remember," she said dryly, knowing she shouldn't say it even as the words started coming out of her mouth, "someone at this table getting pretty damn excited at how I came off." She looked at Dell, who cast an embarrassed look at Kathleen. It was mean to say, especially in front of Kathleen, but it was true. She could go back to the bathroom at the bar and pin Dell against the wall and reach up her skirt, and Dell would come in a second, standing, panting there in the bathroom stink. She was almost too easy. With her, there was no hurt or vulnerability to overcome, no sense of surrender. No thin ice to crinkle soundlessly, the way there was with Kathleen, who had come to butches late and had that barrier there that Chris had to coax and sweet-talk her way through. Nope, Dell just lay down on her back and opened her legs, and climaxed with noisy enthusiasm. Chris had to admit it, she liked a woman to be kind of moist-eyed and overwhelmed after coming. It made you feel like you'd accomplished something. With Dell it felt as though *anyone* could make her come like that.

Dell flushed. "A nice thing to say to the person who played Cupid between you," she snapped. "You're really full of yourself, you know that?

160

Chris rolled her eyes. Dell always bragged that she was their Cupid: she had worked with Kathleen, and was the one who invited her to come hang out at the bar. But Chris was certain she'd had no intention of bringing them together. She'd thought Kathleen was safe to bring to the bar because she was straight and married, and after Kathleen and Chris got together, Dell had been meanly jealous, and even tried to scare Kathleen off by telling her she thought Chris had a violent streak.

Kathleen sat down and poured beer into a glass. "C'mon girls," she said mildly, sending an imperceptible but vicious kick Chris's way, a skill she'd acquired raising two teenaged siblings. "Talk about water under the bridge." She couldn't believe what a baby Chris was being, and how rude.

All that week, Chris left the house at 7:00, sneaking out with her book bag before Dell awoke. With time to kill before her 9:00 class, she crossed under the Drive to the lake and sat bundled on a cold bench, trying not to freak out the old Russian people who gathered there, watching the iron heave of the water, the occasional jogger going by with a swish of nylon or Gortex. One rainy morning she went instead to the Coffee Chicago near Pathways, sat in the smoking section drinking a cup of fancy coffee and watching young people with fashionable glasses read the paper and tap away at laptops.

Class that week was dreary; Anna had them doing a phonics interlude. Chris kind of liked it, though: it was drudge work, like assembly-line work, and she knew how to put her head down and suck it up. Anna had them put their fingers to their throats to feel the number of syllables in a word. After a little while of this, Antwan grabbed his throat with his whole hand and rolled his eyes back in his head and made gagging noises. Cheryl didn't come on Monday, and a rumor went around that she had been arrested for assault, or for dealing. Then she showed up on Tuesday, completely nonchalant, speaking thickly with a newly-pierced tongue. Oh great, Anna thought, *that'll* help her pronunciation. There were a few mandatory and furtive jokes about blow jobs that made Vanessa blush and Cheryl cast a quick look at Anna — to see, Anna thought dryly, if she got it, or was shocked, or had ever heard of a blow job. Brandy made Cheryl stick out her tongue, and gazed at it with horrid fascination. "Don't food get stuck in there?" she asked.

At the end of class Anna stopped by Renée's office, to check in and tell her about Cheryl's return. "Did you notice her tongue?" she asked.

"I sure did," Renée laughed, wrinkling her nose, "and it makes me feel pretty old!"

Anna leaned against the doorway and smiled. "Seems kind of symbolic, don't you think? We sent her to anger management and she mangled her own tongue."

Renée shook her head comically and lifted a finger. "No," she said, "she didn't mangle it, she *decorated* it."

When Chris got home on Wednesday, she found Dell and Kathleen in the living room, drinking beers and giggling over an old photo album. They had Oprah on the TV, with the sound off. Kathleen had taken a rare sick day, to spend the day with Dell. "Lord, this was some roll of film," Kathleen called out. "Remember that one, honey, where you look great in every picture?"

Chris approached and peered down at the pictures. They had taken that roll over a week of vacation, when a bunch of them had rented a cabin up in Wisconsin. There were some at the beach, some barbecuing in the yard, lots of group shots of lounging lesbians with beers in their hands, looking up at the camera through sunglasses. Everybody looked goofy in at least a few shots, caught chewing, or with their mouths slack, but not Chris. "Oh yeah," Chris grinned. "Just goes to show you the power of a good haircut."

Kathleen and Dell looked at each other and cracked up.

"What?"

"We were just talking about butches and their hair," Dell said, still giggling. She pointed to other butches in the pictures: Jo, Perry, Sue Black still cocky before she got messed up by the cops. "Man," Dell said, "You guys are like old ladies that way, always with a hand up, patting or smoothing."

Chris instinctively smoothed her hair, making Dell and Kathleen collapse laughing against each other. "Hair is important," she said haughtily, and walked down the hall to the bedroom.

There she found the closet open and her school books scattered over the floor. Kathleen had obviously rummaged through it to find the album, and had left her stuff out there in plain view. For a second, it was hard to catch her breath. Chris gathered her books carefully and stacked them back into a shelf in the closet, closed the closet doors. She stayed there for such a long time that Kathleen came looking for her. Her hair was down and her face rosy. "What's up?" she asked playfully, sliding her arms around Chris's waist and bringing her face to Chris's neck.

Kathleen had clearly had a few. Chris clasped her wrists and freed herself. "I found my books from school scattered all over the floor."

Kathleen looked down at the floor, then at her. "Oh, I was trying to find the album."

Chris raised her eyebrows at her.

"What?"

"Dell could see them."

Kathleen groaned. "C'mon Chris, stop. I'm so tired ...."

"Of what, Kathleen?" Chris spoke tauntingly. "Of being supportive? Of my going to school? Of having an illiterate for a girlfriend?"

Kathleen swiftly and silently closed the door so they wouldn't be overheard. She was going to say she was tired of fighting. A space inside her chest wrenched open. That vacation, she had been remembering, she had sunned herself in Chris's gallantry. She remembered thinking, even back then, that she had had a perfectly nice husband, but that there was something about a butch's care that was so different from, so much sweeter than, a man's. And she remembered carrying Chris's secret like a jewel on a chain, hidden under clothes.

"I'm tired of all those accusations," she hissed. "So you're learning to read: what, I'm supposed to stop my whole life for that?" She started crying, and then was furious at herself for crying. She hated when women resorted to tears in arguments. Now Dell would see that her eyes were red, and would think she was being treated badly by Chris.

Chris stood there glowering, and then got a funny look on her face. "You know what?" she said. "No, you're not." She opened the door and left the room, and in a second, Kathleen could hear her down the hall talking intently to Dell. She thought, *Oh my God,* and sat heavily on the bed, panic swirling before her. In a few minutes she got up and went into the bathroom, washed her face and examined her eyes as she patted it dry. Then she went into the living room. Chris was sitting on the arm of the sofa, her heavy face surprisingly bright, saying, "You can see why I haven't wanted anybody to know." On the couch, Dell was rubbing her face from her relaxed and silly buzz into attentiveness, nodding rapidly.

Kathleen came up quietly and sat next to Dell on the edge of the couch, but Dell's gaze was fixed on Chris.

"It's my thing," Chris said, "and I've preferred to deal with it alone, in my way."

I see, Kathleen thought.

"Chris," Dell said, her sharp face grown warm, touching Chris's knee, "I'm so touched that you trust me enough to tell me."

Kathleen thought, There's Dell, always making it about herself. This wasn't about trust; this was about Chris getting back at Kathleen. This was about spite, about bringing Kathleen down to Dell's level. She got up and went to get dinner started, avoiding the sight of Chris's rapt face.

The training session met in a small classroom on the fourth floor of the Harold Washington Library. Anna got there early, emerging from the El onto quiet Saturday-morning streets that, darkened by tall buildings, had the feel of canyons. She waited in a small line with people sipping coffee, some smoking, until the building opened at nine. Once upstairs, she occupied herself shyly, peering at the glass cases with models of the library made by different architectural firms, trying to decide if the model that had been chosen was in fact the nicest. In the corner of her eye she saw people going into the classroom, some of whom she'd waited in line with that morning. At 9:10, after people had stopped going in, she entered the small, pristine classroom.

Anna introduced herself and welcomed them, said what a good and important thing they were preparing themselves to do. She handed out packets to everybody, then had them pair up and introduce themselves, then each other, to the class. There was a professor on sabbatical, several nuns, a few college students and retired teachers, three women, two middle-aged and one about eighteen, from a Baptist church, a tall short-haired white woman who worked in a women's law firm and who hummed pleasantly in Anna's gender radar, two young African-American men in white shirts and conservative ties from a South Side agency that prepared public aid recipients for their move off of welfare.

What effect does illiteracy have on people's lives? Warming to an audience that was quietly attentive, Anna listed some of the answers. "They have to remember everything aurally," she said, "and they have to remember the first time. They don't know how to use the legal system, so they can't protect themselves from being exploited at work. They order hamburger from every restaurant. They don't write checks. They can't read to their children, or help them with their homework." She paused, then went on: "They can't go to a 12-step program. They can't read the instructions on prescriptions. Sometimes they decline big promotions at work for fear of having to read."

She had the class turn to the page titled "Who Is This Student?" in the packet, and read through it, about the gifts of experience adults bring to learning, about their defense mechanisms and sensitivity to non-verbal forms of communication, about their long histories of self-doubt and resignation.

They nodded thoughtfully and took furious notes.

The first part of this first lesson was designed to emphasize that in adult basic education, the learner is in charge. "That means you always start with them," Anna said. "You ask: Where are the instances where, if you could read better, things would be better?" She waited. "If a learner needs a doctor, you bring in a Yellow Pages. If a learner needs to get someplace in the city, you look at a map together. Reading exercises must be relevant to the actual life and skills of the reader. Which letters do you start with?" She waited.

The class considered, then one of the men from the agency raised his hand. His name was Shay. He had a shaved head and a goatee; his bulk stretched the shoulders of his dress shirt. "Their name?"

"Exactly," Anna said. "Their name. They own the material."

She talked about some of the problems their learners might come in with, and asked them to name the appropriate learning tool for each one: maps, menus, schedules, job applications, newspapers, the Bible, prescription labels. She introduced them to the idea of LEA, Language Experience Approach, and went through the steps of it. They talked about how to coax a story out of a learner, how to listen quietly and ask good questions without pressuring. An older woman raised her hand and said it seemed as though it might be hard, since the two of you were potentially from such different backgrounds.

"It can be hard," Anna said, thinking of Chris, how she made Anna feel like a voyeuristic shmuck every time Anna asked her questions. "Why should they tell you about their lives? Maybe you'll judge them, *they* don't know. If they have a job, they probably think it's too boring to talk about. And often there's such a severe alienation from writing that they can't believe there could actually be some connection between it and something real from their lives."

The boyish-looking woman raised her hand. "What's your name again?" Anna asked. She thought she had said Star, but wanted to make sure before embarrassing herself by saying it aloud.

"Star," she said. Anna wondered whether she was a dyke, and decided that she wasn't her type, even though she was very nice-looking. She was maybe forty, tall and slim, built around the shoulders, with dark hair and very white skin.

"I find in the work I do," Star said, "that sometimes if you share something about your own life, that can make them more comfortable sharing with you."

"Certainly," Anna said, thinking *oy, she's a sharer,* "although you don't want the LEA session to become about you."

"No, of course not," Star said. "I'm just saying...."

"No, I know," Anna interrupted; "just that it doesn't hurt to look for points of commonality between you."

At the lunch break she headed to the Subway across the street, shadowed by one of the volunteers, an older white man with strange propulsive speech patterns who clutched his notepad to his chest. He reminded her of the time during her own training session that she had seen Dan Irwin browsing in the library bookstore after lunch, and how, before approaching him, she had rehearsed some smart question to impress him with.

The man following her wanted to tell her about the experience he'd had tutoring youngsters in an after-school program. She nodded, getting in line, watching through the plastic barrier the gloved and expert hands of the workers laying cheese and lettuce and tomatoes on meat and tuna, and said, "That's great." Up ahead Star was paying for her lunch; she turned and noticed the man talking Anna's ear off, and gave her a wink so subtle Anna wasn't sure at first that she'd winked at all. Then Anna turned pink.

She got her sandwich and paid, and gave the talkative man the slip by sliding, while he was paying, into the last space at a table with Star and the two men from the agency, Shay and Brandon. The moment she sat, Star leaned forward and said, "You know, I really wasn't advocating talking on and on about myself, I want to make that clear."

Ripping open her potato chips, Anna sighed, oppressed by the feeling that she'd been ungenerous, and by dislike of Star for making such a big deal out of it.

"I understand," she said. "Really."

Star didn't take her eyes off of her; she pushed forward ponderously. "It's just that I feel I've found a way to talk to clients that works for me," she said.

"Good for you," Anna said.

"Good workshop so far," Brandon said to her.

"I'm glad you're liking it," Anna said.

They talked about the workshop, and Star's attention gradually came around to it. "Are you happy with how it's going?" she asked.

Anna paused. Shouldn't she be? Was that a sensitive question or a hostile one?

"Yes," she said.

They talked about Shay and Brandon's work and the dilemmas placed on their clients by the new welfare system. They talked about where they lived, white North Side women, black South Side men, and marveled how they were all lifetime Chicagoans, and yet were totally unfamiliar with each others' neighborhoods. They eyed each other, and shook their heads about it.

Star sat back and lay her hands flat on the table; they were large and strong, Anna noticed, and she had rings on three or four fingers and her thumb. "Isn't this something!" she said grandly. "Now if we could only have this kind of dialogue on a larger scale, this real *talking* between black and white" — she gestured back and forth between the women and the men — "there might be some hope for us. And not just hearing each other talk," she added, "but" — cupping her hand around her ear — "*listening.*"

They looked quickly at each other; Anna saw Shay's nostrils flare, his eyes blink rapidly. She sat stiff with embarrassment, while Brandon tilted back his cup and let the ice slide into his mouth, and chewed it vigorously.

Anna began the second half of the session with some statistics for them to mull over. 25-30% of people in literacy programs have high school diplomas. 45% don't make it beyond twelve hours of training. Only 15% still stick around after six months to a year.

Someone gave a low whistle. "Exactly," Anna said.

They went over the different kinds of learners, and then Rachel, one of the older women from the South Side church, asked what to do if your program gave out state-mandated tests. "It seems to me, especially from what you've said," she commented, "that that's getting off to a demoralizing start."

"Yes it is," Anna said. "Let them know," she said, "that those tests are not very good or very important. Also, if you're given material to teach, ask them how they want to learn it, and ask them how they'll use it in their life."

For the rest of the time, she talked more about Whole Language Approach. It uses, she explained, reading, writing, listening and speaking in every lesson, and it's writing that most needs to be integrated. She spoke about daily journals, dialogue writing, the three techniques for teaching words: sight words, phonics, word patterns.

After class a few of them clustered around her, to tell her about the informal tutoring they'd done so far, or about a case they knew that completely illustrated something she'd said, or that completely contradicted something she'd said. She stood by the board listening and answering, enjoying herself, noticing that Star was lingering on the edges of the conversation, sometimes listening, sometimes looking around the room or down at her nails. She was tall, Anna noticed, and she felt a wisp of jealous hostility seeing that her purple jeans hung from her narrow hips just the way Anna wished hers would. "Thanks," she smiled, as the last students said goodbye, "See you next Saturday." She looked at Star and raised her eyebrows.

"Hi," Star said.

"Hi," Anna said.

"Oh heck, I'll just come out with it," Star said.

Anna stiffened: what on earth?

"Would you like to go out for dinner tomorrow night?" Star asked. "You know, to talk about some of the ideas we discussed today?"

Man, was that lame, Anna thought, as a voice came out of her mouth saying, "Sure."

She had no idea why the next night, after a rather stilted dinner in Wicker Park during which Star failed to laugh at her jokes and was revealed to be a vegan, and Anna, drawing her out about her life, repeatedly thought her unattractive and uninteresting, Star was up in her apartment being kissed by her on the living room couch. *What the hell,* she thought, there was an ice storm going on outside that had made their ride home from the restaurant an adventure, and Star wasn't driving anywhere anytime soon. And kissing two women in the space of two weeks: who on earth would have anticipated such a sexual bonanza?

Star was a big girl! — a triathlete, strong and sinewy, with small breasts. Anna focused on enjoying that, rather than wishing her body softer and her breasts bigger. She got up on her knees to get some purchase on her. "Whoa!" Star said, laughing through her nose, as Anna straddled her knees and took her by the hair, kissing her. She let Anna do all the kissing — Anna couldn't tell whether she was respecting that Anna was the butch, or she wasn't a very good kisser. "Put your tongue in my mouth," Anna murmured close to her lips. They touched tongues. "More," Anna said, looking right in her eyes till they split into four, then eight. "More!" — until Star was pushing and their tongues were thickly intertwined.

About an hour later, Star was naked and fragrant in her bed, Anna having brought her to two thunderous orgasms, and Star having called her "little but mighty." Anna lay next to her with her hands crossed behind her head, secretly shocked and thrilled that her sex skills had transferred from Patricia to another woman. Star was lazily trying to get her to take off her underwear and t-shirt. "Oh come on," she teased, propping herself up on her elbow and lifting Anna's shirt as if to try to peek under it, "let me see whatchya got under there."

"No," Anna protested, clamping her forearm to her shirt.

Star lay back down and sighed. "Okay," she said, "It's fine with me if I can just lie here like a slug. But butch or no butch, watch out, 'cuz I really, really want to touch you."

She really did, it turned out. Anna awoke at 6:00 the next morning to the feel of powerful hands on her back and Star's mouth on hers. She stirred awake and Star said "Hi," then took both her wrists in one hand and flipped her over, reached into her underwear with her free hand. Anna tried to heave herself up, but Star gently maneuvered her weight onto her and pressed on her till she stopped. She audibly sucked on her fingers and then pushed them into Anna and started fucking. Anna lay on her face, her mouth dry and her eyes still crusty with sleep, her heart pounding. Star leaned toward her and whispered in her ear. "You can take it," she said.

That morning, Anna got a late start. She and Star left together, exclaiming at the glittering trees, putting on sunglasses, tottering on ice. She was relieved to remember that their cars were parked blocks away from each other. Star bent to give her a kiss on the cheek, and said, "See ya later, slugger." Then she turned and walked off. *Oh brother,* Anna thought. Hugging herself, she reveled in feeling cold and alone, wintry. But when she got to her car, she stopped and groaned. It was encased in ice. She struggled to get the door open, pulling till it broke free with a crack; she got the car started and turned the defroster on high. The ice flaked off the scraper in tiny white chips. Cursing, Anna pounded at it with the edge of the scraper. It took a long time for the car to warm so that the ice slid off in sheets.

She got to Pathways about ten minutes late, and ran up the stairs still sweating, her fingers and toes numb with cold. All morning long, some poltergeist had slowed her down; now she knew how her students felt all the time. She entered the classroom and took quick stock. They were all there, even Vanessa, which was positively shocking for the morning of an ice storm. As Anna took off her coat and hung it over her chair, both Antwan and Brandy gave her comical, significant looks and tapped their watches, the gesture she made when they were late. "Okay okay," she laughed, putting her hands up to her cheeks to warm them. Chris was over in the back corner, her legs outstretched and her arms folded across her chest.

Anna shuffled through her bag looking for the exercise she'd brought for today, growing increasingly impatient, then thinking, *Damn.* Her shoulders sagged. She'd left it at home. She stood there for a second, trying to figure out what to do. Then she turned toward them. "What should I have you write about this morning?"

Just as the words came out of her mouth, she saw a note glide from the palm of Cheryl's hand into Antwan's. Annoyed, she stared him down and he looked back intently, quietly holding it tucked and still in his hand. What kind of moment was this? Her mind flickered back to fifth grade, a note passed to her from Jack Silver, all the way across the classroom. It asked if she would go with him, and Jack had promised, "I won't use you," a possibility Anna had pondered for a long time, and which sounded alarmingly and excitingly dirty.

Should she confiscate the note? Christ, they were grownups. She was still staring at Antwan, who was performing unconcern, gazing into space and whistling noiselessly. But then a thought came, as belated as everything else she'd done that morning. They had passed a note! Cheryl was no doubt making fun of her in writing!

She turned toward the board, grinning. The moment she turned, Antwan unfolded the note. Cheryl had written, impeccably, "She got laid," and Antwan's mind snapped smartly around the words. His face suffused with merriment, he slipped the note into his pocket. Anna picked up a piece of chalk and jiggled it in her hand, reminding herself to tell Renée, who would get a big kick out of adult learners passing notes. She wrote on the board, "Sometimes I wonder why..." She wheeled on her heels and called "Cheryl! Read this aloud," enjoying watching Cheryl jerk to attention at the sound of her name.

Chris saw the note and shook her head. What was this, second grade? She tapped her pencil on her notebook and looked at the words going up on the board. All weekend she had punished Kathleen for almost blowing her cover. She had taken a job with Keith, probably their last outdoor job for the winter, and had been thankful to be out of the house during the day. At night, she turned stiffly away from Kathleen in bed. But punishing her didn't really make much sense, because she was excited and relieved about having come out to Dell. Telling Dell had felt like eating a lemon snow-cone, her mouth cold and tangy, her molars smarting. Did she look dopey, like those clog dancers at the guitar school, bosoms bouncing in enthusiasm? She remembered Dell's avid face as she told her, and how she kissed her goodbye the next morning with rare softness. Not that there wouldn't be fallout! Chris could just see Dell, talking knowingly about her, taking advantage. And Kathleen: she'd had no right forcing the issue. Kathleen hated her being in school. She was sabotaging her in small ways all the time, urging her not to come back, taking a dislike to Dennis. To Dennis!

She looked down at her notebook, wrote down the words from the board. She drew a line out from there, and let it dribble down the page. Anna came over and glanced at it, then looked at her with her eyebrows raised. "I'll tell you what," Chris said, noticing as she looked at her that Anna's lips were chapped and that she kept licking them, "Just give me some boring phonics or cloze thing today, okay? I'll work on it here by myself."

Anna pulled up a chair and stationed herself next to her, too close, as usual. "I'll tell you what," she said, "We'll do an LEA: you dictate, I'll do the writing."

Chris smiled. Her hair was still matted from gel, having dried in the cold air outside. "Just give me an exercise," she said. She was a little surprised at her own pigheadedness, but really, she wasn't in the mood to discuss her life and her feelings.

Anna looked at her, bit the inside of her lip. Chris sure knew how to suck the energy out of a room. "Fine," she said, and stood. She took a few minutes to look through the exercises she had on her, and selected a cloze exercize. She brought it over and dropped it on Chris's desk. "There," she said, keeping her voice light, "That ought to bore you sufficiently."

Chris laughed faintly, and settled down to it. "Once __ a time," she read, "there was a little ____ named Goldilocks." When she got through it, she snorted. She had a daring impulse to write *baby dyke* in the second blank, and her mind turned around the transgressive possibility of marking in the wrong answer — and two words instead of one! — on purpose.

After class, she dropped the worksheet on Anna's desk, and as she turned to go, Anna asked her to stay. "Sit down," she said, motioning toward a chair.

"I'm kind of in a hurry."

"Just sit down for a second, okay?"

Chris sat down and stared at her, then glanced down at the book she was holding. Anna opened it and started to read:

I didn't want to be different. I longed to be everything grownups wanted, so they would love me. I followed all their rules, tried my best to please. But there was something about me that made them knit their eyebrows and frown.

Anna felt an irritation at her peripheral vision, and looked up. A man in a wool cap had popped his head in the door. "Excuse me, we're busy here," she said.

"Sorry, you seen Greg?"

"No."

"Because I was supposed to meet him here at noon." He lingered stupidly, as though, Chris thought, this was their problem. Her stomach was on edge; she didn't know what Anna was trying to lay on her.

"He's not here," Anna said, getting up and going to the door to propel him out. After she sat back down, she said, "I'm going to start over."

I didn't want to be different. I longed to be everything grownups wanted, so they would love me. I followed all their rules, tried my best to please. But there was something about me that made them knit their eyebrows and frown. No one ever offered a name for what was wrong with me. That's what made me afraid it was really bad. I only came to recognize its melody through this constant refrain: "Is that a boy or a girl?"

Looking down at her lap, Chris's face slowly reddened.

You can take it, Anna thought. "Here, it's a novel, a fiction book. Remember what that is? It means it's a made-up story. It's called *Stone Butch Blues.* Read it if you want, I'm lending it to you." She tossed it at her. Chris fumbled and it fell on the floor face down, its pages splaying open. Anna was getting up to collect her things and put on her coat. Chris looked down at the book; there was a picture of a butch on the cover, wearing a jacket and tie. That must be the butch in the story, she thought. She looked at Anna, who had her back turned to her. She was clearly dismissed. Chris bent down, wincing from the twinge of pain in her back, and picked up the book with a large lined hand.

P A R T   T W O

CHAPTER TWELVE

Anna needed to make it up to Terry for making out with her girl-friend. Normally she could have waited a few weeks and let Terry cool off, but it was the holiday season, and she was a bereaved single Jew on the eve of Christmas. She had figured out something hard right before Thanksgiving, when all her friends had left town and she had spent an evening weeping in the shower, bitterly wondering what Patricia was doing and trying to figure out who she could wrangle a last-minute invitation from: that when you're single, you have to be enterprising, because no one will leave their fireside to look for your tracks in the snow. She could've gone out east to visit her mother and her brother Julian's family, but she knew that would entail a lot of sitting around worshipping his son Gerry, who was named after her father and whom Anna privately referred to as The Baby Jesus. She couldn't afford the flight anyway, and was embarrassed for them to know that. So in the end, she had Thanksgiving dinner with an old friend from Oberlin and her husband, who irritated her all evening by explaining to their obnoxious children in scientifically-reasoned detail why they shouldn't grab the carving knife or eat pie before dinner. Was it so very wrong, Anna wondered, to simply answer "Because I said so?" She vowed never to go just anywhere again, just because she didn't want to be alone on a weekend or holiday.

She couldn't stand Christmas; the music and the hot mall air and the local news stories paramilitarily enforcing the holiday spirit put her in a foul mood. One day, trying to grade papers in Coffee Chicago, she thought the frenzied holiday muzak would drive her crazy. After some

deliberation, she finally asked a staff person to turn it off, and to her surprise, he laughed and thanked her and put on some R&B instead. When
she told Scott about it later on the phone, he asked if he'd told her his
latest theory, about Rudolph the Red-Nosed Reindeer.

"No," Anna said.

"Well first of all," he said, "Rudolph has a RED NOSE. Get it? And
second of all, he'll work on a night when all the others refuse." He paused
significantly.

"It's about Jews?" Anna ventured.

"Exactly! It's a song about the Jew who keeps the 7-Eleven open on
Christmas Eve." Anna laughed. Scott loved Jews with campy abandon;
Anna called him a matzo queen. He had a theory that *The Munsters* was
about the rich Jewish family that wants to move into your neighborhood
and join the country club. Hence all those episodes of Hermann wreak-
ing havoc on the golf course, and the blonde daughter Marilyn — the
daughter who passes as a *shiksa*.

She met Terry at Einstein's on a Saturday morning. When Terry
walked in, her face red from the cold, her hands jammed in her parka
pockets, Anna's stomach turned nervously. Terry joined her in line, and
they silently peered up at the menu on the wall. Anna peeked over at her,
noticed that the skin around her nostrils was peeling from repeated
blowing. They ordered and paid and put their food down on a table, and
Anna rose to fill her coffee cup, grateful for a reason to leave the table for
a few more seconds. Finally, she sat, cupping her hand around the hot
cup. Terry looked at her. "Well?" she demanded.

Her hair was shaggy and her eyes narrowed, and her outright belligerence made Anna laugh. "I'm really sorry I kissed your girlfriend,"
she said. "It won't happen again."

Terry raised her eyebrows. "You don't look very sorry to me at all,"
she said.

It had been inappropriate to laugh. Anna composed her face and
said gravely, "I know, but I really am."

Terry sat back in her chair, her face glum. "So that's it?"

"I don't know what else to say," Anna said, wondering whether if she told Terry that she would never in a million years consider Janice as an actual girlfriend, it would be helpful or hurtful. "It was a spontaneous thing — I certainly didn't plan it." Especially, she thought, since it was Janice who had jumped *her*.

"You know, Anna," Terry said, "We're grown-ups, there are consequences to our actions."

Anna looked at her in surprise. This didn't sound like mordant, witty Terry at all, the Terry who was rarely disappointed in her friends because she saw them so keenly for who they are, and who counseled with an utter lack of judgment people who were sick or dying because of something they'd done. That was the thing Anna admired most about her, why she was able to be generous about Terry's crabbiness and general nihilism.

"You'd think you'd have some empathy for my position," Terry was continuing, with a tight smile, "given Patricia's affair with what's-her-name."

Anna flushed. Terry wanted to hurt her, she thought: fair enough. "You know, Terry," she said, "You try to figure out a way to think about these things that's different from the old fucked-up story of secrecy and betrayal. You think, well maybe it's good that your girlfriend has found someone else to share the burden of taking care of her, because God knows she's a handful. Or maybe you can make erotic hay out of competing with this other woman, or maybe you can take that energy she has that comes from sleeping with a new person, and tap into it when the two of you are in bed." She found herself unexpectedly emotional, tried not to let her voice quaver. "Maybe it's a way of loving her, decking her with garlands as she goes off to meet a new lover, being there when she comes back home."

Terry was regarding her with a mix of incredulity and pity.

"But what does our culture say about that?" Anna asked, prompting her with a weary wave of the hand.

"You're pathetic, you're fooling yourself, she's fucking you over."

"Exactly," Anna said, stung by the enthusiasm of Terry's answer even though it was the answer she was looking for. "And that's so fucked, it so much doesn't leave room for all these other possibilities."

"For Christ sake," Terry cried. "She *left* you for her lover."

Anna shook her head; she didn't believe that. "She left me because she wanted to leave me," she said.

They were quiet for a few minutes. Terry finally picked up her bagel, examined it, and took a bite, catching cream cheese with her finger as it squirted from the side. "So what are you saying?" she asked as she chewed.

Anna shrugged. "I don't know. That I'm sorry. That my kissing Janice doesn't necessarily mean all those things we're taught to think it means."

"That I should be cooler about this?"

"I'm not saying you're not cool," Anna said. "I'm not saying that."

Terry bit her lip, and said suddenly, "It made me feel like you don't care about my friendship."

Anna's face filled with dismay at the unfamiliar sight of Terry wounded. "I do. Terry, I've been lonely. I jumped at the opportunity to do some kissing. That's all."

They ate bagels and sipped coffee for a little while, Anna fighting back the urge to barge into the conversation again and protest how much she cared for Terry. The truth is, when Janice reached out and touched her face, Anna hadn't given a damn about Terry. It didn't mean that she didn't care about Terry's friendship, but she guessed that was too fine a point for Terry to parse at this moment. And anyway, did it really matter? Even sitting here with her angry friend, she could feel the muscles in her thighs, the soreness of her mouth from kissing Star. She felt awed by the fact that two women had opened their arms and pulled her in. Two! Which might mean, she thought wildly, that it was no accident.

"Terry," she finally said. "If it's any help, I've just started seeing somebody."

Terry looked at her in amazement.

Anna nodded.

"What's her name?" Terry asked.

Anna cleared her throat. "Star," she said.

Terry leaned forward and cocked her ear toward her. "What?"

"Star," Anna repeated.

Terry raised one dark eyebrow, mischief giving off faint light behind cloud cover. "Is that the name she gave herself at the lesbian feminist commune?"

Anna laughed. "I've been afraid to ask," she said.

"Are you spending Christmas together?"

"Nah, I've just slept with her once."

They sat and finished their bagels without speaking, letting reconciliation steep gently around them and gain flavor. People in parkas bumped and scraped against them; Anna moved her chair forward to let a woman with a stroller through. She and Terry weren't quite friends again – that'd take some time – but they'd said the things they needed to say. Terry told her that for Christmas, she and Janice were driving up to a cottage on the Upper Peninsula, to have some quiet time together. Anna nodded, surprisingly not disappointed. Monica too was going away, with Martha; they were flying to the Caribbean to give their relationship one more shot. Anna and Terry got up and put their coats on, and as they stepped out into the cold and Terry accepted her muffled embrace, Anna realized that she didn't envy any of them one bit: the couple in distress going into isolation, to process.

This was going to be the first Christmas in their house. And now, early Christmas morning, in her house coat, stuffing the turkey with onions, apples and parsley, Kathleen was sure it was going to be ruined. A cup of coffee was cooling on the counter. Chris was shoveling the walk outside; hearing the scrape of the shovel on the sidewalk, Kathleen worried about Chris's back, and then thought: oh well, she's a grown-up. Last night Chris had suddenly, after twenty years, revealed she didn't like Kathleen's cornbread stuffing, which had hurt Kathleen's feelings more than she could have ever imagined. Kathleen rinsed parsley and shook it dry, cut off the stems. It was too wet, Chris had informed her; she liked it more crumbly. And she acted as though she wasn't being mean at all, just honest and helpful. Why she had never said anything for two decades was beyond Kathleen.

These days, Chris was walking around looking as placid as the man in the moon gazing down upon earth. Coming out to Dell without consulting with her first! As though to say to Kathleen: *Don't think you're so special.* It was almost three weeks later, and despite trying to get into a warm and forgiving Christmas spirit, and despite the unwelcome knowledge pressing at her mind that she didn't really have a leg to stand on, Kathleen just couldn't get over that; a bad feeling seemed to hollow her out whenever she thought about it.

Kathleen had tried to bring it up, but Chris just asked her why she should care, that if Dell ended up lording it over her, that was *Chris's* problem.

And to that Kathleen had no retort. Because she couldn't figure out how to argue that it was her problem too, even though her heart kept telling her it was.

She finished packing the turkey cavity, her hand numb with cold and wet up to the wrist, then turned the tap on and waited for the water to get hot. Chris thought Christmas was a crock; it was totally up to Kathleen to create any holiday spirit, and then of course Chris totally benefited from it. Kathleen washed her hands vigorously in the hot water, dried them on a dishtowel. Last night she had gone to mass by herself, and in the glow of candles and song she had closed her eyes and thought of her mother, who the whole time she was dying of ALS, never mentioned the disease aloud, and of her little brother Danny, whose querulous questions Kathleen had viciously shushed, having no tolerance for his 7-year-old nonsense, the tears and the bedwetting. Her lips moving silently with the liturgy, she suddenly regretted her harshness. He had just been a little boy. The feeling did not last long: regret was not a major emotion in Kathleen's repertoire. The way she saw it, you did the best you could do at the time. And Danny had turned out just fine. He was a VP in sales in Miami, bringing in close to six figures, in a good marriage.

Kathleen opened the oven door and put the turkey in, feeling as she knelt the pressure of moist heat against her face.

Keith and Margaret and the girls came over that afternoon, bearing pie and a pitcher of eggnog. The moment they walked in the door, cold air rushing in, Jessica shot her mother a furious look. There had apparently been a fight about Jessica wearing a dress, and now Kathleen wasn't even wearing one.

"You made her wear a dress?" Chris exclaimed, casting a sympathetic look at the sullen sixteen-year-old, who took off her parka and handed it to Kathleen in silent rage. "Why?"

Keith put his hand on Chris's shoulder and squeezed. "Oh my God, Chris's having a flashback," he joked. Normally the sober provider, he liked to be naughty around Chris.

Chris shrugged his hand off. "Ha ha," she said.

"You're not helping, you two," Margaret said, as Jessica ran into the bathroom and slammed the door.

Keith was sent to coax her out, and after some fierce whispering that broke once or twice into a strangled lament, they eventually emerged, Keith's hand atop Jessica's head, her eyes puffy. "Chris honey, will you carve?" Kathleen said in the fake chirp she used when she was giving Chris the cold shoulder. "And everybody else, dig in." They served themselves in the kitchen and ate around the coffee table in the living room, since Chris and Kathleen couldn't yet afford a dining room table. Keith said grace, and sitting on the couch, her head bowed, Chris grudgingly let herself be disarmed by his words of gratitude. The whole time Kathleen was preparing for Christmas, Chris had felt she was overdoing it. She had spent a fortune on food and presents — money that Chris, frankly, would have spent differently. Kathleen always bought the most expensive present for the Secret Santa bag at work, and then came home with some piece of crap like a scented candle or a figurine of a St. Bernard. And why did they need stuffing *and* mashed potatoes, when it was just the Seryneks? But sitting with their friends in the fragrant house, a heavy plate on her lap and the tree glittering in the corner, she thought: you had to hand it to her. Without Kathleen, Chris would never have a sense of family at all. Even the sullen teenager felt like a homey touch.

When they finished eating, and Keith and Chris had cleared the dishes and stacked them in the sink, they settled back into the living room with eggnog — the adults' spiked with brandy — and opened presents.

Keith and Chris stretched out on the floor beside the tree, faces flushed and sweaters rising up the gut. Keith leaned toward her and whispered, "What's wrong?" and when she frowned he said, "You guys having a fight?" She shook her head dismissively. Keith raised one eyebrow, then settled back. He reached lazily up to the tree and fingered an ornament of Daffy Duck quacking "Have a Gay Christmas!" that Kathleen had found years ago in a sale box in a gay bookstore. "Cute," he said, and Chris grinned.

Kathleen got Chris a jigsaw for cutting a new hole for the dryer vent, and Chris got Kathleen a white cotton sweater. Kathleen had done the shopping for the girls, a box of magnetic poetry for Zoey and a gift certificate for pottery supplies for Jessica. Seeing that even Jessica was pleased, accepting the girls' kisses on her cheek, Chris was impressed by Kathleen's knack for buying the right things for them. Margaret said "Keith honey," and gestured him toward a gift under the tree; he reached and handed it to Chris, and as Chris pulled a book out of the wrapping paper and held it so Kathleen could see the cover, Kathleen gave her a strange smiling look. Adrenaline surged through Chris. "Oh, wow!" she said, taking in the picture of a ledger and dollar signs. It was a book on managing their finances — a gesture, Chris realized instantly, toward the class she was supposedly taking. Blood pulsing in her temples, she felt the full stupidity of that lie, and wished that she had told them something closer to the truth and more plausible, like she was going back to study for her GED. For a second she wondered what difference it would make if they knew the truth. "Thank you, guys," she said, getting up to give Margaret a kiss, avoiding Kathleen's eye. And after they'd left, as she labored in steamy water over a crusted casserole dish, and Kathleen stripped bits of turkey off the carcass, laying them onto a big doubled strip of aluminum foil, Chris wiped a sweaty temple with her shoulder, the words "how to manage" ringing savagely in her head.

On New Year's Eve Chris and Kathleen drank champagne as they watched the ball drop in New York, commented on how Dick Clark never aged, and toasted to Chris's settlement arriving in the coming year. After that, school being out till the 20th, there was nothing left for Chris to do but work on the house. Chris woke up every morning thinking of another project: a bathroom fan causing too much of a draft, which she had just disconnected and stuffed a towel in for the time being, the paint starting to peel on the outside window frames, the decrepit blinds left on the bedroom window from the previous owner. Normally she would have been energized by the thought of these repairs. She had finally finished laying the bathroom floor, and going in there gave her enormous pleasure every single time. But she would never have even tackled that project if she'd known how many others they would need to throw money at.

Meanwhile, Kathleen was deep into *Stone Butch Blues*. Way deep into it.

She picked it up on Sunday morning, while straightening the bedroom. Chris was brushing her teeth. "What's this, honey?" Kathleen called.

Chris spat and rinsed. When she came out of the bathroom she saw Kathleen sitting on the edge of the bed in her nightgown, reading. She got right back into bed and spent the whole morning reading, didn't even shower, while Chris installed the new medicine cabinet they'd bought for the bathroom and ran over to the hardware store on Clark to get shades cut for the bedroom. When she returned, stomping into the house and kicking off her boots, she heard Kathleen cry out. She stiffened, and ran back to the bedroom. Kathleen was still in bed, looking like a crazed person with her unwashed hair sticking out and her glasses low on her nose. Her eyes were glistening as she held up the book.

"Wow," Kathleen said.

"You scared the crap out of me."

"Sorry," Kathleen said, obviously not very sorry, bringing the book back in front of her face.

Half an hour later, having screwed the hardware into the window frames, Chris tried to lay in the shade and saw that the old guy who had waited on her had cut the shades too short. "Shit," she said. He'd estimated too much space for the hardware. She'd thought he was measuring it wrong at the time, and had come right out and said so; but when he lay out the numbers of what he was doing he confused her, and in the end she had avoided what she knew would become an unpleasant tussle. She fiddled unhappily with the shade. You could pry open the plastic piece and lengthen it that way, but the shade looked bad and fell off every time she tried to snap it open. Now she'd have to go back. She fished into her jeans pocket and put her fingers on the receipt. Looking irritably over at the bedside table, she saw Anna's book laid face down, right next to a half-full cup of coffee with milk filming on the top and drying stains on the outside.

"What?" Kathleen asked, coming into the room, her breasts loose under her nightgown.

"I messed up the damn shades," Chris said. "Are you going to even get dressed today?"

Kathleen looked at her. "It's Sunday, I'm spending one day in my nightgown."

"And could you not put that book down like that?" Chris said. "You're gonna get it wet, and it doesn't belong to you."

Kathleen looked slowly over at the book, then picked it up and got back in bed, pushing vigorously at the covers with her feet to free them. The sight of her fat lazy wrinkly feet was too much for Chris.

"Are you going to be reading that book all day?"

Kathleen closed her eyes with consummate forbearance, and rested the book on her stomach, her finger holding the page.

"I have to go back to the hardware store," Chris announced.

"So what are you accusing me for! It's not my fault. I have a right to spend one goddamn day in bed enjoying myself."

Chris was rolling up the useless shade; she held it vertically for a second and the plastic rod shot out of the bottom. "Shit," she said, bending to pick it up. "It's not even your book, my teacher lent it to me."

Kathleen raised her eyebrows and gave her a vicious smile. "Oh, so you want to read it? Fine." She sat up and hurled it at Chris, whacking her in the shoulder. "You can tell me what it's about later," she said with the same smile.

Chris stared at her, then looked down at the book, which was lying on its back with the front cover curled up. This was the second time someone had thrown it at her.

The truth was, she'd opened it herself, a few days ago when Kathleen was at work. She brought it to the kitchen table to look at while she drank her coffee.

But the book didn't start the way she expected, the way Anna had read it, about how the butch didn't ask to be this way. It started with a very long title she didn't understand, *acknowledgments,* and a paragraph saying "thank you, Amber" that she couldn't get through. The print was the tiniest she'd ever seen; she had to hold it close to her face to make it out. Who was Amber? It was like picking up the receiver in the middle of someone else's phone conversation. When she flipped forward a little, her heart in her stomach, she found Chapter 1, but that didn't start the same way either, it started with a letter to someone named Theresa. And this print was different; it was squiggly and distracting, and also very, very tiny.

Chris swallowed, felt the coffee taste in her mouth turn to ashes. She obviously could not read this book. Well what had she expected? — that three months at school would turn her into a college professor? That she could just waltz in and open a book and start reading?

But then why had Anna given it to her? That was weird. If her teacher thought she could read this, she was even further behind than she thought. She opened to where Anna had written her name on the first page, and ran her thumb over it. *Anna Singer,* in the same writing as the comments on Chris's homework.

She got up and made herself some toast with butter and raspberry jam, ate it efficiently, then put her plate in the sink. She went into the bedroom and took her pocket dictionary out of her book bag, went back into the kitchen and looked up *acknowledgment.* There were six different definitions, all impossible to understand. She decided to skip that part and go on to *Dear Theresa.* "I'm lying on my bed tonight missing you, my eyes all swollen, hot tears running down my face." It took her twenty minutes. When she read it, she felt scalded. She flipped the book over and looked at the photograph of the spiffy he-she in a coat and tie speaking at a podium. Was that the same butch as was talking to Theresa like that, bawling all over herself? She thought: *what a pussy.*

At work Monday morning in her cubicle at Illinois Masonic,

Kathleen entered data and wondered whether that Jess Goldberg in the book was going to get herself killed. Jess reminded her exactly of Chris when Chris was younger, only much nicer, if truth be told – although Kathleen suspected that maybe the book wasn't realistic that way, that maybe, if you're writing a book about your life, it's only natural to portray yourself as a nice person. She felt a little bad because the book portrayed the working girls as brave and tough, and she had always thought of them as lowlife, thought of herself as a much better class of woman for Chris. And reading this book about all the violence in the world of a he-she made her feel *really* bad about being mean to Chris lately. It made her remember all the things Chris had been through in her life, things that Chris had told her about when they first fell in love. Chris had said: These are some things you should know about me. She was being conscientious, so Kathleen wouldn't think later on that she'd been sold a bill of goods.

Kathleen took off her glasses and breathed on the right lens, wiped it with a tissue. Sometimes she marveled that Chris even got up in the morning. And now all these new hard things: not working, trying to learn how to read – a task Kathleen worried was too much for someone in her fifties. What if she never learned to read? How would she deal with that humiliation?

She looked out the window into the alley off of Clark St., dumpsters and brick garages flat in the wan winter light. She wondered what would happen if she offered to read the book to Chris. She'd read her plenty of things before: articles from the paper, and of course the bills and stuff that came in the mail. But she'd never sat down beside her and read her a whole book. This book would make her flip out. It was about a he-she growing up in Buffalo, in the fifties.

She looked at the computer screen. Here was a poor slob in Wheeling whose HMO wasn't going to cover some big treatment he'd just had. She turned back to work, tapping at the keyboard with skillful fingers.

Well, first of all it was a big surprise when Kathleen came over to the couch after dinner, the book in her hand, took the remote from the table and turned off the TV, and flopped back next to her and read the whole *Dear Theresa* part out loud. Because suddenly Chris remembered being little and snuggling in the crook of her mother's shoulder, being read to. Remembering made her freeze with a strange panic. Her mother's nails on the page were long and polished; she snarled the bad guys and cheeped the little animals and children, hamming it up. And here was another thing she remembered: her mother's warm breath on her ear.

And second of all, she was still mad at Kathleen for being such a huge jerk.

So when Kathleen finished the he-she's tale of woe and put her arm around her and squeezed, and she looked in her face and saw tears in her eyes, Chris rolled her eyes and removed her arm, and got up off the couch, saying, "Don't be a sap."

Because third of all, good God, she couldn't believe her ears.

That night before bed, feeling a lowering ache in her back, Chris remembered the bottle of leftover Percocets in the back of the bathroom closet. She fished around the junk on the top shelf — extra toothpaste and trial-sized samples and empty plastic bottles — till she laid her hand on the bottle. It was more than half full; she'd stopped taking them when she started school. Chris opened the bottle and shook out two pills, swallowed them slurping tap water from her hand. She put the rest into the medicine cabinet. When she came to bed, Kathleen had already drifted off, curled toward Chris's side of the bed. Chris lay awake, trying to become mesmerized by her light even snore.

What Kathleen had read was full of crying and sex and fighting, and getting creamed and bloodied and humiliated by the cops, and her shame and her stone, and saying *you understand* to this Theresa, who Kathleen explained was at one time her femme. It was about a butch in the bars. They wrote books about that!

She just couldn't get over it.

Chris closed her eyes and waited for the pills to take effect. Her mind was like a mouse on a wheel in a cage. The book was exactly like her life, exactly. Only she didn't think of her life as that violent. Had it been? She thought of it as a hard life, as a hammer pounding a wall. She never thought of it as a drama that you'd write about, discussing all your miseries and pain. Why would you want everybody to know about it? What if straight people read it? Anna Singer must have read it. That thought brought a surge of mortification; she curled her knees up to her chest and hugged them with a groan. It took her an hour and a half to fall asleep.

The next night they sat on the couch with the book and a couple of beers. Chris lay down, her butt pushed up to where Kathleen was sitting, her knees bent over Kathleen's lap, and smoked a cigarette with her eyes closed as Kathleen read. It was a new thing, very still and quiet except for Kathleen's rich grainy voice, the hum of the refrigerator in the kitchen, the slam of the next-door neighbor's car door. She tapped ashes into the ashtray on her stomach. Rufus, lying at their feet, let out a yawn that ended with a tiny squeak. Kathleen stroked one foot, and Chris enjoyed the feel of her strong thumb, the rub of the sock against her arch. She opened her eyes and looked at Kathleen's profile, the glasses sitting on her nose, her strong chin and broad face with wisps of hair coming out of where she pulled it back.

It was confusing. Because it was so very nice, because Chris felt herself warming to Kathleen and appreciating the swell of her breasts under her sweater, but then, within moments, there was another expression of Jess Goldberg's parents' hatred for her, and her heart began to race. The thought swarmed up her throat, her mother again — her mother, who would get Chris all relaxed and snuggled up, and then say something that sent terror through her like a poison. *Your father thinks you should go away for a while. Why can't you just try, honey, for me?* The memory shocked her, and she struggled upright to breathe.

Kathleen stopped reading and considered her. "Pretty rough, huh," she said. She lay a commiserating hand on Chris's straining back; Chris could hardly bear her touch. "You okay?" Kathleen asked.

"Yeah," she said.

She and Kathleen started meeting on the couch every night, even the nights Kathleen worked late. Jess Goldberg was turning ten, and the shit was really starting to hit the fan. By this point, Chris had moved off the couch and was sitting in the lounger, her face rigid with concentration. And as she listened, she began to marvel: Jess had trouble in school just like she had! That night, washing her face and swallowing two painkillers, Chris thought about it; she thought maybe it was no wonder she'd had trouble in school given the shit she had to guard against every single moment of the day. But then again, Jess Goldberg didn't use that as an excuse not to learn to read. Even when she was committed by her parents, she spent her time in the mental hospital reading poetry. As far as Chris could remember, she had spent her time in the loony bin staring into space, fantasizing through the drugs' luscious syrupy haze about being an Indian warrior moving silently through the forest, or about her gym teacher from school, and how Chris saved her from great danger. What an idiot. It was her own damn fault if she couldn't read.

Over the next few days Jess Goldberg was gang-raped twice, once by the football team at school, and later by the cops. Listening to the book had become an agony. Chris sat very still during the second scene, where they lay her handcuffed over a desk in the precinct, noticing that Kathleen was casting little looks her way as she read, to see how she was reacting. She closed her eyes, trying to ignore being watched. Jess Goldberg started talking about being in the desert. "Wait," Chris asked uncertainly, "is she in the desert?"

"No, honey, she's imagining it," Kathleen said gently, "so she can act like she's not really there."

Jess Goldberg imagined sand and wind and sky. The ash grew long on Chris's cigarette and Kathleen stopped reading and said, "Honey!" right before it dropped off onto her sweatshirt; she jumped up, cursing, and brushed it off. It had burned a tiny hole. She looked down her chin at it and her eyes blurred. "Shit," she said.

"It's okay, you can still wear it around the house," Kathleen offered.

Chris threw herself down on the couch beside her.

"Do you want me to go back to the beginning?" Kathleen asked.

"Shit no!" She moved closer to Kathleen and tried to be more vigilant, trying to follow, her eyes nervously scouting ahead, to get the bad news before Kathleen's voice caught up with it. Only it was hard to see, because the print was so small, and because Kathleen was farsighted and held it away from herself on her lap. Chris cupped her hand under Kathleen's and tried to bring the swimming sea of print closer to their faces.

"What are you doing?" Kathleen asked.

"Trying to see," she said.

Kathleen considered. "Well I can't see it from this close," she said.

As she held it closer, Chris's vision popped onto little words here and there that she could read. *I walked, I felt, fuck. Fuck:* that surprised her, a dirty word printed and official in a book. Kathleen sighed, and then let go of the book; it fell out of Chris's unprepared hand onto Kathleen's lap, shut. Chris picked it up. "What page were we on?"

"I don't remember," Kathleen said, giving Chris a studied patient look. "Do you want me to try to find it?"

Chris bit her lip. She knew it was the end of one of the chapters. "Sure," she said, handing it over. "If you want. I'm going to the john."

Rage swelled through her; in the bathroom she sat on the toilet and took a breath. She hated this book, every aspect of it, from the terrible violence that made her want to puke to the gushing conversations about love and courage that also made her want to puke.

It was time to get some glasses. Because she really needed to get cracking with this reading thing. They might look like crap, but what was she anyway at this point — just an old bulldagger with an aching back and a girlfriend who gave her an inferiority complex. This old dog, Chris thought, her jeans around her knees, rubbing her face with her hand, definitely needed to learn some new tricks. Earlier that night, before Kathleen came home, she'd been watching the Bulls beat the Pacers, appreciating Michael's fadeaway jumper. He was getting older, and that was how he was adjusting to his loss of quickness driving to the basket. He could do that, she thought, because he had drive and discipline.

By the time they got to Chapter 16, Chris had gotten reading glasses and started back up at school, and Jess Goldberg was passing as a man.

The eye doctor told Chris she needed bifocals, so she could see both close up and far away. But bifocals, which they called progressive lenses nowadays, cost a fortune. Even Kathleen, who was usually hot to get things fixed right away so they didn't get more broken, whistled when Chris told her the price, and asked "Are you sure it's worth it?"

But ever since the eye doctor appointment, when the doctor had put a machine over her face that made the letters on the wall look as crispy as cornflakes, it was more and more evident how badly she saw, and how irritating it was to have to strain all the time. The doctor had been surprised that she'd never had glasses before. If she didn't count the fake ones, she thought wryly. He'd put drops in her eyes that expanded her pupils, and Chris stumbled out onto a brilliantly sunny afternoon feeling the light hit her like a blow to the head. She sat at her El stop and closed her eyes, moving her wallet from her back pocket to her front, but even closed, her eye felt so violently open it drove her nuts. She could get regular glasses, to see far away, and a pair of $10 reading glasses from Walgreen's. That might save her about $100, the doctor had said. But she'd have to keep switching glasses back and forth, and that would be a huge pain in the ass.

The next day she went to the Pearle Vision Center on Lawrence, and peeked in the window. There were no customers, and the salesman looked like he might be a fellow sister. But when she went in, he called her *sir,* then turned red and apologized belligerently. He was one of those femmy balding guys with a whistling *s* and a big fat wedding ring so you shouldn't get the wrong idea. Chris shrugged and told him not to worry about it. She never minded people making a mistake. What she couldn't stand was the hysteria in their recovery: when they giggled, or apologized like this guy, or whispered to their co-worker. It was like they were saying they hadn't meant to make you feel bad, but they believed you *should* feel really really bad.

She'd been told not to get them too small, that the lenses needed to be big enough for the prescription to change in increments. She put on a pair of wire rims, peered into a mirror, and immediately saw it had been a mistake to come without Kathleen: how could she see what she looked like in glasses when she needed glasses? She tried to turn away from the sales guy, so he wouldn't watch her scrutinize her own face. But he saw her falter, and came over and said "Try this," flipping the mirror over. Suddenly, the bottom half of her face loomed hugely, as though it was about to charge her, or eat her. It had a gigantic mouth, reddened by chapping, with big black broom bristles at the top corners. Chris felt nausea lick up her throat, and tried not to recoil; the guy would enjoy that.

When she left, she couldn't believe she'd bought glasses from that closet faggot. They cost $327, and she had slapped it on the credit card she and Kathleen used for special purchases like furniture or dental work. She was just too tired to contemplate shopping all over again, and at this place they would be ready in 24 hours. She secretly liked the idea of surprising Kathleen, who would be appalled at the cost but wouldn't be able to say anything because she had spent so much over Christmas, and because she always acted like the boss of Chris's health.

So when they sat down to read Chapter 16, she put them on, and Kathleen sat back in surprise. "You got them! How much were they?"

Chris told her.

She winced. "Geez, Chris."

"I have to see, don't I?"

"I guess so," she said. "Let me look at you."

Chris was gruff under her scrutiny. "You look *very* intelligent," Kathleen said.

"Yeah, right, a regular professor."

"No, really," Kathleen said. "Well you *better* look intelligent, you paid enough money for it."

Jess Goldberg was taking the hormones and passing as a man, because she could no longer take the abuse she got every day as a butch. She had lost Theresa, the love of her life, because Theresa didn't want to be with a man. Now, after a long stretch of sorrow and loneliness, Jess had asked out a straight hard-boiled waitress named Annie. She arrived one evening at Annie's apartment, filled with hope and need, secretly packing her dildo in a small canvas bag.

Kathleen and Chris laughed all the way through the dinner scene, where Jess shocked Annie over and over by being considerate and helpful and good with her child, a thing Annie had never experienced with a man before. "She didn't know what hit her!" Chris laughed, adding suavely, "A dose of butch lovin'." She came closer to Kathleen, and put her arm along the back of the couch.

And then it looked as though Jess was going to have sex with Annie, needing it so badly she was willing to risk being revealed and humiliated. "Holy shit," Chris muttered as Kathleen read about them getting into bed together. "Is she ever gonna get in trouble."

"Shush," Kathleen said, and read:

I looked at her with a question on my face. "I'm just gettin' over my period," she said. I shrugged. "So?"

Emotions played across Annie's face: disbelief, anger, relief, pleasure. Pleasure was the unmistakable emotion still on her face as I began to tease her thighs with my mouth. She gave in to her own desire and, in doing so, reached her orgasm with an almost relaxed trust.

They looked uncertainly at one another. Chris massaged her temples with focus and confusion. "Did she make her come to orgasm just by touching her thighs?"

Kathleen laughed. "No, hon, I think they left out the part that she really touched with her mouth."

"And she did this when Annie had her period?"

"Apparently," Kathleen said, giving her fastidious lover the once-over.

Chris sat back in her seat with a surprised grunt. Anna Singer had read this and given it to her, a book about menstruation and oral gratification.

"But hold on," Kathleen said, and prepared to continue.

"Wait," said Chris, easing the book out of her hands. She looked down at the print, tiny but sharp in her new glasses. "Where did you stop?" she asked.

Kathleen pointed. "My mouth," Chris read. "Was. Near. Her." She turned beet red: could it be? What else could it be? "Nipple," she said. "Here," she said, laughing breathlessly, "you read."

Kathleen looked at her in shock. "Honey, you're reading!"

Chris laughed, her face still hot. "Oh big deal, one sentence."

"Honey," Kathleen said, laughing, tears starting to run down her face. "You read: 'My mouth was near her nipple!'"

"Well don't keep saying it!"

Kathleen went to find a tissue, and came back mopping her face and blowing her nose with a big honk. She sat back down next to Chris and gave her a smack on the cheek, then picked up the book and began to read the next scene. As Chris held her breath, Jess went to the bathroom and slipped on her dildo, and made love to Annie passing as a man, surprising her yet again by taking responsibility for birth control and by being considerate about Annie's needs, and giving her three orgasms. Then, claiming she couldn't come with the condom on, she pulled out and faked ejaculation. She ducked back out to the bathroom, took off the dildo and harness, and slipped a sock in her briefs. She and Annie fell asleep in each others' arms.

"Jesus Christ," Chris said. She sat bolt upright as Kathleen read the passage, her fingernails digging into the knees of her jeans, terrified that Jess would be caught, and then incredulous and a little outraged that she wasn't. Her mind was flying. Wouldn't Annie notice there was no dirty condom left anywhere? How did Jess keep her from touching the dildo harness?

Kathleen continued:

> She put her hand gently between my thighs and squeezed the sock. "I got a lot of pleasure out of this tonight," she said. "It was like magic." My body tensed, and she withdrew her hand.
>
> I stroked her hair. "All magic is illusion," I admitted.

Kathleen looked at Chris with her eyes wide and her mouth a big O. "My!" she said.

"All magic is *bullshit*," Chris protested; "No way she'd squeeze a sock and think it was a cock!" She laughed at the involuntary rhyme.

Kathleen sat back and took a swig of beer, then looked at her provocatively. "You don't think so?"

"The only way I can see it would be if she squeezed through jeans," Chris said. "But Jess Goldberg was only wearing briefs."

"It's magic, honey," Kathleen said, grinning. "Jess Goldberg was obviously a very, very good cocksman."

"Bullshit," Chris said sourly. "Nobody's *that* good."

"You know what I think?"

Chris looked at her. Her cheeks were a little pink, and she was being mean, surefire signs of arousal.

"Shut up," Chris said. "I know what you think."

"What?"

"You think I'm jealous, but if you think that, you're *way* off the mark."

"Am I?" Kathleen asked, closing the book and putting it on the coffee table. "Well I'll tell you something, I've never mistaken you for a man."

Chris raised her eyebrows. So she wanted to play like that? She sidled over, taking Kathleen's hair in her fist. She looked at her through her glasses, tilting her head back to get the right focus from the bottom of the lens, watching Kathleen's face waver and wince and sharpen. "Get up," she said, pulling her up by the hair, gentle and steady, careful not to yank. She twisted Kathleen's right arm behind her back and held her that way, trapped, by the hair and the arm, and kissed her, shoving her tongue into her mouth. Kathleen made a noise and Chris's glasses steamed up.

She reached to turn off the halogen light, grabbed Kathleen's hand and tugged her up the steps out of the living room. Kathleen dropped the book and turned to pick it up, and Chris turned back toward her, starting to say *Forget the book*, coming back down. Then the stairs blurred and she stepped down too far, her heel sliding off the carpeted edge of the step, and Kathleen cried out and held out her arms and Chris sprawled on her ass. Pain lurched up her back. "Sonofabitch," she hissed. She'd forgotten about walking down stairs in progressive lenses. She looked at Kathleen, whose face was flushed from either desire or ridicule. "Well there goes the mood," Chris said dryly, and they both laughed. Kathleen reached out to grasp her hands. "Up you go, champ," she groaned, pulling Chris to her feet.

Chris took a long time in the bathroom, washing her face and brushing her teeth, waiting for her mortification to subside, taking an extra Percocet in case she'd reinjured herself. She got stiffly into bed. Kathleen was propped up on all the pillows, watching a *Mad About You* rerun.

Chris grabbed one of the pillows and eased it out from under Kathleen, settled back on it and turned her head toward her. "So how many orgasms did she give to that Annie woman all together? Was it seventeen or eighteen?"

Kathleen laughed. "Four," she said, clicking off the TV.

Chris folded her hands behind her head and gazed into the quiet darkness. "That Jess Goldberg was some Casanova," she mused. "Either that or a big fat liar."

She wasn't exactly a liar, Kathleen thought, turning away from Chris and pushing her rear end gently into her, it was just that she was a little full of herself. Maybe Jess Goldberg was the cocksman of the century, maybe she wasn't. But it made Kathleen laugh to think that it never once occurred to Jess that maybe Annie knew all along she wasn't a man. That Annie might be playing along to make Jess *feel* like a man, spinning her own femme magic.

CHAPTER THIRTEEN

Chris gulped the chalky tablets down with a full glass of water, feeling a residual bitterness against her throat. She went into the living room, picked up the book and settled in the recliner. It was late afternoon and she had finished her homework. She sat with the book closed on the bulge of her gut for a few minutes, her eyes drooping in meditative gloominess, almost dozing off. Then she sighed awake and opened it carefully at the note card they were using as a bookmark. She wanted to hear it again, the scene between Jess Goldberg and Annie, but she refused to ask Kathleen to read it to her, because the last thing she wanted was for Kathleen to sense her interest in it. She knew she had to back up a few pages, and she knew there was a coffee stain on the right bottom of the second page of the scene. Kathleen had not only been careless enough to make the stain, but had treated it with infuriating casualness, wiping it with her thumb, clucking "Oh well, can't be helped."

At the time Chris had been livid, but now she was glad it was there to mark her place. Trying to get her bearings in this novel still made her head ache. Even with the help of the chapter numbers, she got impossibly turned around in it, an embarrassment for someone who took pride in her keen sense of direction. She needed Kathleen to help her — at the very least, to find her place. That need came both as an ache and a fury. For it was new to Chris how Kathleen took advantage.

She found the little break where the new scene began, saw the word "Annie" dotting the rest of the page. Something about Jess Goldberg's going on the hormones and passing as a man had gotten under her skin. How was it that Chris walked around Chicago freaking people out right and left, but still had the nagging sense that Jess had shown her up? It was stupid, because Chris had never wanted to pass anyway. There had been a lot of talk at the bar about taking the hormones, but Chris had never seriously considered it. Frankly, the idea of hair all over her body and of smelling like a man gave her the creeps. And another reason glimmered, unarticulated, at the back of her mind: she was so frightened of doctors that it was beyond the realm of her imagination to take a step requiring their help.

As she sat and fingered the book, Chris regretted that decision as another failure, as the lack of courage to go all the way, to walk the walk. And then, as she thought about Jess Goldberg acting the dashing and sensitive man with Annie, astounding the hard-boiled waitress — who was, face it, something of a bitch — again and again, and as the Percocet scattered its strange merriment, her sense of irony revived and she began to rebound. Maybe she was an illiterate bulldagger with big boobs, but she had taken her lumps like a man, and at least she wasn't a phony like Jess Goldberg. Passing was one lie she had never told. It was true that whenever people addressed her as a man she didn't correct them, but rather hastened out of there with her head ducked, dreading the catastrophe of the correction. But she had never deliberately set out to fool anybody, she thought with a ringing righteous feeling, especially any woman who trusted her enough to have relations with her. She had had the courage to be herself.

She heard the key in the back door and got up to meet Kathleen. Kathleen's face was red from the cold. "You know," she said to Chris, tossing her keys onto the table and peeling off her gloves, "I've been thinking it'd be real nice to build a stone wall in the back yard. You know, a semicircle, around a raised planting bed."

"Hello!" Chris chanted. "How are you? I'm fine, honey, how are you? Oh, I'm just fine and dandy, thank you for asking."

Kathleen stared at her, and moved around her to pick up the mail.

"We got other things to worry about," Chris said. "Like paying off the credit card. And painting, and the roof."

"Oh come on," Kathleen protested. "The inspector said we wouldn't need a new roof for five, six years. And I don't think it'd be that expensive, just the price of the stone. I've been talking to Carl down the street — you know that wonderful wall he has on the side of his house? — and he says it's not hard at all to build one yourself."

Not gonna happen, Chris thought. She hovered with her hands in her pockets. "Hey, tell me something," she said. "Isn't it kind of two-faced that Jess comes off as such a great person and all when she's in bed with Annie, when she's lying to her the whole time about being a man?"

Kathleen looked up wearily. "Were you even listening to me?"

Her parka was still on; Chris reached for her shoulders and slid it off. She put her nose near the back of Kathleen's neck till it was tickled by the fuzz. Kathleen was flipping through the mail, slitting envelopes open. Offers to refinance and consolidate their debt, the mail of the new homeowner. Good Lord, there were a lot of people out there waiting for them to fail. She turned and looked at Chris holding her coat with a hungry look on her face, and said, "Honey, put it back in your pants, I just walked in the door."

"Fine," Chris said. She dropped the coat on the floor and left the room.

It wasn't, Anna tried to explain to Scott on the phone, after soldiering through a conversation about the presses competing for his book, that Star didn't have a sense of humor at all. She was in fact a cheerful person. And it wasn't even that she, Anna, didn't find Star funny, although Star's idea of a joke was an elevator door closing on a man's tie. The problem was that Star didn't laugh at her jokes.

"Now that's just rude," Scott said.

"I know!" Moreover, Star wasn't a belly laugher, but rather a nose laugher. How could you be with someone who never cried from laughing, who never fell back weakly in her chair? "And furthermore, she's one of those lesbians who knows all lesbians," Anna said. "*All* lesbians."

Including someone Anna had known in high school and hadn't even known was a lesbian, and including Anna and Patricia's ex-couples therapist, who, Star informed her, had just had a baby girl and was putting an addition on her house. This enraged Anna.

"I see," Scott said, "that the case against Star is airtight."

She wore a big class ring from Purdue, cheered the Boilermakers on TV with alarmingly martial roars. When she dressed for work in suits with skirts, she looked to Anna like a barely-passing transsexual, her adam's apple abulge, her nyloned legs flatly flesh-shaded. Verbally, she was a real clunker. She was educated in the social sciences and worked in bureaucracies, so she talked in terms of *communication skills* and *having issues* and *utilization* and *output*. She called herself a people person, and used *impact* as a verb.

You couldn't love a person like that, Anna thought. It was a fervent critique. And yet, she was an athlete, with hard arms and long sloping muscles in her thighs. And while one moment Anna was praying that Star would never meet any of her friends, the next she was in bed with her, pulled against her powerful body, pheromonally smitten, like a dog rolling in stinky grass.

"Can't you just have sex with her?" Scott asked, his attention for the intricacies of lesbian coupling clearly starting to wane. When he and another man were attracted to each other, they just did it. He had once said that one of the great things about being among gay men was that they could just go ahead and be the assholes they all were.

"I guess," Anna sighed, feeling stupid and boring, the lesbian of the joke who brings a U-Haul to the second date. "But I just feel that it's going to end in tears."

Chris heard the toilet flush, and the grind of the shower turning on. She went into the living room and turned on Channel 9, where the Bulls were playing the Clippers. They were playing without Pippen, who was sitting on the bench in street clothes, with some injury or complaint or whatnot. She sat there, bored by the meaningless February game.

When she heard the water go off she went back into the bedroom and loitered outside the bathroom as Kathleen toweled off. "No really, Kath," she said. "I can't see acting like that. Pulling one over on this lady and then bragging about it."

Kathleen emerged from the bathroom wrapped in a towel, her hair wet around her shoulders. "Chris, you know that Annie and Jess are not real people, right?"

"What do you mean?"

"It's just characters in a book."

Chris felt her face get hot. Of course, she wasn't stupid, she knew that they would never come ringing the doorbell. She looked at Kathleen's pink gleaming skin as she stepped into underpants and put on a clean bra. They hadn't done it in months, ever since Dell, ever since Chris — Casanova that she was — had fallen down the stairs. Not that they'd been at it like bunnies before that, what with Chris's back, and now, the book.

Kathleen put on a sweatshirt. Chris came up and slipped her hands under it. "Chris," Kathleen sighed, grabbing her wrists to make her let go. "I just got home from work." Chris slipped them free and backed Kathleen against the wall, holding her there with her body weight and her knee pinned between her legs. "Stop it," Kathleen said. Chris slipped her hand down Kathleen's panties, felt the coarseness of her hair against her palm. She pushed two fingers into her. Kathleen was moist from the shower, but not slick, and Chris pried her open carefully, felt the skin pull around her fingers. She felt clumsily with the dry fingers of her other hand for her clitoris, had trouble finding it in the folds of her labia. She felt a slight swelling and tried to approach it suavely, sidelong.

Kathleen leaned her head against the wall resignedly, thinking *Ouch*, feeling the ungratifying movements of her lover's fingers jamming against her pubic bone, cutting her with a jagged nail. And what on earth was she doing with that other hand? Kathleen tried to stand it for a while, then said "Lower." And then again, "Lower." She heard the cluck of Chris's irritation but her fingers moved and suddenly felt like silk, and Kathleen felt herself sigh open and gather around Chris's hand. If this is what Chris wanted, she thought. Chris's forehead leaned on the wall next to Kathleen's head. Kathleen closed her eyes, trying to focus. She was sweating profusely from her shower; the sweatshirt would have to go into the laundry. She whimpered. She wouldn't be able to come standing up. "Let me lie down."

Chris wheeled her from the wall and pushed her down onto the bed with a thud, lay down on top of her with her mouth near Kathleen's ear. "I know they're not real people," she whispered, her hand moving hard in and out, the friction now perfect, both tight and slick. And suddenly this wasn't enough for Chris. She said "Hang on," jumped off of Kathleen, who yelped with dismay, and went into the closet, emerging with the strap-on. "Oh come on," Kathleen complained, closing her legs defensively and drawing them up. She had been about to come, and was ready to get it over with; she wasn't in the mood for a huge scene. Chris ignored her, stripping off her jeans and stepping into the harness, expertly slinging the heavy dick on over her underwear and pulling the cinch tight. Then, approaching the bed, she spat on her hand, looking down at her flushed lover, and rubbed the spit onto the dildo. It bobbed in her hand, gave off a faint smell of latex.

She lay down on top of Kathleen, parted her legs with her knee and started to enter her. There was the familiar shock of being inside her and feeling nothing, the disappointment of the dildo's artificiality that surprised her every time, it felt so real till then. But as she pressed herself against its base she started to warm with each thrust. It took Kathleen some time to work through the pain. But eventually, as she knew it would, it became fringed with a shivery feeling. Kathleen wrapped her legs around Chris, and turned her energy toward getting off on hating her. She trilled on the edge of coming. And then Chris felt Kathleen go absolutely still and murmured "There you go!" and Kathleen arched up, her neck straining and a blotchy flush spreading over her neck and chest. Chris felt a widening in herself, an arching open, a glow in her core.

Kathleen fell back on the bed. She licked her dry lips, turned her head away.

Without feeling it, although she was still inside her, Chris knew that Kathleen's cunt was rippling like water broken by a stone. She turned her head toward her lover, spoke into her hair. "Just because Annie and Jess weren't real people," she said, "don't mean their sex shouldn't make sense."

Kathleen caught just the tail end of the sentence. She groaned. "Since when does sex ever make sense?" She shifted and eased the dildo painfully out of her; it made a marshy sucking sound as it emerged. She twisted and reached for a Kleenex. "Is this how you're gonna be from now on?" she asked, reaching down to wipe herself. "Let it go, Chris, it's just a story."

The moment Anna hung up from talking to Scott the buzzer rang. There was a tinny sing-song: "It's me." Which reminded Anna of another complaint she had: that Star had the presumption not to identify herself on the phone when she called, prematurely in their relationship, before Anna could reasonably have been expected to assume it was her. She just said "Hi!" and Anna was put on the spot, supposed to recognize her voice, too embarrassed to ask "Who is this?" Anna buzzed her in, heard her footsteps come lightly up the stairs and opened the door, and then there was Star, her nose streaming and her face lit up. She closed and locked the door, then stooped and lifted Anna right off her feet with a cheerful groan. "Whoa!" Anna cried, grabbing Star around the neck, feeling awkward and heavy, fretting about Star tracking in slush. It was a relief when Star deposited her on the bed and fell down on top of her, her boots and winter coat and gloves still on. Anna lay under the weight of all that, shifting her rib cage so she could breathe, felt herself nuzzled on the neck by Star's warm lips and cold nose. She put her hands into Star's thick hair, then yelped "Ow!" as Star, shifting to take off her gloves and coat, accidentally dug her elbow into Anna's side. "What a baby," Star sniffed, and Anna's eyes widened with indignation and she grabbed Star and flipped her on her back, sat panting on top of her, looking critically at her rangy confident face.

But Anna was no match for Star in weight or strength, and a second later Star flipped her back, held her wrists with one hand and unbuttoned and unzipped her jeans and thrust her hand inside them. Anna struggled, her arousal irritating to her, and then said, "No, really, stop. And take your dirty boots off, okay?

Star took her hand out of Anna's pants and removed her boots, letting them thunk to the floor. She grabbed a pillow and plumped it, then turned lazily on her back like a farm boy with a straw in his mouth, her arms behind her head, one knee propped up. She was wearing a navy wool sweater Anna recognized from the J. Crew catalogue, and had a look of satisfaction on her flushed face. Anna thought: she thinks she can flip me like so many pancakes.

Anna got up and zipped her pants, opened her closet and pulled the tie of her terrycloth bathrobe out of its loops. She returned to the bed and sat down. "Hold your hands over your head," she said.

She watched Star's face work its way toward comprehension, and then coarsen with resistance. "You've got to be kidding," she said.

Anna looked at her steadily, until her face broke into uncertainty.

She tied her up and made her struggle and beg and come and cry, and afterward, Anna picked at the knots, cursing, suddenly in a panic to release her as quickly as possible. Star's wrists were chafed, and Anna rubbed and kissed them. Star's eyes welled up again; she pulled her sweater down over her bared breasts and stomach in a gesture that broke Anna's heart, it was so much like a child's. She turned heavily onto her side and curled her knees to her chest, her naked ass and thighs coiled, her face raw and streaked. Anna took off her own clothes and crawled into bed behind her, covering them both with the comforter. She had to hike herself up onto her back, like a jockey, to get her arms around her. She kissed Star behind the earlobe. The wool of the sweater was scratchy against her chest.

They dozed for a little while, and then Star sighed and struggled up and sat cross-legged, reached for a Kleenex and blew vigorously. Her eyes were red and her nose bulbous; she attempted a smile that came out as a grimace, and Anna's heart lurched with something like

love toward this woman who prided herself on her strength, and who
was allowing herself to be seen looking ravaged and ugly. Anna reached
out and touched Star's hair, which was matted on the side.

"I've never had that done to me before," Star said, her voice wavering. She had never been with a butch. She didn't even think she liked
butches much. Once she had been at a Butchiest Dyke Contest at Paris
Dance, but she'd been turned off, she said, by all the male attitude. "It
looked like they were trying too hard," she said. She wondered anxiously if Anna thought of her as a femme, and Anna shrugged. She did: she
could make soft sounds come out of her, she could shape even those
broad shoulders and big hands into femme, thinking of her as the big
girl who didn't count as sexy at the prom, but who started looking delicious in her thirties. But, not wanting to prescribe how Star should be,
she picked her words carefully. "I think of every woman I'm drawn to
sexually as femme. Maybe not a femme, but femme."

Star pondered that, and Anna wondered if the distinction was too
fine for her. "Because I don't think of myself as weak or frivolous," she
said sturdily.

"That's not what femme is," Anna insisted, shaking her head. "It's
more like what you just did: being strong enough to make yourself vulnerable to me."

Star sighed a shaky sigh. "I didn't feel very strong."

Anna put her arms around her neck. "Are you kidding me?" And
Star embraced her back and Anna kissed her red sore face, and her eyes,
and her hair.

Chris was whistling in the bathroom. Coming down from her
orgasm, her vagina sore and pulsing, Kathleen recognized the tune as
"Yankee Doodle," and her heart surged with annoyance, then something like devastation.

If someone had asked just a few months ago, she would have said that
she cherished Chris's stone. She accepted without question the way the big
show was her own orgasm, and believed she should be happy she had a lover
who was so focused on her pleasure. It was *definitely,* she used to joke with

Dell and the other girls, better than a poke in the eye with a sharp stick.

But now, after so many years, a complaint that may have been murmuring all along was making its full voice heard, and Chris's stone began feeling mean-spirited to her, like a slap in the face, as though somehow it was okay for Kathleen to lower herself by spreading her legs, but Chris was above all that. Was this something new, or had Chris's stone always been so punishing, and Kathleen just hadn't seen it? She thought about the way Chris, who wasn't a big kisser, nuzzled her ear after she came, whispering how sexy she was, and the way she hitched up her jeans and drew up the zipper with a flourish. What had seemed like evidence of hearty appreciation suddenly seemed arrogant and patronizing. Just then Chris emerged from the bathroom, still whistling that ridiculous tune. Kathleen got up heavily and peeled off her sweatshirt and bra to throw into the laundry, and put on a different bra and a flannel shirt and sweatpants. She went into the bathroom and washed her hands and face, then headed to the kitchen to make dinner.

After that afternoon when Anna had taken her in hand, it was as though somebody had given Star a telescope and she was amazed by the sight of Mars. She started to accept Anna's hand at the small of her back as they entered a room, to relinquish the car keys, and to dress for Anna's eye. Anna noticed the little touches — a sweater with a graceful dip in the neck, tight wool pants that made her ass look full and luscious — and was touched and surprised by them. Star blushed under Anna's thoughtful compliments, which were designed to show her appreciation without applying too much pressure to Star's gender expression. For Anna it was walking a tightrope, like complimenting a woman on her weight loss without making it seem as though she looked fat before. Anna loved knowing that with Star, she walked it with skill and assurance, offering compliments that felt designed without being calculating, and she attributed that assurance to Star's generosity, because Patricia had been able, at any moment, to make her feel clumsy. But that was complicated too, because secretly part of her denigrated Star for her very easiness, feeling that she just wasn't put-together with the exquisite complexity of Patricia, and that it just wasn't that hard to gratify a woman that simple.

Star began adjusting Anna's collars and stepping back to appraise. In bed, she crooned to her and gradually coaxed her clothes off. She reached for Anna — at home, on the street — with proprietary affection, and pulled her into her authoritatively. No one had ever done that to Anna before. Sometimes, her face drawn in against Star's breasts, Anna got a whiff of the maternal, and before she recoiled, she let herself feel tiny, gathered, suckled.

In the dead of winter, Chris continued to go to the shabby classroom, which was either stone cold or boiling hot. She'd changed the refill number on the prescription for her pain killers from 1 to 4, so she was on them every day now, feeling just a little woozy, and strangely competent. It had been her first forgery, which made her smile to herself and decide that this literacy stuff was really paying off.

She met Dennis one afternoon a week at a coffee shop, and he hooted and hallooed and poured lattes down her, the sweat standing on his forehead. "Tell me something," she said to him one day, after making her way painstakingly through a short paragraph on Martin Luther King, and being congratulated by him with a painful thump on the arm as she wondered what the hell she'd just read.

"Shoot, boss." He'd taken to calling her *boss*, which was stupid, but an improvement over some of the names he'd called her, like *amigo*, and *bud*.

"How is it that I can read these words, but I can't really read yet?" She hadn't told him about reading *Stone Butch Blues* with Kathleen. As nice a guy as he was, he just wasn't part of that world, and she didn't know how to explain it to him. The words just weren't in her.

"Whaddya mean, boss, whaddya think you're doing right now?"

"Don't try to make me feel better, okay? It's just bullshit."

Dennis hung his head. "Gotcha," he said.

"No really, sure I can make it through this paragraph, one word at a time, and if I really bust my hump I can make the words connect up with some meaning in my head. Like, I think I could tell you what I just read, like I was standing up in front of the class and giving a report. But it's not really *reading* reading. I can't do it without making a big production out of it. Don't people do it just, like, naturally?"

Dennis considered. "It's like you know what to do on a bike — turn the handles in the opposite direction of the tilt — but you're not yet *riding*, correcting instinctively, without thinking about it."

Tears sprang into Chris's eyes from the rightness of that, and she laughed out loud. "That's it! And no fucking way I can start by myself! — I still need Daddy to push the seat."

Dennis grinned and thumped himself on the chest. "Well Daddy's here for you," he said.

"Eww," Chris protested, "Don't be disgusting." She had a powerful urge to ask him if he'd ever read a book that ripped up his insides like a power drill. But she sat back and kept her mouth shut, worried it'd make her look stupid and melodramatic. Somewhere in her mind, she believed that she was overreacting to *Stone Butch Blues,* that experienced readers read not only effortlessly, but also with unruffled composure.

That night, reading at home at the dinner table over spaghetti and meat sauce, Chris and Kathleen arrived at another big surprise: Frankie, one of Jess Goldberg's bull friends, ended up being girlfriends with another he-she, Johnnie. Unable to accept two butches together in bed, Jesse derides Frankie and walks away from her.

They looked at each other, shocked.

Kathleen let the book swivel shut around her finger, then reopened it and pressed it down with her palm.

"Careful," Chris warned.

Kathleen nodded, not listening. "Well it's not like butch-and-butch has never happened in the history of the world," she said, adding softly, "Carmine and Ariel."

Chris was suddenly angry. "Why are you always defending it?" she demanded. "Just because it happened doesn't mean you have to write about it for everybody to see!"

Kathleen snorted. "Doesn't mean *I* have to write about it? I didn't write the damn book."

"I didn't mean you!" Chris shouted, watching Kathleen hold the place with one hand as she took a forkful of spaghetti and twirled it around. "Do you have to treat me like a moron all the time?" And then the thing happened that she'd known all along would happen, but hadn't quite unanchored her tongue to prevent: a glob of spaghetti sauce whirled off Kathleen's fork and splattered right on the page where Jess Goldberg was stalking off in disgust.

They stared at the stain. Kathleen said quickly, "We'll buy her another one."

Chris was murderously silent. Where would they get another one? What would she tell Anna Singer: that in her household, instead of reading books like human beings, they mangled and destroyed them? She took a napkin and dabbed at the mound of sauce, taking off the chunky surface, leaving a red blotch with smeared-looking print underneath. It looked obscene to her, as though she had gotten her own menstrual blood on it.

She flung herself from the table, giving her chair a vicious slap to the ground on her way out, then on second thought, turned around and grabbed the book and marched it over to the garbage and stuffed it in.

She put on her boots and coat and went outside, slamming the door behind her. She crunched down the front steps she'd sanded and headed east, toward the lake. She was having trouble catching her breath, had a brief panicked sense that she might be having a heart attack. She stopped and stooped, her hands on her knees, her head lowered, until she calmed down. When she straightened, blood rushed to her head. Cold wind was cutting at her cheeks, and she took a deep breath against it.

Why did Kathleen keep sabotaging her? And what was Anna Singer going to think of her? Feeling for icy spots on the sidewalk, her legs tensing unpleasantly in the effort to walk without sliding, Chris's mind whirled around the idea that Anna already thought of her as crude and ignorant, and that this was just going to confirm it. What had she been trying to prove by giving Chris that book? She had to know it would stir up the poisons in her. Chris had felt all along that it was some kind of test, but now she started feeling that Anna wasn't just testing her ability to read; she was testing something much more fundamental, like her ability to handle herself. Chris found herself feeling unexpectedly respectful of, even a little cowed by Anna; she'd clearly underestimated her power to hurt her.

A clump of young men formed out of the darkness up ahead, and Chris put up her hood to make herself bigger and more intimidating, like a hiker in the woods encountering a bear. But as they drew nearer Chris heard a delighted laugh, and familiar with the raucous guffaw of straight men together, she knew that these men, though a little west of their habitat, were gay. They passed her chattering, without paying attention to her.

Small houses began giving way to brick apartment buildings, and as she looked into bay windows warmed by light and caught a glimpse of a bookcase here, a woman eating alone at her dining room table there, the blue glow of televisions, she felt as though she was watching a movie about people who lived cozily in their homes, and wondered at how other people's houses looked more inviting from the outside than she felt her own was. She shoved her hands in her pockets – she'd forgotten her gloves – and wished she rented a small Chicago apartment, in a courtyard building, with a tiny tiled bathroom with its tinted window painted shut, with creaking wood floors and hissing radiators. You could relax in a place like that; if something wasn't the most beautiful it could be, you'd just let it be, because that was a feature of the apartment. And if something broke, you could call the building manager and harass her, as many a renter had done to Chris back in the day, when she managed those four buildings down in Cal City. You didn't have to make everything perfect, and there wasn't a long chain of expensive repairs stretching off into the dismal future.

When Chris got home the house was dark and Kathleen was already asleep. She found the idea of lying in bed next to her intolerable. She headed into the kitchen and put the kettle on. Kathleen had taken the book out of the garbage and set it, its damp cover curling up, on the counter next to the toaster, where it gave off a faint stink.

Chris began sleeping on the couch, sometimes not even bothering to brush her teeth. She lay awake smoking, attentive to when the Percocet was taking effect, tapping ash carefully into the ashtray perched on her stomach even as she had fantasies of grinding it out on the blanket and letting everything go up in flames. It wasn't like those weeks before she had started school, when she lay in bed in exhausted despair, letting herself get filthy. This feeling was different: torn open, bared, still, sleepily alert, wolfish. Time stretched out around her and everything seemed big and slow. She found herself thinking all kinds of weird things. Like how, when she first left home, when she was staying in shitty furnished rooms in boarding houses and working shitty jobs that she'd quit after a few weeks after being harassed by the boss, or figuring out that she was inhaling something dangerous, she would wonder with a cry in her throat who to ask questions of, who would tell her what to do, who would tell her she was okay, or doing the right thing. It took her a long time to discipline herself not to want that anymore. She did it by digging sharp objects into her palm, by denying herself small pleasures — chocolate, cigarettes — if she let herself abandon herself to longing. Until she stopped: until she felt alone and fierce on a mountaintop, her lips dry, deadwood everywhere, wind roaring by her with the sound of battered corrugated metal, rocks quivering beneath her boots.

She hadn't let herself want to be taken care of again until Kathleen.

In the quiet living room, Chris began to dream. She was in the desert, or back in the bar. Sometimes there were butches in her dreams, slinging back drinks and talking trash. They weren't the butches from her life, but the ones from *Stone Butch Blues* — Jan, Al, Rocco. In one dream her mother appeared, calling her *presh*, short for *precious*, and when Chris awoke she lay there like a child in the stunned moment of silence between the first wail and the next, when the breath is fighting to come. They had been making meatloaf. She felt tears burn her eyes and remembered her hands and her mother's working the cold squishy mixture of hamburger and eggs and ketchup and mustard, and her mother taking off her wedding ring afterward and running it under the faucet. And out of the blue there came to her another memory, her mother saying: *For heaven's sake, when you walk it looks like you have a shovel up your ass.* And the whole series of deliberations that criticism touched off: suddenly picturing, as she walked innocently down the street, an actual shovel shoved up her ass. Wondering which end up, and turning it this way and that in her imagination, till she finally decided it must be the shovel end up, not the handle.

She'd awake in the middle of the night and shove some Percocet into her mouth before she could remember too much of what she had dreamed, and then she'd ride its smooth wave back into sleep. She never dreamed about being beaten or attacked, but she had a dream about losing her finger. In the dream her Aunt Gloria had bitten it off — and Chris was pondering the empty air where a part of her body, her own pulsing flesh and blood, had once been.

Kathleen didn't say much about her sleeping on the couch, except to ask her once if she could put the sheets and blankets in the closet when she got up in the morning; they coexisted in silence, and stopped gathering in the evenings to read. Kathleen had finished the book on her own long ago, so it was only Chris who was left hanging. At first she didn't know how she could bear not knowing what happened, and briefly contemplated an apology to Kathleen for all her sins if Kathleen would only finish it with her. But her pride quickly won out, and if Chris wanted to know what became of Jess Goldberg — it didn't yet occur to her that Jess's narrating the story meant she had to survive it — she kept her mouth shut. She mustered the austere knowledge of the stone butch who is accustomed to, and even glories in, being aroused without being fulfilled, who finds the moment of lying in the tall grass more delicious than the taste of the prey.

After a few days, as Kathleen was putting on her coat to go to work, she said to Chris, "There's a bookstore called Women and Children First on Clark, somewhere around Foster. They'd probably have another copy of the book there."

Chris continued to hunch over her coffee, but felt grudgingly impressed that Kathleen knew that. After Kathleen shut the door behind her, Chris mused on the name of the bookstore, found it clever.

It was what Anna had always yearned for, a femme who wasn't too insecure or ambivalent or downright lazy to roll up her sleeves and figure out what Anna wanted. Often, when Star fucked her, Anna didn't come, her body was so arched open and aghast and deranged. Or when she came it came as a great aching bass shudder, with no momentum or melody. When they stopped she'd be sore and panting; she'd clamp her legs together and roll into the fetal position, while Star flopped happily behind her and gave her a big squeeze. Kissed and nuzzled, Anna would lie there, absorbed in the thud of her own body.

She had always felt guilty about blaming Patricia when it was quite possible it hadn't been her fault at all, that Anna had irreparably undermined her fragile confidence. Now, it seemed strange and a little threatening that the femme who could take her in hand wasn't really a femme at all, but rather someone who was basically gussied up as a femme. But what did it matter, really, if this rather large and often butch woman was willing to act the femme for love's sake?

And was it really so wrong for Star to gloat periodically over her own prowess? Maybe not, but it was hard to take. Anna, who made an ethic over her own no-nonsense home run trot, felt showed up by Star as she dogged it around the bases, looking around for applause, after scoring with Anna. One night, after giving Anna one particularly hard-won and spectacular orgasm — she had almost lost her attention completely but then electrified her by clamping her hand to Anna's throat — Star grinned and told her she was cute as a button.

A pained look came over Anna's face. "Cute as a button?"

"Absolutely," Star said.

"Not commanding?"

Star laughed and shook her head.

"Not senatorial?"

"Nope."

Anna leapt up and tackled her and tickled her till Star was gasping and it wasn't fun anymore.

CHAPTER FOURTEEN

By the time Chris emerged from Women and Children First clutching a paper bag with *Stone Butch Blues* inside, she thought someone should write a sitcom about her adventures trying to buy it. She had procrastinated for days after Kathleen destroyed Anna's copy, until she despised herself for her fear sufficiently to drag herself onto the Clark St. bus and ride up there. She got off at Foster, walked the wrong way for a few blocks, and then, as the west side of Clark grew increasingly industrial, and the east side taken up by what promised to be miles of cemetery, she turned and walked back. The store was on the corner of Farragut, on a commercial stretch where chain bagel and coffee places and cluttered, badly-lit pet shops and antique stores mingled hospitably, rainbow flag stickers in the corners of their windows. Loitering in her worn and cracking leather jacket, Chris shaded her eyes at the window of a feminist crafts store whose smell of perfumed soap and candles, perceptible even through the closed door, immediately oppressed her. She turned away and hesitated at a café door a few shops down, then entered. It was warm and dark, redolent of smoke and spices. Hippies sat on pillows on the floor eating large salads. There were tables further back where people were eating lunch, and further back still, books and ponchos and bangles laid out for sale. The café's eclecticism felt safe enough, even pleasant. With a mild impulse to claim this territory, Chris went up to the counter and looked at the chalked menu, but the ornate handwriting swatted her eyes away. Averting her gaze to the display of baked goods, Chris ordered a cup of coffee and a bran muffin.

Once she got them, though, she didn't have the patience for them; she felt she was just procrastinating, and that as usual, she hadn't gotten the best food. She ate her muffin hurriedly and gulped her coffee. Then she left the café and walked the block to Women and Children First and pushed her way firmly inside. Amid the display tables and shelves, her practiced mind swiftly took in the variety of genders and flavors of the women in the store, their hair, clothing, piercings. There were some oddballs, and the voices of children from the children's section in the back. The atmosphere of conscious safety was relaxed, fluty. Sometimes, in places like these, the sense of safety was tendentious, and then the danger was that she herself could be treated as a danger.

Lacking the skill to browse, Chris walked over to a table and lowered her head, pretending she was studying the books, staring at the colors of their jackets. How would she find the book she needed? She felt someone approach, then a voice over her right shoulder asking if she needed help. She whirled around. A well-heeled middle-aged lesbian with graying hair was smiling at her, her face unflinching at the sight of her.

"No, thank you," Chris said.

After the woman walked away, Chris wheeled and walked quickly out of the store. Standing out on the curb, the door closed behind her, she wanted to kick herself. Why hadn't she just asked if they had a book called *Stone Butch Blues*? She wanted to go back in, but now she couldn't without looking like an asshole. She stood self-consciously on the curb, then turned and trudged back to the bus stop.

It took a week before she got up the nerve to try again; unaware that people drop in to see what's new on the shelves with no intent to buy, she imagined that if the salespeople remembered her, they'd be surprised to see her again. This time, a Saturday morning, she almost made it to a salesperson, when she turned the corner around a shelf and caught a glimpse of Anna — sitting cross-legged on the floor absorbed in a book, laughing to herself and absently picking her nose. At the sight, Chris panicked, and bolted. Out on the street, her heart pounding, she thought: what were the odds of that? And heading home on the bus, she wondered who would have been more embarrassed if their eyes had met: her, looking for a replacement for Anna's mangled book, or ol' Ms. Singer digging her way to China.

Earlier that morning, Anna was sitting up on the air mattress in a t-shirt, a clipboard propped on her knees, drinking coffee and grading papers for the freshman composition course she was teaching this semester at Northwestern. When these students' writing was bad, it was bad in a wholly different way from that of her adult learners: full of platitudes and generalizations and pumped-up vocabulary, as they struggled to produce the language they sensed was prized by the university. And even though Anna had some empathy for their struggle, and was good at helping them produce writing in which you could hear a voice that sounded halfway honest and human, grading always felt like a pointless drain. When the phone rang she gladly put down the paper she was working on.

It was Star, singing "Oh What a Beautiful Morning."

Anna sighed, thinking that Star was like an uncle who liked to shmooze waitresses and pull quarters from behind kids' ears. She set the clipboard on the floor and stretched out on the bed, enjoying taking up the whole thing.

"Hi," she said, when Star had finished.

"Hi sweetie."

Anna wanted a day to spend by herself, which Star had accepted good-naturedly. Star was going to spend this afternoon training at the pool, she was saying, and had just been invited to a party in Bucktown that night. She hesitated before asking, "Sure you don't want to come? There'll be lots of babes there."

"I'm sure," Anna said, knowing she was disappointing Star, who wanted to show Anna off to her friends, and knowing that Star was trying hard not to pressure her.

But Star was philosophical about it, and they hung up after a spirited exchange of fiber-optic groping. Anna stretched and yawned. If having Star in her life gave her a sense of well-being, it was because Anna knew, with a ruthlessness that was a new and surprising development, that she was expendable. Anna had worked her tail off to make her relationship with Patricia work, performing amazing feats of emotional daring in her attempts to understand and comfort and appease. Being able to give all that up came as a temporal revelation; suddenly she felt as though she was luxuriating in time.

She knew Star was in love with her, and she was still waiting to see if there was any component of not being over Patricia that was keeping her from falling in love back. It didn't seem likely. Yesterday, Star had been singing to the radio in the car, and Anna had thought, She thinks she has a good voice, she thinks it's *lusty*, but it's just loud and annoying. And then she shushed herself, because nothing seemed quite so appallingly ungenerous as being critical of a lover's voice. But then again, the song was "Mama's Got a Squeeze Box," and Star was shooting sidelong suggestive glances intended to express the idea *"woo-woo!"* – placing Anna in the position of "Mama," which hadn't helped her case at all.

She was a total bitch about Star, she knew, even as thinking about that moment irritated her all over again. As she lay in bed, listening to the radiators knocking on and the steady hiss of steam from the humidifier, Anna thought about the serious talking-to Janice had given her about her complaint that Star wasn't smart. Janice had urged her to think through what counted as smart for her, and what kinds of valuations had been put upon smartness in her family. Scott, on the other hand, had said briskly, "Ah, well if she's not *smart*.... You'll just have to dump her."

Star sure was smart sexually, though; she had tuned right into what Anna needed, submitting to her with courage, dominating her with energy and passion. She got points for that. And Anna was allowed to be temperamental with her! The other day Anna had plunged into a black mood for a few hours, and Star had patted her and said "It's okay, sweetie, I'm here when you surface." And when Anna did surface, brimming with emotion and gratitude, Star had grinned and slapped her hand to her neck, yelling "Ouch! Whiplash!" Star brought her things – breakfast in bed, aspirin when she had a headache – without her even asking, and at first Anna had been so disconcerted and mortified by that, she hadn't known how to act. When Star made a sandwich for Anna she cut slices of fruit onto the plate; Anna came to call those lunches "Mommy lunches." It deeply impressed her that she no longer had to be on her best behavior in order to get ministered to. She felt freed, but also very sad, because it was dawning on her how well-behaved, how placating, she'd been for so long.

Anna looked at the papers scattered around her, and instead of resuming her grading, flipped on the TV and turned to *Sportscenter,* where Stuart Scott was bellowing "BOO-yah!" If she was a nice person, she'd go to this party with Star. There was, she was thinking, a strange dark side to being able to express a wider range of emotion. When she was difficult, a secret part of her felt like, well, like Patricia, or her mother. It was hard to describe, but sometimes she felt like one of those big round soft butches who cram themselves into severe men's clothes and wear woolly cowboy haircuts and just look awful. When Star called her a "woman," — as in "what a beautiful woman you are" or, playfully, "you mah *woman*" — Anna flinched, feeling as though Star, out of her manifold crudeness, was inadvertently speaking the truth. Now, sitting up and setting her papers on the floor, Anna wondered uncomfortably whether *all* butches were as misogynist as she was.

She'd finish grading later this afternoon. She got up, and pulling on sweatpants, she wondered who the reviewers were for her book, and when she'd hear from the press, and whether she would end up being an academic. She would certainly try again in the fall, for at least one more job cycle. The prospect made her sigh, but so did the arduous prospect of trying to piece together a decent living doing this other work. At the moment she couldn't even afford to buy a new bed, although she had bought a new coffee table, with wood legs and a tiled top, that she liked a lot. She pulled up the blind onto the alley. There was a clear blue sky, and Anna knew she should get out of this heated air, which was crisping the insides of her nostrils and making her throat sore. She touched her toes and groaned, and decided to walk the ten blocks or so to the bookstore. After a shower and coffee, she left the house, striding in her hiking boots onto the soaking grass as she crossed streets on the diagonal.

When she got there, she dried her feet vigorously on the mat at the door and entered the warm crowded store. She went to the new fiction table and scanned the titles. Then she wandered over to the gay and lesbian section to see what was new. Lots of books about cross-dressing and transsexualism. A title caught her eye: *Dagger: On Butch Women.* She grunted with surprise; how had she not seen it before? She pulled it off the shelf, immediately disliking its cover, with its supposed-to-be-shocking profile of a butch woman wearing leather and chains and brandishing a knife. Dagger: get it? It annoyed her. It tried too hard; it was what TV newsmagazines would call "provocative." She flipped to the table of contents and scanned till she noticed an article by Shar Rednour and Susie Bright called "The Joys of Butch," and perked right up. To her mind, Susie Bright was a sex-writer goddess.

The article was in conversation format, and Anna, sitting on the floor, read quickly, smiling and snorting. Near the end, Susie announces, "OK, here's my number one criticism of butches in bed," and as she read that, there crept over Anna a delicious anxiety. With Shar egging her on, Susie says,

> When you're femme, and you're trying to get your way in bed, you do so by making little moans and mews and moving your body a certain way…. Lots of wiggling, and if she is doing something you don't like, you very sexily wiggle into a new position or do something incredibly seductive to lead her down a different path, right?

> …And you would never, ever, want to hurt her feelings or her ego by slowing down this little locomotive that's inside her…. And so many times I've been stopped dead in my tracks by some butch putting her hand out to stop me, just saying, "No, I don't like that," or "Stop, you're not doing it right." Well, that's direct. So when that happens it's hard for me, as it would be hard for her, to just keep on trucking….

To which Shar responds, "It's a *nightmare!*"

The passage cracked Anna up, delighting her with recognition and a strong whiff of relief: she sat on the floor with waves of chortles breaking over her, reached with a forefinger to scratch an itch inside her nose.

It was there she sat when Chris walked by and caught a glimpse of her and fled.

The third time, though, a week later, Chris strode in, found the first salesperson, asked for the book and brought it to the register. She didn't look around; if Anna was in there, she didn't want to know about it. She lay the book on the counter to have it rung up, and found herself looking into the face of a young he-she, a row of tiny earrings festooning the edge of her ear, her baby face full and fringed with light beard fuzz. Chris blinked. "Hey," she said.

"Hey." The butch turned hurriedly toward the register. She was tall and heavy and big-breasted. Chris felt her peeking shyly back as she rang her up without a word, and felt the brush of her cupped hand as she slipped change into Chris's palm. She looked at Chris brightly as she handed her the bag, as though she was about to say something, then said, "Thanks, man."

"Thank *you*," Chris said affably. She ducked her head and high-tailed her way out of the store. Once on the street she let herself smile. She hadn't mother-henned a youngster for a long time; and she regretted not being better at making new friends, and feeling too shy to go back in and introduce herself. That kid had balls to go around like that, Chris thought — big boobs *and* peach fuzz, and those outrageous earrings drawing the eye to her face.

When she got home, the house was empty. Chris made herself a grilled cheese sandwich. When she was done eating, she washed the grease off her hands and dried them carefully with a clean towel. She got the destroyed copy of *Stone Butch Blues* from the bedroom dresser, set it on the kitchen table and carefully tore out the title page with Anna's signature on it. She placed that page under the title page of the new copy, and began to trace, feeling silly, like a little girl writing the name of her third-grade future husband. She traced the word *Anna* and took the page out to compare. It wasn't bad, just a little wobbly. She put the page back in and biting the inside of her lip, approached the flamboyant curve of the capital *S*. Just as she thought she'd pulled it off, she saw that her left hand had badly smudged the word *Anna*.

Her heart sank. "Fuck," she said.

She sat back in her chair. It was her luck to be left-handed; God had to make everything about her queer. And now what? She couldn't give this copy back to Anna Singer. And she couldn't, she just couldn't, buy it again. Her mind shot to the possibility of asking Kathleen to do it, since she had messed up the book in the first place.

Half an hour later she heard Kathleen's voice; she had stopped on her way in to chat with their neighbor, Joanne, a nurse Kathleen had befriended, although neither she nor Chris could stand her husband. Chris peeked out the living room window. Kathleen was standing on the sidewalk wrapped in the big, colorful fleece jacket she wore in the winter, her arms crossed in front of her, nodding at Joanne, who was on the front stoop. At one point she put her head back and laughed, and was so pretty that Chris thought: a Kodak moment. And memory came to Chris, a lonely hollow whistle, of combing her hair before going out, and Kathleen coming up behind her in the bathroom mirror, her eyes crinkling with mischief. But with admiration too; wrapping her arms around Chris from behind and kissing her neck. No one had ever seen Chris so fully. Chris let herself be haunted for just one minute by nostalgia. Then she heard the stomp of Kathleen's boots on the front steps. She went into the kitchen and thrust the new, ruined book deep into the already-full trash, pulled out the garbage bag, twisted it closed, and opened the door to the back porch, where she tossed it into the garbage bin.

"Hi," Kathleen called, coming into the kitchen. "Whatchya doin'?"

"Just taking out the trash," Chris said, washing her hands.

Thunder rippled outside, more a grumble than a roar, and coming to the front of the classroom after the mid-morning break, Anna wished there could just be normal February snow instead of this meteorological circus. Outside it was damp and leaden, with lumps of dirty snow on the soggy grass, cars sugared with ice and slush. She could hear them slash through wet streets. She wrote a word on the board, her shirt sliding part way out of her pants as she raised her arm. The chalk hit the board with a glassy thud. The word was *prediction,* and Anna was asking if they knew what it was.

"That's when you look in your crystal ball," Brandy said through wet bangs, with an air of satisfaction.

"That's right," Anna said: "you look in your crystal ball to see what's going to happen in the future." She looked at Vanessa regarding her dubiously, and said, grinning, "Not really a crystal ball, she's speaking metaphorically."

"Oh!" Vanessa laughed.

"Vanessa, what kinds of things get predicted?"

"The future," Vanessa said, confused and darting a look at Antwan on her right, as though she was being asked to answer a question they'd already answered.

"What kinds of things about the future?"

The weather, Antwan thought, leaning alertly on his forearms on his little desk. He had been taking his sweatshirt off and putting it back on again, unable to figure out whether it was hot in the room or cold; now he was in his t-shirt, goose bumps rising from his arms. Next to him Cheryl, twirling her pen and popping her gum, announced: "I can read palms."

Anna paused and considered her, weighing whether to go down this path; she had the school's one overworked overhead for only 45 minutes, the maximum they were allowed to check it out. The others looked at Cheryl as though she'd said she could walk on the moon. "No kidding?" Brandy asked. Once, a mother of a friend of Watson's had read her future in the cards, and had told her to beware of a man with big hands. That man, of course, was Kenneth, with his big hands that grasped the wheel of an 18-wheeler, that could close completely around her arm when he squeezed or shoved her.

"I could tell you," Cheryl said, "if you will find love." She caressed the *l* and sang the vowel.

Antwan sniffed, and she wheeled gleefully toward him.

"I can!" Cheryl insisted. She fixed Antwan with a stern eye, then said, abruptly, "Not you." She looked away until her gaze rested on Anna. "Ms. Singer found love. And you —" she gestured toward Chris, making Chris freeze, "you lost it."

The others looked expectantly back and forth at Anna and Chris, until Anna laughed and said "Lucky me." Cheryl sat back with a cool knowing nod.

"Well, listen," Anna said. "This is what we do when we read: we predict what's going to happen. When we read a sentence, we get a feeling for what's going to happen next." She asked Antwan to turn off the lights, then went to the back of the class and turned on the light of the overhead. She had covered a sheet of paper with a paragraph printed on it, and now she revealed the first three words of the paragraph:

Maria Lopez takes

"Okay," she said. "This is how this story starts. What are some ways you think the sentence might end? Can you predict what comes next?"

Brandy craned around and stared at her. "Brandy, look at the sentence, not at me," Anna gestured. "How do you think it might end?"

"Two aspirin," Chris said, adrenaline stunning her as it often did when she spoke in class.

"Good, Chris! Maria Lopez takes two aspirin for her headache. What else could come next?"

What comes next after she writes the story? Brandy wondered. She looked wonderingly at the projector, and at Anna's face, illuminated like a half-moon by the light of the lamp. Probably tutoring, and then lunch, and then go get the kids. But she thought Ms. Singer had already wrote the story, and it was lying there under a black piece of paper.

"The bus," Robert said faintly.

"Who said that?"

"I did," Robert said.

He was sitting right next to Anna; she looked at him and said, "Well, as it happens, Robert, that's exactly how the story goes." She pulled the black sheet away to reveal the rest of the sentence:

Maria Lopez takes the bus to work every night.

She stood back and let them contemplate it. "Go ahead and read that, Robert," she said, hoping her bravado would transfer over to him.

Robert read it gingerly, word by word, as if cracking nine eggs. "Okay," Anna said, "close your eyes and say that sentence again."

He did, and it came out as a real sentence this time. He opened his eyes and blinked at her, then smiled faintly.

Anna read, "Maria Lopez takes the bus to work every night. Okay, now what? If you were reading this story, what would you be expecting to come next? Can you predict what comes next in the story?"

"She gonna get mugged, or raped," Cheryl called out quickly. She was begrudging Robert his right answer.

Brandy nodded. "Somebody's gonna get in trouble," she said, ruefully.

Vanessa wondered aloud, "Who taking care of her kids?"

"I don't know," Anna replied. "You think the next sentence might be something like, She leaves her kids with their twelve-year-old cousin?"

"I hope not!" Vanessa cried.

"I bet the bus breaks down," Antwan said, and Anna laughed. "Maria Lopez takes the bus to work every night," she read, and then riffed, "But one night the bus died at her stop, and wouldn't start up again, despite all the efforts of the driver. Everyone sat there worrying until a talented and handsome mechanic arrived on the scene."

Vanessa and Brandy raised their eyebrows: was that the story? "That's right," Antwan said complacently, thinking: *handsome!*

Anna pulled the black sheet down another sentence: *She works the night shift at the electric company, as a telephone operator.*

Picking her laborious way through the first few words, Brandy was baffled. Wasn't there supposed to be a handsome mechanic there? She had been looking forward to a story about a handsome mechanic. And then everybody in the class was laughing, and Vanessa hooting, "I talked to that heifer last night!" Brandy quickly joined in, crying "What? What?" and they all laughed more strenuously than the joke warranted, until Anna raised her voice above the din and called, "So Vanessa, predict what comes next: tell me the next sentence of the story."

Vanessa hesitated, suddenly sorry she'd said the h- word and feeling a sinking feeling that she wouldn't guess right. Anna read the two sentences again, giving her a smooth push and letting go. Vanessa ventured: "She tell people they got to pay their bill on time." She slid an anxious glance toward the paper lying on the projector, then at Anna. "Did I get it right?"

"It's a great prediction," Anna replied. "If you were reading this story, you might think, when you get here, that it's about people calling Maria Lopez about their electric bills. It's definitely a good answer. Let's look at the next sentence." She slid the black sheet down.

James O'Brien takes the same bus to work.

She stood quietly while they looked at the screen. Vanessa signed audibly and adjusted the shoulder pads of her blouse. Who was James O'Brien? And what was the point of guessing if they kept getting it wrong?

Anna read the three sentences aloud. "Hmm," she murmured, "now there's a new person in the story."

Chris's eye twitched as she looked up front. She was stoned and alert and curiously trembly; she could feel emotion in her throat. That was just how reading went, she thought, welling up with world-weariness. They made it seem as though it was going to be a joy, but the truth was, you were always being thrown a curve. She thought about Jess Goldberg's story, the sudden rapes and brutalities. Frankly, she wouldn't be surprised if James O'Brien turned on Maria Lopez and beat the living crap out of her.

Looking at them slumped at their desks from behind, Anna discovered that even the back of the head can look defeated. She suddenly realized that they were discouraged over not getting the right answers. She walked over to the door and switched on the lights, stood before them with her hands on her hips as they blinked in surprise.

"Getting it right isn't the point," she said firmly. "Here's the thing, you guys: good readers risk making mistakes. They make predictions as they read, and then they revise them as they go."

Chris took this in with shock. That must mean she was a fantastic reader, she thought dryly.

Antwan, who had been staring at the screen even as the letters washed out in the light, turned toward Anna with a sudden idea. "Did they get together?" he asked. A white man and a Mexican lady: he pondered whether that boded well or ill.

"Maybe," Anna said.

"No, they was taken hostage," Robert said.

"Hostage!" Anna cried.

Brandy sighed. "Somebody's gonna get in trouble," she said.

Anna snorted and turned the lights off again. She pulled the black sheet down another sentence, the light illuminating her fingers and their raggedy bitten nails. *He is a security guard at a warehouse.* They were silent.

"Did his gun go off?" she heard Vanessa whisper to Brandy.

Brandy gave her a meaningful look. "Uh-oh," she said loudly: "trouble."

Antwan slammed his hand on his desk and cried, "Shut up! Man!"

Anna started. Then, as adrenaline made its hot glide through her, she wanted to laugh, he was so much the picture of male exasperation.

"Antwan," she said, "take it easy." He shifted and muttered in noisy resignation and started leafing ostentatiously through the used pages of his notebook as though looking for something more satisfying to do. Anna pulled back the paper over the next sentence, and then, because prediction seemed to be turning them all into nutcases, over the next as well:

Maria and James depend upon the #490 to get to their jobs. But now the CTA wants to cut some bus lines, because there is a budget deficit.

She stood there quietly, resting her arms on the sides of the machine, watching Chris look at the sentences with an intensity that looked painful, and at Cheryl's lips moving in profile. Antwan was looking down at his desk, refusing to play anymore.

Cheryl's lips curled into a faint smile. "Somebody *did* get in trouble," she said.

"See!" Brandy crowed.

"What do you mean, Cheryl?" Anna asked. Brandy looked at Cheryl urgently.

"They gonna lose their jobs if they can't take the bus there," Cheryl shrugged.

"You're right," Anna said. "So what's this story about?" She read the sentences aloud, emphasizing the clause about the CTA cutting bus lines. She knew she should call on someone else instead of taking the easy route by letting Cheryl answer.

"The bus," Cheryl said.

"Good. Get that, everybody? Who can read those sentences for me?"

There was a pause, while a man shouted in the hall and another voice, a woman's, murmured querulously. An argument was in progress. Heads whipped toward the closed door. Anna promised to read to them and let them go home as soon as somebody read the whole paragraph aloud. There were no volunteers, although their faces turned reluctantly back to her. Anna strolled around them, waiting for a raised hand.

Half-listening, Brandy trembled for the woman arguing outside, whose voice was faltering under righteous male indignation. Her frosted lipstick smudged and her pale face puffy with exhaustion and allergies, she sat back and sighed. They always beat you in an argument about why they were right and you was wrong. At least Kenneth had never laid a hand on the boys, except when roughhousing. Next to her, Chris sat perfectly still with her hands in her lap, the sentences duly transcribed in her notebook for future puzzlement and annoyance. She looked over and saw Cheryl doodling cubes, inking them so heavily they soaked through the page. On the previous page she had drawn an open palm, its lines, the creases of the finger joints, the folds in the skin between thumb and forefinger drawn with such confident precision the hand seemed to take flight. Chris wondered, Where did she learn that? She'd seen that kind of natural skill before in carpenters, the old-timers.

There was a timid knock at the door and Joyce from the GED class came slinking in, grimacing and murmuring apologies, to take the overhead away. So Anna, keeping the room dark, read the passage herself. She read it musically, trying to bring it alive as a story, and Chris, closing her eyes, let herself be swayed and satisfied by a narrative she already knew. When Anna continued on to a new part of the story, about the community protest over the cutting of vital CTA bus lines, Chris felt the words as foreign, as a disturbance, and stopped listening. Yesterday, Kathleen had opened the credit card bill and laid it with bitter pomp on the kitchen table. She had made herself a cup of tea, laid two butter cookies on a plate, and sat down with them and the calculator, trying to figure out how much of the settlement this debt would take up, when the check finally came. It wasn't too bad; there would still be enough money to pay off the medical bills and do some repairs on the house. "If it ever comes, I'll be able to stop freelancing for a while," Kathleen announced. "Finally get home at a decent hour."

Chris had wiped her nervous hands on her jeans. Neither of them could tolerate debt; they'd lived a lot of their lives paying cash because they couldn't even get a credit card, and had turned necessity into an ethic. She knew this was the moment to thank Kathleen for busting her ass to keep them afloat over the past half year, but feeling Kathleen soliciting it, seething till she got it, she couldn't quite bring herself to choke it out.

"Don't get me wrong," Kathleen said without looking at her, "I got nothing against your spending the year studying instead of working."

But? Chris wondered.

"It's just I'll be glad to have a little help, is all."

That was it. Chris closed a fist thoughtfully over her mouth. "Yeah," she said. She put her hand on Kathleen's shoulder and squeezed. "Thanks," she said, maintaining the pressure till Kathleen looked up and her face broke out of tense absorption into something softer. "You're helping me do something real important."

Kathleen saw the struggle on Chris's face and welled up. "Oh Chris," she sighed, squeezing Chris's hand, "Let's just hope it's worthwhile."

Anna read from *Bastard out of Carolina* for the last fifteen minutes of class, and sent them home after announcing that Family Night would be held a week from Friday. "It's a gathering of people who have supported you. Bring your spouses or parents, and especially your children. There will be refreshments and a bookmobile. Not this Friday, *next* Friday," she called over the rustle of coats. "Don't show up this Friday!"

As they started to filter out, Anna wondered what had gone wrong with this exercise. They obviously thought it was a capricious and somewhat mean exercise in guessing the right answer out of hundreds of potential answers. She hiked herself onto the desk and tried to think it through. When it was taught to her, she had thought it a wonderfully clever exercise, one that made explicit the unconscious but vital things people really do when they read. But Vanessa's discouragement and Chris's tuning out suggested that it had defeated them; each time a new sentence announced a shift in what they thought was the right topic, they had looked crestfallen, as though she had offered them just one more opportunity to get a passage wrong. That was interesting. You could romanticize the first time you read a beloved book all you wanted, but their response to her exercise showed that part of reading was not only taking false steps, but also being confident and flexible enough to regroup and rethink when the maze shot you into a blind turn. You needed a sturdy *ego* to do that, it occurred to her. That was one reason, she imagined, why many people — and particularly the youngest readers — loved to reread their favorite books: because they could let go of all that alertness and anxiety, and float in the story.

She looked up with a smile as Vanessa came back into the room to get her things. "Hey there," she said.

"Hey," Vanessa smiled, easing herself into her winter coat. "My boy Jordan got a B+ on an essay he wrote!"

"No kidding!" Anna said. She knew Vanessa worried about Jordan as he approached adolescence, hovering sternly over him in a way he seemed to tolerate with remarkable good nature for a twelve-year-old. She didn't let him go to a sleepover at a white friend's house, because, she told Anna, she was sure that if something bad happened or something got broken, it would be Jordan, the only black boy there, who got blamed. To Vanessa, Jordan was a roll-your-eyes kind of child. Vanessa had once said that playing baseball, he'd often overrun the bases hoping that when the ball got thrown his way it'd be overthrown, and he could take the next base. "He just hafta be brilliant," was Vanessa's commentary on Jordan.

"And I helped him with it."

Anna's eyes lit up. "Really! How did you help him?"

Vanessa raised her head with a conscientious look, as though she had prepared a recitation. "I told him to brainstorm," she said. "We drew those circles, what do you call them."

"Image clusters," Anna said. "What was the essay about?"

"If violence in rap music make kids violent. It was suppose to be just what he thinks."

Anna put her hand on her heart and comically wiped away an imaginary tear. "Vanessa, you helped him! It does a teacher's heart good."

Vanessa laughed at her antics and turned to go, but then turned back, having just remembered something. "Can you help me write a petition?" she asked. "I want to write one for Smith House for all the parents to sign."

"What do you want to write on the petition?" Anna asked.

"That some of the daycare teachers need a drug test."

Anna paused, remembering that Vanessa was worried about her daughter's teacher. "Do you mean," she asked, "that you think they should do better background tests on their workers before they hire them?"

"Yes!" Vanessa said with gratitude.

"Okay, sure," Anna said. She wondered if it would get Vanessa in trouble, but if writing a petition wasn't using writing to empower herself, nothing was. "Let's do it tomorrow in class."

As she exited onto the gloomy street, where it was still spitting a cold rain, Anna found Chris waiting for her. "Hey," she said, noticing that she was no longer intimidated by Chris's approach.

Chris handed her *Stone Butch Blues,* thinking she should thank her, but saying instead, "Here."

The book was surprising to the touch, giving off slight staticky mist on her fingers. Anna glanced at it and noticed immediately that this was a brand new copy, its spine pristine, the top cover uncurled. She opened it to the title page and found her name on it. That was strange. This wasn't her book. Some drizzle landed on the page and she closed it quickly, smiling quizzically at Chris, who was turning to go. Anna opened her mouth; she had been enjoying the masculine companionship of hanging out with Chris on a street corner. "Were you able to read it at all?" she asked.

Chris turned and considered. "Not really," she said.

Anna made a regretful face. "Yeah, after I gave it to you I realized it would probably still be too hard."

Chris looked at her with hurt incredulity, and put up her hood. Why hadn't she said something then, when Chris was thinking the whole time that she was behind in her reading?

"I'm really sorry," Anna said quickly, reaching and touching her arm. "I was just so excited by the idea that you'd be interested in it, because it's about a butch in the '50s who fights for social justice."

Chris looked down at Anna's hand, her face half hidden by her hood, and Anna took it away. Chris had never thought of the book that way. She had thought it was about a butch in the '50s who gets the shit knocked out of her. She had obviously gotten the whole book wrong.

"Chris," Anna said impulsively, "wanna go have a cup of coffee? There's a Coffee Chicago just a few blocks that way."

That was the café where Chris met Dennis; where did Anna think she lived, in the projects somewhere? "I know," she said, with a belligerence that surprised Anna.

But Anna pressed on. "C'mon, Chris," she coaxed, "You and I should have a lot to – " she hesitated "– say to each other." She had been about to say, "learn from each other," but altered mid-course. "And I could tell you about this amazing book."

Chris looked anxiously at her watch. She'd stumbled into another misunderstanding, and couldn't handle the idea of having to perpetuate it over coffee. In fact, something about the idea of sitting face-to-face with Anna at all panicked her. So even as she hissed scornfully to herself, *Coward,* she said to Anna, "I'm sorry. I have somewhere I have to be."

Anna shrugged and said with a smile whose skepticism Chris caught, "Okay, maybe another time." Watching her put the book in her bag and turn up her coat collar against the dismal afternoon, Chris regretted that she wouldn't hear from her teacher how the book had ended, and wondered, with sudden avidity, what Anna Singer thought it was they had to say to each other.

CHAPTER FIFTEEN

To Chris's shock, Kathleen wanted to go to Family Night at Pathways. At around 11, Chris took the blanket and pillows and was making up the couch, when Kathleen came in and made herself comfortable in the recliner, transgressing the understanding that made this Chris's bedroom at night. "I wasn't even planning on going myself," Chris protested, kicking herself for having let the whole thing slip in the first place, which she had done with the vague notion that an event like that would make Pathways seem like a classier place to Kathleen, a notion that now seemed really stupid. She perched on the end of the couch, her temples pulsing strenuously. "To them, we're freaks," she argued. "And I'm not making small talk with people we got nothing in common with." She stared at her determined lover, terrified that being seen among those people would be the final dagger in Kathleen's esteem for her.

Kathleen nodded her head and looked at her nails. "I'm just curious," she said. "And I want to get a load of this Anna Singer."

"Why?" Chris demanded.

"I don't know," Kathleen mused. "Because she seems to know about queers and such."

Chris looked at her grimly. "I'll tell you what," she said, "*you* go. You'll love it: all those people you can feel superior to."

Kathleen didn't bite; instead she laughed and narrowed her eyes knowingly. Then she got serious. "Plus," she said, her broad face pinking with emotion, "I just think that going to Pathways is one of the most important things that's ever happened to you."

Chris was stumped. She couldn't argue there: hadn't she wanted all along for Kathleen to acknowledge precisely that, and to show some interest in her schooling? She rubbed her face in exhaustion. "Can we talk about it in the morning?" she asked.

She was going to have to go, and to take Kathleen, even though the idea dizzied her with dread.

Chicago began to thaw in earnest. The sidewalk off Anna's courtyard was plastered with newspaper ads, their colors bleeding. Water streamed over paper and garbage into the sewers, and when she walked or ran in the neighborhood, Anna smelled a faint sewage stink. The lake lay still and gray under great mists. The city had turned on the water fountains along the lakeside paths again; at the end of her run, her hands cold and her body steaming, her t-shirt drenched under her sweatshirt, Anna bobbed her head down to the warm bubbly stream, and when she swallowed, her mouth was flooded by an organic, silty taste.

Hip-hop thundered from open car windows. On the campuses, students walked to their afternoon classes on 60-degree days in shorts and flip-flops. In Anna's and Chris's neighborhoods, subcontractors were completing their work in kitchens and bathrooms, and coming outdoors to pour foundations, lay landscaping ties, build decks and put up fresh siding. The newspapers reported the discovery of a human skeleton by sewer workers investigating a back up in an Uptown sewer, and, later that week, the discovery of a fetus, two or three inches long, under a seat on the Blue Line — which forensics specialists were examining to determine whether or not it too was human.

There was a week of heavy rain. On the fifth straight day, Chris and Kathleen stood in their bedroom staring glumly up at the brown sketch of a water stain on the ceiling. Rage welling in her, Chris cursed their home inspector and demanded that Kathleen find the document he had written. Kathleen sighed and went to call Keith, who gave her the number of a roofer buddy of his.

On a rain-lashed night in Star's apartment, Star gave Anna a tiny wrapped package. Inside was a silver ring, which Star emphasized was supposed to be worn on her third finger. Sitting cross-legged on Star's bed, Star beside her, Anna turned it over in her hand, her eye twitching. It had crescent moons and dancing goddess figures on it. As a gift for Anna, it was a terrible mistake. She looked at Star and cleared her throat.

"You don't like it," Star said quickly.

"I love the gesture," Anna replied, placing a conciliatory palm on Star's back.

Star stood and plucked the ring out of Anna's hand. "That's okay, I can take it back."

Anna peeked at her stiff, disappointed face. She understood what a risk Star had taken, and how much complex and ardent calculation must have gone into this gesture. This was one moment she really didn't want to be difficult, but she couldn't help it; she couldn't even pretend for a minute that she would ever wear that ring.

The next day, coming home from work, Anna found a long letter, together with two readers' reports, from the press that had been considering her book. She read the press's letter in terrified gulps, standing at the open apartment door, her dripping umbrella still wedged under her arm. They were interested in the book! — that was the first thing she saw. But her heart sank as she realized that both readers thought it needed one more chapter drawing together the larger cultural context for the novels she had written about, and making a stronger case for the importance of her argument to studies on the Victorian novel as a whole. Her first reaction was crushing disappointment and rage. Over the next few days, she pored over the readers' reports again and again, reading them to her friends on the phone and bringing them to her lunch and dinner dates for perusal and consultation. She argued passionately that the reviewers were asking her to have written a different book altogether than the one she'd written. But gradually, Janice and Monica and Scott helped her see that the press really wanted the book, and that the readers praised her work for the qualities she herself most valued in it: her elegant writing, the ingenu-

ity and originality of her readings. Anna herself, her friends reminded her, had always known that her argument lacked a certain breadth.

It took an entire week, but finally Anna let go of her indignation
and faced the real issue: did she really want to write another chapter of
her book? Each chapter had taken her nearly a year to write, and the
thought of embarking on that research, those long stretches of paralysis and confusion punctuated by short anxious bursts of insight, filled
her with dread. And yet, if she didn't, and gave up on the book, she'd
essentially be giving up her academic career.

The trees in Anna's neighborhood began sprouting small buds,
impossibly green, and at night, she was awoken by the sound of yowling
cats in the yard below. Squirrels and crows made a racket in the dawn
hours. And one morning, as she was racing out the door to class, Anna
received a phone call from Renée, telling her that Brandy was in the
hospital, having been assaulted by her boyfriend.

Twenty minutes later, when Anna gravely told her class that she had
some bad news, she found that they already knew Brandy was in the hospital. Indeed, the rumors making their way around Pathways were grisly.
Brandy's boyfriend had cut her throat, they had heard; he had kicked her
repeatedly in the head; he had raped her right in front of the kids. And in
one rumor that seemed suspiciously to Anna like adult-learner urban legend, he had piled all her notebooks on the kitchen table, soaked them in
kerosene, and forced Brandy, at knifepoint, to light the match. All morning Anna felt nauseated – by the fact of Brandy's assault itself, but also by
the riotous abandon with which the rumors multiplied. And because
Renée had gone to the hospital, she couldn't find out what had actually
happened.

On the board, she drew an extended semantic map around the word
abuse: kinds of abuse, victims of abuse, causes of abuse, consequences of
abuse, resources for escaping abuse – Cheryl's favorite, which Anna
declined to write on the board, being "cutting off his nuts." It didn't help,
she was thinking, that Antwan was wearing a t-shirt with a skull and cross-
bones on it. She heard Cheryl's gum popping, and the groan of a chair leg

on the floor. Vanessa was shifting uneasily and clearing her throat. "Write by *consequences of abuse, death,*" she said, stumbling over *consequences.*

Anna wrote it on the board, and had her back turned when Vanessa declared that her sister had been killed by her boyfriend.

Anna turned; for a moment, the only sound in the classroom was the fierce buzz of fluorescent lights. Then Robert said "Mine too."

The two of them looked at each other with wonderment.

"Her boyfriend killed her?" Vanessa asked.

Robert nodded.

Anna came slowly to the front of the classroom and sat on her desk, her mind spinning to the reading she'd been doing from *Bastard out of Carolina.* What had Vanessa and Robert been thinking as she read them that story of abuse and survival? She was surprised that Vanessa, normally so voluble, hadn't said anything before.

"How did he do it?" Cheryl asked Vanessa.

"He threw her out of the window," Vanessa said, her lips tightening with old anger.

A murmur made its way around the class. Anna looked at Robert, erect at his desk, his eyes clear amid the stubble on his face.

"That's so sad," Anna said. She asked them their sisters' names and how old they were when they died. She wrote on the board, "Tonya Harris, 1974-1992" and "Deborah Ruth Day, 1959-1980."

"Is it okay to write that on the board?" she asked, turning with sudden alarm. They nodded without looking at her; they were staring at the names on the board. Anna waited, trying to imagine the relation of a functionally illiterate person to the engraved record of a loved one's death. They must know what's on their sisters' gravestones, she thought.

Chris looked at the names of the dead on the board, shutting out the lesson in the practiced way she did when she felt it wasn't relevant to her life. She felt bad for Vanessa and Robert, she really did, but she also had the idea that they must be so used to that kind of violence in their lives, that these deaths didn't devastate them the way they would devastate other people. And these, she thought, were the people Kathleen was going to see her in the company of. Kathleen would scorn these people, she knew it; she wouldn't see them as real people with intelligence and feelings.

"Do you know if there's anything else written on their grave-stones?" Anna asked. Her demeanor had grown patient and soft, and she was turning over in her mind the exercises she had had planned, a backup option if this lesson turned out to be too raw.

Robert had a look on his face as though he wanted to say something. "It don't look like that," he said, when Anna gave him a querying look.

She held out a piece of chalk toward him.

He stood and put on his jacket, the blue blazer he wore every day, and took it from her. His fingers were remembering the feel of the stone as he traced them over the engraved letters. At the board he wrote, with a labo-rious and noisy clack:

> Deborah Ruth Day
> Born 1959
> Died 1980

"Thanks, Robert," Anna said.

"On my mother's gravestone it say *Resting with Jesus,*" Antwan offered.

Anna gestured him up to the board. "In fact," she said, "anybody who wants to, come on up to the board."

They came up, everybody but Chris, and jostled for chalk; Antwan snapped his piece in half and gave one to Cheryl. Anna watched them deliberate and write. In a few minutes the board was covered with their dead. Antwan's mother, Lois Johnson, and his cousin Edward LaFebvre; Cheryl's boyfriend, Germaine Washington, dead at 26; under his dates she had written, "Freedom evermore from pain," and she was drawing an out-line of the tombstone around the words. Robert wrote his father James' epitaph, just the simple name and dates, and Reggie Jr.'s.: "Answered his country's call." After a few moments' consideration, Anna got an extra piece of chalk from her desk drawer and began writing her father's name.

Everyone stopped writing to watch.

"Keep writing," she said. She wrote,

> Gerald Issac Singer
> 1943-1976

Beloved son, husband, and father

One by one they took their seats, swiping their hands on their legs to wipe off the chalk dust. Anna stood at the side of the board and wondered if she should have them read aloud. If she didn't, they might not pay attention to the epitaphs that weren't their own. Should they read? Should they sit in quiet contemplation? Should they testify about their dead, whose presences, she knew, animated that classroom each and every day?

Chris was doing the math, realizing that all those people had died young, most of them probably from violence. She saw Anna pausing and thinking. Just let it speak for itself, she wanted to tell her: if people talk they'll just ruin it.

Anna asked, "Does anybody want to tell us something about someone whose name is on the board?"

"Is that your father?" Cheryl asked Anna.

They all turned to regard her with avid curiosity. Anna nodded.

"What did he die from?"

"A heart attack," Anna said.

They pondered the board in thick silence, until Cheryl exclaimed, with a burst of aggravated laughter, "Brandy ain't dead yet!"

Then everybody laughed, and Vanessa put her hand to her face and shook it; there was a sheepish feeling that they were jinxing Brandy.

When Anna let them go she thought that someone should land in the hospital every day, it created such intense focus. But why the hell had she told them her father had died of a heart attack? Christ, many of *their* dead had been *murdered*. She had made that whole honest, tentative moment into a lie. She was wearily packing up to go, thinking about walking over to the hospital, when Antwan approached her.

"Hi," she said with a mechanical smile.

He put his arm around her shoulder and gave her a friendly squeeze. In the damp warmth of his arm pit, pulled toward his chest and face, Anna smelled a pungent blend of sweat and after-shave, and found herself eye-to-eye with the pores and bumps and leftover stubble around his chin, and his lips, which looked, close up, disconcertingly luscious. "I could tell you was having a hard day," he said.

Anna turned toward him and eased slightly away. "Thanks," she said, feeling like a teenager trying to ease a boy's arm away from her breast without seeming hostile or rejecting. "That's nice of you, Antwan."

"Okay then," he said awkwardly, and picked up his backpack. "See you tomorrow."

Anna stopped in Renée's office on her way out; she had just returned from Weiss Memorial. "She's okay," Renée said, hanging her coat on the rack, "or as okay as you can be under the circumstances. She has a broken jaw, which has been wired, and two cracked ribs, and she's pretty badly bruised."

"I'm relieved," Anna said, her hand on her chest, "after all the brutal rumors going around. So she just got beat up?"

Renée made a sour face. "Yes, that's all," she said.

"Should I head over there?"

"I wouldn't," Renée said. "She's in a lot of pain. They just gave her a shot and she was going to try to sleep."

"Okay," Anna said, turning to leave.

"One good thing, though," Renée called out: "With that jaw wired shut, she'll get a lot of practice writing."

Anna laughed. "Talk about your silver linings."

All the way down the stairs, on the El and on the street, putting her key in the door, imagining the mess of writing with which Brandy would communicate with her jaw wired shut, Anna could smell Antwan rising spicily off her shirt and hair.

Anna visited Brandy the next day. She was in a room with an elderly woman, a circular curtain drawn around her bed to give her some privacy. Anna peeked into it and then stepped inside. Brandy was alone and dozing, her mouth sagging on one side like a stroke victim's, her face disfigured with bruises. When she awoke and saw Anna standing hesitantly at the foot of the bed, she lurched upright and tried to smile;

Anna caught a glimpse of the hardware threading her gums and felt a shudder shimmy up her spine. "That's okay, Brandy," she said, "You don't have to play hostess." Brandy laughed sniffing from her nose and gestured humorously with her hands, a gesture that expressed the sentiment *That's life*.

She was a grotesque parody of herself, battered and ballooned, addled from pain medication. Her hair was matted and stringy; somebody ought to wash it for her, Anna thought. Amid the clutter of cups and tissues and kids' toys on the table next to her was a wide-lined pad of paper and a pen. The pad, Anna noticed, was unfolded and unmarked.

"How about I just ask yes or no questions?" Anna asked.

Brandy nodded eagerly, and Anna tried not to flinch at the eagerness on her face, the utter lack of self-consciousness with which she greeted her teacher here in a hospital bed, scantily dressed and beaten to a pulp. When she leaned forward, her gown opened and Anna could see her nipple, huge and pink, studded with goose bumps. Brandy gestured toward the foot of the bed for Anna to sit down, and Anna looked around for a chair, but seeing none, said she didn't mind standing.

"I'm sorry this happened to you," she said, training her eyes on Brandy's so she wouldn't have to see her breast.

Brandy shrugged self-deprecatingly.

"Are the kids okay?"

Brandy gave an emphatic nod.

Anna nodded, reached into her bag and pulled out a sheaf of papers clipped tightly together at the left margin. "I brought you some exercises, for if you get bored," she said. She had considered having Brandy keep a journal, but had decided that she would be more likely to pull off easier, more structured homework: punctuation exercises and simple fill-in and synonym exercises. At the end of the packet Anna had added optimistically a sheet titled "Hospital Vocabulary," with a list of numbers, and then a few blank sheets, marked with dates starting today, and sentences that began "Today the nurse..." and "Today I felt..."

Brandy's face clouded as she reached uncertainly for the sheaf, making Anna wonder with a pang whether it was appropriate to give homework on a visit to a battered woman. Homework and lessons left and right, on abuse, murder, the hospital. Either she was a total boor, she thought, or she was turning into quite the adult literacy teacher.

A nurse drew aside the curtain with a clatter and entered with a milkshake with a long straw in it. "How ya doin', Brandy," she sang ear-splittingly, with perfect nursely condescension. "I brought you something to eat." She handed the cup to Brandy and closed her gown where it had opened, then took the straw and pushed it into the gap between two of her teeth. "Think of a nice juicy steak," she said as Brandy began to suck on the straw, and Brandy tittered obligingly.

Anna stood. "Okay, I should go," she said. "Brandy, feel better, okay? We expect you back soon."

Brandy nodded with that same anxious face and at the last moment, reached out her hand. Anna took it. It was clammy. She's not coming back to school, Anna thought — Brandy, who was there rain or shine, for whom school was the one sure thing. Who was, Anna realized, in her classroom, such as she was, Anna's own one sure thing.

Brandy squeezed her hand hard.

Pathways looked especially bare and institutional at night, flooded with fluorescent light, darkness hugging in at the windows. Anna looked at her watch as she trudged up the stairs to Family Night; she had tried to get there half an hour after the event began, but as usual, had arrived earlier than she wanted. The library door was propped open, and Anna entered shyly. A smattering of people, none of her students yet, mostly teachers. They stood around holding plastic cups filled with punch; conversation was low and self-conscious, punctuated by false hearty laughter. Anna took off her coat and hung it up. A few teachers called out to her, asking how Brandy was faring, and she shrugged and waggled her hand so-so.

A display table of bookmobile books had been set up, some for children and some for adults, and it had been decorated with flowers and toys. Anna approached it and smiled at the sight of a little Lego truck next to a children's book about trucks, and a primitive horse made of Sculpy with its nose dipped toward *The Black Stallion*. Someone had taken the trouble, she thought appreciatively. Probably Renée. She picked up a book, then put it down again. Time to be a grown-up. She turned toward the room.

Vanessa and her kids were taking off their coats, Jordan slumped and sulky. Anna grinned at the sight of him, thinking there must be a thousand things a teenaged boy would rather be doing.

The library was beginning to swell with noise and heat and motion. Out of the corner of her eye, Anna caught a glimpse of Chris entering stiffly with her lover. A wave of charged surprise passed over her. Kathleen was wearing a big fleece coat and clutching a purse; Anna noticed with appreciation her red hair and tall bosomy figure, congratulating herself on her own large-spiritedness the way young people do when they find older people attractive. She checked her fly and headed toward them. Chris had steered them directly to the dessert table and was cutting herself a piece of cake, but Kathleen took notice of Anna's approach, uncertain at first, then brightening. Their eyes met smilingly. Kathleen touched Chris's arm, and Chris straightened, juggling a paper plate with a piece of cake on it, licking icing off her thumb. Anna extended a hand to Kathleen and said "I'm Anna Singer."

"Oh," Chris said.

"Yes," Kathleen said, "I'm Kathleen Petty."

"Hi Chris," Anna grinned. "I'm so glad you guys came!"

"I had to drag her," Kathleen said drolly. She had the manner of a stoic person who has to put up with a lot of nonsense from others; and yet, Anna felt herself singled out by a warm teasing regard.

"I'll *bet* you did," Anna exclaimed, while Chris rolled her eyes. Her leather jacket was still zipped up to the chin, and Anna's approach had seemed to freeze her at attention with the plate in her large palm, a plastic fork lying neatly next to the cake.

"What's that, carrot cake?" Anna asked. She looked at the table, the orange cake with white icing and plates of pale sprinkled butter cookies, and wrinkled her nose. "I come from a family that fails to see the point of desserts that aren't chocolate."

Chris shrugged. "Your loss, I guess," she said, cutting herself a forkful.

But Kathleen laughed. "Well I come from rural Indiana," she said, "and if you don't like white food there – your marshmallows, your mashed potatoes, your Cool-Whip – you'll just about starve."

"Yum," Anna exhaled, "Cool-Whip!" and Kathleen laughed again, giving her the once over. "How is it?" Anna asked Chris, thinking even as she spoke that she should stop beating this dead horse.

"Not bad."

Anna turned toward Kathleen. "So Kathleen," she said, "what kind of work do you do?

"I work in a hospital, doing insurance billing," Kathleen told her.

"Aha," Anna said, imagining a tiny cubicle, the tapping of long-nailed fingers on keyboards, the jocular/hostile stickers and cartoons on her computer monitor. *I can only please one person per day. Today is not your day. Tomorrow's not looking so good either.* "So you're the person who Xeroxes my insurance card?"

"I don't actually do the copying, but the Xerox ends up with me."

Chris swiveled and put her cake down, announced "I'm boiling," and took her jacket off. "Let me take your coat, Kath." Kathleen unbuttoned her coat and Chris moved behind her and slid it off her shoulders. Anna watched the small gesture with appreciation. The coats draped over her arm, Chris headed to the coatrack at the other end of the room. Renée was organizing a reading circle, and Anna watched her waylay Chris to help place chairs in a circle.

"No really, how did you get her here?" Anna asked, half-jokingly.

Kathleen narrowed her eyes in mock menace, then touched Anna's arm and leaned toward her. "I have my ways," she said.

Anna laughed. "Well she's doing great."

Kathleen looked quickly at Chris, then back at Anna. "You mean in school?" she asked.

"You sound surprised." Anna bristled on Chris's behalf. "She's a terrific student."

Kathleen nodded thoughtfully. A little black girl in pigtails was watching Chris swing chairs around. Chris stopped abruptly and looked down at her, then said something inaudible. The little girl looked keenly at her face, whirled and ran and wrapped herself around her mother's leg. Kathleen, her face watchful and immobile, sniffed softly.

"What did she say?" Anna asked.

"'I'm a girl,'" Kathleen murmured. Then, as though she'd revealed too much, she turned brightly back to Anna. "So," she said, in a way that made Anna think she was going to elbow her and make a sexual joke, "That was quite a book you lent us."

Anna looked at her uncomprehendingly.

"*Stone Butch Blues,*" Kathleen said.

"Oh!" Anna said. "Did you read it?"

"Well Chris of course isn't ready yet, but I read it aloud to her." Renée was walking around the room rustling up children, a book under her arm, touching parents and telling them they could come listen too.

"Really! What did you think?"

"Oh, I thought it was marvelous. Chris on the other hand...." She was still watching Chris, keeping a protective eye on her, perhaps, or taking the measure of her in this environment, Anna couldn't tell.

"What do you mean?"

Kathleen turned to her, smiled a social smile that was meant to charm, but whose execution was mirthless. "It's like reading about your own life," she explained. "Only the person in the story is a hero, and you're just a poor slob."

Anna looked at her sharply. At that moment Chris rejoined them, her face red with exertion, her shirt bunched up above her belt. Renée quieted the people in the circle and started to read from *Where the Wild Things Are.* Anna smiled at the selection; Renée loved Sendak, the glum whimsical Jew. She felt Kathleen next to her, heard Chris's slightly labored breathing, and leaned companionably onto this little island of queers amid a sea of small children and mothers. She liked Kathleen less and less as they talked, and wondered: was Kathleen exhibiting an acute perceptiveness to

Chris, or did she think of Chris as a poor slob? The line was so fine between empathy with your partner's abjection and *buying into* that abjection. You needed your partner to hold the line, to stand resolutely behind your best self-image even as she let you give voice to your secret fears. Patricia had been terrible at that; at times, when Anna sank into self-hatred and paralysis about her work, she could see Patricia's face flicker with anxiety, as though she were thinking: What if she really *is* mediocre? Maybe, Anna thought, she should suck it up and finish her book just to show Patricia. Because the reviewers had really liked the book, and she knew now that if she could write this one chapter and get it out there, it would be well-regarded.

The reading circle was in full swing. Tisha was sunk back on Vanessa's lap, sucking her thumb, and even some of the bigger kids were lurking around the circle's edges to hear Renée's voice, whose blend of briskness and mischief was delicious to the ear. Anna closed her eyes, her throat aching at the sight of mothers and children savoring this moment of quiet animation in their perilous lives.

On their way home, on the Lawrence El platform, Kathleen said to Chris, "I think she's dreamy."

Chris turned to her with a face so pained and perplexed Kathleen felt laughter surging in her chest. "You're kidding."

"Hell no!" Kathleen laughed, a delicious raunchy note sounding that Chris hadn't heard for ages. "A butch like that?" She mused sexily, running her fingers over her throat. "She's the kind that would ask you how your climax was and how she could do better next time. She'd go down on you and consider it a privilege."

Chris looked around quickly to make sure nobody on the platform had heard. "And that's what you'd go for," she said, heavy on the sarcasm. Until she had seen the two of them talking so animatedly together — *conversing* really, not jawing, or making a commotion in front of the ballgame, or commenting on the food at dinner — until she'd seen Kathleen laugh out loud and touch Anna's arm, it had never occurred to her to regard Anna in that light, as part of her own universe.

Kathleen shot back, "If I was twenty years younger...."

She knew Kathleen was just teasing, but she felt taunted. Chris was grim and thoughtful on the train, her hands dangling between her knees. They walked down the quiet street with their hands in their coat pockets, and Chris opened the front door and let Kathleen in ahead of her. Then she said abruptly, "I'll tell you what: I'm going out. Don't wait up." Kathleen turned in surprise, and Chris shut the door hard between them. She walked back down the steps and headed toward Ashland, wishing there was a bar she could live with in her own neighborhood. She would have to hail a cab, and head way out west. She hated to spend the money, but finally hailed a cab and directed the cabbie up to Irving Park and then west, to an old bar she'd been to a few times called Nook and Cranny, affectionately known to its regular clientele as "Nookie's." It was run by a butch named Nan Rice. Nan had survived in the neighborhood by being such an aggressively good neighbor — organizing block parties and fund-raisers for local playgrounds — that since the days of the raids, with the exception of the occasional homophobic escapade of drunk high school boys, the bar had existed side by side with its blue-collar neighbors in relative harmony.

The driver's eyes had been flitting from the road to the rearview mirror for so long Chris was sure he'd run them off the road. Chris considered having him drop her off a couple of blocks away, but then she wondered who she was kidding, and had him drop her at the bar. After all his bug-eyed antics Chris decided to live dangerously and stiffed the bastard on the tip; he lurched off with a squeal of tires and a "fuckin' bulldagger" that made her grin harshly and give the streaking cab the finger.

She crossed the dark street. Nook and Cranny was an uninvitingly windowless stucco building on a corner, with a small neon sign. You still got buzzed in; Chris rang the bell and waited to be scrutinized through the small window in the heavy door. The buzzer sounded and she pushed her way in to the welcome smell of smoke and booze. Two bowling teams were in there, talking and laughing noisily, big women bending over the pool tables in shiny brightly-colored bowling shirts with their names stitched on the backs. Wood paneling, NFL team pennants and framed pictures of the bar's sports teams all over the wall, a TV tuned to the sports news mounted on a stand over the bar, liquor bottles encased in cabinets with glass panes: not much had changed in the years since Chris had been here. She approached the bar. She didn't know the bartender. But sitting on a stool slumped over a beer was someone she was surprised and glad to recognize: the little baby butch from the bookstore.

"Well well well," she drawled as she slid onto the adjoining barstool.

The kid looked over, and slowly, recognition dawned over her face. "Hey," she said, awkward and evidently delighted, fishing for something good to say. "How'd you like the book?"

"Pretty wild," Chris said, without missing a beat, and promptly ordered a Miller on tap and a tequila shot from the bartender, a tough bird with muscular arms and an attitude like she'd been aggravated all night long, and you just might be the last straw. Just like Jack from the old days, Chris remembered, who had had no time for indecisiveness; just give her the damn drink order.

She lit a cigarette, twisted around and peered back into the room, exhaling. "Looks like guys' night out," she said, settling happily as the glasses were set hard on the bar before her.

"Our luck," the kid said morosely.

Chris craned her head comically down toward the top of the bar till she was looking right in her face. "Why the glum face," she joked, "you just get dumped by your girlfriend or something?"

"As a matter a fact," the kid said into her beer, "yeah."

Chris grimaced. "Ouch." Then she straightened and grinned. "Broads, whatchya gonna do."

The kid didn't like that, she could tell; she obviously wasn't at that stage of the breakup yet. Chris tossed back the shot, set the glass on the bar, wiped her hand on her jeans and extended it to her. "Chris Rinaldi," she said.

The kid shook it firmly. "Sam Solarcyk," she said.

"Hey there Sam Solarcyk." Chris withdrew her hand and flexed it playfully, as if shaking out the pain. Sam offered a grudging grin.

They sat in companionable silence, drinking steadily, and Chris got a quick fierce buzz on. Recklessly, she called for another shot.

When the bartender brought it to her, Chris asked her, "How's Nan making out on the bar?"

The bartender wiped her hands on a towel. "Nan passed about a year ago," she said. "Cancer. Bar's being run by her lover, Cassie."

A pang pressed at Chris's chest. "Shit," she said, stricken tears coming to her eyes. She raised her glass, and gestured to Sam to raise hers too. "To Nan Rice," she said. "She made a home for people that didn't have anywhere else." She tossed back the shot and shuddered.

The bartender looked at her in surprise. "You friends with Nan?"

"Naw," Chris said. "This wasn't my bar. But somehow it still feels personal."

The bartender nodded.

When she left them, Chris sat shaking her head. "You kids got no idea," she said to Sam.

The kid looked at her uncertainly, the desire to ingratiate herself warring on her face with a look of being fed up. "Is this where I get the lecture about how you old bulls got busted so we young ones can have a life that's all sunshine and roses?" she asked. "Well get a good look at my face lately?" She turned fully toward Chris and lifted her chin, displaying its full deviant splendor. Chris, who had been about to take serious umbrage, was disarmed. She reached and clamped Sam's shoulder hard.

"In the old days you'd of got your ass kicked for talking like that," she grumbled.

"In the old days I'd of been dead long before *you* could kick my ass," Sam retorted. Chris released her, grinning to herself. She felt a rapport with this kid she didn't know how to describe. Was it antagonism or affection? She couldn't tell, and the open-endedness of the feeling made her light-headed.

"Where do you know so much about the old days?" she barked good-naturedly.

Sam slugged back her beer. "I'm not an idiot, I can read."

Chris looked at her drink and sloshed it in the glass, her mind shifting into low gear. This could go so many different ways, she thought.

"It's not just idiots don't know how to read," she said, looking intently at Sam. "Some real smart people don't know how."

Sam caught the intensity of her gaze and became alert.

"Things happen to people."

"I know," Sam said. "It was just an expression."

Chris took in her green painter's pants and sneakers, and the black t-shirt that pressed against her breasts and biceps, struggling to get a read on her. "Maybe where you come from," she said, "people are protected from circumstances."

The kid blushed. "Okay man, you're right, that was a dumb thing to say." She held out her hand, and Chris slapped it, then grabbed it. The kid obviously couldn't imagine that she was talking about herself. Chris thought comically: What the hell does an illiterate have to do to out herself around here? The sense of two understandings coming this close to collision gave her a thrill. She studied Sam out of the corner of her eye. She was chubby in the beautiful way of children; Chris imagined her skin to feel baby-silky.

"How long you been working at the bookstore?" she asked.

"A year and a half."

"They treat you okay there?"

"Yeah," Sam said. "They don't give a damn what I look like, as long as I know my way around books."

Is that so, Chris thought. And suddenly she was quite drunk. It took her aback, because she prided herself on knowing exactly what her body could take and how to modulate her buzz, and she hadn't expected to be so shitfaced so soon.

Next to her the kid was welling up. Chris noticed it and a rush of alarm, and then pity, came over her. "I don't know what I'd do without that job," Sam said, a catch in her throat, "especially now."

Chris tried to get her bearings in the surging room, as women in bowling shirts came up to the bar and bawled out drink orders, crowding up around and behind and between her and Sam. Chris welcomed the commotion; her heart was beating hard, and emotion was pooling in her heart, and there was a disconcerting warmth between her legs. Someone jostled her arm hard, and she yelled "Hey!" jerking it away and whirling around, and the woman put up her hands and murmured placatingly. Then the crowd around the bar receded, and it was just the two of them again.

Chris thrust herself up from the bar and stood carefully. "I gotta go to the john," she said.

"Me too," Sam said, scraping her stool back and getting up to follow. Chris, whose lifetime strategy was to allow no one behind her back, felt her padding in sneakers behind her, warm and dangerous.

In the bathroom she lurched into a stall and sat down on the toilet. She heard a thunderous stream coming from Sam's stall, the creak and rattle of the toilet paper roll and a noisy yank. Her head was pounding, and she had burst into a flop-sweat. She peed and lingered for a minute, listening to Sam wash her hands. When she emerged from the stall, Sam was staring at her reflection in the dirty mirror above the sink.

Sam's eyes met hers through the mirror. She turned, her face ugly with drunken anguish. "Who else will love me?" she asked.

Chris stumbled forward, pulled Sam's head roughly toward her, felt her soft cheek against her face, and the fuzz of her jaw. She ruffled her hair, then stroked it, and they both grew still. Chris felt the sweat trickle down her sides. They swayed for a moment like bears.

Chris put her lips to Sam's warm neck. She pulled Sam's shirt out from her pants and lay her hands on the bare skin of her waist, surprised as her thumb grazed a navel ring. "Whoa," Sam panted, her hands starting to flutter over Chris's. Chris pulled back and looked into her flushed and muddled face, felt her hot beer-scented breath. She grabbed her by the ears and butted foreheads with her, just hard enough to hurt, then released her as she heard the sound of approaching voices and the door opening onto the racket of the bar.

Sam turned to the wall and fumbled to tuck her shirt back in. Two women who had come in looked uncertainly from her to Chris, with a look of wanting to say something jocular. Moving as casually as she dared to the mirror, Chris took out a pocket comb and drew it coolly through her hair. She heard the honk of Sam blowing her nose, and the slam of the stall doors as the women closed them. She walked out of the bathroom and back to her seat, where she fished a twenty out of her wallet, flung it onto the bar, and exited hastily onto the street.

The air was raw and wet. She walked quickly east, keeping her eye out for a cab; the venomous taste of blood began coating her throat. Crap, she had a nosebleed, and she hadn't even been fighting. She tipped her head back, stopping her nostrils with her fingers; she had no Kleenex on her. When she straightened and pulled away her bloody fingers, nausea came over her in such sudden spasms she vomited onto the street. She was staring at her own puke and blood, heaving and choking, when she remembered the Percocet. Jesus, she thought, you probably weren't supposed to drink on painkillers. And as she straightened and tried to catch her breath, she had a vague and comforting thought: it was the drugs that had made her act that way.

She knew that sick and bloodied, she was a magnet for trouble, but on this late night she didn't pass a soul. She was irrationally disappointed by that, wanting to make good on all this bloodshed. It was a good few miles before any cabbie would pick up a pervert with a bloody face. The one who finally did, a Spanish guy, said "Jesus, man," his eyes steady in the mirror, and handed her some Kleenex without looking back. "Who fuck you up?"

Chris had to laugh. Her head pounded as her thoughts scrabbled back to the scene in the bar bathroom, but on its heels came a strange bitter mirth. Well, she thought, I guess I'll never be able to show my face at the bookstore again.

She got home around 2:00, letting herself in quietly and peeling her jacket off, laying it over a kitchen chair. Her heart began thudding, and nausea seized her. She vomited into the kitchen sink, trying not to wake Kathleen, not to cough. She ran the tap and rinsed out her mouth, then stooped and washed her face with cold water, rubbing with her forefinger around her upper lip and nostrils to wash off the crusted blood. She wiped her face with a dish towel and walked stealthily to the hall closet to take down her bedding.

Kathleen was standing in the doorway of the living room, ghostly in her nightgown. Chris moved to pass her, shifting the bedding a little higher in her arms to conceal her face. But Kathleen reached out and touched Chris's chin, tipping her face toward the moonlight coming through the dining room window. She raised her eyebrows.

"It's just a nosebleed," Chris said.

"Oh yeah," Kathleen snorted, indicating that she wasn't born yesterday.

Chris jerked her face away.

As Anna drove home from Family Night, she thought about what Kathleen had said about reading *Stone Butch Blues,* and tried to fathom why Chris had pretended they hadn't read it. It was possible that Chris felt too vulnerable to share her reaction, but it disappointed Anna and pissed her off that Chris refused to see her as someone who might understand that response. Every effort Anna made, Chris received with withering disdain. And it burned; it made Anna want to say *Fine, you know what? You're on your own.*

She crawled down Wayne Ave., which was lined on both sides by parked cars, then saw the brake lights going on in a car right in front of the walkway to her building. She eased into the space when the driver drove off, thinking about Chris and Kathleen, whom she realized she didn't like, a realization that always surprised her, she tended so strongly to liking people. Part of her felt a little sheepish about huddling up with Kathleen at Family Night. But it had felt gratifying in a slightly spiteful kind of way — as though Anna had been zinged back into regular ol' butchhood. After Star, and the three-ring circus they had going, that was a big relief.

Her footsteps were clammy on the wet walk. Anna opened the downstairs door and in the dimly-lit vestibule, thought she saw a piece of paper in her mailbox. Strange, she thought; she had already taken in the mail. She opened the mailbox, and into her hand fell an envelope with her name on it, in handwriting that made her legs grow weak. It was from Patricia.

She ran upstairs and let herself in, the keys trembling in her hands. She turned on the hall overhead, ripped open the envelope and read:

Hi there — I was in Chicago to do some research and see Janice and Terry, and thought I'd stop by and say hi and pick up my books. Sorry I missed you. I'm off early tomorrow to a conference in Toronto, so maybe next time…. Hope you're doing well, P. P.S. Here's the extra mailbox key.

The note was marked with the date and time. Anna looked at her watch; Patricia had written it ten minutes ago.

Anna removed her coat and closed the front door, went into the bedroom and flung herself on the bed. Her mind savaged the messages conveyed by Patricia's prose: she was claiming Janice and Terry as her friendship territory, she couldn't use Anna's name in salutation or farewell lest Anna, still pining to be intimately addressed by her, take it the wrong way, she was surrendering her claim to the private domain of Anna's mailbox but had been holding the key to it all along. She was so important and had professional obligations of such urgency that she could spare only a minute to drop in on her profoundly less important ex-girlfriend. *Fuck her,* Anna thought, exhausted and bored by her own persisting vulnerability, her own tears.

The phone rang, and she picked it up. "What're you wearing?" Star was murmuring huskily.

Anna choked back her tears and said, "I can't, Star, not right now."

Star chuckled. "I know, I'm so bad," she said.

Anna thought: She thinks she invented phone sex. "Patricia was just here," she said, with a touch of drama.

There was a moment of silence, then Star said, "Wow!"

"Yeah, wow is right."

"How was it seeing her?"

"I didn't see her," Anna said. "She was here just briefly, maybe ten minutes before I got home, and left me a note."

"Really!" Anna fancied she could hear relief in Star's voice. "What did she say?"

"Oh, the usual about rushing off to her next important professional event. Listen," Anna said, knowing this was a bad idea, but knowing that Janice and Terry were with Patricia, and scared to be alone, "Can I come over?"

There was another pause. "Sure," Star said.

An hour later Anna was naked in her bed, having been given a cup of tea and made love to too wistfully for her to get really turned on. Her back turned and her butt thrust against Star's stomach, she began to drift off, but Star was talking, evidently awake and beginning to warm to a theme. She was talking about how her best friends Sharon and Dee had warned her not to let Anna manipulate her. It was totally understandable that Anna still missed Patricia, she said, but she was thinking about how she had to take care of Star Montague. That's how she said it, referring to herself in the third person, like an athlete at a press conference. Anna winced at the formulation, and at being considered a girlfriend who manipulated. It was so much more complicated than that: she still genuinely wasn't over Patricia, and was trying to conduct a relationship under that condition. She lay still and alert, galled but also hoping just a little that Star would take charge and break up with her. But she didn't: she sighed loudly and tossed for a while, and in a few minutes Anna drifted to sleep, still Star's girlfriend.

Early that morning, when it was still dark outside, a blaring nauseous headache woke Chris. She stumbled into the kitchen so she wouldn't wake Kathleen and threw up in the trash till there was nothing left to come up, then began dry heaving and cramped so severely she sank to her knees. She knew there were six Percocets left in her bag, which was on the floor of the front hall closet, and no refills left. As she struggled for breath on all fours, blood pounding in her head, the thought came to her that she was in trouble, so violently sick, but her mind still scrabbling over her stash. She sank to the linoleum and curled herself fetally, moaning softly, and later, when Kathleen got up, she found her there.

CHAPTER SIXTEEN

When the recognition that she was addicted to painkillers came to Chris, it came not like a thunderbolt, but like something once forgotten, swimming its way back into memory. Back in their bed, on sheets that smelled of Kathleen, Chris lay quaking with nausea and chills, and thought, in a small voice in a dim corner of her mind, *Oh yeah*. She'd doctored the prescription; she'd hid the pills and taken them on the sly. She'd hungered for the next pill, and taken more as she grew tolerant and the buzz faded. She'd mixed drugs and alcohol. Even as these thoughts came to her, their significance flickered like a dying neon light, their hum an irritant. In one lucid moment she remembered hearing about movie stars who went into rehab because they were addicted to painkillers. That, she thought, was what she had, it made sense now. As she lay still trying to breathe steadily through the next wave of nausea, Charlie Sheen wandered into her mind, and the guy whose name she tried and tried to remember, the one that played Charlie Chaplin and kept ending up back in court. Spoiled movie stars who had never had to dig deep. Puking and panting, humbled as she was, Chris took comfort in her own discipline.

She had expected Kathleen to huff and puff about her coming home plastered, but she was surprisingly gentle. She set a plate of saltines, a bottle of ginger ale and a glass on the bedside table, and Chris tried to wash the alcohol through her by draining glass after glass, its mild sweet bite welcome in her foul-tasting mouth. She got up often to pee, and she vomited all day long, her face pulsing as her gut twisted and convulsed.

On Sunday afternoon, when Kathleen was in the kitchen, Chris made her way to the closet, found the remaining pills, dumped them in the toilet, and stuffed the empty bottle into an empty Kleenex box deep inside the bathroom trash.

She awoke the next morning even sicker than she'd been the day before. Dressed for work, Kathleen stood over her fretting over whether she could leave her alone. "You've really done it now, Chris. I wonder if you need to go to the hospital."

Chris closed her eyes in weak protest. And Kathleen's heart wasn't in it: it just wasn't their habit to bring in doctors, except as a last resort.

Kathleen did go to work, and Chris was sick all that day: vomiting, chilled, her head splitting. The sheets were soaked with sweat. When she could collect her thoughts, fear swarmed through her, fear that she had irreparably harmed her body, her liver or her kidneys. She slept the shallowest of sleeps, half thinking and half dreaming. In those hours of laborious mental churning, Sam came to her again and again and Chris reached out for her strenuously, rooting like a pig, making obscene keening sounds. She dreamed that her teeth were falling out, and she was tonguing the bloody gaps in her mouth. She dreamed of a *Tribune* article about a murder in her neighborhood, and when she awoke that dream confounded her for hours because she could remember reading the actual words, and knew that wasn't possible.

All afternoon she lay sweating and shivering in the dark. She couldn't stop yawning. She called for Rufus, but he came only to the bedroom door, and stood there wagging anxiously and yawning back at her, refusing to come in. Desperate for some familiar noise, she turned on the TV, then sank back into delirium to the strains of women screaming at men who denied their paternity of the women's babies. She dreamed again, busy and exhausting dreams that demanded a logical explanation for every strange detail, and corrections and shifts in direction when she couldn't figure out the logic. In one dream she looked at the stump of her pinky and noticed it was on the wrong hand; looking quickly at the other, she saw she was missing *both* pinkies. She looked away, and knew with terrible dream-knowledge that when she looked again, she would be missing *three* fingers. She awoke in tears and fumbled for the clock. It was only 4:10. She turned off the television, and for the next two hours she listened fiercely for Kathleen's return.

When Kathleen came home from work, Chris's ear, made acute by panic, heard her keys dropping on the kitchen table and the squeak of her sneakers on the kitchen floor. Her heart was thudding with dreadful impatience, and she called out weakly, again and again, like a baby seal stranded on hot sand. She was beginning to weep when Kathleen finally appeared at the bedroom door. "Kath," Chris whispered, and when she came to the bed, Chris rose and grabbed her with a sob, burying her face into her stomach.

"What's this all about?" Chris was crying and clutching her so hard she cried out, and struggled to loosen her grip. "Chris, you're hysterical." Chris smelled rank from sweat and vomit. When she let go, Kathleen patted her damp head, listening to the strangled sound of her sobs, reaching with a grimace to ease off one sneaker, then the other. She was frightened, but something was quickening in her too. "You're freezing," she said. "Let's get you into the tub."

She ran a bath, and remembering the bubble bath she'd been given by a co-worker, took it out of the closet and poured some under the faucet. She came back out to Chris. "Up up," she clucked, and Chris raised her arms so Kathleen could wrestle off her t-shirt. Kathleen felt muscled, maternal; she found it wasn't hard to lift Chris out of bed, that she knew just the right leverage. In the bathroom she took off her own clothes, and climbed into the tub after her, easing herself behind Chris into the hot water. Chris's teeth were chattering; Kathleen took a washcloth and dipped it in the water, then draped it over Chris's shoulders. She pulled Chris back against her breasts till Chris's whole torso was submerged. "There," she said. "Warmer now?" She heard Chris's ragged breath. She held her and murmured to her, ran the hot washcloth over her temples and eyes.

"Is it dark outside?" she heard Chris ask hoarsely.

"Yes," she said.

After a while she sat them both up, their bare bodies rumbling on the bathtub floor, and water sloshing over the edge of the tub. She tipped Chris's head back and ran water over it from the hand nozzle, and scrubbed shampoo into it for a long time, using her nails on Chris's scalp. She lifted Chris's arms one by one to soap her armpits. She took Chris's hand and put the bar of soap into it, closed the fingers. "Here," she said, "wash between your legs." When Chris was completely lathered, she pulled the plug from the drain, and rinsed them both off.

She handed Chris a towel, but Chris just stood there trembling with the towel in her hand, so Kathleen paced around her dripping body, rubbing between her thick thighs and under the breasts drooping over her belly. Rufus had ambled into the bathroom, and was licking Chris's wet calves. "Rufus, stop it," Kathleen snapped. The vision of Chris as a large inert woman upset her, and she hastily wrapped Chris's bathrobe around her, pulling the belt closed.

That night, Kathleen put fresh sheets on the bed, poured fluids into Chris, and fed her Cream of Wheat from a spoon. She slept a cool gentle sleep; when she awoke at dawn she saw that Chris was looking at her.

They gazed at each other in the faint dawn light. Chris's eyes were dark, almost slate, the skin under them purple. Her chin was sagging onto her hand. Kathleen remembered in half-sleep that she had worried at the beginning that she was too into Chris's looks. But now she saw that Chris would lose them so gradually, Kathleen would get used to it as it happened.

"Listen," Chris whispered. "I think I might be going through withdrawal of that drug I was taking for my back."

Kathleen frowned. It was the first rational sentence Chris had uttered in days. "You mean Percocet?"

Chris nodded.

"Damn," Kathleen said, struggling to a seated position. "Why didn't you say something?"

Chris shrugged.

"How much were you taking?"

"More than I should of," Chris said.

"How *much* more?"

"I don't know, Kath, I'm saying I took too much, every day."

"How did you get that much?"

Chris groaned and crooked her arm over her eyes. "Shh, don't shout."

"Chris, if I'm gonna help you, you have to tell me things." The more Kathleen thought about it, the more the information came as a relief; at least she knew now what was making Chris so sick. "When did it start?" Kathleen fixed her with her eyes.

Chris thought about it. "I think in January, when I was home a lot," she said. "When we started reading together."

The meaning of those words resonated around them. Kathleen shook her head. Then she had a thought. "You know what, I'm pretty sure that with narcotics you're not supposed to go off them all at once."

She watched Chris grasp the implications, and met her avid glance. "But to go off them gradually, you'd probably have to notify a doctor that you're in withdrawal," Kathleen said.

They both knew that was out of the question. Chris bit the inside of her lip and turned her face away.

Kathleen took that day off from work, and the next as well. She went to Jewel to stock up on crackers, Cream of Wheat, cans of chicken noodle soup. She lingered at the health food section, where she'd never shopped before, thinking she might be able to find a home remedy for Chris's problem. She read the bottles of so many vitamins and supplements her head spun, and she began to suspect they were just a big marketing scam. Finally, though, she bought a bottle of St. John's Wort, remembering a health segment she'd seen about it on the local news. Maybe, she thought, Chris could use it as a substitute for the Percocet, as a mild and natural mood elevator. She was proud of her ingenuity, and as she paid for her groceries, her heart rose as buoyantly as it had the first years of their relationship, when she couldn't wait to get home.

She spent the next two days in bed knitting and watching TV, Chris curled beside her and Rufus asleep on the floor, the room dark and close. From time to time she dozed, and awoke feeling as lazy and powerful as a lion. How had they come to this point? she wondered, looking at her quivering lover and curling her warm feet around Chris's cold ones. Something was coursing through her, sweet and clear. If someone had told her that Chris would be out of work and battling the DTs, and that it would not be one of the worst moments in Kathleen's life — far from it, really — she would never have believed it.

The phone rang and rang in the hall, and they let the machine take it. When Kathleen played the messages back, she found two messages from Anna Singer, and promptly erased them.

Anna had the following nightmare: She was on her way to visit Star, and left later than she thought she should. She pulled into a gas station to buy a bag of Smartfood and a Butterfingers. When she came out, she couldn't find her car, so she kept asking people to direct her to the Citgo station, until she ended up in a dark room, a huge Citgo sign blaring like a freakishly huge moon through the open window.

Star called that morning as Anna was getting ready for work, and Anna told her she had had a dream about getting lost.

"Where were you going?"

"To visit you," Anna said.

There was a pause. "*Oy vey,*" Star said.

After they hung up, Anna thought: *Citgo.* Did they even have Citgo stations in Chicago? Sit? Go? Smart or Butterfingers? The wordplay brought to her face a faint smile. But then the idea surged toward her that she had waited too long to break up with Star. She had finally capitulated to going to a party full of Star's friends on Saturday night — all of them lesbians, a boisterous mix of lawyers and P.E. teachers — and they had welcomed Anna by appraising and teasing her. The whole time she had felt like a terrible person, knowing that the very lesbian who was wringing her hand and telling her how much she loved Star and how happy Star seemed would soon come to regard Anna as a total loser. They spent the night at Star's and had drunken, woozy sex, and

Sunday morning Star brought her a steaming cup of cappuccino in bed. How could she leave Star now? — this woman who had opened her heart to loving Anna when Anna was putting out only about 50% of her charm, who had shown her that being loved shouldn't require an effort to be loved. And now Anna was about to devastate her. For Anna there was a powerful ethical distinction, a legacy of her father's suicide, between those who left and those who were left. It was almost unbearable to think of herself as the jerk who tramples on a woman's heart. And yet, she could no longer let this go on, when she knew she was never going to fall in love with Star.

That evening, feeling a sense of urgency, Anna called Star and set up a date for the next evening. Star's voice was cautious, and several times Anna got the feeling that she was about to blurt out a critical question, only to rein herself in. "I'll see you tomorrow," Anna said over and over in a voice meant to be hypnotically reassuring, realizing even as the words came that Star was likely hearing, "That's the only certain thing I can offer you."

The next evening Anna dressed in clothes she could hunker down in, but which weren't so casual they would be insulting to Star, giving her the impression that Anna didn't care at all what she thought of her. She drove over to Star's with her heart in her throat. She had NPR on in the background, and the moment her attention drifted to it, the interviewer was saying, "Tell me about the cotton that grows in those riverbeds." She snorted. Patricia used to drawl, at moments like that: "It really is *all* things considered, isn't it!" See, Anna thought: now *she* was funny.

As she let Anna in, Star's face was stark and shut, as though Anna was a last-minute customer coming in at closing time. She had just returned from a run, and was wearing training pants and a t-shirt with an unzipped hooded sweatshirt over it. She turned her back on Anna and walked into the kitchen. Anna followed, noticing her strong leggy stride with rueful appreciation.

In the tiny kitchen, Star had cracked two eggs into a bowl, and she had the kettle on. She fussed at the sink while Anna nosed around in the cabinet for a clean mug, moving aside the Chicago Gay, Lesbian, Bisexual and Transgender Pride March mug and settling instead on a Chicago Gay, Lesbian, Bisexual and Transgender Film Festival mug that was a more pleasing size and heft. Anna dropped a tea bag in and added hot water and sugar, casting anxious glances at Star's back. Finally Star turned, wiping her hands deliberately with a dish towel.

"Star," Anna said, her eyes big and her face tight.

Star waited.

"I think we have to break up."

Star's face suffused with tears; it was the news she had evidently been preparing herself for. "Say the truth," she said. "We don't have to break up, you are breaking up with me."

"I'm breaking up with you," Anna said.

Star began to cry, without trying to cover her face. "Why?" she asked.

Anna was stricken. She had thought she'd be able to improvise this breakup, but it was becoming clear that she couldn't. For this was the question she didn't know how to answer; she just couldn't imagine telling someone who loved her that she didn't love her back. "Star," she said, stupidly. And then reached for the only thing she could think to say: "I'm not ready, I'm obviously not over Patricia."

Star cast her a brooding tearful look. "You know," she said, "for whatever reason, I don't think you're capable of loving anybody."

"That's not true," Anna began to object, and then suddenly wondered about the protocol of this argument, wondered whether it was more ethical to just let Star believe that, so that she could despise Anna and move on. How despicable was Anna willing to be made out to be? Anna's mind, after its instinctive recoil from the prospect of not being liked, buzzed around this question, until finally she decided: *somewhat* despicable.

Star was nodding with knowing bitterness, as though she had told Anna a piercing truth about herself that Anna couldn't handle. Anna saw it, but held herself back from arguing, sat stolidly, prepared to take her punishment like a man. But Star wheeled and walked into the bedroom. When Anna got there she found her flung on her back, her arm crooked over her eyes, crying. She was trying to say something, but the words were unintelligible, punctuated with sobs and hiccups. Anna heard: "I don't know what you want me to be."

Anna looked down at her, stricken. "Star," she said. She wanted to say "honey," but at the last moment decided that using an endearment would be giving a mixed message. "Star, it's not that, who you are is wonderful."

"I'm not femme enough for you," Star said.

"Oh my God no," Anna said, aghast.

"It scared you, how I fucked you, didn't it." The words came out in a spray of tears and spit. "You wanted a nice obedient woman on her back, and you just couldn't take it yourself."

"I loved how you fucked me," Anna protested.

Star sat up, her eyes growing hard. "You did not. You had to humiliate me back, by tying me up."

Anna blinked. "What?"

"It was humiliating," Star said brutally. "It was like rape. I haven't even been able tell my therapist about it."

Dismay and shame flooded over Anna so wildly she had to sit down. Star was just trying to hurt her, she told herself; she was just trying to hurt her. She said, "Star, don't. You don't want to do this."

"Do what?" Star demanded. "It's the truth."

"No it's not."

"Then *why?*"

Anna looked at Star, at a loss. Was it wrong not to tell her the truth, as much as that would hurt?

"I'm just not ready to be involved with somebody," she said.

Star reached for a Kleenex and blew her nose. "It's just," she wavered, "that this really speaks to my abandonment issues."

Anna nodded sympathetically, knowing that Star was referring to her parents' divorce. She was relieved that Star was turning away from the whole rape thing, and sorry that Star's thundering cliché made it that much easier to break up with her. "I'm so sorry," she said.

They sat cross-legged on the bed for a few moments. Finally Star said, in a flat nasal voice, "You'll never find somebody who loves you as much as I do."

Oh yes I will, Anna thought; and made a mental note to pay attention to that confidence in the future.

After a decent interval Anna managed to maneuver herself out the door, officially broken up with Star. She gave Star a bear hug on her way out; Star was stiff in her arms, her shirt damp and cold, and Anna could feel the slime of tears on her cheek. In the car she took a deep breath, and exhaled shakily. It took her a few moments to start the engine and drive off. She drove with extra care, and went over to Janice and Terry's.

Janice welcomed her in, and led her into the living room. Anna's battered sensibilities gratefully took in the woody warmth of the room, its light-colored furniture; she had always felt comfortable here, and that comfort made her teary. "You broke it off," Terry said from her seat in front of the television, glimpsing Anna's ashen face.

"Yeah," Anna said.

Janice turned, arrested by the waver in her voice. "Oh honey," she said. She found the remote control on the couch next to Terry and turned off the TV, giving Terry a deliberate look.

Terry gave her a look back and turned obediently toward Anna. "How'd she take it?"

"Pretty hard," Anna said, sitting down on the couch. Janice sat down at the edge of the chair opposite. "I feel so bad. She really loved me." Her eyes welled up again.

"She really did," Janice said warmly. "It was lovely how she gave herself over to you."

Anna nodded, her eyes bright with crisis. "It feels awfully arrogant, like bad karma, to turn my nose up at love. I'm giving this up and getting nothing in return. How many more times will someone offer herself to me that way?" Terry sniffed in recognition and nodded. "It's so strange," Anna continued. "On the one hand, she knew exactly what I wanted. And on the other, she wasn't acute enough to really know me. I felt as though she was loving somebody who didn't necessarily bear much resemblance to me."

"You're saying she was a good fuck, but nothing more," Terry said, never one to waste time and mental effort on excessive nuance.

Anna regarded her with annoyance. "I was trying to express something a little more fine-tuned than that," she said.

"Whatever," Terry replied. She was in a provoking mood. "So tell me something," she said, stretching out her legs on the coffee table. "She wasn't a femme, was she? If you ask me, she was kind of a bruiser."

"Terry!" Janice exclaimed, shooting a horrified glance toward Anna.

"What?" Terry said. "I'm just asking."

Embarrassed by Janice's response, Anna shrugged, determined to stand up calmly to Terry's fighting words. "How can I account for how I see another's gender?" she ventured. "To me, she was a bruiser who, at my touch, melted into femininity." She looked keenly at Terry, refusing to blush. "Not to brag."

Terry laughed. "Of course not."

"Or sometimes she was just a big ol' bruiser and I was her fag lover. Or sometimes her genders were at war, and she needed me to help put her at rest." Or sometimes, she thought, Star was big and strong and Anna was a little girl. Never a woman, but sometimes a girl.

Or sometimes, apparently, she was Star's rapist. That was just breakup talk, she told herself, talk designed to hurt her back.

Terry sat back and stared at her with disbelief. Janice had gotten up from her chair wondering where the cat was. Anna looked down at her chewed-over cuticles, narrowing her eyes and trying valiantly to focus. There were certain arguments, she thought, that you didn't have to get into if you didn't want. Especially when feeling so sad. She looked up, just as Janice reentered the room holding Jake in her arms, her chin buried in his fur. "You know what, Terry," Anna said. "I don't feel like arguing with you. I don't notice you ever having to justify *your* sex life. What's *that* like? Who are *you* to other women?" She narrowed her eyes. "I peg you as a vanilla egalitarian type, with a dollop of enraged sadism held at bay, but coming out in small cruelties you can't quite control.

Would that be accurate?" She knew it was accurate from certain hints Janice had given out over time.

Janice, who had been about to sit down, stopped in her tracks.

"Okay," Terry said uncomfortably, "You don't have to be an asshole."

"*I* don't have to be an asshole!" Anna laughed, flushed, realizing she'd wanted to accost Terry this way for years. "You started it! And furthermore, I'm feeling kind of sad right now. So you could lay off."

Janice sat down next to Terry and plopped the cat in her lap. "Okay," Terry said, looking down at a blinking Jake as though wondering what he was doing there. "Forget about it."

Anna sat back and folded her arms. Terry had some bone to pick with her, it was clear; maybe she wasn't happy that Anna was on the loose again. The thought made Anna a little more complacent. She was going to turn the conversation back to Star, but she was quickly realizing that breaking up with somebody didn't warrant a ton of sympathetic attention from friends. "Anyway," she said. "How are you guys doing?"

Terry and Janice looked at each other, then Janice laughed and leaned forward and ran a finger down Terry's cheek. "Terry's mad at me because I got appointed graduate field representative for next year, and she thinks that'll be too much work when I have a book to finish."

Anna frowned. "It *will* be, won't it? Don't they give that job to people who already have tenure? Doesn't that put you in charge of graduate admissions?"

"Yeah," Janice said, visibly relieved to change the topic. "But it's a long story." As she told it to Anna over the next half hour, it involved a series of senior colleagues going through gothic life crises, and some algorithm of obligation by which Janice had no choice but to assume the position. After a few minutes Anna's eyes glazed over and she stopped listening, the thought of her own stalled career rearing up and blocking everything else out. She was thirty-two years old, and had no book, no real job, no money, and no girlfriend. How the hell had that happened, to a person who was smart, ambitious, loving?

Janice's face was pale and beautiful with heroic resolve. Anna

JUDITH FRANK

glanced several times at Terry, knowing that she must want to kill her. Man, she thought, her wacky friends. Without Star, this was what was left.

She was so engrossed in the drama of breaking up with someone for the first time in her life, it kept slipping from Anna's mind that she needed to follow up on Chris. But by Wednesday, when Chris hadn't shown up for three days, she finally called her house, because at Pathways, if a student missed more than five classes in a row without some kind of reasonable excuse, he or she was suspended for a month. The idea was that they could use that time to weigh their commitment to their studies, and that only those who committed in earnest would return. She was reluctant to call Chris at home, certain that it would make Chris feel intruded upon, and thinking irritably that Chris was probably just sulking because her girlfriend had been nice to Anna. But she had to call: she had let Chris's absence go on for too long.

Her stomach churned as the phone rang, and she was relieved to get the answering machine. The message was minimalist, in Chris's voice, gruffness trying to sound friendly, and instead sounding like a caustic parody of friendliness, or like the friendliness of an autistic person who's been coached how to mimic human emotion. Anna left her home phone number and asked Chris to call.

But Chris didn't. On Thursday, Anna got home and checked her machine: still no call. It occurred to her that if she called at night she'd be more likely to reach somebody, so she picked up the phone and called Chris again, and again got the machine. "Hey Chris," she said. "Hey Kathleen. It's Anna Singer again. I'm kind of worried about Chris. Could you give me a call as soon as possible and let me know what's going on?" When she hung up she had a brief moment of dissatisfaction with the message: she had portrayed her worry as personal, and had failed to convey that Chris was required to report to her. Irritated with herself, she considered calling back, but decided that that would look too neurotic and incompetent.

On Thursday afternoon, after Chris failed to show for the fourth day in a row, Anna stopped in Renée's office.

"How many days has she missed?" Renée asked, rummaging through some papers on her desk.

"All week," Anna said, and felt an apprehensive dive in her stomach.

Renée looked up abruptly. "For God's sake, Anna, why didn't you say something?"

"I've been calling her house and leaving messages, but she hasn't called back."

"Anna," Renée said, "You know the rule. You needed to let me know. I might have to suspend her."

Anna opened her mouth to justify herself, but then closed it. She didn't know what to say. She had meant to tell her; how could she describe the blur of knowing-and-yet-forgetting that had prevented her from doing so all week? She had simply let it slide, letting Chris's absence be obscured by Brandy's hospitalization, and her own personal dramas of Patricia and Star and the reviewers' reports on her book. And then there was her antagonism toward Chris, her temptation to let her be screwed by her own refusal to be helped. That realization came pulsing hotly into Anna's face, and promptly backfired into anger at Chris and at Renée, before whom she always seemed to be standing like a guilty child, trying to explain herself.

"I've been trying to reach her," she said with angry haughtiness.

Renée raised one eyebrow at Anna's tone. Anna maintained dogged eye contact. "Anna," Renée said, "You're going to have to reach her." She raised her voice and continued as Anna opened her mouth to protest. "It's the right policy to suspend students for missing a lot of class, but we need to give them every chance to account for themselves. I want you to do whatever it takes to give Chris that chance."

Anna took off her glasses and rubbed her eyes. "Where does she live?" she asked. "Somewhere in Lakeview, isn't it?"

Renée bent and opened her file cabinet, removed Chris's file and wrote the address on a slip of paper. She offered it to Anna, then snatched her hand back as Anna was about to grasp the paper. "I want you to report back to me this weekend," Renée told her.

Anna nodded. Renée held out the slip again and Anna gave her a look, then reached out and plucked it from her hand.

"Goodbye," Renée called loudly as Anna stalked out of the office, in a teaching-Anna-some-manners voice. "Have a good weekend."

Anna had wondered how Chris could afford to live in Lakeview, but later that afternoon, as she wound westward on the small one-way streets west of Whole Foods and the Y, she began to get the picture. Chris and Kathleen's house was as far west in Lakeview as you could get, far from the fashionable area along the lake nicknamed Boys' Town, right on the El tracks off of Ravenswood that ran on a small grass hill only slightly above street level. Their block was a hodgepodge of styles, unsightly to Anna's eyes: sagging clapboard houses with peeling paint, a few dying businesses — auto parts and dry cleaners — and scattered among them, freshly-renovated apartment buildings sporting immaculate siding, with signs in front advertising expensive one- and two-bedroom condos with wood floors, fireplaces, and every conceivable kitchen amenity. And right near the tracks, yellow-brown brick ranches and split-levels like one sees all over Chicago, with iron railings up the concrete front steps and an old-fashioned awning over the one picture window facing the front — houses that are improved and impeccably landscaped in the suburbs, and squat and densely-packed and exhaust-darkened on the major thoroughfares. Chris and Kathleen lived in one of those houses, the last on the block. Good for them, Anna thought. Someday somebody would buy this modest and unprepossessing house for a lot of money and add another floor to it, with two bedrooms, two bathrooms, and an exercise room or a hot tub.

Anna pulled up and parked. Okay, she thought, opening the door and heaving herself onto the street, yanking down the bottom of her leather jacket. She could hear the sound of hammering in the distance, and a big dog barking a few houses down. The sky was white, the trees sparse, although a young elm had been planted on Chris and Kathleen's small patch of lawn. Through their front window Anna could see that it was dark and still inside. She walked up the front steps and rang the doorbell next to the big black mailbox, which was marked with their names on a strip of masking tape.

There was no answer. She rang once more, worried about hassling them if they were in fact inside: maybe somebody was sick, or they were having a fight, or a meal.

But the house remained still. Anna turned in relief, thinking there was still time to sneak away; nobody would know she'd been there, and it wouldn't be her fault that she couldn't reach Chris. Then she caught sight of a woman trudging up the street in a coat and white sneakers, with a plastic bag of groceries in each hand and a purse slung over her shoulder. She walked down the street toward her with her hands in her pockets.

"Hello," she said as she approached. "Anna, remember?"

"Of course," Kathleen said crisply, with no token of surprise. "Hello."

Anna reached out for one of the bags, which was full of plastic bottles of Jewel-brand ginger ale. "Can I take that?"

"No, I'm fine."

It was a rebuff, Anna thought, because the bags were clearly cutting into Kathleen's hands. "I came because...." Anna said, and hesitated: "Did you get my messages?"

"Yes," Kathleen replied, trudging up the steps and fumbling for her key. She opened the door onto a dark hallway, gestured for Anna to come in, put the grocery bag on the floor and started flipping on lights. She walked down the small flight of stairs to the sunken living room, peered at the thermostat, muttered to herself and adjusted it. She faced Anna with a look of studied agnosticism. "You'll have to discuss it with Chris," she told her, picking up the grocery bags and disappearing with them into the kitchen.

"Oh!" Anna said, absorbing the information that Kathleen was angry at her. It was surprising; just a week ago Kathleen had been openly flirting with her. Anna stood uncomfortably in the small foyer with her jacket on, something preventing her from following Kathleen into the kitchen. A series of scenarios galloped through her mind:

Chris had decided to quit school, Chris had suffered a catastrophic beating, Chris and Kathleen had broken up, Chris had skipped town. Anna stood there feeling like a fool, unzipping her jacket as though preparing to stay for a while, then zipping it back up. In the carpeted living room, in the dreary late-afternoon light, she saw a couch and recliner aimed toward the large television. With the exception of two coasters the coffee table was bare, and the room was bare of books; on the walls hung a single picture, a Monet print in a cheap black frame, crooked by just a few degrees. There was a closed cabinet containing a hodgepodge of trophies and figurines. It seemed to Anna like a home that had been settled into and tended, but not recently — a home whose aged occupant has died and whose children haven't yet broken it up.

Kathleen emerged to hang her coat in the front closet, and looked surprised that Anna was still there. What the hell? Anna thought; a minute ago she had acted as though she'd been expecting Anna's visit all along. "Is she home?" Anna asked.

"Oh, she's home," Kathleen snorted enigmatically from inside the closet. She turned toward Anna and Anna's fingers went again to her jacket zipper, but stopped when she saw that Kathleen hadn't brought out a hanger to offer her. "She's been sick," Kathleen said, a strange private amusement or hostility playing on her face. "You can go on back and see her if you'd like." She gestured toward the bedroom.

Anna glanced down the hall; all the doors were closed. "What does she have?"

Kathleen looked at her challengingly. "Some kind of flu," she said, like a teenager offering up an insultingly blatant lie. It was an unpleasant effect on a middle-aged face, and all of Anna's courtly feelings for her vanished at once.

"Aha," Anna said.

"Go on back," Kathleen insisted. "It's that door on the right."

Anna was balking. "Don't you want to tell her I'm here first?"

Kathleen waved a hand. "Nah," she said breezily, "It's fine, she'll be glad to see you." She walked toward the kitchen, saying over her shoulder, "I'll be in the kitchen."

Anna stood in the foyer looking down the gloomy hallway at the four closed doors. She did not relish walking in on Chris, but Kathleen had signaled that she was finished talking with her, and she couldn't just leave without getting to the bottom of Chris's absences. She walked down the hall and knocked lightly on the first door on the right. There was no response. "Chris?" she called into the door's crack, then turned the handle gingerly and peeked into the darkness, where she was greeted by a mop sitting in a pail and other cleaning supplies, and the pungent smell of Pine Sol.

She closed the door in a hurry and glanced back toward the kitchen. "Kath?" She heard Chris's voice, muffled and wavering, in the next room. She knocked on the door and called out, "Chris? It's Anna Singer. Kathleen told me it was okay to come say hello?"

There was a long silence.

Anna opened the door a crack and peeked around it, smiling a frozen smile that felt stupid and painful. "Hi," she said. "Kathleen told me to come on in." She opened it and entered the room. It was illuminated only by the tiny television on the dresser, next to which glinted a tray with moisturizer and perfumes, and scattered earrings. The air was close; the smell of Chris's body odor hit her, and the fake citrus smell of deodorizer from the bathroom. Chris lay slack and slumped on a mess of pillows, in a wrinkled t-shirt, her bare feet and hairy calves sticking out of covers she'd kicked aside. Chris seemed not to have registered her presence; Anna approached, inserting herself cautiously into her field of vision, her stomach tight with anxiety. Finally Chris's eyes wavered toward her, and Anna held her breath, and they caught her gaze.

"Hi Chris," Anna enunciated, over the TV's low flicker and blather. "Kathleen told me to come in."

Chris struggled to straighten up. Her eyes were haggard and yellow. Anna watched her, hands thrust in her jacket pockets, puzzling over what she was seeing. "What's happened to you?" she finally asked.

Chris pulled out a pillow, punched and plumped it weakly and stuffed it back behind her. Emptied of ferocity, she moved with the frail deliberation of an old person, which distressed Anna and frightened her. She thought of the strange friendly voice on Chris's answering machine message, and wondered whether Chris had a mental illness she wasn't aware of.

When Chris finally spoke, her voice was low and dry. "Didn't Kathleen tell you?"

"Not really," Anna said, reminding herself of a police detective who has separated the two suspects in the hopes that they'll blurt out different stories.

"It's a terrible flu," Chris said. "But I think I'm getting better."

"That's good," Anna said. "Have you been to the doctor?"

Chris looked vaguely in her direction. "No," she finally said, adding after a moment, "Do I have to?

"Here are the rules, Chris." Anna paused and waited for Chris's eyes to meet hers. Talking to Chris was just like talking to Brandy, she was so flaccid and addled; Anna felt a rush of impatience and anger. "You need to either show up Monday," she said clearly, and more angrily than she'd intended, "or produce a note from your doctor saying why you've been absent for so long."

Chris sighed and nodded.

"Or else they'll have to suspend you for a month."

"Okay," Chris said.

"Okay what?" Anna asked in exasperation. "Do you think you'll show up on Monday? Do you think you can get a doctor's note? I've been calling and calling trying to get you to respond, so it wouldn't come to this."

Chris sat up and regarded her keenly, the Chris Anna recognized. "I'll take care of it one way or another."

Anna stood and stared at her, and finally nodded. "Okay," she said. "Did you get what I said about them suspending you?"

"Yup," Chris said crisply.

Anna bit her lip. "Because it would really be a shame, Chris, you've come so far. With another year or so, you'd be reading your tail off."

Chris closed her eyes. Anna stood there with her hands in her pockets till she considered herself dismissed. "I hope I'll see you soon," she said, and left the room.

Anna closed the door softly, her heart pounding. She couldn't wait to get out of there. Walking quickly down the dim hallway, she contemplated poking her head into the kitchen, where she heard Kathleen running the faucet, to make sure that Pathway's rules were heard by a fully sentient person. But she didn't; she couldn't face what she somehow knew would be a look of glittering enigma and triumph on Kathleen's face, the message *See? See what I'm living with?* Anna slipped silently out the front door, took the front steps two at a time and walked quickly to her car. For whatever reason, Kathleen had wanted her to see Chris looking pathetic and deranged. She hated Kathleen. She got in, started the engine and drove away.

She had planned to head straight to the gym, but what she had seen at Chris and Kathleen's house, and the dead weight of this leaden Thursday afternoon, produced in Anna a trembling sense of dread, and she turned the car toward home instead, speeding up onto the tail of a driver who had pulled unhurriedly into her path from a side street, and tailgating her punishingly. When she got home she threw herself on her bed, kicking her shoes off with frenzied impatience, trying to cry and choking instead, drawing her legs up to her chest. She couldn't rid herself of the image of Chris, her hair dank on her forehead, her face pasty and wasted. It was one thing for Brandy to look like that, another for this warrior to be brought so incomprehensibly low. Anna lay there in her clothes and shoes, her hatches battened down, drifting in and out of chilly sleep for several hours, till she awoke so cold she had to rise. She would take a hot bath.

But first there was an obligation to fulfill, and that was calling Renée to report on her visit to Chris's house. As it rang she fretted for a few moments with irrational ferocity over whether she would be recognizable as "Anna" or whether she needed to identify herself as "Anna Singer." When Renée answered, Anna said quickly, covering the bases, "Hi Renée, it's Anna calling, about Chris Rinaldi."

"Yes, Anna," Renée said. "Did you go over there?"

"I did," Anna said. "And I'm not sure what to tell you." She described Kathleen's strange evasive hostility, the dubious claim that what Chris had was a bad flu, Chris's dissociation. "It's hard to explain how out of it she was," Anna said, her voice suddenly shaky.

Renée was quiet.

"Chris said she'd take care of it," Anna continued, her voice now even. "I don't know what that means, whether she plans to get a doctor's note or to show up on Monday, or to blow us off altogether. But I made it clear what's required."

After a pause, Renée said, "You know, I wonder whether what you were seeing had something to do with drugs."

There was a long pause on Anna's end. "How so?"

"It's just a hunch, and I probably shouldn't speculate, but when students disappear inexplicably there are often — maybe not often, but regularly enough — drugs involved. And her disorientation...."

Anna's mind revolted against that idea; Renée was being rote, she thought, her experience limiting the range of her imagination. "I can't imagine someone like Chris on drugs. Her whole self-image is wrapped around her self-control."

"Maybe you're right, Anna," Renée replied, "But I've seen a lot of this kind of thing."

When they hung up, Anna started a bath. The more she thought about it the more she believed Renée's interpretive range was limited from over-exposure to indigent people. Chris wasn't like them. But Anna's mind was too keen and experienced to hold that thought for more than a few minutes, before its lame self-delusion became apparent to her. Her father had been a drug addict carrying on a medical practice. Anna held her fingers under the faucet till the water scalded them, then adjusted the temperature and added bubble bath, as a series of thoughts shifted into place. Was that what she had been seeing in Chris? The panic that had made her flee their house — that panic — it was so funny, she thought, even as it rose again and flailed against the current of her breathing, how decades later she could still be knocked off her feet by someone's oblivious glance failing to meet her own. Anna took off her clothes with trembling fingers, and stepped gingerly into the hot and foaming water.

C H A P T E R   S E V E N T E E N

By Saturday Chris was starting to feel better. Kathleen had her up on the stripped bed with a tray of soft-boiled eggs and toast on her lap, and stood beside her with crossed arms as she ate. She had moved through the bedroom like a tornado earlier that morning, straightening and dusting and stripping the bed and throwing the bedclothes in the wash. "How's that going down?" she asked now, with a probing look. From the next room the dryer sounded like the ocean.

Chris nodded, chewing on a spoonful of egg. Her hair was wet from showering, and she was wearing sweatpants and a faded Northwestern sweatshirt. Her face was haggard, but being free from nausea made her feel almost euphoric.

"Good," Kathleen said. "I think you're through the acute phase of withdrawal." She had been talking discreetly with Joanne next door. She and Chris now understood that Chris had gone about her withdrawal all wrong, that you were supposed to go off Percocet gradually and that there were even drugs that could help temper the symptoms. But what else was new, Chris thought, hearing that; it was just like the emergency exits whose alarms she'd set off by walking through them, or the furniture she'd assembled ass-backwards without the benefit of instructions. In the end, you might screw up, but you still got outside, and you still got an assembled table or TV cart. She could afford to be philosophical about it now, with her gut still and her body scrubbed, and the mellow salty taste of egg yolk in her mouth.

"But we can't get complacent," Kathleen warned, sitting on the bed. "In a way, you're through the easy part. The hard part is staying off it."

Chris shrugged. "Where am I gonna get it, Kath?" she asked wearily.

"Well you've seen all those ER episodes where people come into the ER pretending to have migraines and such."

Chris looked at her and saw that she wasn't joking. "Yeah, I'm for sure gonna wander into the ER! Me and hospitals, we're like this." She held up two fingers pressed tightly together.

"This is not a laughing matter," Kathleen said.

Chris mopped up egg yolk with the last piece of toast, and chewed it without looking at Kathleen. Some kind of crazy energy for imagining problems and how to solve them had been unleashed in Kathleen, and it was making Chris dizzy. She knew it was tied in with the fantastic care Kathleen had been giving her, so it wasn't right to knock it. But she was hungry and calm and clean for the first time in days now, and she didn't feel like making her mind race into this and that dire scenario.

"Are you done with that?" Kathleen asked. Chris handed her the tray; she was taking it out of the room when she stopped and turned. "Oh, I forgot," she said. "Keith called last night, and wants you to call him back. He says it's important."

Left alone, Chris looked at the clock on the bedside table. It was early; she still might catch Keith at home. She reached for the phone and dialed, but got the machine. She put the phone down and sank back into the pillows. The brief sense of well-being she'd had had dissipated, and she felt suddenly clenched and clawing. She stared ahead of her, bewildered, while every bright and savory thing – the morning light, the taste in her mouth, the faint smell of Dove emanating off her body – withered and turned to ashes. She thought: *so this is how it's gonna be.*

Keith called back that afternoon. "Margaret says you're under the weather!" he yelled into the phone through a roar of background noise.

"Yeah," Chris said loudly, and coughed, her voice rusty. She had been napping, and the noise was inexpressibly jarring. "What the fuck's that noise?"

"They're sanding down some beams," he shouted. "Hang on!"

There was the sound of muffled thunder as Keith cupped his hand over the phone; after a few moments, his voice came back clearly. "That better?"

"Yeah," Chris said. "What's up?"

"Chris, there's this contractor I know, Jason Paciorek. His business has been growing too much for him to handle alone, so he's looking to hire a project manager. You know, someone who can take charge of a couple of his jobs, and help him out."

Chris sat up, hardly able to make sense of what Keith was saying, it seemed to come from a world so far away from the desert island she'd been inhabiting for the past week.

"He's a real crunchy type – big lesbian clientele, goes down to Guatemala with Habitat for Humanity and such."

Lesbian clientele? Chris tried to pay attention.

"Don't you think you'd be perfect for the job?" Keith was saying. "Think about it: a job where you could use all your skills only it's not manual labor, it's brainier than that. I told him all about you, Chris: how much experience you have in all aspects of building, what a strong work ethic you have, how you're tough enough to work in a man's world but can talk to women. Of course, I had to hide the small problem of your personality, seeing as you'd have to be, uh, personable." He giggled. "But hell, you could change your whole personality for a job like that, couldn't you?"

"Piss off, Egg."

"Anyway, I gotta go, but I wanted to tell you I gave him your number. His name is Jason Paciorek, and he's gonna call, okay?"

"You gave him my number?"

Keith hesitated. "Yeah," he said. "I hope that's okay."

"Sure, thanks," she said, her chest constricting. She felt as though if she didn't get off the phone that very moment she'd faint.

Man, she thought after she'd hung up, Keith didn't know what he was messing with. Chris slept fitfully the rest of the day, and when she was awoken at nine by Kathleen's coming to bed and realized that Jason

Paciorek hadn't called, she was relieved, thinking he might have had second thoughts about hiring someone. On Sunday she awoke with Kathleen breathing regularly beside her, and looked over at her, taking notice of the fact that after a long while, they were once more sharing a bed. It came to her with an sudden unpleasant jolt that Anna Singer had been in this room too. Or had she dreamed it? Chris turned her mind away from the idea with the thought that she couldn't afford to dwell on it. Tomorrow she had to get up and go back to school before they kicked her out. She remembered something Kathleen had told her yesterday: that Dennis had called, and would be out for a while because his mother had broken her hip, and he was taking her to rehab and trying to get her into a nursing home. She felt bad for him and also for herself, because she knew that his goofy affection would have eased her transition back to school.

A pang passed over her, a kind of aching nostalgia for the week that had passed. That struck her as perverse; for God's sake, she'd been in drug withdrawal. *Get over it,* she told herself. It was time to get over it. Even as she had that thought, she was seized by a wild craving, and her mind shot to all the places in the house where there might be a forgotten pill.

She moaned and turned toward Kathleen, rolling her by the shoulder so she was facing away from Chris. Kathleen turned easily and scooted backwards till she was snugly spooned. Chris draped her arm over her and lay breathing into her shoulder blade, trying forcibly to turn her mind away from wanting the drug, and toward this job. When you thought about it, Keith was right, it was the perfect thing. The only problem was reading, and what she could get away with. She tried to anticipate what she might be called upon to read. Trade catalogues? Contracts?

After a while Kathleen awoke and turned. She put her hand on Chris's cheek, scooted closer, and kissed her softly on the lips.

Chris felt her lips, and smelled her morning breath. Up this close, Kathleen had four eyes and two mouths. "Tomorrow I gotta get back to school," Chris said quietly.

Kathleen stiffened, and then pulled away. "You can't," she said. "You can't hardly shower and dress yourself."

Chris laughed. "Give me a break, Kath, I can too."

Kathleen threw back the covers and got out of bed. She went into the kitchen and returned with a small glass of orange juice and Chris's St. John's Wort. She was giving Chris the silent treatment. "What did I do?" Chris demanded, but Kathleen just marched into the bathroom and turned on the shower.

And then the call came. The moment he asked for her Chris knew it was Jason Paciorek, and her hand began to tremble. She asked him to hold on, and got up to close the bathroom door so she could hear him over the noise of the shower. "Hello," she said when she returned to the bed. She was breathless.

As he explained to her why he was calling, Chris noted that he had a nice speaking voice, warmly masculine. He laughed about the building boom, and pretended to be exasperated by all the money flying around. He told her that he'd heard good things about her from Keith. Then his voice became businesslike. "I need someone," he said, "to take care of three to four projects at a time, coordinating the subs and serving as the contact person with the client. I, of course, would meet daily with you, probably twice a day at the beginning."

"Right," Chris said.

"So does that sound like something you'd be interested in?"

"Absolutely," Chris said.

"Good!" he said. "I have to tell you, I do have another person interested, so I'd like to interview the two of you. Does that sit okay with you?"

Chris's heart sank at the thought of having to hustle for this job. "Sure," she replied. "When would you like to meet?"

Chris heard him mumble to himself as he thumbed through his date book, then answer a question someone in the background was asking him. He laughed self-consciously. "My calendar is so full I don't even have time to interview an assistant this week! Oh wait, how about this coming Thursday? Say 2 pm?"

"That's fine," Chris said.

"And you might want to bring a résumé. Just so I can glance over where you're coming from."

Chris caught the word *résumé* and committed it fiercely to memory. "You bet," she said.

You bet, she mocked herself as she hung up the phone. *Right, sure, absolutely, fine!* She sat on the edge of the bed thinking scalding thoughts about her performance on the telephone. That other person would just have to string two sentences together and they'd get the job. And the thing is, she had really liked Jason Paciorek, a thing she couldn't say about most people.

Résumé. It sounded French.

The shower stopped, and Kathleen came out in her bathrobe, toweling her hair. Chris watched her contemplatively.

Kathleen looked at her. "What," she snapped.

"That call was from a contractor Keith knows, who wants to interview me for a job."

Kathleen frowned. "As a sub?"

"No," Chris said, "As a project manager. I'd be in *charge* of the subs. Or some of them, anyway."

Kathleen stopped drying her hair and let her hands fall to her sides, the towel grazing the floor. "Wow," she said.

Chris watched with satisfaction as it sank in, then wondered how they had gotten here, to this point where Kathleen was surprised whenever Chris succeeded. It hadn't always been that way. Kathleen had always had great confidence in her ability to provide. Once Chris had lost a job at a confectioner's factory with lucrative overtime, and despite Chris's raging anxiety about paying the bills, and her best efforts to make Kathleen feel that anxiety too, Kathleen had persisted in taking it in stride. "Aren't you worried?" Chris had demanded. And Kathleen had touched her cheek and said "Darling, we'll be okay, you always land on your feet."

But sitting on the bed with Kathleen blinking at her like an owl, Chris suddenly wondered what Kathleen had meant by that. Land on your feet: that didn't mean she was good at stuff, it just meant she was lucky.

"Do you think you'll need to be able to read?" Kathleen asked.

"I'm not sure. Probably at least a little."

"Well it's worth a try," she said unconvincingly.

"Yeah," Chris said.

"Although…" Kathleen's face grew red with what Chris imagined to be the strain of trying to be supportive, and then failing. "I just don't want to see you set yourself up for a fall."

She arrived early at school the next day, hoping to catch Anna before class. She had looked up *résumé* in the dictionary, and with a great deal of difficulty — she spent at least twenty minutes on the word *résumé*, which meant a new beginning — she had figured out that it was a summary of previous job experience. Jason Paciorek wanted to know what other jobs she had had in her life.

The question of who could help her had required some tortured thought. She couldn't ask Dennis, because he had enough on his plate. And not Kathleen, no way: she had already given a huge vote of no-confidence, and damned if Chris was going to let her take the wind out of her sails any more than she already had. Chris had figured out that Anna must have called the house several times when Chris was sick, and Kathleen would never have even told her if Anna hadn't actually shown up. It was as though Kathleen only loved her when she was knocked on her ass! — and she, for one, did not plan to spend the rest of her life on her ass, no matter how much Kathleen got turned on by that.

She was going to have to ask Anna Singer for help.

The labor Chris's mind had to go through to settle on that conclusion was prodigious; it galled her to approach a person who obviously got off so much on helping her. But she reached for the statement that Anna always made in class — that they worked from the needs of the learners — and decided, with the righteous anger of a person long unused to asking for anything, that it was her turn. That Anna had seen her in her bedroom now felt unreal to her, like an event from a long ago acid trip; she was grateful for the delirium that had allowed her not to feel that contact.

Anna was in the empty classroom writing on the board. She was wearing jeans and boots and a black sweater, and when she turned to see who it was, Chris noticed that her face was tense and unhappy. But at the sight of Chris, it sweetened a little. "Hey, you're back!" Anna exclaimed. She came up to Chris and extended her hand, and taken by surprise, Chris shook it. Her own hand was ice cold in Anna's warm one. "In the nick of time, my friend," Anna said, smiling faintly.

"Yeah, listen," Chris said. She hesitated. Anna looked different, even with that smile, as though somebody had drained the personality right out of her. It was her same face, but what she would look like, Chris thought, if she'd grown up poor.

"Listen," she finally plunged in. "I'm interviewing for this job, and I'm supposed to bring in a résumé."

"What kind of job?"

"A project manager for a contractor."

Anna nodded slowly.

"It's the person that takes charge of a few of the contractor's jobs, coordinating the work."

"Cool!" Anna said. "That sounds like interesting work."

Chris snorted softly. "More interesting than anything I've ever done, I'll tell you that."

As they spoke, Anna tried to kick her mind into gear. Over that weekend, depression had descended like a fat pig of a god lowered onto the stage, to dispense its dreary justice. Rage had flared in her at the friends who hadn't called. She had spent the weekend in bed, hoping that if she just let it come and have its way with her, it would leave quietly, sated.

It had been an enormous struggle to get to work. Now, with her pallor and her rapid speech, her uncanny focus on Anna, Chris was making her nervous, and it took an effort not to recoil from her. Anna wondered if this job really existed, and what motivation Chris could possibly have to lie about it; she wondered if it was a job that Chris could handle from a reading standpoint, and then wondered whether that was her business. Chris was staring at her, and Anna felt the weight of it. Resentment crept over her. First Chris had blown her away with her scorching oblivion, and now she was acting like nothing had ever happened.

Robert and Cheryl were coming in. The day was cool but dank, and Cheryl was plucking her blouse away from her body and wiggling it to produce some air after having climbed the stairs. "Good morning," Anna called in their direction. Then she turned back to Chris. She wanted to punish her, but she was Chris's teacher, and it was her job to work from her needs. "Okay," she sighed, "We'll figure out a way to make this work."

When class started everyone was there but Vanessa, who was missing her second day in a row. "Anyone know what the deal is with Vanessa?" she asked.

They shrugged as though to say: *what are you asking us for?* Anna remembered stories she'd heard of other classes where the students threw each other parties when one of them had a success, and thought with a sinking feeling that she had utterly failed to help her students bond.

"It's just that she's hardly ever absent," she fussed. The class felt ruined without Vanessa's attention, which was sometimes scattered but often fervent. She went to the board and erased the words she'd written before class, in preparation for a review exercise on vocabulary they'd learned over the past week. If she returned to that later, she'd just write the words again; she didn't want them distracted by them right now. "Chris needs to write a résumé for a very interesting job," she said. She wrote the word on the board. "Anybody know what that is?"

Chris's eyes widened in alarm: Anna was doing this with the whole class! They'd never get it done this way. And what if she didn't get the job? She'd look like a total loser to this group of losers.

They were quiet. Cheryl was gazing intently at the board, eyes narrowed, arrested by the effort to bring it to mind. She looked at Anna. "Is that where you write down all the jobs you had?"

"Yes!" Anna said. "For what purpose?"

"To get a new job."

"Right. Now you don't need a résumé for a lot of jobs. Sometimes they'll just hire you from talking to you, or sometimes they'll be satisfied with calling up references, people you've worked for who can vouch for you, say you're a responsible worker."

Anna had them begin a résumé by writing a heading and their name and contact information. She circulated around the classroom making sure they'd all done it, then came back to the front of the class. "Now," she said. "The résumé basically comes in three, actually four parts. There's the part you've already written, the heading and your name, and your contact information. Then they start with your *objective* for a job. You write what kind of thing you're looking for, what your goals are. Then you write your education. Then the jobs you've held." She swiftly wrote the four parts on the board. "So you write here, *objective,* and then a colon."

Chris looked at the board, her mind suddenly numb with foreboding. Education? How the hell would she write something when there was nothing to write? In her strenuous handwriting, she copied the word *objective* in the right place, and drew a heavy colon, two tiny circles filled in.

"Good," Anna said. "Now let's think about your objectives, your goals for a job."

As Anna passed by her desk Chris cleared her throat. "This is gonna take forever, with everybody doing it," Chris said.

Anna nodded. She knew Dennis was out with his family crisis for a while, and couldn't help Chris.

"The interview's on Thursday," Chris said.

Anna looked at her. "Shit," she breathed, "why didn't you say so?" She stood with her hands on her hips, her mind scrabbling. "I'll tell you what, I can't today, but I'll meet you here tomorrow afternoon for a tutoring session. See me after class and we'll figure out a time."

Chris exhaled. She caught a glimpse of Cheryl, who was regarding them with curiosity.

"Okay, again," Anna said. "What are your objectives, your goals for a job?"

There was a long pause as they gazed at her, stumped.

"Anybody?"

"*What's* the question?" Cheryl called, and at the same time Chris said, "My goal is to *have* a job."

It dawned on Anna that they didn't know how to say what puzzled and annoyed them: that it wasn't as though they got to think about what they'd like in life, then go out and achieve it. "I know. When you think about it, this objectives thing is for bourgeois people."

"Booj-wah?!" Cheryl cried, looking wildly around the room to drum up an incredulous response.

"Middle-class people," Anna explained. "Middle-class people, people who already have money, are supposed to think: Now how could I be most fulfilled in life? And then try to get a job that helps them realize their full potential."

An anxious yawn was making its way up Chris's windpipe; she really didn't want to know about the philosophy behind the résumé, she just wanted to write one.

"It's hard sometimes to come up with your objective. Once when I was in high school I was looking for an after-school job, and I applied at a supermarket near my house to be a cashier. And the manager asked me: Why do you want to work at a supermarket?

"And I totally blanked," Anna continued, holding her hands up helplessly and laughing again. "I couldn't think of one response that wouldn't be total bullshit." Their faces tilted toward her at the word *bullshit*. "What should I have said? 'I love food?' 'I love adding up numbers?' 'I'm a people person?'" That last she uttered with withering scorn. "And you know what? I still can't think of a good answer for that question. I wanted to make money, for Christ sake." The moment she said that she was glad Vanessa wasn't here to hear her take her savior's name in vain. She was being too loose, and they were also getting off track.

Chris tapped her pencil doggedly against her paper. "So what should I put here?" she asked.

"Well let's think about it," Anna said. "There's not one right answer. Let's try honesty first. What *would* you like in a job?"

"A lot of things," Chris said. "I'd like to win the lottery and never have to work again."

"Okay," Anna said. "But the question is: what kind of job would make you feel like you were using your full potential?"

They were silent, and Anna willed herself to be patient. When she finally spoke she spoke gently. "You guys, you can say what you'd like."

"A longer lunch break," Antwan said. "They just give you a half hour."

"Benefits," Cheryl said, her face taut, knowing that a more sophisticated response was being called for.

"I'm not just talking perks," Anna said, "although of course the more perks the better."

Chris opened her mouth. Her face wooden and her voice dead, as though trying to drain all the emotion from a statement about her desires, she finally ventured, "I'd like a job where I didn't have to be on my feet all the time, and where it wasn't just repetitive motion, and where I could use my head without having to read too good. Too well."

"There you go!" Anna said. "Write that down, Chris."

Chris looked at her dully, then stared at the page.

"What about other people?"

"A job where there ain't no boss in my face all the time," Antwan said.

"Good, Antwan. But how would you say that in the language of the résumé? Remember, it's about you and your abilities and desires."

She'd lost him; his face, so different when alive, deadened again. But Robert was speaking on the other side of the class. "Being self-employed," he was saying.

"And what kinds of skills would you want to be using?" Anna pushed.

"My leadership skills," Robert said. The words sounded like nonsense to him when they came out, like they always did; talking in class was beginning to remind Robert of being stoned on reefer, where your mind took what you said just a second before and revolved it around with amusement.

"Your leadership skills indeed, Robert!" She turned back to Antwan. "See what he means? You talk about what qualities you have that you'd like to use in the job."

She had a sudden idea. "Robert," she said, "write down an example of a time you used your leadership skills, okay?"

That would keep him busy for a while, but she also needed to occupy the others and go sit with Chris; this discussion had taken them far afield, and Chris was looking flushed and panicky. It had just been so tempting to reach out and try to pull out of them their desires, and some kind of recognition that they had abilities. She rubbed her chin, thinking hard. "Cheryl and Antwan, what kind of talent do you have that people don't know about? I want you to confess. Write it down." She wrote the question quickly and firmly on the board, then added: What kind of job would let you express that talent? She looked at their faces, then wrote that down too.

"How long should we write?" Antwan asked.

"I want at least two sentences."

She pulled up a desk next to Chris. Chris had scrawled a mess of words, with streaks of eraser smudge, laboring to get out her ideas. The words "I want a job where I don't have to be on my feet all the time" were perfect. "Look," Anna pointed. "I think that must be the longest sentence you've ever written."

"Yeah, but it's not right yet," Chris said.

"Yeah, but Chris, pay attention. You've written a whole sentence, and it's pretty long!" She stared at Chris till understanding passed over Chris's face.

"But I can't use it," Chris insisted.

Anna's mind churned over how to phrase those sentiments in the numbingly gung-ho jargon of the résumé, and how to help Chris mimic that language without just writing it herself. "Let's figure out," she said, "how to write that in a professional-sounding way. Like instead of *job*, we'll say *position*." She made a stuffy face to cue Chris into the language they were after. "A position allowing me to use...." Actually, they'd say *utilize*, she knew, but Anna despised the word *utilize*, it was so patently puffed-up and technocratic.

"Problem solving," Chris said suddenly, then looked at Anna with an uncertain grin. "Don't they like you to say that you're big into problem solving?"

Anna's face broke into a smile. "Now you're talking. 'A position allowing me to use my problem-solving skills...'" She looked at the piece of paper in front of Chris; Chris was working on *position*. "You know how the *shun* at the end is spelled," she commented.

Chris looked at her. "Maybe you could write it, just this once," she said.

Anna took a breath. She had gotten them into a bind with this objectives thing; she should have just launched into Chris's previous work experience, which would be straightforward, not this circus of inference and circumlocution. If she was going to have Chris write her objectives, she should have done that last, if they had a little extra time. Now she was faced with teaching Chris shitty writing, and she was wasting Chris's time. She reached down with her pen and wrote in clear script, "a position allowing me to use my problem-solving skills to help people with their home design and construction needs." Then she lay the pen on the paper and shoved it neatly toward Chris.

Chris stared at it, not allowing the gears of her mind to engage, feeling as though a Percocet would have softened these fancy words from the mind of her teacher, and made them unthreatening. It would do: it had long words and the phrase "problem-solving skills." She wondered if the fact that she had written a whole sentence meant she wasn't an illiterate anymore. Her mind told her that it wasn't a real sentence, like Anna's was. But then she stopped, and resisted her automatic self-doubt. It was a real sentence. Did that mean she wasn't an illiterate anymore?

"Okay," she said; "Now what?"

Over at the other end of the classroom Robert was sitting still, his hands folded on his desk, indulging himself in thought. He couldn't say he'd been a leader in his lifetime. He'd tagged along after Reggie Jr., his cousin and boyhood companion, for the lion's share of his childhood. Junior was a year older and his daddy played in the Negro Leagues, so everybody wanted to be near him, he had that spark and gloried in it. Then, in 'Nam, Robert had kept his head down as much as possible, praying that if he just followed orders, he could live another day. It would be hard to call him a leader, hard indeed.

And yet, he was alive while others had died: first Junior in the waning days of the war and then Junior's parents, and of course his own father long ago. The way he saw it, he was so unremarkable he slid through life leaving barely a ripple, so death had not hungered at the sight of him. That idea gave him just the faintest pleasure, which, as he had in the past, he immediately tried to dispel; it smacked of a sense of superiority over the dead. No, death had not hungered at the sight of him, the way Ms. Singer's eyes did not light up with expectation at the sight of his raised hand.

It confounded Robert again and again how fragile human life was, and at the same time, how hardy.

Next to him Antwan wrote: "My talent." After that his impulse was to write "auto mechanics," words he had written often even before he really learned to write, but Anna had said to write a talent that nobody knew about. He was pretty good at making those textbook covers out of paper bags, something he did for his little brother. He sang pretty good. He had been in the church choir when he was a boy, and in the school choir at Thurgood Marshall, and he had relished the music and the discipline. He still remembered the tenor line of songs whose melody he had forgotten, and their words could come out of him at any moment without his awareness even touching what they meant: they were a collection of sounds etched into his bones.

What kind of job would let him use that talent? A job as an R&B singer, he thought with muffled mirth. He could be the artist formerly known as Antwan. A memory shivered unpleasantly in him: Marvin Gaye stuffed under his shirt, dragged with Lamar to the back room of the record store by that cracker security guard. Then it suddenly occurred to him that he could find himself another church choir, and the shiver became a thrill.

Sheila would think he was finally turning respectable. Well, she could think that if she wanted, it didn't hurt him none.

That wasn't really the assignment, he remembered. Joining a choir wasn't a job. That cop pushing Antwan to his knees, with a force that made Antwan crumple: it was the last thing he remembered. He didn't even remember how old he was at the time, if his mother was still alive or if she was dead.

He peeked over at Cheryl's paper, but she was bent over it, and her secret talent remained secret.

Anna made an appointment with Chris for the next afternoon. They'd meet back at school, in the lounge. For the rest of the class she reviewed vocabulary. Afterwards, walking out past Renée's office, she saw Vanessa inside, sitting down with Tisha, who was dressed in a bright yellow raincoat, on her lap.

She stopped and went inside.

Smith House had refused to continue taking Tisha after Vanessa had given them the petition she'd written, with nineteen signatures on it.

Anna's heart sank, and she looked at Renée. Renée's eyes were hard.

Tisha was leaning against her mother, sucking on the ear of a stuffed animal. "Can't Desirée take care of her?" Anna asked Vanessa.

But Vanessa's half-sister had left, it turned out, as suddenly as she'd come. "And I depended on her," Vanessa said, astonished all over again at this unexpected turn of events. "Now I don't even have no babysitter." She'd looked into a few other places for low-income families, but both of them were an El trip from her house, with at least one transfer, and would get her to class an hour late every day.

"Well an hour late is better than nothing," Anna said. Her mind was flailing around for a solution, but it felt limp and hopeless. She had harmed Vanessa by trying to help her take charge of her child's care and education. This world was so cruel and stupid: what the hell was the point?

"I'm going to speak to the people at Smith House tomorrow," Renée said. "Meanwhile, I was thinking that Vanessa could bring Tisha to class until she finds another daycare." She raised her voice a little, teasingly, to the child. "So Tisha's coming to school with her mommy."

"Oh! That's fine," Anna said. "Did you suggest that Vanessa bring something for Tisha to do when she's here, like crayons or a puzzle?"

Vanessa shook her head and Renée said "No, I didn't, but that's a good idea." She looked over at Vanessa, who was nodding.

"What's your bunny's name?" Anna asked Tisha.

Tisha's face broke into light, just like her mother's. She held the stuffed animal out toward Anna as though Anna had asked for it. "Bunny," she said.

A few minutes later, Anna headed down the stairs feeling as though she couldn't get out of there fast enough. In her world, she was thinking, if you got billed incorrectly for something, or your insurance wouldn't pay, or you were wronged or damaged, you called customer service, or the manager, or a lawyer. You had recourse. She opened the door onto the street, rage pumping through her, and threaded her way through a crowd of black teenagers outside the next-door bodega, who were laughing loudly, smoking, smacking gum, eating snacks out of shiny bags. The sidewalk was damp and sticky under her boots, and there was a fine mist, not quite rain, in the air. It didn't work that way in Vanessa's world, and she should have known it.

Anna unlocked the door to her car, got in and unlocked the Club on her steering wheel. She had hurt Vanessa with her own naïveté, and she hated herself for it.

CHAPTER EIGHTEEN

On Tuesday, Anna got there at 4:00, just as Rosie was closing up
the office, her purse hanging on her forearm as she struggled with her
giant ring of keys. She looked at Anna in a disheveled way through big
pink-rimmed glasses, and said "Oh, did you forget something?"

"No," Anna replied. "I came to work with a student in the lounge."

"Oh great," Rosie breathed. "Only you know, Carl closes up the
building at 5:00?" Carl was the afternoon security guard.

Oh shit, Anna thought, looking at her watch. But then she remembered that she herself had a key that she rarely used. She said, "Well
that's okay. I have a key, so I can lock up after we're done." She found
it on her key ring and held it up to show Rosie.

"I don't know." Rosie shook her head worriedly. "Carl doesn't like
people to be here after he closes up." She had been hired by Renée's
predecessor, and had what Renée called a can't-do attitude.

"That's okay Rosie," Anna said. "Carl and I will take care of it."
She went into the lounge, where shafts of the remaining daylight
gleamed on spots of the imposing mural, showing the brushstrokes
on the oiled surface, and turned on the light. It was close and messy
in there, and smelled of microwave popcorn. She wrestled a window
open, then walked around straightening chairs and picking up
garbage left behind by students: empty bags of chips, candy wrappers, soda cups with watery soda left at the bottom. Dust motes rose
off the table. There was a piece of lined yellow legal paper with a
tortured outline on it for an essay on the student's opinion of the

most beneficial household invention of the last fifty years — a GED question; the student was trying to make a case for the microwave, but had obviously run out of steam after claiming it was very convenient. *Can you be more specific?* Anna thought with weary expertise; it took a lot to whip up a scintillating answer to a GED question. She crumpled the paper and shot a jumper into the wastebasket from across the room, and looked up triumphantly when Chris came in, her bag slung over her shoulder and a cup of coffee in her hand.

Chris didn't even greet her; she put her coffee down, took her jacket off and sat down at the table, and unpacked her bag with resolve. She took out the piece of paper on which Anna had written her objective and flattened it fastidiously; Anna, sitting down next to her, saw her own handwriting again with a pang of embarrassment. From here on in, she thought, they would do this right. Chris's body was hunched and heavy, and she reeked of cigarette smoke. Her breathing was labored. She tapped her pencil on the line below the sentence Anna had written, a gesture Anna was already learning to hate. "What goes here?" she asked.

"You could say hello," Anna said.

"Hello," Chris intoned.

"Oh, that was touching," Anna said, mockingly wiping away a tear. She remembered Chris's hairy legs splayed outside the covers of her bed, and resentment and distaste heaved inside her at this huge lump of an ingrate who refused to acknowledge even her existence, let alone her help. Chris turned to stare at her and Anna met her gaze with belligerent steadiness. "Okay," Anna said, "this next part is your employment history. So go ahead and write that down: *employment history.* Capitalize the E and the H, because it's like a title." Anna sat back and crossed her arms with a satisfaction she knew was sadistic as Chris's pen hovered uncertainly above the page. Chris wrote a capital E, then stopped. "Say the word, Chris, syllable by syllable. You know the suffix *ment.*"

Chris said "em," and the rest of the word stuck in her craw. She turned to Anna, her face dark and pinched. "Why can't you just help me?" she demanded.

Anna put her pen down on the table. "I *am* helping you, Chris. This is what that looks like."

"You're making everything take a long time on purpose," Chris said. She was turning red, anger seeming to stupefy her.

"It *takes* a long time," Anna said heatedly. "Writing a résumé is hard. There's no magic wand you can wave over this paper even if you're already a good writer."

Then, looking at Chris's face, Anna saw a glimmer of panic amid the turgid anger, like the glimmer of light on rough water, and it yanked at her conscience. She was pontificating, and that wasn't doing anyone any good right now. "Don't panic," she said.

"I'm not panicking," Chris interrupted.

"Well you're certainly wound up," Anna said gently. "Listen, we'll get this done."

It took fifteen minutes for Chris to write "Employment History," and when she'd done it successfully, Anna stood to stretch her back while Chris peeled the lid off of her coffee and gulped down the lukewarm remains. "Now," Anna said, walking away from her, then turning and facing her from across the room. "Here's where you list the jobs you've held. It's done chronologically, in order of time, with the most recent job first and then moving backwards in time job by job."

Chris's mind was churning. Job by job? "Jesus," she said, "I'm fifty-two years old, I've held a million jobs."

Anna nodded. "Well, let's start at the beginning, or actually the end. What's the last job you've held?"

"I screwed PC boards onto computers."

"Where?"

"Howell Electronics."

"So what should we call your job? Computer technician?"

Chris looked at her with that look of incredulous pity Anna's students occasionally laid on her. "Assembly line worker."

"Okay, so write down: Assembly line worker, Howell Electronics."

Chris sighed and began to labor. Watching the uncertain waver between letters, the slanted stroke of each letter made by Chris's mangled hand, a yawn constricted Anna's throat and she thought about how much of her job — indeed, how many of her waking hours — entailed sitting still and waiting while someone next to her struggled to write something down. It made it so hard to sustain a sense of purpose, sitting with people who were damaged or demoralized, in a space that felt shabby and improvised, working on a text that was more likely than not a hodgepodge of scrawls and half-hearted sallies, destined for the trash. They didn't even have recycling here at the center, which meant that her students' words were not even worth the paper they were written on. But this text, this one: Anna felt her heart clench with determination to will this one into reality, into the fully-dimensional world where written language was taken up and received, like dead people's souls by angels. As the words began slowly and angularly to form under Chris's pen, Anna began to think about the challenges of this résumé. Chris had probably been a drifter, holding jobs for short periods before being fired or moving on. How would they represent that on paper without making Chris look like someone who couldn't hold a job? She decided that rather than listing jobs in reverse chronological order, they should brainstorm a quick list of all the jobs, and then distinguish between the ones worth mentioning and the others. Meanwhile, she watched and murmured *"Good."* When Chris sat back in her chair, Anna told her how she was seeing the problem. "You've had a lot of jobs," she said. "And it's important to write it in a way that doesn't make it seem that you can't *hold* a job. Let's get as many of them down as possible, and see how we can organize them in the résumé so your employment history looks purposeful."

Chris took in the intimation that she couldn't hold a job with the stoicism of a person who doesn't flinch at the sight of snakes or needles. "So we're not writing backwards anymore?"

"No," Anna said.

"But won't that take much longer?" Chris asked. "That's like writing a whole 'nother thing besides the résumé."

"I know," Anna said. "But sometimes you have to get it all out before you can organize it properly." She thought for a few moments.

"I'll tell you what," she finally said. "You dictate, I'll write the list."

Chris looked at her as though there must be a catch. But Anna was thinking that it wasn't like writing it for her, as she'd done impatiently that morning; it was cutting Chris a little slack so she could think freely without having to struggle with her own incompetence. "Okay," she said. "Shoot."

Chris scratched her ear, then sat up and reached for her jacket. "Do you mind if I smoke?"

"Yes," Anna said. "I'm sorry. I'm an ex-smoker and it really bothers me. Even the smell of smoke on your clothes bothers me." The moment she said the last part she regretted it; had it really been necessary to tell Chris she smelled bad?

Chris looked at Anna, stung, and shot a glance over toward the open window. "How about if I sit over there on the window sill and open the window a little more? I'll blow the smoke outside." She headed that way before Anna could answer,

Anna gave her a heavy look, defeated by the pretense of compromise. Chris moved a few plants off the sill that sat atop the radiator, and brushed dirt and crumbled leaves off it with her hand before perching herself on top of it. She took a soft pack of cigarettes from her breast pocket, pushed a cigarette up and removed it from the packet with her teeth, and lit it with her hand cupped around a lighter. She inhaled deeply and blew the smoke out the window with a sigh that taunted Anna with its performance of satisfaction.

"Okay, Chris, let's have it," Anna said.

"Okay. Well back in the stone age I worked on the assembly line of American Can Company, and also at United Card Factory. Those were both back in Hammond."

"Did you live in Hammond?" Anna asked, writing.

"Actually, Cal City. It used to be called West Hammond."

Anna looked up. "Sin City," she said, smiling faintly.

Chris made a wry face. People liked to get all shocked and excited about Calumet City's reputation, about the sex and the crime on the strip, but to her it had just been home, a place wild enough to draw attention away from queers like her. What other godforsaken jobs had she held there? "I worked in the stockroom of Goldblatt's in Hammond, and at a fruit market called something-or-other, Jansen's. I was a custodian at U.S. Steel in Gary for a little while." A week and a half, to be exact. Her foreman had been a real vicious motherfucker to her and to the black lady — what was her name? — who worked with her and liked to listen to gospel music; you'd mop a floor and he'd go spill some vile shit all over it.

Anna took notes, her mind whirring over how to organize this stuff. Chris stubbed out her cigarette on her shoe. "Well," she said, looking up with combative jocularity, "that just about covers 1962."

Anna held up her hands and waggled her fingers in a gesture that said *gimme.* "More. Cough it up, Rinaldi."

Chris laughed to herself, warmed by getting her balls busted, as though she was tough enough to take it. And it was good, because remembering these godforsaken jobs was like rubbing the finish off a burnt pot with steel wool, and her mind was that pot. "Oh, I tended bar on and off, which in that town made me a combination bartender and bouncer."

Anna looked up, remembering things she'd read about the old bars. "Did you have those pedals down below the bar to call security?"

"Yeah. But sometimes we just closed the doors and took care of the jerk by ourselves." Chris sniffed and touched her nose with the knuckles of the back of her hand, a gesture whose bravado made Anna grin.

"What other jobs did you hold?"

"Well I was a handyman and apartment manager at a bunch of apartment buildings. This one Polish landlord hired me on and off for a bunch of years in Cal City."

Anna nodded, writing. "So you did repairs. What kind?"

"All kinds," Chris said. "Plumbing, carpentry, landscaping, electric, painting. Roofing."

Chris shifted uncomfortably on the windowsill, her face working as Anna's hand scurried along the page. She could feel the turn of her ankle and the grip of her boot on the roof's rough surface, and the hot scrape of shingles on her palm.

Anna was poring over the piece of paper in front of her. "Okay," she said. Her eyes were bright; she was moving into the zone, the space where her intelligence became supple and empathic, and she felt herself on the brink of having an impact. "So it seems that when you first started working in Cal City you were looking for stockroom and factory jobs, but you increasingly moved toward taking custodial and handyman-type work. Does that sound accurate?"

Chris settled herself into one of the worn easy chairs. She fished a candy wrapper out of the side of the cushion, and careful not to get some slob's chocolate smears on her hands, leaned over and dropped it into the trash. She had never thought of her jobs that way, but what Anna said was more or less true. "Yeah."

"How come?" Anna asked.

Chris cleared her throat. "I don't know, I didn't plan it. Oh, I guess I didn't want no manager breathing down my neck."

Anna nodded. "That makes sense," she murmured. "It must have also been a relief not to be working with gangs of men. And to do a variety of things instead of just one thing."

That was exactly it. And as she spoke, Ms. Singer's face took on a thoughtful beauty that made Chris's heart leap up weirdly, as though her name had been called out as the winner of a contest.

Anna put down her pen and stretched. "I have an idea. Let's arrange your jobs by category rather than listing them by date. The factory and stockroom jobs, and the handiwork you've done. We'll list all the kinds of repairs you did, and we'll make the fact that you had a lot of jobs work in your favor, by showing that you've acquired a lot of the skills you'll need to be a project manager. We'll make it look as though you've been working systematically to become a project manager."

Chris took note of the half-smile on her face, anxious and stimulated by the idea of taking all the shit jobs she'd had and turning them into roses. She thought, *She's getting off on being smart.* "I never had no intention to be a project manager," she said. "It just got suggested by a friend of mine who knows the guy."

"Still," Anna said. "The purpose of a résumé is to tell a story about your life that makes it look as though getting this job is the logical climax of it, the inevitable climax, the job toward which all the other jobs have been pointing."

A look of skepticism froze on Chris's face. A thought came into her mind and careened recklessly out her mouth. "Look, I ain't no Jess Goldberg."

Anna's face opened with surprise. She heard the cutting way the name *Goldberg* came out of Chris's mouth. "You're not?" she said, leaning back and stretching with her hands folded behind her head. "What do you mean?"

Chris had blown her cover; now Anna would know she'd lied about not having read it. She cleared her throat. "Nothin'," she said.

"No really."

Chris shrugged. "I don't know what I mean."

Anna laughed. "Oh give me a break, Chris, you know exactly what you mean."

There was a rustling in the next room, followed by the crash of a chair knocked to the floor. They looked at each other quickly, then Anna stood because it was her job to be in charge, and because it was important to her to look brave in front of Chris. At the doorway she ran into a large man's belly.

"Whoa!" he said, throwing his arms out, then looking Anna over. It was Carl, the security guard. He was white and middle-aged, red-faced and puffing from the stairs, a handgun holstered at his hip. Anna stepped back, and he peeked into the classroom and saw Chris. "Well *hello* ladies," he said, smiling broadly. They both stiffened at his choice of words.

"Hi Carl," Anna said. "Listen, we need to stay here for another hour or so, okay? I've got a key, and can lock up."

Carl was still smiling, the smile turning foolish. Looking at him, Chris could tell he was high, and noted that she seemed to have a new expertise.

"Well I don't know," he puffed, wagging his head comically. "Guess I could let you stay, for a small pay-off."

There was a pause.

"Just kidding," he said. "Actually, I can't. Because if something happens, and there's a break-in or vandalism or what have you, that's my balls, excuse my French."

Anna sighed and let her shoulders sag theatrically. "C'mon, Carl. We've got some important things to finish here."

Carl shrugged. "Nothing I can do."

Anna stared at him, then snatched her jacket off the back of a chair. Chris took her papers and put them in her bag, thinking that Anna was going about bullying him the wrong way, by acting all pissed off, when what she should do was mention that Ms. Wallace had told her to tell Carl to make an exception just this once. Everybody was intimidated by Ms. Wallace.

They had to push past Carl, who was still blocking the doorway with his huge gut. Chris paused for a second, chest-to-chest with him, and looked him evenly in the bloodshot eyes. Then she followed Anna out, and they trotted down the stairs to the sound of tapping boots. Right inside the opaque glass doors to the outside, they paused and looked uncertainly at each other. There was still a lot to do. "Okay," Anna said, "what time is it?" She looked at her watch: it was 5:20. She thought for a few minutes, growing increasingly irritated by the passive implacability of Chris's demand; she was just standing there like a lout. "Why don't we just go over to my house," she finally said.

"Okay," Chris said, with no hesitation at all, and they pushed their way out onto the noisy street, Anna stifling her surprise. "I didn't bring my car today," she said, and gestured with her chin toward the El station.

They trudged up the stairs. For a while, standing on the rickety Lawrence El platform next to Chris with her hands in her pockets, Anna felt bulked up and powerful, and suddenly understood what teenagers got out of joining gangs. They strode into a crowded car as people piled out, and Anna swung around a pole and lowered herself onto an open seat. Chris followed and landed heavily next to her on the last remaining seat, almost on top of her, then scooted over. They sat with their feet planted and their knees open.

Anna hugged her backpack to her. Straight people were heading home from the Loop: secretaries and store clerks and men in sales. The women wore dresses and pumps and the men white shirts and ties. As her awareness opened up to take them in, Anna felt their eyes darting at her and Chris, and annoyance flared into a panic reflex so complicated her vision blurred. She was terrified that she looked grotesquely masculine to them, and at the same time she feared that next to Chris, she looked *feminine* to them, and they thought she was Chris's girlfriend, and that this is what a lesbian couple looked like. Her knee touched Chris's as the train swerved, and she moved it away. If they didn't know how to look at you, you were nothing. She thought of Patricia, whose eyes had brightened unfailingly at the sight of all things butch: buzz-cut bartenders, teenagers with hands like farm boys, k.d. lang crooning like Elvis and Amy Ray brandishing her guitar like an exultant god. That seemed so long ago now. Anna caught the eye of a young woman with a double chin and pancake makeup looking at her over her paperback; the woman looked back down with stifled irony — *whatever* — and a vicious hatred knifed through Anna at her ignorant complacency. People like her said things like *she keeps a lovely home,* she thought, and talked of *starting a family;* they were people who had baby showers, whose husbands spent their leisure hours acting like adolescents and thinking that was charming. Anna knew they regarded her as beyond their pale, beyond anything they could love or even give a shit about, and sitting on the train next to Chris, she hated them for not knowing that she would rather lie down in a hole and die than be part of their world.

By the time the train pulled into the Bryn Mawr station and they tumbled out onto the platform, Anna was drained to her very core. Did Chris feel that hatred every single day? She grasped the railings as they headed down the stairs.

It was a warm cloudy day, and Anna and Chris walked swiftly down Bryn Mawr, cutting through crowds of black and brown people on a sidewalk littered with garbage, past bodegas and discount stores and the Queen of Africa hair salon, the smell of cheap spicy food tickling their nostrils. The moment they crossed Broadway it was quieter. They walked past a small, well-tended playground with new mulch on the ground and a sign on its gate menacing potential drug dealers, walked in what Anna hoped was companionable silence. She was trying to shrug off her black mood with a wide stride. She peeked over at Chris. "So did you like *Stone Butch Blues?*" she asked.

"It was interesting," Chris said, pronouncing all the syllables.

"What did you mean when you said you aren't, when you said that thing about Jess Goldberg?"

Chris looked at her blankly. "What thing?"

Anna laughed mirthlessly and shook her head. "You're a piece of work, Chris, you know that? They should give you a Ph.D. in pretending you don't know what the fuck I'm talking about."

Shocked merriment pushed itself into Chris's face and she laughed a painful spurt of a laugh. "I mean I'm no saint, like she was."

"Aha." Anna chewed on that. "You think she was a saint?"

Actually, it wasn't exactly what Chris meant. Suddenly she thought she had read the whole book wrong.

They turned the corner onto Wayne Ave. Anna was still looking at her. "So you're telling me you're a worse person than Jess Goldberg?"

Chris didn't answer. The Mexican girls were hanging out in a doorway smoking, their forearms laden with bangles. They looked at Anna and Chris with their mouths open, and Anna greeted them as they passed. Anna gestured to her to turn, and they headed up a courtyard sidewalk to her building. Anna opened the door and retrieved her mail. Then she opened the door to the stairway, and Chris followed her upstairs to her apartment.

"This is my apartment," Anna said, waving her hand around. "I'm going to make some coffee."

Chris followed her into the kitchen, too shy to relax and look around. "Let's sit here," Anna said, gesturing to the small round table covered with newspapers. She swept the papers off the table and tossed them in a neat stack on the floor.

Chris peeked at a framed photograph on the wall, in black and white, of a handsome black cat walking toward the camera with its tail in the air. She sat at the kitchen table as though huddling in a lifeboat, as though the domesticity around her, the sheer personal quality of these rooms, might overwhelm her. Anna made a pot of coffee and sat down beside her. "Okay, let's see," she said, as Chris took out her papers. "Where were we?"

Anna created three categories — factory, stockroom and loading dock, and custodial/repairs — and began to coax. *What else?* she asked, and *What kind?* Somehow, Anna was realizing, leaning back with her hands crossed expansively behind her head, now that they were outside of Pathways, now that she had called Chris on how difficult she was, she felt as though it wasn't such a big deal to push Chris ever so lightly. She felt entitled. And as she applied her suave managing hand to Chris, Chris's face grew startled by memories of the work she'd done — unloading truckloads of M&Ms, snapping wheels onto toy cars — more complex and human than Anna had ever seen it.

Steam began to rise from the gurgling coffeepot, and Anna got up, asking Chris how she took her coffee. "Black," Chris said. Anna set a mug before her. It was excellent, Chris found: bold and strong without being bitter.

Some of Chris's jobs Anna wrote down, some she didn't. She found Chris's jobs interesting, which dumbfounded Chris. She murmured as she wrote, and sometimes she gave out a low chuckle, or a small exclamation. Chris wanted to say: frankly, only someone who had never worked a day on her feet could find working on a loading dock or in a toy factory interesting. But she didn't, instead she squirmed like an idiot and had trouble meeting Anna's gaze as a strange feeling stole over her that she couldn't name, that had something to do with the quality of attention directed her way by Anna's disconcertingly warm eyes. That had something to do with seeing, suddenly, what the appeal of Anna would be as a lover.

That thought propelled her off her feet and out on the fire escape to smoke. Sitting in the dusk on the dirty railings of the back stairs, her heart thumping unpleasantly, she inhaled deeply and shot smoke upward into the warm rank air of the dumpster-lined alley, and the sound of a gunning engine cut into the darkness, and the screech of a cat a few yards away.

It wasn't just a skill she was learning, she thought, like wiring a fuse box or changing spark plugs, the same kind of thing only harder. Writing turned her head around; it brought things before her that she might not want to see, like one of those multiplexes with wide screens and Dolby sound, music tickling her ear from behind and images galloping at her as though they might burst from the screen. It made her wish there was a woman with big hair sitting in front of her blocking the view.

There were assholes she hadn't thought about for decades. Women who took their purses out of the front hall right in front of her eyes and stashed them somewhere so she wouldn't steal from them. Millrats or canning guys whose wives had called to get some repair done, who would be home in the late morning standing up in the kitchen slurping huge mouthfuls of cereal, milk slobbering down their chins as they told her she was doing it all wrong. Sometimes they'd grab the wrench right out of her hands, when their wives had been begging them to do the fucking repair for months. And once those guys sitting around watching the game when she had come to put in a phone jack in the living room. She had felt their eyes on her, a stillness, a current of communication among them, and had pretended the wire took her to the door, where she slipped out and raced downstairs, taking the stairs two at a time. It was funny, she met the guy whose apartment it was plenty of times after that and never got a bad vibe from him. But together, an awful smell had come off of them, the smell of mayhem.

Sitting out on Anna's fire escape, she wondered: did it count as a bad event if things evened out? Because there were, after all, those hippies who offered her some hallucinogen she didn't even recognize, and she'd had to crawl — literally crawl, on her hands and knees — back to her cave of an office, where she spent an hour weeping over the beauty of a documentary on beavers on the tiny black-and-white TV. And those folks on the Cal City Gold Coast, who obviously thought they were living on the *Chicago* Gold Coast. When the husband was there they barely gave her the time of day. But one day when she went to replace the dishwasher hose, the wife was alone, and seduced her right there on the kitchen floor. She didn't consider it cheating; she thought of screwing her as giving a little something back to the community she'd come up in.

Things got even; she'd evened the score. For every asshole a hippie with some great funky stuff; for every assault a guy pinned by her knees, his mouth a bloody mess; for every insult a woman reaching out for her, breathing hard.

She stubbed out her cigarette and flicked the dead butt down into the alley, her mouth tasting stale and her head aching. Lord she missed her high. Her mind sugared, fairy-dusted. The way emotion expanded her chest, her throat catching with gratitude as it took hold, like cracked hands cupped toward the rainy sky.

As she stood to head inside, she heard the buzzer sound and Anna exclaim to herself and head to the door. She reseated herself and hastily lit another cigarette. She heard the musical sound of a woman's voice, and Anna's pleased response. They murmured for a while, and their voices got louder as they approached the kitchen. Anna poked her head out the kitchen door and said "Come meet my friend Janice."

Chris groaned to herself at the thought of having to socialize with Anna's friends. But she followed Anna in and was immediately disarmed by the sight of a good-looking gal about Anna's age, with straight brown hair and a rich emotional face, the kind that laughed and cried easily, the kind that she could instantly imagine welling up with passion. "This is my friend Janice," Anna was saying. "And this is my student, Chris. We're working on a résumé she needs for a job interview."

"Hi Janice," Chris said, taking Janice's hand in her own, which caused Janice to blush. She felt rough-hewn and dangerous next to Janice but not like a brute, and that told her that this woman liked butches.

Anna gave her a funny look, and thought: *check out the ladies' man.*

"I won't interrupt you, I'll only stay a second," Janice said, obviously disconcerted and stimulated in Chris's presence. "I just came by to pick up that book we were talking about."

"Oh right, let me look for it." Anna left the room and as Janice perched on a chair, her hands folded stiffly on her knees, Chris leaned against the stove with her ankles crossed and her palms resting behind her on the stove's edge. "Are you a teacher like Anna?" she asked.

"Yes."

"Where do you teach?"

Janice cleared her throat. "The University of Chicago."

Chris let out a soft whistle. "Does that mean you're a professor?"

"Yes."

"You must be *really* smart."

Janice laughed at the teasing look on Chris's face. "Oh yeah, I'm *really* smart."

"I probably shouldn't even be in the same room as you," Chris said.

Janice nodded gravely. "Probably not, but I'll allow it just this once."

"Allow what?" Anna asked, coming back into the room with a book in her hand. Chris and Janice laughed, and said "Nothing" at the same time, and laughed again. Anna looked at their flushed sheepish faces and felt something verging on humiliation. She held the book out to Janice, saying "Here you go, sweetheart. I marked that chapter we talked about."

Janice took it and stood to go. "I'll let you two get back to work," she said. "It was nice meeting you, Chris."

Chris nodded with ironic good nature, and said "You bet," and Anna caught the slightest of winks.

On her way out, Janice turned back abruptly. "Oh. And good luck with your résumé; I hope you get the job."

Anna let her pass, and escorted her to the door. When Janice turned to say goodbye, Anna leaned her face in close to hers. "You flirting with my student?" she grumbled.

Janice backed up nervously, not about to let herself get kissed again.

Anna reached out and grabbed her belt loops, pulling her hips toward her, knowing even as she did so that she was making herself obnoxious to Janice, but unable to help herself. "In my house, you flirt only with me, you hear?"

Janice rolled her eyes and disengaged Anna's hands. "Maybe you two can measure your dicks after I leave," she whispered, and slipped out the door.

"I'm just saying," Anna called after her as she galloped down the stairs. She strained for a joke. "It's only common courtesy."

She shut the door with a bitter taste in her mouth. She looked at her watch; it was almost 7:30. Indecision and irritation crowded inside her as she wondered what to do about dinner and how to get this résumé typed. She had the savage hope that Chris had heard the murmuring between her and Janice, and was sitting in the kitchen feeling excluded and awkward. They still had to organize this fucker, put the dates in, and get it typed. If she did that with any semblance of pedagogical integrity, it would take a while.

Chris was sitting at the kitchen table staring into space, and again Anna bristled at her passivity. Chris turned her head toward her as though it were a massive stone. "That your girlfriend?"

"No," Anna said, wishing she could say yes. "Listen, Chris, there's still a bit more to do. We have to arrange all the jobs in backward chrono- logical order and put the years in, and it needs to be typed. I'm assum- ing Kathleen will be able to type it for you?"

"No," Chris said quickly, the lie emerging smoothly. "They don't let her use the computer at the office for personal stuff."

Anna's mind was whirring about the right thing to do. It would only take her about half an hour to type the résumé, but Chris should learn how to deal with this kind of problem, and plus, Anna wasn't her secretary. "You know," she said, "the two of you can rent time on a computer at Kinko's."

Chris froze. "Look," she said. "I can't ask her to do it."

"Why not? You can ask me but you can't ask her?"

"I can't," Chris said doggedly. "Look, if you don't want to help me...."

Anna looked at her with amazed hurt. "Why do you keep claiming I don't want to help you?" she cried. "What the hell do you think I'm doing here, with you in my house?"

Chris absorbed her words the way she'd learned to absorb a blow; you just made sure you kept breathing. The rebellious thought that she wasn't just sitting there, she was dredging up her whole grubby asinine life for Anna to know what a loser she was, welled up in her, but she let it go. She could take it, she thought, if it meant not having to ask Kathleen to help her. She met Anna's angry eyes. "Please," she said.

Her supplication make Anna catch her breath. When it came down to it, here was a person who hadn't caught many breaks in life, who was asking for her help. "Okay," she said, "I'll type it. But first I'm ordering a pizza." She picked up the phone. "What do you like on yours?"

Chris took a deep breath and cleared her throat. "Whatever. Pepperoni."

Anna dialed and gave her phone number to the pizza person. She ordered a large pizza with onions, peppers and pepperoni. When she hung up she put the paper in front of Chris and told her to number the jobs in reverse chronological order. "Remember we talked about what chronological order is?" She shoved the pen toward Chris. "It's in order of time. Here you need to do it backwards. Just put the numbers here, like number 1, number 2."

Chris labored over the paper, numbering the jobs under each category, writing down the years to the best of her memory. A trickle of sweat came down her right temple, and her face had a fierce scowl of concentration. Anna stood and stretched, poured herself a glass of water and drained it. When the pizza came twenty minutes later she paid for it and brought it into the kitchen, put slices on plates for herself and Chris, and opened beers for them. "Thanks," Chris muttered, noticing that Anna drank Coronas. Chris folded a slice lengthwise in her hand and took a huge bite out of the end, and took a gulp of beer from the bottle while her mouth was still full. As Anna stood against the refrigerator eating and watching her, she tried not to be resentful that Chris hadn't offered to pay for half the pizza. If Chris got this job, she thought, she'd probably make twice as much as Anna was making helping her get the job.

When Chris was done she handed the paper to Anna, who perused it quickly and said "Okay," while Chris tried not to be intimidated by how fast she read. "It's good enough. Why don't you go sit in the living room and watch TV." She went to the refrigerator and got them each a second beer.

It was the first time Chris had gotten up from being huddled at the small kitchen table. She set the beer down and put her hands on her hips, arching her back to stretch it. Then she took up her beer again, walked into the hall and stood at the threshold of the darkened living room. She flipped a light switch on the wall, but nothing happened; she entered and turned the knob of the halogen lamp, bringing the room to light. The room was crammed with books, in the built-in bookcases along the wall, stacked or face down on the coffee table and the end table. Chris settled herself heavily onto the couch. In front of her, the windows overlooking the courtyard were a great dark blank, and they made her feel cold. She reached for the remote control on the coffee table, and cleared her throat. "Have you read all these books?"

"No, not all of them. But a lot of them."

Chris was quiet for a few minutes before she spoke again. "What are the rest of them for?"

Anna was in the dining room she used as a study, cleaning the papers off her desk. "What?"

"Why did you buy all them other books and not read them?"

"Oh," Anna said. She swiveled in her desk chair and contemplated Chris. "I bought them because I thought I'd like to read them. Because a friend recommended them, or because of what it said on the book jacket." She got up and took a hardcover book, *When Work Disappears,* off the coffee table, sat down next to Chris, opened it and brushed her fingers down the left-hand flap. "Here they write what the book is about. Or sometimes on the back too." She flipped it so Chris could see the back cover, then opened it the other way and showed Chris the right flap. "And here they tell you something about the author." She laid it back down on the coffee table, then slapped her hands on her knees and got up. "But then I didn't have time to read them, or I wasn't in the mood." She headed back into the dining room, then turned. "Did you know that in newspapers there are book reviews, where people write their opinions about books that have just been published?"

"Sure," Chris lied.

"Yeah, that's another way you decide what book you want to read," Anna said, and sat down at her desk.

She untucked her shirt and spread her knees, sniffed. She began tentatively, grudgingly, but as she typed Chris's jobs, her fingers rapid over the keyboard, she warmed to the task, reorganizing them, renaming some and omitting others. She ended up dividing the category of factory and stockroom into two, and called them *Factory* and *Stock/Inventory*. She decided to create an *Education* category after all — without it, there was a gaping hole right in the middle of the résumé. Underneath it she typed: *self-educated.* Her mind was alert and agile. She formatted as she went along. Not too fancy with the fonts, not too attention-hogging; she used bold face but no italics. Declarative, in a competently masculine way. This motherfucker was going to work, unlike every job letter she'd written for herself.

In the living room, Chris was flipping channels and being reminded of all the times she sat in front of the TV drinking beer while Kathleen paid the bills or made calls to the insurance company. Anna had good cable, she was noticing, even though she apparently couldn't afford a nice TV cart. She didn't live that much higher on the hog than Chris and Kathleen did, but for some reason Chris couldn't account for her apartment looked classier than their house. Maybe it was the books, she thought, but there was something else too, the pretty shabbiness of the faded rug, and the casual clutter of magazines and coasters and little pictures in frames grouped over the fireplace, a clutter that had an almost graceful look. There was a picture on the wall that somebody seemed to have actually painted instead of one bought in a poster store. Chris paused at a home improvement show on HGTV, where they were showing a house before and after it was renovated. She watched the contractor's advice and disagreed with him. As a project manager, she would make decisions about tile and paint color and closet space. And give instructions to subs. She wouldn't mind lording it over them, that was for sure. She would have to take a firm hand.

Then suddenly she felt she was jinxing herself by letting herself want it too badly. Turning to a wildlife show, she tried to make her mind blank. The beer wasn't doing it for her; it just gave her a headache. She tried to imagine herself high, her mind light and soaring. She could do it for just a moment, but then it became like flying in a dream, and the ground came rushing up toward her.

Eventually Chris heard the sound of the printer, and when it stopped, Anna came out of the room.

"There," Anna said. "What do you think?"

Chris took the clean white sheet in her hand, and looked at it. It took her a moment to absorb what she was seeing; a fuse seemed to blow in her head. *You already know what the sentence says because it's your words.* Her words? They looked so sleek — there was her name, at the top in bold letters, like a logo — she could hardly recognize them. It was as though they had been bought by a big conglomerate, and now half the old workers were going to be laid off.

Her hand shook slightly and she stared blindly at it as she struggled to produce an appropriate reaction. Finally, she looked at Anna, whose face was plumped with triumph, and said, "Thank you."

CHAPTER NINETEEN

The house was quiet and dark, light coming only from the kitchen, along with the odor of cooking meat. Walking into the kitchen with her jacket still on, Chris looked quickly at Kathleen, who was eating at the table, and then up at the clock. It was 8:50. On the stove stood a steak on a broiling pan, drops of fat congealing on top of it. "You made dinner!" she said to Kathleen, who was pushing her knife and fork against the remains of a baked potato with frigid precision.

"Of course I made dinner," she said.

Chris took off her jacket and hung it on the back of a chair. "I had pizza," she said, knowing even as she spoke that the words were unwise. "I'm sorry I didn't call. I was at Anna Singer's writing a résumé to bring to my interview Thursday."

Kathleen put her silverware down and wiped the corners of her mouth with her napkin.

"Look," Chris said, before Kathleen could say anything, removing the pristine papers from the envelope and holding them in front of Kathleen. Then as Kathleen reached for them, she pulled them back. "Are your hands clean?"

Kathleen shoved herself back from the table and stood. "Do you want me to look at it or not?"

"I want you to look at it with clean hands," Chris said.

When Kathleen took the papers, after washing and wiping her hands, she was still seething. She'd made a nice meal, and now it was spoiled. She put her glasses on and stared at the papers in her hands. Chris froze, thinking she saw something wrong with them. Kathleen looked up. "Anna Singer wrote you a résumé? How'd you get her to do that?"

"She didn't write it for me," Chris said, "we wrote it together."

"Really?" Kathleen said. Her mouth turned up in a deadly mechanical smile. "You wrote: 'a position allowing me to use my problem-solving skills to help people with their home design and construction needs'? And then typed that out?"

Chris flushed. "We came up with it together."

"Aha. And you called yourself self-educated?"

"Where?" Chris demanded. She was pretty sure they had never used that word; had Anna used it when Chris was thinking about something else? Chris looked down at the paper Kathleen proffered her, her distraught vision raking over the page. Then she snatched the résumés from her hand and stalked from the room, looking to make sure she hadn't wrinkled them. She had, just a little. She went into the bedroom and flattened them on the dresser, stood there thinking furiously, her knuckles resting on the dresser. Had Anna added things without asking her? After a few minutes she heard Kathleen come in behind her.

"Look," Kathleen said. "I'm sorry."

Chris turned toward her in surprise.

Kathleen sat on the edge of the bed. "I'm just trying to protect you."

"Well don't protect me," Chris said bitterly.

"I'm just saying you don't want to mislead this guy, because it might come back to bite you later."

"I'm not gonna mislead him," Chris said.

"Well you are if you give him a résumé you didn't write, and pretend you wrote it. What if he finds out you can't read?"

Chris put her hands to her ears. She wanted to say that she could read, but that wasn't entirely true; she wanted to protest that it wasn't pretending, but that too was complicated — she was and she wasn't pretending. "Leave me alone, Kath," she said.

"I'm just saying…"

"Just don't! Leave me the fuck alone."

Kathleen came to her feet. "How dare you talk to me like that?" she demanded.

Chris's head was pounding. "How *dare* I?" she mocked, coming toward Kathleen with her hands dangling. "What the fuck am I, your child?"

Kathleen snorted, eyeing Chris's hands. "You might as well be! I've taken care of you since I've known you. You wouldn't have a house without me, let alone a bank account." Her voice slithered with contempt. "When I met you, you thought North America was the same as *Canada*. You didn't know you were supposed to pay taxes. I would send you out for aspirin and you'd bring back laxatives."

Chris stopped in her tracks, amazed. "That's such bullshit!"

Kathleen laughed and nodded knowingly. "Is it? I had to make you use deodorant because my friends were all whispering that you stunk. Dell had to *beg* me to buy you some deodorant."

Chris had been about to ask what friends — Kathleen had never had many friends — but the mention of Dell made Kathleen seem credible, and took the wind out of her sails. Her hands grew slack. "Dell?" she wavered.

Kathleen saw that she had Chris on the ropes, and while part of her wondered what was happening to her, why when she had cooked a conciliatory dinner and resolved to stand behind Chris during this job thing, another part was ripping loose from its moorings and tearing violently into the wind. "Dell," she said. "Who, by the way, has known for years that you're an illiterate."

"What?"

"Oh please, did you really think she didn't know?"

For a moment, Chris thought she might suffocate. She was still for a long time. The image came to her mind of Dell's face as she confessed to her, but she refused to let it take, knowing the terrible humiliation that would flood her once she did. Until she took this in, she knew, she could go on living her life.

Kathleen looked at Chris's stupefied face and was suddenly frightened. She began to cry. "It wasn't just something happening to you,

you know, it was happening to me too," she cried.

Chris stepped up to her and stared woodenly at her streaming face, and bloodied her nose with a tremendous open-handed blow.

Anna went into the kitchen and turned on the light, revealing the remnants of the meal: a few slices of hardening pizza in the box, dirty plates and beer bottles on the table, Chris's napkin crumpled on top of her plate. She cleared the table and set the dishes in the sink, but she didn't have it in her to deal with the pizza box or wipe off the table. Instead she went into the bedroom, took off her clothes and got into bed. She turned on the TV and found an NCAA tournament game. They were down to the Elite Eight.

She thought of the urgency on Chris's face as her eyes devoured the printed résumé.

She wondered how many steps it would take for Chris's résumé to actually arrive in the contractor's hands, and remembered the New Age cat book she and Patricia used to read, which claimed that when you were away from home, if you visualized your cat in its favorite situation, that vision would be communicated to your cat, and calm it. They had mocked the book, but routinely visualized George playing with his teepee toy whenever they traveled. Now, sliding down the sheets and closing her eyes, Anna tried to serenely imagine Chris's résumé held in the contractor's hands. She imagined his hands as big and blunt-nailed, with a wedding ring. Her mind wandered and she found herself thinking about the pep talk she'd give Chris if she didn't get the job, and a bright little fantasy came upon her about making a nifty unassisted double play at first base in a softball game that Chris happened to wander by and witness.

Then she froze. She hadn't prepared Chris to be interviewed. She needed to remind her that this guy's presumption would be that Chris knew how to read. Her heartbeat quickened. If she didn't prevent that from happening, her help was just half-assed; it was just Vanessa and the daycare center fiasco all over again.

Anna took a breath in an attempt to ward off a full-blown panic attack. She looked at the clock. Way too late for tonight. But then she remembered: the interview wasn't till Thursday afternoon. And Chris had to show up in class: it was part of the agreement they'd made about her long absence. On Thursday, Anna remembered, Kevin O'Connell was coming in to introduce the students to the Internet on the center's two ancient computers. They could do it then, while the rest of the class went to the computer room.

She glanced at the score; Duke was stomping all over the tournament's lone remaining Cinderella team. She should brush her teeth, she thought. She should try to still her clamoring mind. It was late, and there was nothing she could do. She reached behind her head for the vibrator she kept stashed at the mattress's edge, and pushing her most standard fantasies to her mind's forefront, brought herself to orgasm and sleep.

Kathleen had staggered from the room with her hands cupped around her nose. Chris went into the closet and took out a backpack, and packed it quickly, her ears straining, wondering where Kathleen was and what she was doing. She could hear the tap running in the kitchen. Her rage had not abated, but it had become mixed with bewilderment. In the space of an hour, she had gone from writing a résumé to smacking her girlfriend. What did that say about her? And yet, the provocation.... The humiliation over Dell burned in her as she stuffed toiletries into the pack, closed it, and swung it onto her shoulder.

Outside there was a drizzle and a funky smell in the warm air. She quickly walked the nine blocks to Keith and Margaret's. She was thankful to see that the lights were on. Keith answered the door in sweats and a t-shirt, and taking one look at her ghastly face, beckoned her in. "Can I crash on your couch?" Chris asked.

"Sure."

Toby, their alpha cat, was sitting on the newel post, his eyes challenging and his tail wrapped around his body. Margaret came downstairs in her bathrobe. "Hello," she said, shooting a quick questioning look toward Keith.

"Hi, Margaret." Chris smoothed her wet hair back with her hands. "Hope I didn't wake you. Keith said it was okay for me to crash here."

Margaret put her finger to her lips. "The kids are sleeping," she said. "Let me take your jacket."

Keith went to get some bedding with what seemed to Chris to be a hangdog air. She went into the living room and sat on the couch, and Margaret followed her in. Margaret was a person who gave off a frosty aura, and it had taken Chris and Kathleen years to learn not to take it personally. For animals alone she reserved an ardent warmth; Rufus always greeted her with adoring moans. She sat down opposite Chris, and Toby jumped on her lap. "What happened?" she asked, running her hand over his arching back.

Chris shifted. Her face was still damp, and she ran a sleeve across it. "A really bad fight. Something it's hard to forgive."

Margaret raised her eyebrows. "For you to forgive or Kathleen to forgive?"

Just then Keith returned, his arms laden with bedding. "Here you go, kiddo," he said, letting it fall on the couch next to Chris.

"Thanks, Egg."

After they went back upstairs, she made up the sofa bed, then set up in the tiny wallpapered powder room, setting the shaving bag she used for toiletries on the back of the toilet and making an effort, as she washed her face in scalding water, not to sully the shell-shaped soaps lying in dishes. Back in the living room she stripped down to her underwear and undershirt, and settled into bed with a groan. After a few minutes she heard a soft noise on the stairs. She opened her eyes and let them adjust to the darkness, and saw Jessica's bulky dark shape stealing toward the kitchen. She was wearing a jacket. "Hey," Chris whispered, and the shape froze. Jessica came over and peered down at her with a sullen face, refusing to give an adult the satisfaction of surprise. "Where you goin'?"

"None of your business," Jessica whispered back, looking furtively over her shoulder.

"Your mom thinks you're asleep," Chris said, "You're not running away or nothin', are you?"

"No."

"Okay." Chris had never liked Jessica very much, which made her feel guilty, because Jessica was a rebel, and technically Chris believed in kids being rebellious. But the trouble with her was, you could never catch her eye, and as ridiculous as it sounded, seeing that she was all of fourteen, her sarcasm made Chris feel stupid. So she was surprised when Jessica sat down on an ottoman, with her hands in her jacket pockets.

"What'd you do, get in a fight with Kathleen?" she asked.

"Yeah." Chris crossed her hands behind her head.

"Did you hit her?"

Chris blinked and ran through some calculations. The phone hadn't rung since she'd gotten there. "How'd you know?" she finally asked.

Jessica shrugged.

After a pause, Chris asked, "Do I look like the kind of person that hits their girlfriend?"

The question floated out into the darkness. Jessica was quiet. Then she said, apologetically, "Kinda."

Chris accepted her response with a grunt.

After a few moments, Jessica stood. "Well," she said, "I gotta get going."

"Where you going?"

Jessica shrugged again. "Just out with some friends."

"You guys doin' drugs?"

"What is this, the inquisition?"

Chris smiled. "You're in luck, kid, I'm too ignorant to know what the inquisition is."

Jessica's shoulders seemed to relax. "It's just an expression anyways," she said.

Silence, as Chris found herself feeling unexpectedly tender. "You wanna stay here and watch some TV with me?"

Jessica rose. "Nah, I gotta go, they're waiting for me."

"Okay," Chris said. "But no drugs, and no getting in a car with a drunk person, okay? Because otherwise I'll have to personally kick your ass."

"What are you, my father?" Jessica huffed, but Chris could see her teeth gleam in the darkness.

"Shit, I'm much scarier than that wimp," Chris said. Jessica laughed a startled huff, then turned to go. "I'm the kind of person that hits her girlfriend," Chris called softly as she slipped into the kitchen and out the back door.

Over the next few days, as Anna mulled over an end-of-the-year project for her students, the phone began to ring. Her birthday was the weekend after next, and it was a momentous one: not only her first since Patricia left, but the birthday on which she would turn the age her father was when he died. Scott, who was coming in from Ithaca, called to give her his flight information, and Janice finally called too, to urge Anna to have a party. Her enthusiasm for thinking through how to mark this occasion slowly dissipated Anna's anger at her. But Anna was ambivalent about a party. "To be honest, I have no idea what to do," she said to Janice. "What's the proper way to celebrate the emotion: you're dead and I'm alive?"

"By having a delicious meal with people who love you," Janice replied decisively. She added, "You know, your father would be proud of you."

Anna snorted. "You think so? Think he'd be okay with the whole lesbian thing?"

Janice laughed. "He'd love the whole package," she said warmly, making Anna's heart hurt.

She was on the couch, and when she and Janice hung up she sat there tapping a pen against a pad of paper, musing on their conversation and trying to invent a project that would put in play, in a meaningful fashion, all the things her students had learned during the year. How to write a sentence with a subject and a verb, how to write a paragraph, how to punctuate. How to write what matters rather than the alienated rote crap they felt was called for. The essays, from her class and the others, would be collected into a book and "published" on the computers, then put on display in the Pathways library.

The living room windows were open to the mild afternoon. Anna closed her eyes and tossed the pad of paper on the floor and lay down, her hands folded behind her head. She loved Janice. When you had her attention you felt bathed in attention. So when Janice neglected her, Anna felt utterly desolate. But was she asking too much? — was it reasonable to expect of your friends that they'd keep track of your daily whereabouts? Maybe she just needed a girlfriend really badly. When she and Patricia had been together, they'd had a category they jokingly called "a really interesting thing I just thought of" — those things that popped into your mind, and for which you were each other's only possible audience. Like you'd had a sandwich earlier in the day on bread that you thought was too fancy: and then the two of you would agree that bread shouldn't have rosemary or jalapeños in it. Or you'd remember the moment in your twenties when you realized you mustn't wear polyester anymore, and the two of you would muse about social class and the cotton/polyester divide.

She brought her mind back to the task at hand. She wanted her students to write something risky, something with genuine drama. What if they wrote a story about a moment where their lives had changed, and tried to describe what difference that moment had made in their lives? Her mind rejected that idea as unoriginal — that's what she was implicitly asking them to write, after all, each time they did an LEA. But by the end of the weekend, that was the idea that stuck with her, and she had decided that she could make it stand out to her students by giving it a title: Turning Points.

She drove to class Thursday morning with her windows open and the radio on. Up at Pathways, she walked stiffly past Renée's office without turning her head. When she came into the classroom, Antwan and Cheryl were hanging out the open windows, Antwan blowing great gusts of cigarette smoke outside, Cheryl craned out and yacking with someone down below. "You crazy!" she heard Cheryl calling, and after a pause, a cackle. Cheryl glanced inside and saw Anna, and drew back as though she'd been caught doing something wrong. "I got to go," she said out the window in a stage whisper, and swung her feet off the ledge and onto the floor. It was her very special way, Anna thought, of making Anna feel like a parole officer.

Vanessa came in with Tisha, who was clutching a plastic bag to her chest, her hair ribbons bringing a burst of color into the dingy room. Behind them Chris and Robert were coming in, both awkwardly flattening themselves against the door frame to let the other in first, looking vaguely past each others' knees. When they were all seated, Anna told them about their assignment. "It'll be called Turning Points," she said, "and here's the idea. At one point in your life you were headed in one direction." She held out her hands, palms facing each other, at the end of outstretched arms. She saw that Tisha was taking out of the bag a coloring book and crayons, laying the crayons one by one in a neat line on the little desk. "And then something happened," Anna said. She paused dramatically, and turned her palms upward into a more receptive pose. "And after that, you had to turn in an entirely new direction." She dropped her hands to her sides. "And here are some questions we might ask: What kinds of decisions did you have to make? How did you change as a person? How did it make you think of your future differently?" She stood quietly at the front of the room and let it sink in.

"How long it got to be?" Antwan asked.

"A page."

They took in their breath.

"Wait — we learning the computer today?" Cheryl asked.

"Yes, in a few minutes," Anna said. "I just wanted to plant the seed of the project in your minds." She looked at their stricken faces and laughed; all of the morning's buoyancy had faded. "I see from your faces that I've succeeded! You'll see, you guys. We'll do it little by little, and I'll help you.

"Your first task is to brainstorm about an event," she said. "I want you to keep that in the back of your mind for the next few days. Then on Thursday, we'll start working on it in class." There was a rustle as they prepared to leave. "Wait!" she said, her voice rising. "Listen. The thing about a project like this: it's not easy to write about something so personal, and so dramatic. I'm hoping that you guys will find it in yourselves to open up and be honest and thoughtful about your lives. I hope we know each other well enough by now to do that."

She dismissed them to the computer lesson. Vanessa stood and bent over Tisha's desk, looking defeated at the prospect of packing her up again. At the door, Cheryl whirled around, her earrings swinging. "You writing one, Ms. Singer?"

"What?"

"You gonna write a turning point?"

"No," Anna said.

"You should," Cheryl said. "You should be honest and thoughtful too." Her eyes brightened with helpfulness. "Write about when you turned gay!"

Anna was so completely nonplussed, she actually choked. Cheryl walked off with a grin, and only then did Anna remember to go into the hallway and call Chris back. Through spasms of coughing, she said, "I just wanted to say a few things before your interview."

"Okay," Chris said.

They came back into the classroom, where Vanessa was sweeping Tisha's crayons into the bag with a single swoop of the hand, and Tisha's face was clouding up. "Don't you cry," Vanessa warned.

"Vanessa," Anna said, "why doesn't Tisha stay with us for a little while, and you go on ahead? Is that okay with you, Tisha?"

Tisha nodded solemnly, and Vanessa didn't hesitate; she gave her daughter a noisy kiss on the cheek, grabbed her bag and left the room.

Anna pulled two chairs opposite one another. She and Chris sat, and Anna cleared her throat and appraised Chris. She was a wreck, her jeans stiff and dirty, her face sallow and her eyes even more haggard than usual, almost purple, her hair uncharacteristically greasy. She hoped Chris didn't plan on going to her interview like that.

"I just wanted to remind you that he'll assume you know how to read," Anna said.

"Right," Chris said.

"He might ask how you'd handle working with subcontractors who are mostly male," Anna continued, "although I don't think he's allowed to be specific about that. He'll probably just ask a general question about management style."

"Okay."

"Good. And oh, one more thing. Let's see how to put this." Anna looked at her shrewdly. "You're a rough-hewn kind of person," she said. "You give off the impression of being very competent, but not taking any crap. Now our clients are middle-class people with lots of opinions, some of them half-baked, and lots of anxiety about all the money they're spending and all the chaos that's going to be going on in their houses. How will you make them feel comfortable?"

Chris rubbed her nose with a knuckle and considered. "Shoot," she said to Anna, "this is sounding more and more like a big fat dud of a job."

Anna laughed. "Well, when you think about it… Some of them will be straight couples with kids and a lot of money." She made a squeamish face, and Chris chuckled in spite of herself.

"You're gonna have to come up with an answer to that, Chris. Firm handshake, smile, eye contact…. You're gonna have to tell this guy that you'll listen respectfully to their opinions."

"I'll listen respectfully to their opinions," Chris intoned. "I'll tell them that this is their house, so they're in charge."

"Okay," Anna said. She leaned forward toward Chris, resting her elbows on her knees. "Hey, how come you look like such a wreck? Those clothes look like you've slept in them for a week." She was reaching for the language of male affection, the way men insult each other over their baldness or paunch or big feet. "Are you nervous?"

Chris gave her a look loaded with sarcasm, as if Anna was an idiot for stating the obvious.

"Are you?" Anna pressed.

Chris snapped "So what if I am? It don't help to whine about it, especially right before the interview."

"You know, Chris," Anna said, "Talking about something isn't always the same as whining."

At that, Chris looked so genuinely startled that Anna laughed. Then she got serious again. She reached forward and put her hand on Chris's shoulder, grasped it, took a long look into Chris's face. She could see every bit of fuzz on her cheeks, the tiny broken capillaries around the bridge of her nose. She released Chris's shoulder and sat up, slapping her hands down on her knees. "Good luck, man. I'll be thinking of you."

Half an hour later, Chris let herself into Keith and Margaret's with her spare key. They were at work, and the kids at school. She went into the master bathroom, taking in the smells of shaving cream and aftershave, and stripped, stepped into the scalding shower, shampooed and conditioned her hair and scrubbed herself with soap. She dried herself with the closest towel, and rubbed her hair vigorously. She wiped the medicine cabinet mirror with her palm and looked at herself through the blur of the wet streak she left: too-long hair sticking straight up, skin puffy and yellowed underneath her eyes, wrinkles starting to pucker the corners of her mouth. She caught a glimpse of her breasts, which had stretch marks on the sides and hung heavily, nipples pointing down. She opened the medicine cabinet to make her image vanish. Reaching in, she took out the three prescription bottles and turned them over, one by one, peering at the labels. She fumbled for her glasses, wiped the steam off the lenses and perched them on her nose.

She could read the labels. Pretty much.

She couldn't make out the names of the medicines, but she could read how much you were supposed to take, and which ones were for Keith and which for Margaret. She just read them, without sounding them out or making a big production out of it. She placed the bottle on the edge of the sink, closed her eyes as tears rushed in. Hadn't she dreamt of this moment? But now, as it turned out, it was a whole can of worms. How much more convenient just to ignorantly OD, like a dog lapping up a puddle of anti-freeze. Now, because she could read, she had to make a decision.

She tore some toilet paper off the roll and blew her nose. Did every single feeling have to be mixed? Lord, it wearied her. Once upon a time she had been happy or mad or sad or bored. That's it, normal feelings, not this freak show.

She chose the one that said "for pain," and letting her mind click into pure blind compulsion, took two, then another two. Then she went downstairs and found her backpack and took out her interview clothes. Black jeans and a white oxford shirt. She shook out the shirt and scrutinized it, and went in search of an iron and ironing board, which she found in the pantry off the kitchen. She set up in the kitchen, and poured herself a glass of water, which she filled with ice and set on the counter so it wouldn't spill on her shirt. As she ironed and sipped water, she felt her movements to be judicious, her mind to have more foresight than usual. She was extremely conscious of the hot iron, and of pulling out the plug when she was finished. She put everything neatly back where she had found it, and washed the glass she had drunk out of, sudsing it up, swirling copious hot water through it, and setting it upside down in the dish rack.

It was a warm afternoon with a white Chicago sky, trees waving with the outrageously green buds of early spring. Jason Paciorek's business, Paciorek Builders, wasn't far from Keith's house; earlier Chris had slipped her résumé into the mailbox. Chris walked there now, her dress shoes chafing the sides of her pinky toes. On the North Side, construction crews were out in full force. She walked past more than one crew sitting on a stoop eating lunch and eyeing her as she passed, and chuckled grimly to herself at the thought that soon, she might be the boss of men like that. When she arrived at Paciorek Builders, sweating more than she'd wanted to, she pushed open the glass door into a comfortably cool room where a man was bent over a secretary, pointing at a computer screen and giving instructions. He looked up, glasses perched at the edge of his nose, and straightened. "Chris," Jason Paciorek said, and came forward to shake her hand. "Jason." He was a tall man in his late forties with disheveled dark hair and granny glasses hung by a cord around his neck that interacted disarmingly with his masculinity. He ushered her into a small conference room, and she was surprised to enjoy the touch of his hand on her shoulder.

As he sat her at a table littered with catalogues and sample faucets and shower heads, and poured her a cup of coffee from a coffee machine in the tiny kitchenette in the corner, Chris took a breath and felt herself expand. She closed her eyes for a brief moment and felt the room spin. She opened them quickly.

He placed a cup of coffee before her, and sat down with his own cup across the table. "Well!" he exhaled, giving his head a vigorous scratch. "How do you know Keith Serynek? He speaks very highly of you."

Chris's mind whirred for a few seconds; she opened her mouth, then closed it. "He's an old friend of my partner's," she managed to say. Then, unexpectedly, merriment bubbled into her throat and nose, and she snorted. "Well, actually, her ex-husband."

Jason's eyes widened in puzzlement, then amusement. He laughed a clear melodious laugh. "You must *really* be something, then."

Chris smiled. "He's a good guy, Keith," she said indulgently.

He started talking about his business, which mostly did residential renovations, and from that point on, the drugs loosened her way up. Which was a good thing, because when he was done talking, he put her through the wringer. Gave her a blueprint to read, which she made her way around without incident, and then gave her an electrical blueprint, which, when she looked at the electrical symbols, nearly gave her a heart attack, she could make so little sense of it. She thought she blew the interview right there. But he seemed unfazed, and her mind quick and slippery, she realized that probably plenty of people who could read couldn't read electrical symbols. He took her into a room and told her he wanted to put in a floor using four-inch pine planks, and asked how much lumber he should order. When she said 40 planks he smiled and said, "I estimated 39." He asked her where she would start laying the floor, and walked in the wrong direction to fake her out, but she was onto him, and said she would start by the door — that they'd probably put a couch over in the corner, which would cover the cuts. He took her to another room and said he wanted to make it into an office for two people, and asked her to design it.

Later, back at the conference table, when Jason asked her the question Anna had said he would, about her management style, she said "I figured you'd ask that! I won't lie to you, I've had my problems working with men." When he raised his eyebrows at that, she laughed and waved her hand airily. "Oh! not men like you." She leaned forward on her forearm as she would on a bar, and told him, "I'm just looking forward to being the boss for a change." Then she added in a big rush: "Not that I would abuse that or nothing, no way. I'd be tough but fair." She sat back and repeated with satisfaction, "Tough but fair."

She left with her mind spinning, and later, back at Keith's, Chris couldn't tell if she'd been fantastic or a jackass. She knew he hadn't discovered that she read at a low level, that was for sure. She knew she'd told him she was a real go-getter, and that she came from a family of construction workers, which he was really into. Her construction roots, he called it, and returning bullshit for bullshit, she called her family "simple working folks." She laughed so uproariously at his jokes that later the muscles in her face hurt and she cringed at the thought of the buffoonish grinning she must have done, although it had felt genuine enough at the time. And she thought she might have confessed that she was having trouble with her girlfriend, and called it, with a wink, "woman trouble."

She changed back into sweats and fell asleep on the couch, and awoke a few hours later to find Zoey standing over her, clearly trying to be quiet but breathing heavily through her mouth. "Hi!" Zoey chirped, and Chris groaned and shifted. Her head was spinning, her stomach killing her.

"Where's your parents?"

"Not home yet."

"Where's Jessica?"

"Up in her room," Zoey said. "Can I have some microwave popcorn?"

"Sure," Chris said. "You know how to make it?"

"Of course," Zoey said huffily.

Jessica pounded down the stairs and went into the kitchen without greeting her; even from a distance Chris could smell the pot wafting off her. She groaned again. Who was she kidding, thinking she could do that job, with the reading it would require? She could bullshit her way through an interview, but not the job. She crooked her arm over her eyes, dreading whatever was coming next.

CHAPTER TWENTY

The following Thursday, on her way to O'Hare to pick up Scott, Anna threaded her way through heavy traffic on the Expressway, fretting. Chris hadn't shown up since the day of her interview, and it angered Anna that she hadn't reported how it had gone. She had called Chris's house last night but hung up when she got the machine. Her mind revolved around the possibilities: either the interview had gone badly and Chris was spinning out, or she had gotten the job and decided to quit school. Anna suspected the former.

Traffic surged forward and then stopped again, and she sat back with an irritated sigh. Brandy and Chris's absences were sucking a big hole into the class. This morning, the rest of them had come to class unprepared, looking shocked when she brought up their final assignment. But slowly they had started coming up with ideas for turning points to write about. Vanessa was debating between her sister's murder and Desirée's arrival; Antwan shrugged and said "when my moms died, I guess." Cheryl wanted to write about the death of her boyfriend Germaine, and Anna looked forward to clues about what made Cheryl tick with an interest she hoped wasn't too ghoulish and voyeuristic. And Robert wanted to write about the war.

She made the turn-off to O'Hare, and as she approached the airport a massive jet loomed into sight on a bridge ahead of her, dwarfing the cars, and making her think about the jets in her dreams that descended terrifyingly overhead, casting huge black shadows. She'd had those dreams since childhood, and considered them one of her legacies as a Chicagoan.

She parked in the garage and headed for baggage claim. She saw Scott almost immediately in the crowd of people circling one of the conveyor belts. Wearing a leather jacket, a shoulder bag slung over his shoulder, he was eating a bag of popcorn as he watched the suitcases go around. She cut through the crowd and touched his shoulder. "Anna!" he exclaimed with his mouth full, opening his arms to hug her; she could hear the popcorn bag rustle behind her head as his arms pulled her close. He rubbed his cheek against hers like a cat, and she pulled away because sometimes he liked to run his tongue up her cheek.

"Delighted to see you," he drawled. Anna bumbled a smile. She was often in the position of straight man to Scott, whose performances were so varied and mercurial, celebrating so delightedly the razor-thin line between genuine and parodic, that beside him she felt ploddingly wholesome.

His neck was thicker and his face more square than when she'd seen him the previous August; he had begun going religiously to the gym and put on a lot of muscle. She took his chin in her hand and turned his face back and forth in scrutiny. "Look at you," she said. "You're thicker."

"You better believe it, baby," he said. He thrust the popcorn toward her and she took a handful. "Oh my God I'm so glad to be here," he murmured in her ear.

They retrieved his bag and hauled it out to the garage elevators, where they ascended to the floor labeled White Sox, which played a sports-stadium song that would torment them by blathering its nah-nah-nahs in their heads for the rest of the day. In the car Scott opened his window all the way, leaning out into the clammy air and inhaling auto and airplane fumes with gusto. Two years ago, driving to Ithaca for the first time, he had cried and cried, every hour taking him further from a city, past cornfields, through the tiny towns with rickety peeling houses and rusting cars.

He brought his head in and settled back with a satisfied sigh. He tapped her knee briskly. "Remember when I saw you last?" he asked. "Oh my goodness you were a sad puppy."

"I *was* a sad puppy," Anna said, wondering what kind of puppy she was now.

That night she cooked pasta with eggplant and tomatoes and olives while Scott made a salad, and she pondered aloud the problem of marking this birthday. She covered the sauce and shook a box of penne into boiling water, gave it a stir, then turned and leaned against the counter. "I don't know," she said. "Remember mine and Patricia's cat George? When he died, everything was in place for a beautiful ritual. Everything! We had his ashes, and a beautiful garden to scatter them in. Even a beautiful and period-appropriate poem. Christopher Smart, *Jubilate Agno,* the part about his cat Geoffrey."

"Oh sure," Scott said.

"Plus," Anna added, remembering, "it was a student I really loved who pointed me to the lines — her mother was dying of leukemia but somehow she still managed to engage with my grief about my cat.

"Listen to the lines," she said, and recited, too self-conscious to look directly at him:

For God has blessed him in the variety of his movements.
For there is nothing sweeter than his peace when at rest.
For in his morning orisons, he loves the sun and the sun loves him.
For he is a mixture of gravity and waggery.
For every house is incompleat without him, and a blessing is lacking in the spirit.

She glanced at him, blushing.

"Nice," Scott approved, whisking together oil and vinegar.

"And it so fit George, bless his heart," Anna said in a rush, tears surprising her as she remembered her sweet handsome cat. "And yet, even though when I first encountered those lines I cried and cried, when we scattered his ashes in the yard and I recited them, I felt totally embarrassed. I couldn't muster a feeling to go with the ritual."

Scott straightened and reached for a towel to wipe his hands. "Maybe it would help if you were a Quaker, like Emily Sacks; they always manage to have moving rituals with artwork and songs and quilts."

Anna laughed. "It's true!" Emily Sacks was a Jewish Quaker they knew from graduate school. "That woman knows exactly how to spin a seder so it's not xenophobic or phallocentric, and speaks meaningfully to the situation in the Middle East."

Scott stiffened gleefully. "Oh my God, did I tell you about the seder I went to a couple weeks ago?"

Anna shook her head. Of course Scott had been to a seder. Lately, they had invented a new joke about his fetishism of Jews actually being a subtle form of anti-Semitism, and Anna having to police him. At some point right around what she now called "the whole Rudolph-the-Red-Nosed-Reindeer fiasco," she had clamped down and decided that he wasn't allowed to even say the word *nose,* because that was anti-Semitic. They called it the facial feature that dare not speak its name.

"Normally of course I would go to a lesbian seder where the lesbians are all wearing yarmulkes and prayer shawls, and where they set a place for Sarah as well as for Elijah the Prophet, and where *everybody* gets a prize when the *afikomen* gets found so no one feels excluded — " he waved his hand, suggesting that she knew the drill. "But this year my friend Adam's *mother* had a seder, and his father had just died, and I went as a favor to him. It was a huge Long Island seder, and she used an old-fashioned Hagaddah. And here were my two favorite parts, both in footnotes. The first one occurred at the ten plagues, where the text is hammering gleefully away at the punishments leveled on the Egyptians. It claimed that Jews have been slandered as a vengeful people when in fact they're a very loving people." He screwed up his face and protested tearfully, "We're a very *loving* people!

"Can you imagine?" he asked, cackling. "Even the old lady next to me, Adam's great aunt, read it" — he mimicked her pushing her glasses up and bringing the book to her face and scowling at it — "and sat back in her seat and snorted!

"And then, and then!" he said, holding his hand up to make Anna stop laughing. "At the point where you eat the *charoset* sandwich" — he made the guttural *ch* sound with phlegmy relish — "there was a footnote claiming that, contrary to popular opinion, it wasn't the Earl of Sandwich who invented the sandwich at all: it was Rabbi Hillel!"

Anna cracked up again. "That is so Jewish!"

"I know!" Scott laughed, touching her knee. "And gay, and African-American." He brought his laughter in for a landing, huffing happily, then had a sudden thought. "Hey, remember how your grandparents used to think that every black man on TV was Sammy Davis Jr.?"

"I do," she said. It was a tried-and-true source of delight. There was a pause. "But you know what I mean about ritual?" she asked.

"Of course," Scott said, decisive and kind.

After dinner he shaved and put on a different, tighter pair of jeans and a t-shirt. He was going downtown to meet some old friends at a bar, and she knew he wouldn't return till morning. Anna pressed the veiny biceps his short sleeves strained over and made admiring noises, secretly missing the skinny femmy boy she'd always loved, the one who apparently had had no sexual caché in the circles he aspired to. She pressed house keys into his hand and told him to have fun. He left her settled on the couch in front of the TV feeling for all the world like his dowdy mother.

At 6:30 the next morning, Anna heard the click of the front door latch. In half-sleep, she heard the sound of noisy peeing from the bathroom, then water running, the sounds of teeth-brushing and the gagging noises he made when he brushed his tongue. Scott came into the bedroom and peeled off his clothes down to his underwear, and crawled into bed with her, smelling of alcohol, cigarette smoke, tooth-paste, and Ivory soap. When the alarm went off at 7 and Anna stretched and set her feet on the floor, he groaned and flung his arm around her. She laughed and tried to rise, but he wrestled her back onto the bed and snuggled up to her back.

"Scott!" she protested, unpasting his arm from her waist and wrenching herself up. She was annoyed as she got into the shower — there was a twinge in her back where she had twisted it to get up — and scrubbing her face with her hands, she remembered the many occasions she'd been annoyed with Scott when they were in graduate school together. They had spent a lot of time studying together in each others' Hyde Park apartments, eating popcorn they popped in an air popper and sprinkled with parmesan cheese, watching just one more round of *Jeopardy*, just one more episode of *Cheers*. As Anna fought her way through her papers, her insights coming amid anxiety that felt like bursts of shrapnel, Scott would sit still and absorbed over his book, twirling his hair and exhaling cigarette smoke. To Anna he looked like a real scholar when he worked, while she was just a facsimile — the way people's beds on TV always looked more comfortable than hers, their dinners tastier and better balanced. A lot of the work of becoming an academic you could do supine, and that didn't help her morale one bit. Now, soaping herself, she remembered the torturous stretches of writer's block, how once, at the beginning of her dissertation, it had become so unbearable, so unrelieved by the time-honored strategy of alternating writing and research, that she took Patricia's advice and simply stopped writing till she couldn't stand not writing anymore. It took about a month and a half. In the interim she watched a lot of TV and bickered with Scott, who, when roused into actual fighting, was such a vicious and legalistic arguer that he often drove her to tears.

She got out of the shower, dried herself off and walked quietly, wrapped in a towel, into the bedroom. She looked at the smelly and sated man snoring in her bed. He would be getting up around the time she got back from class, she guessed.

When she got to class she found Vanessa and Cheryl and Antwan sitting in a clump of desks close to each other, in heated conversation. Their heads whipped around as she entered. "Good morning," she said.

They glanced at each other. Antwan sat back in his chair exhaling in a whoosh, and lay his hands palms down on the desk. Anna walked to the front of the classroom, thinking she'd silenced them, and erased the previous lesson, about the parts of a plant, from the board. The heat was clanging on even though it was already about 75 degrees in there. Turning toward the class she saw Robert come in; he paused at the door, nervously sensing the tension in the room.

He murmured a greeting and sat down quietly. Just when Anna thought nobody was going to tell her what was going on, Cheryl spoke. "In the pre-GED class," she said, "they reading a book called *Push*."

"Aha," Anna said, nodding and putting her palms behind her on the desk, hopping backward onto it.

"And some of the people in the class is upset with Joyce."

Joyce was the pre-GED teacher. "Do you know why?" Anna asked. She'd read Sapphire's novel, and had an inkling; but she wanted to hear it from them.

Antwan spoke up. "They saying she a racist."

Vanessa slapped at his hand. "But not everybody," she corrected him.

"Who, Joyce?" Anna asked. "How come?"

Cheryl stared contemplatively at her. "She's saying that black people is fat and have AIDS and they daddies have sex with them."

"Who's saying that, Joyce?" Anna repeated.

Cheryl *tsked* impatiently, and recrossed her legs; she was wearing jeans and heels. "Yes! No! the book. But she making them *read* the book."

Anna nodded slowly. "Do you guys know what the book is about? It's about a fat, illiterate, battered, sexually-abused black girl from the projects with AIDS and two kids, one of whom is retarded." She paused, her thoughts churning, watching shock and dismay come over their features. Things were clearly worse than they'd expected. Robert shook his head about all the pain in the world: it hardly made reading seem worthwhile. Antwan crinkled his nose in distaste at the thought of people too ignorant to use a condom, and then immediately yearned for the old days, before Sheila started making him put one on before he could even come near her.

"You're saying," Anna ventured, "that some people feel that by having them read the book, Joyce is endorsing the view that the book puts forth of black people."

"Yes!" Cheryl said bitterly; "that's the kind of stories white folks just *love* to read about niggers."

Anna tried to make her thoughts orderly, but the truth was, it was a thorny question. Which was why she had decided not to read *Push* to her class. "What about the author who wrote the book?" she asked. "Is she guilty of putting forth a stereotype?" And before they could answer she added quickly, because she didn't want it to be a trick question, "And do you know that the author, Sapphire, is African-American?"

They were sitting sideways, aslant, in transient postures, their book bags unpacked on top of their desks. Vanessa still wore her windbreaker, zipped up to her chin. She and Antwan peeked at Cheryl, as always, the group's spokesperson and rabble rouser. Cheryl opened her mouth, then closed it. "I know," she lied. "But that don't make it right."

There was silence. Cheryl was jiggling one leg and looking bored.

Vanessa was deep in thought. "Maybe she just telling it like it is," she said in a remote and doleful voice.

"Who," Anna asked: "the author or the teacher? Let's try to keep them separate."

"The author, what's her name?"

"Sapphire," Anna said. "It's just one name."

Antwan sniffed. "What kind of name is that?"

Anna shrugged and smiled. "Self-expression."

Vanessa's voice rose. "Because sometimes, that's just how it is. They people *like* that! And it don't just disappear if you ignore it."

"It's true," Anna said. "And just so you guys know, the character in the book grows a lot — the book shows how empowered she becomes by learning how to read. How she started out as low as you could go, but still has courage and the drive to learn."

Vanessa sat back with a gleam of complacency, at having been right and at the thought of a person inspired by learning to read.

"But I also get Cheryl's point," Anna said. She told them about the movie — whose name she'd forgotten — that portrays Leopold and Loeb as gay, and after explaining that Leopold and Loeb were famous Chicago murderers, said, "And I watched this movie and I thought: why? Even if they were gay: gay people don't have enough bad press already, now you have to portray us as murderers?" She laughed irately and stuck out her hands at spastic angles, palms up, performing that position, showing that it was a legitimate one. "But! Some people might say, like Vanessa, 'Sometimes, that's just how it is.' You can't just portray gay people as wonderful inspiring heroes. Because in real life, some of us are jerks just like straight people. Just like not every black person is Michael Jordan, not every gay person is Martina Navratilova. Life's just not like that."

They sat gazing into space, sniffing and frowning, *caring about representation,* Anna thought. Her heart rushed toward them in a warm tumult.

Robert cleared his throat. "Or like Sidney Poitier," he said.

Anna lit up at being able to follow his train of thought for once. "Exactly!" she said. "The perfect African-American man."

Cheryl cut through, not listening. "It still don't make it right for Joyce to read that book to those pre-GED students," she said.

"Well that brings us to the next question," Anna said. "You know, I thought about reading you that book." She paused for effect, and it had one; Vanessa's nostrils stiffened, and Antwan averted his eyes. "But in the end, I chose *Bastard out of Carolina* instead. Because it's a book about poor people with big problems, but they're white. I worried that if I read *Push* to you, you'd think I thought that was *you.* While if I read a book about white people who batter and abuse each other, you could relax into the story because it would feel less personal."

"That's right," Vanessa said, settling back nodding and crossing her arms.

Anna looked at them, pondering, her decision suddenly seeming inevitable. What was the argument for the other position again? That she was just being super-cautious, even cowardly, while Joyce had dared to challenge them with a text that was difficult emotionally to digest? She also found herself suddenly tangled in a digression: how would they have reacted had *Renée* read them *Push* instead of Joyce? It probably would have been okay. She ran a quick analogy through her mind, substituting black people with gay people. And while her thoughts gobbled along like chickens eating feed, the worry that she was criticizing Joyce in order to portray herself as the culturally-sensitive white teacher made a cameo appearance.

What was the argument for the other position again? She knew there was a good one, one she even believed in. Oh yeah, Anna thought: that it was empowering for them to see characters like themselves in literature. That claim suddenly seemed like utter bullshit. And then she remembered *Stone Butch Blues* and froze.

When she came home, Scott was at the kitchen table drinking coffee and reading the *Reader,* his hand plunged into his hair. "Can I ask you a really important question?" he asked.

"Sure."

"Does anybody ever *really* know what time it is?"

She rolled her eyes. He had left the coffee can open on the counter, the lid off the sugar bowl.

"How was last night?" she asked.

"Fabulous," he drawled. He had had sex with an Argentinean man, he told her as she tidied up the kitchen, who had afterward threatened to tear his eyes out if he looked at other men. "It was so sexy," he laughed, and added dreamily, "it was like whatchamacallit on *The Addams Family* when Morticia spoke French."

Anna smiled. "Good for you, sweetheart. Listen, I've got to make a call." She closed herself in the bedroom and dialed Chris's number, leaving a firm message this time, that either Chris or Kathleen should call her back.

Chris had been staying at Keith's for a week, and Margaret's pursed lips and the hushed conferences between her and Keith were becoming too much. Margaret was in a constant struggle with Jessica, over her grades and her general demeanor, and even in her dazed and miserable state, with, admittedly, zippo experience at being a mother, Chris could tell she was going about it all wrong. One afternoon Margaret came home from work to find Chris and Jessica slouched on the couch, their feet on the coffee table, watching a VH1 *Behind the Music* show about Fleetwood Mac and eating Chips Ahoy out of the bag. "Don't you have homework to do?" she snapped at Jessica, and when Jessica stalked furiously out of the room, she turned to Chris. "I'd appreciate it if you wouldn't encourage her to eat junk food and watch crap on TV," she said coldly.

"Jesus, Margaret," Chris said. "It's better than her being out on the street. Plus, it's educational — "

Since her job interview, she couldn't bring herself to go to school;

she didn't know why, she just couldn't put one foot in front of the other and haul her body there. She had given Jason Paciorek the number at Keith and Margaret's, but no call came.

Saturday afternoon, after returning from picking up some groceries, Chris came into the kitchen with plastic bags in each hand, and found all four of them standing there, engulfed by a thick silence. She heaved the bags onto the counter and turned toward Keith. Zoey came up and wrapped her arms around Chris's waist and lay her head against her stomach.

"Hi peanut," Chris said, surprised, and then joked, "What's with the long faces, did another hamster die?"

"Now is not the time, Chris," Keith said. He was sober and red-faced. Jessica had been crying.

"Chris," Margaret said, "Excuse us. This is a family matter."

Chris blinked and stalked out of the kitchen, fuming. She had bought toilet paper and cooking oil because she'd noticed they were almost out, and while she was at it she had splurged and bought the smoked mussels that she knew Margaret loved. She settled on the couch, at a loss over what to do next, when she began overhearing the fight going on in the kitchen. "How am I supposed to believe you?" she heard Margaret demand. "We know you've smoked pot."

"But I don't *steal*," Jessica wailed. "You must think I'm totally pathetic."

As they argued, it dawned on Chris that Margaret and Keith thought that Jessica had taken Margaret's painkillers. Her heart crammed itself into her throat. How had they noticed? She hadn't taken more than two or three. But then she made herself go back over and count, and she realized that she had taken more like six to ten.

She rubbed her face with her hands and thought: *poor kid.*

That evening, she packed her things. "I think I've outstayed my welcome," she said to Keith. "But thanks, Egg, you guys have been great." He didn't try to persuade her to stay; he ran his hand through his thinning hair and said "Sorry, Chris, we got our hands full here."

They clasped hands. She left without knowing where she was going, and without telling him she had taken the pills, feeling like a worm for letting Jessica take the heat.

On her birthday, Anna and Scott drove out to the cemetery. Anna hadn't been there for years, since a visit home the Thanksgiving of her freshman year of college when she'd felt the defiant need to tell her father that she'd left home for good. The cemetery was way out west down Montrose; Anna had to look at a map before they set out, and they had to pull over twice to look at it again when Montrose seemed to dead-end, once in an industrial park, and once at a rotary they spun around three times before discovering that the street name changed there for several blocks. And yet, once they pulled through the open gates of the cemetery, Anna nosed the car instinctively in the right direction, through labyrinthine curves and identical stretches of manicured lawn, and pulled up within minutes in front of the plot of her maternal grandparents and their clan, which was marked by a stone bench engraved with the name Grossman. She turned off the engine and looked uncertainly at Scott. "I can't believe I knew exactly where it was," she said.

They got out and Scott stretched and looked around while she crouched in front of her father's grave. Gerald Isaac Singer, 1943-1976, engraved in a fancy mottled marble streaked from weather. She ran her hand over it, brushing off dirt and dried leaves. She traced the curves of the engraved caduceus in the left hand corner, stood and stuffed her hands in her pockets.

Scott had sat down on the bench, with a look of tranquility and satisfaction. She looked at him and grinned. The names Schwartz and Goldblum and Rosenbaum were engraved on tombstones all around them, and he was in his element among the Jewish dead. She sat down beside him, the stone bench cold under her thighs, and he took her hand. They interlaced fingers and looked down at the gravestones. "So he's buried with your mother's family," Scott said.

"Yes," Anna said, "and she'll be buried next to him." She pointed at a headstone. "That's my grandmother's sister," she said; "she's the one my father treated for lung cancer." Her aunt's family was buried there too, her husband and her son Nate, Anna's uncle, who had died of alcoholism.

"Do you think your dad was gay?" Scott asked, out of the blue.

Anna let out a soft surprised grunt; she pressed her palms to the rough stone. "I don't know," she said to Scott. "Maybe. They didn't seem to have a very happy sex life. She has intimated, God help me, that she liked sex with other men better afterward. He was depressed his whole life, and fat as a child." She paused, and after a moment added, "And my mother has always hinted that there was some kind of dire sexual humiliation when he was a child."

Scott, always up for stories of sexual humiliation, cocked his head alertly. "Like what?"

Anna shook her head. Was it being forced to wear girls' underwear? It was one of those strange details that comes slinking out of the fog like a strange animal, a hedgehog or a mole. And if it was true, she thought, was it the underwear itself that was the problem, or the fact that wearing girls' underwear would count as such a mutilating trauma? "I don't know, maybe I'm making the whole thing up," she said.

"Do you think his being gay would make a difference to you?" Scott asked.

Anna shrugged. "Probably not," she said.

They sat quietly in the warm afternoon air, listening to the birds and the contentious racket of the squirrels, looking out at the vast flat stretch of midwestern land flanked by the bustle of highways. "Hey Dad, it's me," Anna called silently, trying it out. But all she felt was a little foolish.

That evening she dressed for her birthday dinner in chinos and a bright Hawaiian shirt, the shirt she always broke out at the end of the academic year, which used to make Patricia shout, at the sight of it, *It's summer, baby!* Wildly colored, roomy but cut short, evocative of a suburban dad presiding over the barbecue grill, it was excellent, exuberant butch-wear. The phone rang and Anna pulled herself away from the mirror to pick it up.

"Happy birthday, honey," her mother's voice said.

"Hi Mom!" Anna said. "How're you doing?"

There was a pause. "I hate to ruin your birthday like this," her mother said, "but I have some news."

The hair at the back of Anna's neck prickled.

"You know how I've been having chronic diarrhea? Well a curious thing showed up on a blood test, a marker that indicates cancer."

Anna took a breath as fear flared inside her. Here we go, she thought. "Cancer where?"

"They don't know," her mother said. "Nothing showed up on the endoscopy I had, or the ultrasound they took of my stomach. Tomorrow they're doing a colonoscopy. I'm in the middle of drinking this disgusting chalky stuff and emptying out right now." Her voice was stoic. "Then they're going to run another battery of tests over the next few weeks." She sighed. "Oh boy," she said. "I wouldn't have told you today, but you asked, and I couldn't lie."

"No," Anna said.

She tonelessly answered her mother's questions about how she was celebrating, the affect sucked right out of her. She thanked her for the $200 gift certificate to Pottery Barn that had arrived that morning in the mail; it was a generous present and a thoughtful one, since there were so many things in her apartment that Anna needed to replace. She didn't tell her that she'd been to the cemetery.

After she hung up, singing faintly "Good luck, Mom," Anna stalked out of the bedroom and into the living room, where Scott was sitting on the couch with his laptop, notes scattered around him. It took her a few minutes to gather enough breath to get the story out. "She's going to have ultrasounds, MRIs, CAT scans, and mammograms," she said. "Find the poison! She won't rest till they find the poison inside her." She clapped her hands over her eyes and spun around, then groped forward, as though playing Pin the Tail on the Donkey.

Scott was staring at her and laughing.

Her face was red; she was imagining her mother, alone in the house, on the toilet, shitting liquid, frightened and forlorn. The image made her weak, and suddenly the very prospect of going out defeated her. But she had to; her friends would all be there. "It's not funny," she said coldly.

"Whoa-kay!" Scott said. "I'm not the one who was making the jokes."

"Let's go, are you ready?"

They drove in silence to one of Anna's favorite restaurants, a *nouveau* Mexican place downtown that combined ascetic decor and flamboyant food in a way that tickled her. Janice and Terry were already there, sitting in a corner booth against an unadorned white wall, and they rose to hug Anna and wish her happy birthday. Terry was wedged into the booth and had to crane to reach Anna; Anna watched her give Scott a reserved wave as he and Janice hugged, and knew she was glad she couldn't reach him to hug him. "We ordered a pitcher of margaritas," Janice said as they sat down.

The waiter had just put down two baskets of tortilla chips, and Anna was deciding not to get her dinner off to an aggrieved start by telling them about her phone conversation with her mother, when Monica came in with Martha. Anna watched as her friends hugged Monica and greeted Martha with delicate courtesy, thinking: interacting with Martha is like a Japanese tea ceremony. In private they had a running debate over whether Martha was a genuinely poor thing or a total diva. Anna had expected a sudden migraine to keep her from coming at the last minute, which often happened. And she'd kind of hoped she wouldn't come, especially since her last conversation about her with Monica, in which Anna had hinted that she thought Martha didn't like her, and Monica had protested "No, she likes you! Really!" in a way that was so egregiously shifty Anna didn't know whether to be more amused or hurt.

Monica looked drawn and tense, as though she and Martha been fighting right before they arrived. By an unfortunate twist of fate, Scott, who was meeting Martha for the first time, ended up seated right across from her. He tried to engage her in conversation, but alarmed her right off the bat by laughing uproariously at something she evidently hadn't meant to be that funny. Next to her his glitteriness seemed almost predatory; her face was exhausted, plump and white, as though she was expecting him at any moment to sink his pointy teeth into her neck.

The pitcher of margaritas arrived, and the waiter took their orders. When he left, Anna stood to pour the drinks into salt-crusted glasses. "None for me," Martha said, and Anna remembered that she never drank because she had once had an alcoholic girlfriend.

Janice clinked her knife against her glass and raised it. "To Anna," she said, smiling. "A wonderful friend and a wonderful teacher. Many, many more years of not only surviving, but thriving as well." They all touched glasses. Anna, pink cheeked, took a hasty gulp and reached for the corn chips.

"Hey wonderful teacher," Terry called. "How's the teaching going?"

"It's going okay," Anna said. "We had good conversation in class yesterday." She set her glass down, tequila burning pleasantly down her gullet, and hesitated when she thought how long and complicated the story was, and how hard to tell entertainingly. But no sooner had she launched into it than she saw that her literary critic friends were fascinated with this case of real-life, high-stakes interpretation. They asked, "So what did you say?" and "What did they say?" and as the alcohol started to take effect everything got more dramatic. When Anna mentioned Chris, Janice interrupted, announcing with mock self-importance, "I met her. She's hunky."

Anna rolled her eyes as the others laughed.

"No really," Janice said. "She's big and bruising with bright blue eyes, and she knows how to use them."

"The thing is, you guys," Anna said, leaning forward on her elbows, "I gave Chris *Stone Butch Blues!*" She slapped her hand comically on her forehead. "How could I do that?" she wailed. "I thought, Oh gee! She'll love a novel about a '50s butch! It'll be so empowering to her! Never mind that she'd read scene after scene of a butch like her getting gang-raped and beaten to a pulp! But now I'm remembering: you know what she said to me one day? She said, 'Look, I ain't no Jess Goldberg.'"

"Whoa," Monica said. "Heavy."

Anna brought her eyes down to the table; Monica always made her feel as though she was treating Chris badly — there was a not-so-secret class solidarity there — and she was sick of it. But Janice was leaning forward on her elbows, frowning. "Yeah, but so what?" she asked Anna. "It's not like you did the wrong thing, giving her that book. It's just that you can't predict how people will read — whether they'll be inspired or demoralized or pissed off by characters who resemble them. You just can't tell: why shouldn't your students be like any other reader that way?" She was warming to her theme. "In fact, you can't even tell whether they'll *recognize* the characters as resembling them. Who knows what she was saying when she said that about Jess Goldberg? That her life wasn't like Jess's, although you might think it was? That she's not as abject as Jess?"

"Actually," Anna interrupted, "I think she might have been saying that she wasn't as *heroic* as Jess."

"She might have meant more than one of those, for all you know," Janice argued.

Scott agreed, and Anna sat back in her chair and ran her fingers around the stem of her margarita glass. Her sense of irony was heightened by alcohol; she was watching her academic friends have an intelligent and nuanced conversation about reading and identification, and all she could think was that it was all very well and good for them to be fascinated, they didn't have to live through the tedious and defeating shit she dealt with every day. But then again, she thought, maybe she should be grateful she continued to be interesting to them. Scott was saying, "It's not clear to me at all that the other teacher made a mistake by reading them *Push*, or that this uproar it caused is a bad thing."

"Even if it makes the students feel put-down and demoralized?" Anna asked. Martha was nodding, as though Anna had just expressed her thought.

There was a pause, and then Scott said, "It's not good if they feel that way. I guess I'm just saying — Janice is saying — that you can't predict they'll feel that way in advance."

"No," Anna said. Their food arrived, and she leaned back as her plate was put in front of her. Her friends had sure let her off the hook. She needed to find Chris: the thought pressed urgently against her. Anna picked up her fork and contemplated the restaurant's interpretation of a burrito. Its tortilla was gashed and twisted open, the beans spilling out, and it was dribbled with riotously colorful salsa. Scott was looking at it with a fascinated frown. "It looks..."

"Martyred?" Anna offered. He let out a spurt of laughter. Across the table, Monica and Martha were exchanging a private communication about Martha's food.

After dinner there were gifts. Scott's was clearly a CD, and Anna opened it with some irritation, thinking that he had been cheap and lazy. It reminded her of the way he used to bring a bucket of Kentucky Fried Chicken to grad school potlucks, banking on his charisma as an undomesticated person to make the gesture look funky. She looked at the CD, Henryk Gorecki's *Symphony No. 3,* and looked uncertainly at Scott.

"It's the music Peter Weir used as the score for *Fearless,*" he said.

Anna blinked, and then the beauty of the gift began to dawn on her. "Oh my God," she said softly. She looked at Janice and Terry. "You guys have seen *Fearless,* right?"

"Is that the one with Jeff Bridges and Rosie Perez?" Terry asked.

Anna nodded.

"Oh yeah," Monica said. "There's a plane crash?"

Anna set it down on the table. "It opens with a man walking away from a plane crash. And the movie's about how he has to cope with the problem of his own survival. Remember? He's married to Isabella Rossellini, and he estranges himself from his family and gets obsessed with this woman, played by Rosie Perez, who lost her baby in the crash." She smiled at Scott. "Scott and I saw it together when it was first released, and Scott had to steer me out of the theater because I was crying so hard." She looked down at the CD again. "So this is the music from the crash."

"Yes," Scott said.

The crash itself was portrayed only near the end, in a slow-motion sequence with no sound but the grave swelling of a symphony — a sequence not so grisly as grandly, sublimely sad.

"How did you figure out this was the score?"

"I rented it again a few weeks ago, and caught the credits at the end," he said.

"What a great present," Anna said, touching his cheek. "Thank you." She looked around the table, flushed.

Janice took her cue and withdrew a flat wrapped object from her bag — an envelope with tickets in it, Anna guessed, or a gift certificate. "This is from all of us," Janice said, gesturing to take in Monica and Martha. "It was Martha's idea."

Anna slipped her finger under the bright wrapping and pried the tape open. Inside was a gift certificate for eight lessons from the yoga center in their neighborhood. "Yoga lessons!" she exclaimed, nonplussed. She could barely bring herself to stretch for ten minutes on either side of a run.

She heard Scott laugh, and Janice said quickly, "You think you won't like it, but we're pretty sure you will."

"Well it's certainly one of those things I would have never bought for myself!" Anna said brightly. "Thanks, guys!"

"I'll go with you," Monica said.

Anna looked quickly at her; she was probably just being supportive of Martha. "Really?"

"Sure," Monica shrugged. "I've done tai chi, and I also have a high tolerance for the New Age."

It was true, Anna thought: Monica held in a delicate balance a cuttingly intelligent critique of contemporary bourgeois life and a readiness to participate in its rituals. "I'm gonna hold you to that," she warned.

They split three flans for dessert, and Monica told them about meeting the new girlfriend of a famous queer theorist they all knew by reputation and about whom they held passionate opinions — even Terry, who was scathing about what she considered the political uselessness of her baroque writing style. "So what does the girlfriend look like?" Janice asked.

"Well, she has a weight problem, but she's a sexy and confident dresser," Monica said. "Very nice." She and Anna nodded at each other with connoisseurial approval.

Scott licked the back of his spoon. "That's what's so great about lesbians as opposed to gay men," he said in an affectionate rush. "You don't care what each other looks like."

The five lesbians put down their spoons and looked at him coldly.

"Present company excluded, of course," he said. "And anyway, I meant it as a *compliment!*"

Martha got up to go to the bathroom, and they all exchanged glances. "She could do without me, couldn't she," Scott said as she walked away from the table.

"Well you've made yourself so charming," Anna grinned.

The check came and Terry took it. Anna scraped her spoon against one of the crusted plates for the last bits of the burnt part, full and sleepy and relieved that her meal was going to be paid for. She caught Scott glancing at his watch; he was getting antsy, she thought, wanting to go out and find his Latin man. Janice leaned over and put her arm around her shoulders. "So were you thinking about your father today?" she asked.

Anna turned with hooded eyes toward Janice, her first instinct to balk. Sometimes Janice felt to Anna like a major pollyanna. Anna knew she was being ungenerous, that Janice was just following up on the cues Anna had been giving her for weeks, and that if she *hadn't* asked about her father, Anna would be mad about that too. So she nodded. For she *had* been thinking about him; she'd been remembering a vacation her family had taken to Maine, a few months before her father died. "I must have been, like, twelve," she told Janice. "And I was already pretty scared. Anyway, we were crossing this river, and there were signs up saying not to cross, because the current was dangerous. I don't know why they crossed anyway." And Anna, letting go of her father's hand, had been knocked off her feet and swept out to sea.

"A stranger dove in and saved me," she said. "I think my father dove in too — at least he did in the version my mother tells — but this other guy got there first. Then he bawled out my parents for crossing there with kids. Anyway, my father walked me back to the hotel. The thing I remember most was holding his hand, and the way the hot pavement chafed my bare feet — I'd lost my sneakers. My dad was silent the whole way."

She looked up; she had arrested everybody's attention. She laughed self-consciously and shrugged. "What could he have said?"

Across from her Monica leaned forward on her elbows, looking at her intently. "I would have saved you," she said.

Anna felt her face contort weirdly, the jump of a muscle under her eye. With some difficulty, she brought her eyes to Monica's face. What do you mean? she wanted to ask. Who said that? Monica was handsome and fierce, buttoned up in a dress shirt. Anna touched her hand, stifling the urge to take it and bury her face in it. Monica turned her palm up and clasped Anna's hand hard, then released it.

Just then Martha came back to the table. Anna and Monica sat back in their chairs and Scott put his napkin on the table and said "Well." He was ready to go. They stood and sighed and picked up bags and torn wrapping paper and car keys. Saying goodbye at the door, Scott set out for the clubs. Janice and Terry waited in front with Anna as the valet brought her car. It was a warm, velvety night, and Anna closed her eyes, hearing the rush of traffic in the distance and the brisk clack of heels of women passing by. "Wanna come over?" Janice asked. "We could watch a movie."

"Nah," Anna said. "I'm sleepy. Thanks though."

Her car arrived and she tipped the valet and got in. She sped easily down relatively empty streets to the Drive, thinking about what Monica had said, and the intensity that had come from her. An ache was struck inside her, and came to a glow. Suddenly there was a blaring horn and the screech of tires. She stiffened; through her rearview mirror she saw a car spinning to a halt, and then the stop sign she'd missed. She kept driving, terrified that the other driver might pursue her in a rage, checking the rearview mirror as her heart roared in her ears. She sneaked down a side street and pulled over and parked, turning off the car and all the lights. Adrenaline was surging poisonously through her. She didn't even know what had happened back there. She'd had such a big meal she hadn't realized she was still drunk.

She drove carefully home, and when she got there, she had a roaring headache. She took some Excedrin, got in the shower and let hot water beat onto her head, excoriating herself for having driven drunk, remembering her mother's mysterious illness and Chris's disappearance and feeling the tequila nausea in her sternum, which rose and rose until she got out, crouched over the toilet, put her finger down her throat, and vomited up her dinner.

Chris walked up the walkway to her house with her suitcase slung over her shoulder, searching for a sign. There were no lights on, not even the porch light. She held her keys up to the street light, found the right ones, let herself in. Rufus barged at her and pushed his face into her hands. She grabbed his head and scrubbed his ears, murmuring "Hey buddy, how's my buddy?" She straightened and called out for Kathleen, but there was no answer. Rufus stretched his head up in a terrific yawn and then shook, the tags on his collar ringing.

There was one message on the answering machine on the hall table; Kathleen had clearly already listened to it, because the green light wasn't blinking. Chris walked over and pressed the button. The message was from Jason Paciorek, and had come in the day before yesterday. "Hi Chris," he said. "This is Jason Paciorek. I enjoyed meeting you the other day. Give me a call, will you?" He paused, then added "Take care." Chris stood there, considering, then played it again. She hadn't gotten the job. If she had, he would have said so, or at least taken greater pains to tell her how to reach him. Plus, he hadn't called back since Wednesday.

So that was that.

She was sitting in the darkened living room with Rufus's head on her lap when she heard the turn of a key. Kathleen came in, turned on the lights and let out a cry of surprise. "You scared me!" she said. She was wearing shorts and a floral button-down shirt, and she still had a bruise on her face, which had turned a sickly yellow.

"I didn't get the job," Chris said.

"No," Kathleen said. "He called back this afternoon. He said that he wants to keep your number, though, in case he has a carpentry job for you in the future." She looked appraisingly at Chris. "He seemed to really like you. He didn't want you to think you blew the interview or anything."

"Well you must be thrilled," Chris said, her voice flat. "Just goes to show you were right that I couldn't do it."

Kathleen's features thickened with anger. She turned and walked away, saying over her shoulder, "I'm not even going to dignify that with an answer."

"What, you deny it?" Chris called without rising. There came no response, so she heaved herself off the couch and followed Kathleen. When she strode into the kitchen Kathleen whirled and flinched a little, which put Chris into a slow burn. Kathleen was putting on a little show, she thought, making her out to be more dangerous than she really was. She had hit her once, for God's sake, under extreme provocation.

Then all her anger drained out of her, leaving her hollowed to the core. She put a hand on the kitchen counter to steady herself. How would they get through this? How could she stay here, but on the other hand, where else could she go? They stood in the kitchen avoiding each others' eyes, and finally Chris spoke. "Why, Kath? Why couldn't you be my friend about this?"

Kathleen's eyes filled with tears. "I can't," she quavered, "I can't do this. You hit me in the *face*."

Chris took a deep breath. "I'm sorry," she said. "That was stupid."

"Stupid?!"

"It was wrong," Chris corrected herself. "I apologize."

Her apology made Kathleen burst into tears. She sat down at the kitchen table and buried her face in her hands. Rufus came up and tried to push his nose through her hands. "I just," she sobbed, "I just — it was like all along I was with a blind person, and suddenly they learned how to see."

Chris was bewildered: what was she talking about? And then suddenly it dawned on her. "Why wouldn't you want me to see?" she cried.

Kathleen grabbed a kitchen towel and wiped her eyes, then blew her nose. She looked up at Chris through small puffy eyes. "Because I liked the feel of your hand on my elbow," she said.

Chris stared at her for a long while. "Well bully for you," she finally said. "I'm glad *somebody* could get a kick out of my being illiterate."

Kathleen's face crumpled with discouragement and fury. "That's
not what I meant and you know it!"

"Yeah, well," Chris said, for loss of a better comeback, and walked
out of the kitchen. She grabbed her suitcase, and left for the second
time that night without knowing where she was going.

As it closed behind her, Kathleen realized that she'd forgotten to
tell Chris that the settlement check had arrived that afternoon. She
blew her nose again, walked over and picked the check off the counter.
She had almost thrown the envelope away, thinking it contained a fake
sweepstakes check, but then she'd opened it and found a check for
$67,384.81, made out to Chris from a team manager at State Farm.

As soon as Anna had settled her stomach with some Diet Coke and
got into bed, the phone rang. It was her brother Julian, calling from
Cleveland.

"Hey there," he said.

"Hey Juju," she said, using her childhood name for him.

"How are you doing on this big day?" he asked.

"Oh okay," she groaned. "I drank too much at dinner. Hey, that's
wild about Mom."

"Yes," he said.

"You think she'll ever find what's ailing her?" she asked.

He was quiet on the other end. Julian couldn't be enticed to bad-
talk their mother. She closed her eyes and wondered why they hadn't
been able to huddle together for warmth when they were kids. In all her
memories, they were alone, in different parts of the house.

She shifted in bed, bringing a pillow more comfortably under the
side of her face. She could hear the sound of Gerry, her nephew, bab-
bling in the background. "What's he still doing up at this hour?" she
asked.

"Don't ask," Julian sighed. He covered the phone and she heard a muffled "Just a minute." Then he came back, and asked, "Was it meaningful to you to turn the age, you know, he was when he died?"

"Yes," Anna answered, "I'm just not sure how." She paused. "Scott's here for the weekend, and we went out to the cemetery."

"Oh yeah?" he asked, and she thought she detected the slightest frostiness in his voice. Julian didn't like Scott, was put off by his affectation. He had once said he didn't think Scott was a happy person.

He cleared his throat. "You know, recently, I bought more life insurance. Nothing had really changed — I had taken it out when we bought the house, and increased it when Gerry was born. And today when I was thinking about your birthday I realized that I've been trying to protect my family. Because part of me doesn't believe I'm going to make it to thirty-three."

Anna was quiet; she let herself ache for this rigid and graceless man, her little brother, and found that it felt sweet. "I know, Juju," she finally said. "But you will."

CHAPTER TWENTY-ONE

Chris spent the night at an EconoLodge, but she couldn't afford to do that more than once, and she couldn' t think of anyplace else to stay for less than $100 a night, unless she took some furnished shit-hole room by the week, which she just wasn't going to do ever again. She was shocked and frightened by how she could go from owning her own house to possibly having to stay in a flophouse, all in the space of one night. After some unpleasant soul-searching — for she had missed her old friend Jack's funeral, and that now seemed inexcusable to her even though at the time she had just been getting out of the hospital after breaking her leg — she finally called Gladys from a pay phone in the motel lobby, and asked if she could crash with her for a little while. Gladys didn't seem surprised to hear her voice, even though it had been almost two years since they'd seen each other. When she said sure, she could use the company, Chris hesitated, and cleared her throat. "Do you think you could come up here and get me?" Gladys laughed indulgently, a sound Chris didn't much care for, and said she would be there in an hour. Chris hung up feeling sheepish and infantile, and planted herself on the lobby's small couch to wait, her suitcase between her knees. Even if her broken leg *was* an excuse for missing the funeral of an important person in her life, there was no excuse for not having been in touch with Gladys over the past nine months, during what was probably the roughest time of Gladys' life. And now she was asking Gladys to be there for her. Chris settled back and sighed. She wouldn't have called her, she told herself, if she'd had somewhere else to go.

An hour passed, and then an hour and a half. Gladys was probably lost, Chris thought; that would be just like her. She rose and found some vending machines near the fire exit, and bought two bags of orange cracker peanut butter sandwiches and a Sprite. Twenty minutes later, seeing a brown Ford Escort pull slowly under the motel awning, she stood and brushed crumbs off her shirt, and wiped the corners of her mouth. She carried her suitcase out to the curb and tossed it into the back seat of the car. Then she got into the front, turned to Gladys and gave her the old grin. Gladys was wearing a pink sweat suit, and her hair was white and wild. "Jesus, Gladys," Chris said, "What the hell are you wearing?"

"Well if it ain't Chris Rinaldi," Gladys said, shaking her head. "Still getting herself in a jam."

Chris grimaced and lay her head back on the headrest, transformed at once into the crabby teenager she'd been around Gladys since she met her. Gladys paid her no mind; she shifted into drive and pulled out, murmuring to herself about how to get back to the Expressway. She seemed to have aged a lot since Jack died, although when Chris thought about it, it could have just been the passage of time that had aged her. And she drove like an old lady. Or maybe she always had? Chris couldn't remember being in a car with her when Jack wasn't the driver. Chris shifted in the passenger seat, trying to muster words to comfort a bereaved person, as Gladys found the turn-off and merged into traffic. Casting a glance over at her, it occurred to Chris that she didn't even really know her very well. It was Jack who'd owned the bar and showed her the ropes as she learned how to be in her new surroundings. Gladys had just been what? — a dingbat femme who wanted to paint the ceiling of the bar black with the solar system on it, or have Heavy Petting Night, where everybody would bring their pets, and they'd dress them up and give them prizes.

It was late, and they moved freely through the open express lanes. Chris stared out the window at the molten skyline that loomed to their left. Her feet were sweating in her motorcycle boots. "Is there AC?" she asked Gladys, and Gladys wordlessly closed the windows and turned it on.

"Thanks," Chris muttered, and then ventured, "People must really miss the old bastard. She was an institution."

Gladys turned her face toward her and Chris was suddenly mortified. What if Gladys wasn't in the mood to think of her recently deceased lover as a bastard?

But a very slight smile played at Gladys's lips. "She was that," she said.

Forty-five minutes later, they got off the Dan Ryan at Sibley, and from there it was only a few minutes to Gladys's small ranch house, which was on a street with tiny houses and neat square patches of lawn. They got out of the car, and Chris felt the unpleasantly sticky night air insinuate itself around her, like someone breathing right in her face. Gladys's neighbor, a black man in shorts and flip-flops, was setting out his sprinkler, and Gladys called out a greeting with neighborly officiousness. "There's lots of blacks here now," she murmured quietly to Chris as she held the front door open for her.

The house was stuffy and smelled of something scented, like soap or flowers; the white-carpeted living room was crammed with knick-knacks and figurines and fading pictures in ornate frames. Looking around, Chris was dumbfounded. This was nothing like the house Gladys and Jack had lived in when Chris had known them. Jack had been a skinny old bull with a laugh gravely from phlegm, who swept and moved stock with a cigarette dangling from the corner of her mouth. Gladys had kept a nice house for her, and they'd always had nice things, like candles and coasters on the tables and such. But these frilly doodads: Jack was probably turning in her grave at the sight of them. There were two obese cats with querulous meows. "Are these the same ones you always had?" Chris asked, stooping and holding her fingers out to them.

"Um-hm," Gladys said. "They're old fellas now."

She led Chris into the guest bedroom and Chris put her suitcase down on the single bed.

"Lord it's hot in here," Gladys said worriedly. "I haven't been able to get the air conditioner out of the basement by myself. I should get you a fan." But when she came back with her own bedroom fan, Chris refused to take it. They wrested open the window, which opened up to the blank brick side of the neighboring house.

Chris took a cold shower and lay on top of the bed in her underwear and a sleeveless undershirt, her wet hair resting on her folded hands, elbows akimbo. What the hell was she doing here? What would she do tomorrow? Her thoughts moved miserably to Paciorek Builders and she felt like a moron for having applied. Jason Paciorek must have seen right through her. What had she been thinking? And then her mind made a surprising shift, like a train bumping sideways over to the next track, and in the place of thinking that he hadn't wanted her, she wondered instead: had she really wanted to work with yuppies with money to burn? She could just see it, sleek straight people in leather coats telling her that they wanted the kitchen to be a place where their growing family could gather. What was wrong with her, that that kind of talk made her want to curl up in a ball and die? And yet, that's just how it was. It would have been like spending her whole life building her parents' house, helping people that despised her, and that she had learned to despise back.

She hadn't been in touch with her parents for decades. If one of them died, would she be notified?

The next morning Chris lay in bed till about 10:00, when Gladys knocked lightly on her door and said "Are you going to get up, dear?" She rose sullenly, sat in the kitchen drinking coffee and blowing clouds of cigarette smoke and staring out the window at the figurines decorating Gladys's back yard, while Gladys took two Eggos out of the toaster and smothered them in maple syrup and set them before her. She had the sweet powdery smell of old people, a smell that made Chris despair. She didn't ask a thing about what Chris was doing down there, or what kind of trouble she was in, and that, at least, felt like a mercy.

That afternoon, when she grew sick of sitting around twiddling her thumbs in front of the TV, Chris went out to the backyard and found Gladys in gardening gloves and an enormous straw hat, pruning back the lilac tree. "I'm going to bring up that air conditioner," she called.

She hauled the unit up from the basement and installed it in

Gladys' bedroom window, knowing she was hurting her back but not really caring, and took the fan into her own bedroom. Then, while she was at it, she set out the plastic deck furniture, scrubbed it down and hosed it off. As she worked, she berated Gladys for safety infractions: fire alarms whose batteries hadn't been replaced in ages, a furnace that hadn't been serviced for as long as Gladys could remember, kitchen linoleum so scuffed and peeling Gladys would surely trip on it one of these days and break a hip. "And do you know what happens to old ladies when they break a hip?" Chris scolded. "It's all downhill from there."

At around 3:00, when she thought Margaret and Keith would still be at work and the kids would be home from school, Chris tried to call Jessica. She had no intention of admitting that she'd taken Margaret's drugs; she planned to frame the conversation as general moral support. But when Margaret picked up the phone, Chris quickly hung up.

Gladys disappeared after dinner, as Chris sat in front of *Wheel of Fortune,* smoking. When Chris got up to use the bathroom, she walked past Gladys' bedroom, and Gladys called to her. She was standing in front of an open closet. Chris approached, electrified by the smell emanating from it. Jack: cigarette smoke, Old Spice, something undefinable and acrid that for a young Chris, had been the very smell of the tough bull. She pulled a jacket sleeve toward her and plunged her face into it, emerging red-faced. "Man," she said, "it's Jack all over again."

"I'm going to send these clothes to Goodwill," Gladys said. "But I thought you might like some of them for yourself."

Chris said "Oh!" She stepped forward into the closet, moved by the gesture and at a loss for words. As she handled the clothes, enveloped in that smell till she couldn't smell it anymore, her hands became uncertain. Gladys was taking out shirts and jackets and holding them up on the hanger against Chris's back. "Those won't fit," Chris said; "Jack was too small for a bull with big boobs like me."

"Just let's see," Gladys said, going behind her and trying to slip a suit jacket up her arms.

Chris turned. "Stop it, it ain't gonna work," she said sharply, grabbing it from Gladys. She held the jacket over her arm, and brushed lint and crumbs off the shoulders. Or was that dandruff? How creepy to be touching a piece of Jack's body, Jack's scalp. In the weeks after Jack died, it occurred to her, Gladys must have come across Jack's hair, or nail clippings, or toothpaste blotches in the sink all the time.

She handed it back to Gladys, went back into the closet, and pulled out a gray wool scarf she remembered folded over the collar of Jack's bomber jacket, beneath her chapped lips. "Why don't I take this?" she asked.

"Is that all?" Gladys fussed, peering into the closet.

"Yeah," Chris said, and then added gently, "Thank you." She watched Gladys stuff the rest of the clothes into garbage bags, folding them loosely and carelessly, and she thought she was seeing a cold side to Gladys, a part she had never seen when Jack was alive and Gladys seemed sweet and soft-minded.

She hung the scarf on the back of a chair in her room, and when she lay down that night she could smell Jack, which made her remember the sinking feeling of Jack creeping around her as she slept on the ratty couch, playing some dumb-ass practical joke like pouring a glass of water on the sheets so it'd look like Chris had peed the bed, or replacing Chris's underwear with ladies' lingerie. That Jack, she thought she was a laugh-riot. She'd been a heavy drinker, although who wasn't in those days? As Chris lay there, her agitated mind conjured the first time she'd moved in with Gladys and Jack, in that apartment on Clyde Ave. She'd been terrified of Jack, who smoked and spat like a man and barely spoke to her; when Chris did odd jobs at the bar on weekends, she always worried she'd do something wrong or stupid. Jack wasn't one of those kind-hearted butches, like the ones in that book Anna Singer had given her. She gave off the attitude of already knowing the information you were giving her, like you were stupid for taking so long to know it. She thought nobody could do things as well as she could; more often than not, she'd grab a tool out of your hand to do it herself. She was always complaining about employees stealing from her at the bar; she picked unnecessary fights with men and then all the other butches had to jump in and fight. Chris closed her eyes, disconcerted to find herself thinking of it that way. For a long time Chris had automatically trusted Jack's judgment, cultivating hatred for the people Jack had a beef with, who she said were poison. What did Chris know? — Jack was the standard for the butch making her way in a dangerous world. But now when she thought about it, Jack just looked like a paranoid.

She had been drifting off, but now Chris froze, wondering suddenly if Jack too had been illiterate.

Naw, she couldn't have been, handling invoices and contracts as she did. Although Chris remembered her signature, big and loopy and deliberate. One of the delivery guys had once teased Jack for writing like a third-grade girl, and had almost gotten his head taken off. But no, she remembered Jack reading the comics out loud to people in the bar. And arguing about a price a distributor had given her, jabbing her finger at the paper and demanding "What does it say right there?" Chris lay stiffly on her side, looking into the darkness. Was the question just a demand meant to make the distributor look like a liar, as she'd always assumed, or was Jack bluffing, actually asking what it said?

No, Chris was making something out of nothing. Jack wasn't an illiterate; she was just a pain in the ass. And yet, they'd let Chris stay with them until she was on her feet, and never threw it in her face. That was something.

The morning after her birthday party, Anna awoke with her head still throbbing. Weak light was coming through the slats of the blinds. She dragged herself out of bed, and went into the kitchen and made coffee. When it had brewed she poured herself a cup and came back to bed, carefully setting the steaming mug down on the floor, and propped herself up on the pillows. With her eyes closed, her head felt like a washing machine on spin cycle. She opened them into slits. In the corner of the room, clothes were spilling out of Scott's open suitcase. On top of the laptop that lay closed beside it was a messy stack of papers, a draft pored over and edited in his crabbed scrawl.

She had to call Chris, she had to; talking about her last night had given Anna the sinking feeling that she had failed to follow through. She had decided that she couldn't get her back into class through sheer force of her will, that Chris was an adult who could make her own decisions. But now she had a bad feeling about it. She'd dropped Chris at a crucial moment, a moment where Chris had taken a huge risk and probably failed.

She looked at the clock; it was 9:15. Too early to call on a Saturday. Anna put her coffee down and dozed for a few troubled hours, until she was awakened by the phone. It was Julian calling to report on their mother's colonoscopy. "Are you still asleep?" he asked in a teasing tone. "Wow, those days are so over for me."

Because you are such a noble and long-suffering breeder, Anna thought, bringing herself up on one elbow, her empathy from last night draining out of her. It was a not-so-veiled subtext of their relationship, how Julian was such a responsible adult, stolidly populating the earth and living for something other than himself, while she was a selfish hedonistic queer.

The colonoscopy had gone fine, Julian told her, turning up no polyps or other signs of cancer. "Well that's good, I guess," Anna said.

"What do you mean you *guess?*"

Anna pressed her temples with her thumbs; her head was still hurting. "Well isn't the whole point that there seems to be cancer somewhere, and if it's not in her colon it's gotta be somewhere else?"

Julian was quiet.

"What's next?" Anna asked.

"A bone scan and a brain MRI," he told her.

"Okay," Anna said, thinking Jesus Christ, a brain tumor?

"You know," Julian said, "Sometimes when you act like you don't care, it's hurtful. That's why Mom didn't call you herself."

"Because I don't care," Anna said.

"Well *do* you?" he demanded.

Anna groaned. The question was unanswerable: she certainly wasn't going to insist how much she cared in order to fulfill her brother's

sanctimonious demand. "I'm going to hang up now," she announced.
She settled back and closed her eyes. How many times had she
steeled herself for her mother's death? Her mother's furious storming
out of the house, refusing to tell her and Julian where she was going —
and this, for Christ sake, after their father had left home, never to
return. The aneurysm, the coma. After a while you just shifted over to
that other place, the groove in the brain that a trickle of terror had
scalded again and again. Her mind pulled her unwillingly to another
scene, harder to let in than her memories of the aneurysm, which had
the benefit of being codified and presentable from years of telling.
This scene was formless, dank. Her mother was running a high
fever. Shaking with cold, her teeth chattering. She was begging Anna
to come into bed with her and hold her, to lend her body warmth.
Anna opened her eyes as the memory came, bringing in its wake a
sludge of nauseating adrenaline. She had held back. She had gone
numb with dread. Then she'd crawled into bed with her mother,
and let her pull Anna toward her and wrap herself around her,
shaking. Her nightgown had been plastered to her clammy body,
and Anna, lying there rigidly, could feel her mother's breasts
against her, smell her bitter sweat.

She took up the remote control and turned on the TV, sum-
moning images and noise to diffuse the implications of the memory sinking in. How could her mother have asked her to do that? And
how could Anna have said no?

Oh Mom, she thought, her eyes filling with sudden tears for the
woman whose husband had left her all alone: *who else was going to hold
you?*

And how could it be, she wondered, wiping her eyes with her
sleeve, that this memory was so traumatic, and yet now, she loved
nothing so much as holding shaking women? Hadn't she made a
whole sexual career out of doing just that?

She pushed back the covers and got out of bed and showered,
and as she dressed she was glad to hear the scrape of Scott's key in
the door. He was starving, he said, so after he'd washed up they went

out to brunch. Before they left the house, Anna tried calling Chris. She hung up when she got the machine.

Kathleen walked down the street with Rufus, taking him out for his last pee of the night. Blurry haloes radiated from the streetlights in the dense air, and she was conscious of the slap of her flip-flops against the soles of her feet, and the *shhtt* of sprinklers. Rufus planted himself on the neighbor's lawn and started chewing grass; Kathleen pulled at his leash and said "C'mon Rufus, go potty." Chris had been gone for nearly two days. Gladys had called last night and let her know, in a whisper, that she shouldn't worry, that Chris was there. Gladys must be what, seventy? God, they were getting old. Where had the time gone? And what had they achieved?

That thought was followed by a pang. At least Chris was trying to achieve something by going to school. Although Kathleen thought of herself as a supportive person, she knew she hadn't been; she'd been a bitch. And all because Chris was threatening to be able to take care of herself? This bewildered Kathleen; she had been chewing on it for weeks. And she hadn't let Chris know that the settlement had arrived. It hadn't been on purpose — in the heat of their argument it had slipped her mind, is all. But shouldn't she be giving Chris a call and letting her know? What was Chris doing for money?

She didn't care, she decided defiantly: it wasn't her fault that Chris walked out. She didn't owe her squat till she returned.

The sense of having been wrong filled Kathleen with guilt, and a quick anger backlash. She yanked at Rufus' leash and said harshly, "Go potty!" He looked at her reproachfully, eased his rump to the ground and, his head craned away from her, scratched vigorously at his collar. "You want to spend the whole night with your legs crossed?" she threatened. She headed toward home, and he trotted behind her, then nosed his way back onto the grass, lifted his leg and peed.

When she reached the door, she heard the phone ringing. She hurriedly led Rufus inside, unsnapped his leash and grabbed the phone. It was Anna Singer, wondering where Chris was, sounding worried.

The next morning, while Scott packed up his things, Anna spread a map over the kitchen table and studied it, her heart hammering with the reckless rhythm of compulsion. What used to be West Hammond, Kathleen had said; it was just this side of the Illinois/Indiana border, with Hammond on the other side. You could take the Skyway or the Dan Ryan.

It was a hot, humid May day, pushing 90 degrees by noon, when she and Scott left the house for the airport. She had decided to go straight from there to Cal City, rather than calling ahead and being stymied by Chris's dull, hostile wonder at what she wanted from her. Scott stared out the window as they drove down Foster, his jaw working, his leather jacket on his lap; Anna knew he was readying himself for the return to the sexless and ascetic life he lived in his small town. He turned toward her and said "So wait, you're following your student down to this place she ran away to?"

"Yeah," Anna said.

"Is that something people do? I don't think I'd ever show up at a student's dorm."

"Well it's not usual," Anna said, "but sometimes....Once this student wasn't coming to class, and my boss, Renée, threatened to come and break down her door if she didn't get there in fifteen minutes. And that worked like a charm; the student never missed another class."

"Yeah, but did she really go break down her door?"

Anna glanced at him in irritation. "Why are you hassling me?"

Scott shrugged and turned back to the window.

Her reasoning chugged and lurched. If she was going to stay at Pathways longer than just this year, she needed to make her work there meaningful. Nothing ever stuck there, nothing — and she was determined to make her work with Chris stick. Scott would never understand that, because he had work that counted for something in the world. Going to a student's dorm! What a lame analogy — trying to get some rich kid with mono or anxiety disorder to come to his Victorian poetry class.

When they pulled up at Scott's terminal, Anna popped the

trunk and got out of the car to give him a hug. He set his bag on the ground and slung his laptop over his shoulder, took his jacket in his fist. "What a time we had, my friend!" he declaimed. "We laughed, we cried."

"Oh please," Anna drawled: "*you* laughed, *I* cried." He was laughing as she put her arms around him. She said goodbye to him as she always did: clinging to him, tears stinging her eyes, and relieved he was going. It had exhausted her to have someone living intimately with her but going out to have sex with others. And the whirlwind of productivity he brought with him! Now she'd have her apartment back to herself.

She headed south on the Expressway, the skyline ahead of her faint in haze that turned dirty on the far horizon. Her stomach felt queasy with anticipation. What did she even want to say to Chris? *I'm sorry about the job. I hope you'll try again. Just because you aimed high and failed doesn't mean you shouldn't have aimed high. I understand that learning to read is hard and humiliating, and I admire your courage. I care about what happens to you. I'm watching.* And then words faded and all that was left was a clenched jaw and moist eyes, and her hands fervently clasping the steering wheel.

She sped past the Loop, exited the Expressway at the tiny one-lane exit for the Skyway, and drove through the industrial landscape to the tollbooth right before the McDonald's that sat crammed on the divider. Anna held out two dollars, but the attendant waved Anna away with latex gloved hands, saying "You're all set" and pointing to the car that had moved through the booth ahead of her.

"What?"

"That car paid for you," the attendant said.

Anna frowned and said skeptically, "Okay," and hit the gas. That car had passed her already, and she'd thought she'd seen three boys sitting in the back seat. But now, drawing nearer to it, she realized that they were women, really cute young ones, peeking back at her and grinning, and that the car had a rainbow sticker on the bumper. She eased her foot off the gas, seized with delight. They'd treated her to a ride on the Skyway! Just like buying her a drink, only weirder.

She let them speed ahead, too shy to pull up beside them and meet their eyes. Their gesture was a sign, she thought: a sign that women would take care of her. She was still smiling when her exit came, the one closest to Sibley. She signaled and began to exit, when something caught her eye. Off on a Hammond side street, a Holiday Inn sign. The hotel where her father had died! She eased to a stop at the light at the end of the exit, and tried to find the sign again through her rearview mirror. But it wasn't there. She craned around, wrenching her neck, till a horn sounding behind her made her jump. The light had turned green. She turned back and began to drive, her heart pounding.

She found the small house whose address Kathleen had given her, pulled up to the curb, and sat for a few minutes. Then she let herself out of the car, went up to the doorway, and rang the doorbell. The door opened to an elderly woman in slacks and a blouse, who smiled expectantly at the sight of Anna's face. "Well hello," the woman said.

"Hello," Anna said gently, wondering who this woman thought she was, and having the confused idea that Chris had mentioned Anna to her. "I was looking for Chris Rinaldi."

The woman's face became so uncertain Anna wondered if she was senile, or if she'd confused Anna with a long-lost child. Then she told her that Chris was out, no doubt at the Starlight, a bar over on Sibley. She gave clear if garrulous directions, backtracking frequently to mention some minor landmark that Anna would want to look out for, as if to keep Anna at her doorstep as long as possible.

Back in her car, Anna put the key into the ignition and paused. Was she really going to follow Chris to a bar? She had to; her only other option was to wait in the old woman's house for Chris to return, and her mind recoiled at the thought of ringing her doorbell again, and of making conversation for what could be hours. If Chris was sitting at a bar drinking alone, that would work just fine. Anna imagined having a beer and maybe bumming a cigarette off of Chris. Surely one cigarette would be okay, she thought with sneaky ex-smoker excitement, if it was in the service of creating a feeling of companionship and trust.

Later Anna would wonder what she was thinking; her judgment had blanked out to zero visibility. She'd ask Scott, "How could you let me go down there?" and he'd protest, "I thought you knew what you were doing!" And met by reproachful silence he'd add, "I thought maybe there was some weird cowboy ethic in adult education, because you're all adults so it's no holds barred. You kept mentioning your boss threatening to kick down that student's door."

"Yeah, but she didn't actually *do* it," Anna cried.

It was a lounge, a low, inconspicuous ranch building, with a pink neon cursive sign. Letting her eyes adjust from the bright light outside, Anna thrust her hands into the pockets of her khaki shorts. She wished she was wearing jeans and boots instead of shorts and sandals, short sleeves instead of a muscle shirt that exposed her arms. An old guy wiping off the bar took no notice of her, nor did a guy with a wispy beard and arms wrapped by a jungle of tattoos, who was slumped over a scotch. She thought uncertainly that she was in the wrong place, but when she heard the crisp crash of pool balls from the next room, she headed over, acting as though she had a purpose.

In a smoky wood-paneled room, Chris was playing pool with another butch, a young one in her twenties. She looked up and when she laid eyes on Anna she froze. Then she looked back down at her shot and scooted the 6-ball cleanly into a side pocket. She shifted around the table, considering, turning her back to Anna.

Anna leaned against the paneled wall and stuffed her hands in her pockets. The butch playing with Chris wore a sweatshirt with the sleeves cut out; she had a bull ring in her nose. There were other people here too, and beer bottles and empty shot glasses and dirty ashtrays littered on tables. Motes of dust turned languorously in the shaft of light coming from the lone window.

It was a close game; Chris knocked in the 8-ball when only one of her opponent's balls remained on the table. "Shoot," the butch muttered, and slapped Chris's hand in a quick irritated low-five. Chris drained the remainder of a beer and set a stack of quarters on the table's edge. Anna said faintly, "Chris," hoping that the two of them could step outside, or sit at the bar, and talk for a little while. But Chris turned and went into the next room, leaving Anna standing there. A few minutes later Chris returned with four shots, holding the tiny glasses in front of her with stiff arms.

Chris set the glasses down on a table, then walked over to Anna and gave her one. Anna took it and jostled the liquid. She held it self-consciously in front of her with two fingers and her thumb. What was Chris doing, she wondered, welcoming her to her world? Challenging her to a duel? Showing that she had disposable income? Chris looked beautiful to her: craggy and haggard, her carriage easy, her blue eyes clear and faintly amused. She was wearing, of all things, a decrepit Grateful Dead t-shirt with a skeleton on the front, tucked into her faded jeans.

Anna drained the glass — it was tequila — as coolly as possible, as though she made a habit of tossing back shots, stifling a gag as its fumes detonated in her mouth and nose and brought tears to her eyes. Within exactly one minute, she was drunk, and Chris was handing her another shot glass. Anna manfully tossed that down too, thinking *What the fuck*.

A pool cue was thrust into her hand, and her heart sank. She was terrible at pool, and here, in front of a bunch of seedy-looking butch strangers, she was going to have to play Chris. Anna cleared her throat and tried to get a purchase on her breathing, wishing she'd brought her inhaler with her, although frankly, it was hard to imagine pulling it out and sucking on it in front of these characters. "You break," she said, as though offering Chris a head start when in fact she was worried she'd chip the cue ball into the air and it would plop weakly against the triangled balls, sending them wobbling inches to the side. That was her normal breaking technique.

Chris broke with a tremendous crash, and proceeded to kick Anna's ass in six straight games. During that stretch Anna knocked a total of four balls into the pocket, one into a pocket she hadn't intended but, when interrogated suspiciously by Chris, lied that she had. She kept her eyes glued on the game, too anxious to look around the room at the people watching her getting whipped. By the end of the third game the other butches were whining at Chris, "Aw c'mon, man, she sucks, give someone else a chance," and "She don't know a pool cue from an enema," which was so bizarre Anna wondered whether she had heard it at all, or whether her reeling drunken mind had made it up.

Chris kept making her drink, and kept making her play. She cut her no slack, and offered no small talk; instead she stalked around the table with martial discipline, her back erect, taking her shots. Anna doggedly hung in, although she had no hope of winning any game, and although with every shot she was making a spectacle of herself, hitting weakly, feeling her ass flapping in the breeze and her shirt riding up as she bent awkwardly over impossible angles, displaying neither power nor finesse. A million times she felt like leaving; but something told her that if she did, she'd never get another chance to talk to Chris. During the sixth game she made Chris miss a shot by saying "So I take it you didn't get the job?" at the exact moment Chris was drawing back the cue. By the end of the game, which Chris won anyway, Anna could barely stand up straight.

By now the onlookers were slouching around and talking desultorily, clearly bored by the pathetic pool playing going on. Anna heard one of them invite another back to her house to watch the game. But there was a sudden silence and coming to attention as a tall heavy butch came into the room with her hands in her pockets. Chris looked at her with something like irony, then racked the balls again and barked at Anna, "Break." Anna, who had had to break all the games but the first, because she had lost them all, groaned and broke weakly, prompting a contemptuous "pussy" from the corner. She whirled and slung a reckless "Fuck you!" in that direction. And then Chris was coming toward her, making her tense all over as she thought *Here it comes,* and pushing past her in the other direction toward the butch who had just entered. No, not a butch, Anna's confused mind registered, *a man* — Chris went chest-to-chest with him, and her face an inch at most away from his, backed him back up against the wall. Anna caught sight of the confusion and hurt that scuttled across his chubby face before Chris's body entirely blocked him from her view.

The butch with the bull ring emerged with more shot glasses, setting them on a table and downing one herself. Chris backed slowly away
from the man at the wall. She picked up a glass and proffered it stonily to Anna. What was this, for God's sake, Anna thought: butch *Lord of
the Flies?* "I'm through," she told Chris, slamming the still-full glass
onto a table, where it shattered in her hand. This time she refused to
flinch; she turned and walked out of the room, her hand dripping with
blood and tequila. She heard the sounds of the bartender calling after
her —*hey! Miss!*— and thought she heard footsteps behind her. She
steeled herself for a blow. And outside, blinking in the hazy afternoon
light, she thought vaguely that she didn't remember air like this from
her childhood, that this was disgusting futuristic air. When she reached
the street and looked confusedly one way, then the other, for her car,
the motion of her head made her stagger. A police cruiser passed by
and she moved her arm to hail it, but then snatched it back. What was
he going to do, arrest all the bad butches who had made her look like a
pussy? Hold her head while she vomited, and tuck her into bed? She
closed her eyes and reeled, and thought: would this be the day she died,
here on the hot grainy pavement of an alien town? She put her hand to
her chest, and passed out on the street.

CHAPTER TWENTY-TWO

She awoke a few hours later on a couch in a small living room whose treacly smell sent a ripple of nausea through her. She took several deep breaths, interrupted by painful coughs. Her hand was throbbing; she saw that it was bandaged, the end of the tape jaggedly diagonal, as though it had been torn by teeth. A blood spot was seeping through at the palm.

Her vision was blurred, her head a heap of garbage and twisted metal; she touched her good hand to her face, feeling for her glasses, but they were gone. She patted her back pocket; her wallet and keys were gone too. She rose and twisted to look at the table behind her, but all it contained was a shell ashtray and a mottled porcelain egg on a little stand. She lay back groaning and closed her eyes, trying to dig in and get her bearings. Where the hell was she? Not the bar, not jail, not the sidewalk or the slums; she was somewhere where a woman had decorated, which, she was able to register, meant she was safe.

She lost consciousness again, and awoke several hours later to see the face of the old woman she had met before, peering intently down at her. Her white hair was wild, her face sweetly grave; she lay a cool hand on Anna's cheek, and Anna closed her eyes. When she came to again, cigarette smoke was lashing the insides of her nostrils. Chris was standing above her, her large hands dangling at her sides, smoke snaking up from the cigarette between her fingers.

"Fuck," Anna said, through dry lips. "What happened?" She was suddenly chilled; goose bumps rose on her bare arms and her nipples stiffened. She crossed her arms across her chest.

"You passed out," Chris announced.

"So it appears." Anna looked around at the room and wrinkled her face. "Where am I?"

"It's the house of an old friend of mine," Chris said.

"Oh," Anna said, closing her eyes and remembering. Sensations came back to her and sickened her — her face stinging as she threw back tequila, the futile thrust of the pool cue, her sandal sticking to something on the floor. She opened her eyes to find Chris considering her.

"I saved your ass, you know."

Anna felt anger gurgle in her throat. Her head was splitting and her mouth disgusting. "What do you mean you saved my ass?" she croaked. "You're the one who got my ass in trouble in the first place." What *did* Chris mean, anyway? Saved her ass from what? Her imagination spun with weak alarm. Some kind of butch defilement? What, they'd violate her while she was passed out? Pull down her pants and reveal her plump woman's thighs? "What, was that fat friend of yours going to rob me or beat me up or something?"

Chris flushed. "He ain't my friend," she said. "They're not my friends. They're just people that happened to be at the bar."

Anna looked at her as keenly as she was able under the circumstances. "Whatever," she said.

"They're not my friends," Chris repeated resolutely.

"Okay! Do you think I could have a glass of water?"

Chris turned and left the room. She returned with a glass, and handed it to Anna. Anna hoisted herself up onto her elbows and took a sip, her throat closing over it with a cramp. The last thing she remembered was standing out on the street. She looked at her watch, which was still on her wrist; it was 5:30 in the afternoon.

"My wallet," Anna questioned.

"Nobody took your wallet," Chris said, mocking her. "I heard yelling outside, and when I came out I saw you lying there. So I brought you here."

Anna closed her eyes for a moment. "You must have thought that was pretty funny, seeing your teacher passed out outside a bar."

"As a matter of fact, I did," Chris said.

Anna opened her eyes. "What did I ever do to you?" she asked wearily.

Chris stared at her.

"C'mon, Chris," Anna said. "Gloves off: what did I ever do to you?"

"To be honest, I have no idea what you're talking about."

Anna laughed, which made her face throb. "You are such a liar! You're all 'to be honest this' and 'to be honest that,' but you lie right to my face, 24 hours a day. *I have the flu,*" she said in a mocking whiny voice. "Yeah right. You didn't have the flu, you had some major drug event. And what was up with that book you gave me back, which wasn't even mine?"

Chris reddened and rose to her feet. She picked up the porcelain egg from the side table and closed her fingers over it. Then she set it carefully back down. "Why did you come down here, anyway?" she demanded. "What were you, stalking me? Trying to humiliate me?"

Anna wanted to cry: Me humiliate *you!* Lying here whipped and bloodied, this was a whole new level of abasement, a supernova of abasement. She opened her mouth to tell all the reasons she'd come down, reasons whose rightness would sweep Chris's arrogance away in a passionate torrent. But her mind became an awful blank and she couldn't think of a single one. The thought that she had been obscenely inappropriate came to her, and terrified her.

"I wanted to know how the job interview went," she finally said.

Chris's mouth twisted with derision. "Did you really think I could get a job as a project manager? Do you know how trained you have to be for that?"

Anna was quiet for a moment, grateful Chris had allowed the subject to be changed. Then she spoke. "Do you really think I was wrong to encourage you?"

"Your encouragement...." Chris spat the word, staring at some point on the ground and shaking her head. She was straining to find the words to say it.

"Yeah, my encouragement, it was really evil, wasn't it," Anna said. "Why couldn't I just be one of those *discouraging* teachers, like the ones of your childhood, who believed you couldn't do squat?" She paused. "Well at least you've found your way back to your friends. They look like they'll do a pretty good job of discouraging you."

"They're not my friends!" Chris barked.

Anna peered at her from the couch, meanly satisfied by her own low blow.

There was a noise at the door, and Anna heard the rustle of some-one coming in and laying keys on a table. A head peered around the corner. "Oh!" the old woman said, looking at Chris, then at Anna.

Chris stalked out of the room, leaving Anna to fend for herself. Anna struggled to a sitting position, blanching at the queasiness plum-meting through her. "Hello again," she said.

"Hello," the woman said, peering at her with consternation. She was tall and stooped in a way that made her posture seem attentive; she wore slacks and a floral sleeveless shirt. "You look like you had a little too much to drink."

"Yes," Anna said. "Sorry."

"Well, you're not the first," the woman said. She held up the bag she was carrying, from Popeye's, and said, "I brought home some din-ner. Feel free to join us."

"Okay. Hey, I'm Anna."

"I'm pleased to meet you, Anna. I'm Gladys."

Anna sank back down on the couch, curling fetally into its crevices, listening to the sound of Gladys and Chris talking in the kitchen. She thought of the scene in the bar and mortification sent her into a full-body cringe. She tried to take comfort in the idea that maybe someday, far in the future, she would laugh at this whole thing. Laugh at herself, a crazy mosquito butch who had come after the big bad bull who gave her a hard time. She let Gladys's easy comment whir through her consciousness — not minding, really, being one of a long line of butches who had passed out perhaps on this very couch. In fact, tickled, relaxing suddenly, letting her humiliation slip like a kite string through her fingers.

After a while she got up and staggered into the kitchen. "Do you know where my glasses are?" she asked Chris. Chris grunted and rose, went into the other room and returned with them. Anna put them on and felt, to her great relief, the familiar crisping of her vision. At the sink she puzzled over her hands, and finally washed the right one by rubbing her fingers on the palm, and left the stinging left bandaged one be. She glanced into the open cabinets and saw boxed food —Pop-tarts, macaroni and cheese — twelve boxes at a time wrapped in plastic, apparently bought in bulk from a food warehouse. There were neatly stacked jars of applesauce and baby food. She pulled out a chair at the kitchenette set and sat, while Chris, her head bent over a piece of chicken, raised her eyebrows. "Can you eat?" Gladys said. "Sometimes you'd be surprised." Anna leaned over and took a drumstick with her right hand, took a tentative bite, chewed, swallowed, and waited. She was surprised at how good the greasy, crusty chicken tasted.

There had been something going on between Chris and Gladys, she slowly began to notice. When Gladys handed a tiny piece of chicken down to one of the cats, Chris said "For Christ sake, Gladys, those cats are already tubs of lard."

"Oh well oh well," Gladys crooned, rubbing a finger on the top of the cat's head as it licked its whiskers and set about raising its paw for a wash.

"So," Chris said, turning with wide deadpan blue eyes toward Anna. "Didn't play much pool coming up, did you."

"Shut up," Anna said.

Chris laughed — not the harsh snort Anna was accustomed to, but a laugh from the throat that came with an appealing flash of teeth. Anna stared at her for a moment, then reached for a biscuit. She broke it open carefully with her fingertips, letting it flake and the steam rise.

"So," she said, "How do you guys know each other?"

They looked at each other. "We've been friends forever," Chris said. "She used to own a bar, with her girlfriend."

"Oh," Anna said, "a lesbian bar?"

"Yes," Gladys said, turning her body toward her. She didn't like Chris speaking for her, Anna thought. "One of the oldest in the country to be owned by lesbians. It was called The Brink."

"I've heard of The Brink," Anna said. "You're a legend."

Gladys chuckled. "Well I wouldn't say I'm a legend. But I could tell you stories."

Chris hunched over her food, sucking meat off the bones and laying them on her plate with greasy fingers. Anna wondered if Gladys was inviting her to ask more, or just expressing general age and experience. Finally she spoke again. "So did you know Chris when she was coming up?"

Chris looked up at her suspiciously, while Gladys laughed. "You bet I did," she said; "she stayed with us when she first came to Cal City, a little bitty butch with nothing but a dirty knapsack and an attitude."

"Really!" Anna smiled, perking up as she realized she had found an interesting new way to make Chris squirm. "How old was she?"

"Fifteen, sixteen?" Gladys asked Chris.

"Sixteen."

"What was Chris like at sixteen?"

"Well first of all, a heartbreaker," Gladys said.

"That's not hard to imagine," Anna nodded.

Chris turned and looked at her with surprise laced with skepticism, as if wondering whether Anna was making fun of her.

"The truth is the truth, Chris," Anna shrugged. "You're old and mean and in a perpetual bad mood now, but that doesn't mean I can't see what was what back then." Her nose filled with merriment: where was this coming from? — she must still be drunk.

"She had what we called, back in the day, bedroom eyes, bright blue," Gladys said, casting glances over at Chris to make sure she was sufficiently tormenting her. "And if you can imagine a butch with

motorcycle boots and baby skin: my! And trouble! Talk about your leg-
ends! Why, once she punched the lights out of a mobster's brother. As you
can imagine, we were all terrified."

Anna looked at Chris, who rolled her eyes and said, "It wasn't
his brother, it was his cousin. And I didn't deck him. Can we talk
about something else?"

It was lore, Anna thought; they'd had conversations like these
hundreds of times. She sat back, then turned to Gladys again. "So
you could make a living running a bar back then?"

"Well, I also had a modeling job at Gordon's department store.
I would dress up in their clothes and go into their restaurant, and I
had to go from table to table telling people how much the clothes
cost. It was called the Tea Room."

"You're kidding," Anna said. "Did you like it?"

A smile played on Gladys' lips. "You know, I did like it. Of course,
what I really wanted to be was an actress."

Chris looked at her in surprise, her hands freezing with a drumstick
in them.

"Oh yes, I acted in a few plays in Chicago, and I performed once
at the Goodman, in a play with Karl Malden in it. But they told me I
wouldn't be successful because I was too tall. They also wanted me to
change my name. I guess Gladys Gutowski was too Polack for them."

"You're shitting me," Chris said. She sounded derisive, which
Anna read as a cover for being taken by surprise. "You were an
actress?"

Gladys flashed a superior look at her. "There's lots of things you
don't know about me," she said.

Chris twisted her mouth bitterly. "Yeah, well there's things you
didn't know about me either," she said.

"I know that, honey," Gladys said gently.

After dinner Anna stood. "Well I should get going," she said.
"Have you seen my car keys?" She looked up in sudden terror.
"Where's my car, anyway?"

"It's right outside," Chris said. "And your keys are here." She leaned back and fished in her pocket, pulled them out and tossed them on the table. "But you can't be driving back in your condition. You'll have to sleep here."

Anna stood there, calculating. It was true, she felt like shit and her blood alcohol was probably still pretty high. Her near-accident a few days ago came to mind, and that decided it.

"I think I have to go to sleep right this minute," she apologized. "I can hardly stand up."

"I'll open up the sofa," Gladys said.

Anna went into the bathroom and closed the door behind her. She peered into the mirror and winced at the sight of her ashen face, her cheeks pulling downward. She unwound the gauze Chris must have wrapped around her hand, pulling it off the gash in the center of her palm, which began to bleed again. Jesus, it was disconcerting to have two hours totally unaccounted for. Where had she been when Chris bandaged her hand? Had Chris laid Anna on the couch and crouched next to her holding her wounded hand, or resting it on her knee, bringing the gauze around and around again? Or had she dragged her into the bar and bandaged it up while Anna lay blacked out on the floor surrounded by jeering he-shes? Anna frowned. Her fantasy life was very sad, she thought, veering between Harlequin Romance, in which case she was Chris's damsel in distress, and prison movies, in which case she was, well, Chris's bitch.

She washed off the cut, gently cleaning around it with the forefinger of her other hand. It throbbed fiercely and continued to seep blood, and pressing gently around it, Anna found one sharply painful spot. She wondered if there was still a tiny sliver of glass in it. How the hell did a shot glass shatter, anyway? The hand probably needed stitches. But she just couldn't see asking Chris or Gladys, who seemed to think that hers was an ordinary scrape, to take her to the hospital, and she couldn't imagine how to get herself back to Chicago.

Chris had left tape and bandages out on the back of the toilet, and Anna clumsily wrapped up her hand again. She scrubbed her face with cold water, and squirted toothpaste onto her finger and

ran it around her teeth and gums. Then she paused. She didn't
know what to do about a shower: she badly wanted to shower, but the
clothes she was wearing were disgusting, the shirt rank with sweat
and the shorts, she noticed for the first time, bloodstained in the
front. Her heart lurched, and she quickly stuck a hand down into
her underwear, then pulled it back up and inspected her fingers.
She wasn't menstruating. It must have been her hand. She stood
there for a moment, strategizing. The key, she decided, was to keep
an aura of cool about her bloodied shorts, as though she had nothing to be embarrassed about.

She padded out of the bathroom in her bare feet and croaked
out Chris's name. When Chris poked her head out of the bedroom,
she asked, "Do you have an extra t-shirt or something? I gotta get out
of this one."

Chris disappeared and reemerged with a t-shirt and a pair of jeans
wadded in her hand. "You'll probably want to get out of those too," she
said, gesturing with her head toward Anna's shorts. Anna thanked her
and went back into the bathroom and turned on the tub. She took the
t-shirt by the shoulder seams and shook it out. It was a black t-shirt that
said *Hooters* on the front. "Fuck," she exhaled.

That night Chris curled on her side in the single bed with a pillow
jammed between her knees. She tried not to let her mind wander back
to the bar, but the more rigid she got, the less controllable her mind
got. The moment she'd laid eyes on Anna that afternoon, blood had
started pounding in her ears, the sound *no, no, no, no, no* raging in her
head like floodwater. You can't just come in here. You can't just go
anywhere you want. Why did Anna's showing up seem worse than all the
horrible things that had happened to her over the past weeks? And then
she had thought: *Okay, you wanna play? Then play.* She remembered cram-
ming shots down Anna's throat, wanting to suffocate her, prepared to
pry Anna's mouth open and pour the tequila down herself, if that's
what it took.

The irony was not lost on her that she'd been furious to see Anna,
and then gone and brought her here to sleep under the same roof as

her. When she'd seen Anna crumpled on the sidewalk with blood all around, her face as pale as blank paper, she'd nearly had a heart attack. She'd knelt beside her and cradled her head on her knees, brushed the hair off her sticky forehead and forced her teeth open with her finger. She lowered her mouth to hers and blew into her mouth until she saw her chest flutter and expand. She lifted her off the sidewalk like a child.

She could still feel Anna's lips, soft and dry. Chris shrugged off the image. She'd have to chalk it up to one of the knuckleheaded episodes in bars that she seemed to be having in her fifties. That thought failed to amuse her. She moved restlessly onto her back, her mind drifting to the conversation at dinner. By seeking refuge at Gladys's house, she thought, she'd ended up right back where she'd started over thirty years ago. Only at sixteen, she'd known exactly what she needed to do — find work and a place to live — and now she had no idea. Was it like the way old people turn back into babies, she wondered, bald-headed and fed with a spoon?

She was so tired. She'd spent the whole year, it seemed, stunned and stoned. She thought of her own house, and she thought of the way her love for Kathleen had drained right out of her. She stared into the darkness at the wall. Would leaving Kathleen be a step forward, or a step back? When did you become sure that the love would never come back? Who could tell her the answer to that, tell her with certainty the thing she craved to know the way in her younger days she'd craved pulling a woman fiercely close? It was a dangerous question, that last one, always had been; the empty space where the answer should be never ceased to devastate her. *Don't be a baby, don't be a fucking baby,* she thought to herself as tears rose in her throat and threatened to strangle her.

She drifted in and out of fitful sleep, dreaming, her dreams an annoyance, like buzzing flies. Pool balls the size of golf balls tumbling over felt; Anna draped in her arms, only she had died, and was naked, and Chris, in a thunder of panic and shame, was looking for a place to dump the body. Jack walking in the front door and seeing her playing cards with Gladys and Anna, Chris fearing she'd been caught doing something wrong. And her tutor, Dennis, who in her dream was Jason Paciorek, crying because his mother had died. His mother, who in her dream was Gladys.

When she came fully awake it was still dark out. She lay breathing in the quiet room and let her dream about Dennis reemerge till she was in the thick of it again, sitting next to him, pained by the grotesque gargle of his crying. She was certain the dream was a premonition about his mother, and her heart ached for him. She fumbled for her watch and pressed on its light, stared at it for a few groggy seconds. 3:26 in the morning. She stumbled to her feet and went to pee.

Anna was coming out of the bathroom, in her underwear and that stupid *Hooters* shirt, with a tremendous case of bed-head and a sheepish look on her face. Chris stepped in and peed, and when she came out of the bathroom, she headed back to bed, then stopped. An urge was coming over her. She found herself walking toward the living room, her toes crackling. She stopped at the threshold and peered in. She could see a great lump that was Anna's shape, and hear her plumping her pillows with her fist.

Anna stopped when she noticed Chris. "Hey," she said. In the dark living room, Chris was hardly more than a shadow.

Chris cautiously felt her way in, taking care not to stub her toes on anything, and set her hand on the arm of the armchair, lowered herself sighing. She let her eyes adjust to the dark and then closed them, felt the breathing presence of Anna settling and pulling covers around her.

Anna sat there alertly, listening to the rumble of Chris's breathing and running her hand through her hair, wincing at the burn of her scalp where she'd fallen on it.

"Have you left her?" she asked Chris.

"Maybe. I don't know."

Anna was quiet for a long while. Then she ventured, "Was she unsupportive about your learning to read?"

Chris grunted in surprise. "How did you know?" she asked.

"It happens a lot, Chris."

"Really?" Chris had the fleeting sensation of liking being called by name, which Anna did a lot.

"Really." Anna lay back down on the pillows she'd stacked and stared up at the ceiling. "You mean you thought you were the only one whose spouse had trouble with the relationship changing? Shit, I guess we forgot to warn you."

Tears burned Chris's eyes; hidden by the darkness, she was able to relax till they subsided.

Anna's body was light and empty now, the sheet caressing her bare legs. "She probably...I mean, not to excuse her, but she probably, you know, liked being the person who read the world to you. You can see how she'd like that, right?"

"No I can't." Chris's voice was thick and bitter. "I can see how she should like me to succeed."

Anna sought an analogy, but then stopped. She didn't even like Kathleen, and certainly didn't want to defend her. "Have you ever tried counseling?" she offered, then waited for a stinging reply. It came, but not right away, and with a quiet pain she hadn't expected.

"You know what? Not everything can be fixed."

"No," Anna said.

"I mean it," Chris said. "You think everything can be fixed. You think even Brandy can be fixed, and you saw what happened to her."

Anna sighed. "Chris, *somebody* in the world has to believe in Brandy."

"Well don't believe in her, pal, because if she lives to see forty, it'll be a fuckin' miracle."

"Yeah well," Anna said, a note of harshness in her voice, "That's what they pay me the big bucks for."

A car started outside, the engine gunning, and a dog barked in a nearby yard. Anna thought what a miracle it probably was that *Chris* had lived to see forty, or *any* of her students, for that matter. Going through danger and heartache she could only intuit from the accounts they consented to give of themselves, accounts so crystallized by the telling over the years that the pain had almost been abstracted out, was left as a hieroglyph.

They sat in the dark without speaking, till finally Chris groaned and rose.

"Hey," Anna said. "What was with that guy at the bar today, anyway? Did he used to be a butch or something?"

Chris sat back down. Ol' Ms. Singer was full of surprises, she thought. "He used to be a butch named Sally, and now he's a man named Sal," she said. Her voice was heavy with sarcasm. "I guess when she turned into a guy she had to turn into an Italian, too."

A surprised laugh tumbled out of Anna. "It's hard to know what to think when they go do that, isn't it. I mean, you want them to feel comfortable in their own skin, but Jesus, where does it leave the rest of us?"

Chris blinked. How did Anna know how to say what ailed Chris, just toss it off even while totally hung-over? You had to give her credit. "I wouldn't of pegged her for someone who would cross over," she told Anna. "She wasn't even that butch." They had worked together once, long ago, in the stockroom of an office furniture warehouse, and she was remembering how Sally used to pretend she was checking something, or counting units, when she was really trying to buy time to rest her arms. Man, Chris had wanted to light into him at the bar this afternoon; but Sal had backed off the minute Chris had looked at him cross-eyed.

Anna smiled into the darkness at the familiar sound of the universal butch put-down. Just then the light in the hall went on, and they blinked and looked at Gladys, who was standing in the hall in a nightgown, her eyes wide awake and her hair flying. Anna struggled upright, while Chris grumbled, "Jesus, Gladys, you look like a ghost."

"I heard you talking," Gladys said. She peered at Anna, who was sitting cross-legged on the couch with the sheet and blanket draped over her legs. "What *are* you wearing, dear?"

"I am wearing a *Hooters* t-shirt," Anna said haughtily. She turned to Chris, noticing for the first time that she too was in her underwear, boxers and a t-shirt. "Do you even *go* to *Hooters?*"

"Naw, somebody gave it to me as a gag gift."

Anna gave her the finger.

"Does anyone want ice cream?" Gladys asked. "I don't know about you, but I'm in the mood for ice cream." Anna and Chris looked at each other, bonding over the crazy lady who had wandered into their midst, and shrugged. Gladys disappeared into the kitchen and came out with three Good Humor drumsticks. Anna grinned at the sight of them as Gladys passed them out and settled on the couch next to Anna, remembering the baby food she'd seen in the cabinets.

They assiduously unwrapped their ice cream cones and sat in silence for a while, eating. The living room was faintly illuminated by the light in the hall. Gladys pulled the paper down to the base of the cone to create a little paper napkin that blossomed open from her fist. She nibbled around at the ring of hard chocolate and nuts and then put her whole mouth over the remaining ice cream, as though channeling some ancient drumstick-eating memory. Her lips came away coated with ice cream.

Chris looked at her and opened her mouth to comment.

"Hush," Gladys said.

Chris closed her mouth. She bit off the tip of her cone and tilted it, and sucked hard. When she'd gotten all the ice cream out, she popped the remaining cone in her mouth and disposed of it in a second.

"I don't sleep much anymore," Gladys confided. She reached for a napkin and patted her mouth. "I read in bed. I often get up and have a little snack."

Chris reached for a napkin, leaned forward and wiped Gladys' mouth where she'd missed a spot, while Gladys held her remaining cone away from her and compliantly leaned her face toward her. Anna watched them with a faint smile, wondering what kind of traumatized kid had appeared long ago at Gladys's door, what kind of explosive encounter had resolved over the years into affectionate and slightly denigrating teasing.

"What kinds of stuff do you read?"

Gladys turned toward Anna and patted her knee. "You're a good person," she said. "I'm glad Chris knows you."

Anna laughed softly through her nose. "Why?"

Gladys thought for a minute. "Because you have a nice open face. Because you're interested in an old broad you don't even know."

Anna raised her eyebrows at Chris as if to say: See?

"Remember Angel?" Chris asked Gladys, her eyes steady, conveying private significance.

"Yes," Gladys said. "And I miss her. Remember Kay?"

"Kay!" Chris said. "I haven't thought about her in ages."

"Jack hated her," Gladys said.

"Jack hated a lot of people."

"You can say that again."

To Anna the conversation seemed to have turned oblique, yet deeply significant, as though they'd all returned to adolescence and were smoking pot together on the grass right outside the school grounds.

"I go to a book club where we read the Oprah books," Gladys told Anna.

"Oh," Anna said. "Which is your favorite so far?"

"*White Oleander,*" Gladys said.

"I haven't read that one," Anna said. "What did you like about it?"

Gladys paused for a long time, considering deliciously. "I liked the girl's spirit. It couldn't be crushed."

"Well I guess I should read it then," Anna said, thinking that you could probably say that about every single Oprah novel.

"Tell me something," Chris said abruptly. "Was Jack really as big a sonofabitch as she made herself out to be?"

"Yes!" Gladys said, with such vigor that Anna and Chris laughed. And Chris understood, suddenly, that it was Jack who had prevented Gladys from being an actress. She could see all the reasons Jack had. That they'd kill Gladys out there if they found out about her. That Gladys would be backstage, at parties, courted by actors, and where the hell would that leave Jack? All of those excuses for Jack's own jealousy and insecurity. Chris had always thought of Gladys as a good-hearted nut, and now that she thought about it, she realized that a lot of the good times she'd had with Jack involved making fun of Gladys.

Her mouth twisted as she thought about what couples do to each other.

Anna was getting drowsy, sitting in the semi-darkness with a blanket over her knees, the pleasant crunch of ice cream cone crumbs in her molars. When she heard Chris ask, "Did you ever read a book called *Stone Butch Blues?*" she closed her eyes in lazy satisfaction.

"Sure," Gladys said.

There was a long pause, which made Anna stop breathing for a second as she wondered what would happen next. "Did you like it?" Chris finally asked.

"It knocked my socks off," Gladys said.

"Yeah, I know what you mean," Chris said. "Wow."

Gladys was quiet for a while. "But I remember that I didn't really get the end. The person the main butch — what's her name? — ends up with."

"Jess Goldberg," Chris said.

"She's not even a femme, she seems to be a man that turned into a woman. What's wrong with ending up with a plain regular femme? There's all this wanting between the butches and the femmes, but for some reason they can't make it together." She laughed. "But then again," she said lightly, "Maybe there's something to that. It's just that sometime I'd like to see the femme get the last word."

"Oh please!" Chris snorted.

Anna drifted off to the melody of the old familiar wrangle.

Chris was pouring herself a cup of coffee, and Gladys was sitting at the table drinking tea and reading the paper in a housedress, when Anna shuffled into the kitchen, wincing from the morning light. She was wearing Chris's jeans, which rode low on her hips and which she'd had to cuff at the bottom four times. Chris saw her look over at the table and hesitate, then look out the window into the backyard, at the figurines of frogs and swans and gnomes and Buddhas sitting out on the patio and the grass.

"She puts little hats and scarves on them in the wintertime," Chris announced.

"I don't want them to get cold," Gladys said.

Chris said to Anna, "The neighbor kids think she's a witch."

Gladys peered over her glasses at Anna, then rose and opened the cabinet above the stove, the one that held the liquor. "Uh oh," Chris said, watching her take down the whiskey bottle, "here we go." Gladys was making her famous hair-of-the-dog concoction: whiskey, milk, baking soda and red pepper flakes. She stirred it with vigor, claiming as she had since 1963 that there was nothing like it to cure a hangover. Anna looked at Chris, who shrugged and said "I can't help you, man, I told you she's a witch." Chris shot Gladys an impressed look as Anna bravely gulped it down. A moment later Anna rushed to the sink and vomited, then puked up the remains of her dinner as well. Chris was laughing as Anna turned on the water full force to wash them down and mute the strangled sounds of her gagging. The smell of regurgitated alcohol and fried chicken rose into the kitchen.

"See?" Chris joked as Anna straightened and wiped her mouth, looking reproachfully at Gladys through streaming eyes. "Nothing like it."

Gladys brought her a cup of coffee and the three of them sat at the table, Anna coughing and sniffing and Gladys reading *Dear Abby*. After a few minutes, Gladys tsked. "Here's a lady whose stepdaughter refused to be a bridesmaid at her wedding with the father."

Anna looked at Chris. "Ain't that a crying shame," she said

Chris laughed, and Anna began telling Gladys some story about trying to find an outfit for a black-tie wedding she had to go to, where wearing a tuxedo would have been an affront to the conservative families involved in the wedding, and how she had found a short, midnight-blue jacket with silver sequins in a department store. And how the whole day of the wedding, her girlfriend had referred to her as Little Liberace.

Watching Anna's eyes crinkle with mirth, her face still pale from vomiting, Chris thought: an *affront* to the families. Anna knew just how to say it, and without using pretentious words, either. She'd done that last night too, and each time, it had struck Chris's ear like a thunk on a xylophone key. Chris narrowed her eyes. Now that Anna was just a regular person, a person who puked and got bed-head, she was starting to see her a little differently. The way she had tossed down Gladys' potion: it was so typical, leaping before she looked, trusting an old lady she didn't even know because she was just like that, a trusting person. The world hadn't been bad to her so why *shouldn't* she trust it? It suddenly occurred to Chris that you didn't *have* to hate a person for that. You could see how it made them willing to try new things. You could call them brave just as easily as you could call them stupid.

She patted her t-shirt pocket for her cigarettes; they weren't there. She took a sip of coffee, agitated by new thoughts. What if she had known Anna back when she was coming up? She immediately reprimanded herself: they never would have even crossed paths. But what if they had? She tried to push her imagination forcibly past the obstacle of her standards of realism. Would they have been friends? There her imagination failed her. Because Anna Singer was from her parents' world, and if Chris had laid eyes on her she would've been compelled to kick her ass. Just like she did yesterday.

Stricken, she looked at Anna, who was unwinding the bandage on her hand and inspecting the gash on her palm. The skin was white and puckered around it. A horrible sense of having done something wrong came over Chris. She looked around the kitchen for her cigarettes, found them on the kitchen counter, stood and took one from the pack. Remembering that the smoke bothered Anna, she opened the back door, went out and sat on the tiny stoop. She lit it and inhaled deeply, and savored the rush of the first drag of the day, the closest thing she got these days to a Percocet high. The sick feeling of having been an asshole was beginning to shift under the calming rhetoric of her value system, the way a bitter defeat is spun by athletes with platitudes about effort and fate. She'd been unfair to Anna. It was like Anna had said last night: somebody has to believe in Brandy. And she'd signed on to believe in this motley crew of illiterates, signed on for what was no doubt a shit-paying job when she could do better. You had to give credit where credit was due.

Inhaling cigarette smoke down to the very last capillary of the bottom of her lungs, Chris was tamping down a subterranean awareness that if she let go of despising Anna, she might love her, might crave the sound of her own name in Anna's mouth.

After she'd finished her coffee and eaten a piece of toast, Anna gathered her wallet and keys and stuffed her dirty shorts and t-shirt into a plastic bag Gladys gave her. She assured Gladys that she was in shape to drive. "Are you sure you don't want to come with me?" she asked Chris, but Chris mutely shook her head. Anna couldn't say that she wanted Chris there for the last few days of class, because Gladys was always in the room, but at the front door she did say, "Chris, I hope I'll see you again sometime." She gestured down at Chris's jeans, and said "In any case, I'll have to get these back to you."

Chris nodded.

"Listen," Anna said, touching her arm. "I'm sorry for everything."

Chris looked down at Anna's hand. "I don't know what you're talking about," she said.

She was trying to tell Anna that it was she who should be sorry, but Anna heard only the usual chilly evasion. She laughed sharply and turned on her heels.

Driving back to Chicago, past the stench of the smoking mills, Anna wondered if she would ever see Chris again. If she didn't, would she miss her? *You don't have to like all lesbians,* Patricia had instructed her when she had first come out. But it wasn't really even a matter of whether she liked her or not. Chris had gotten under her skin. Had she gotten under Chris's? — a do-gooder who had appeared out of nowhere, making mischief on Chris's earth?

She remembered making this same drive last summer, staggered by grief, wondering what would become of her. Now the thought of her father came to Anna, easily, like a child coming home to an unlocked house. She saw him in the family Impala driving south, away from the city toward smoke and flat sky. He drove right past her in the opposite direction, probably high — up onto the Skyway and into the stench, past the mills with their vast clouds of smoke and the flocks of swans sitting on dirty water. He noted with bitter satisfaction how the landscape correlated to the wasteland inside him. He was the age she was now, but she thought of him as younger, as though he were her lover or her teenage son. He let himself into a comfortless institutional room with a Bible in the dresser drawer, sat on the bed and tried to cry. But unpracticed, he could only produce whimpering sounds that were hideous to his ear. Did he think of her as he reached for the pills and hoped to die? — think *My baby, My little girl?* She'd called lovers those names. They say you can't really imagine love till you've had a child, but Anna hated that idea, because it invalidated the love she'd felt in her life, love so fierce she didn't know how she could love any harder.

Next year, she thought, she would start all over again with new students. This time she would come out to them right from the start, give the class no chance to become a circus of speculation. Anna looked at the shimmering city ahead of her. She would send out her hope and effort like homing birds into the sky. If they returned, well great. And if they didn't, she thought, the comfort would have to be in the sending.

CHAPTER TWENTY-THREE

In a sun-flooded studio, sitting cross-legged on top of two folded blankets and singing "om," Anna peeked at Monica out of the corner of her eye and tried to hoist her voice up to the register of the rest of the women in the class. It broke like a pubescent boy's, the one who can no longer sing soprano in the choir. The teacher was named Clarice, and she was willowy and long-haired, and her *om* was clear as a bell. In contrast, Monica, who was tone-deaf to begin with, chanted an interval lower without even noticing it.

It made her laugh and recoil, yoga. Not, as it turned out, the spiritual part: Anna found herself surprisingly receptive when Clarice recited poetry, when she urged them to leave their arrival at class, and the stress of the day before that, behind them, when she invited them to say a kind word to themselves and to their beautiful strong bodies and to their willingness to practice yoga. She moved through Clarice's instructions, watching the person in front of her and then realizing that she didn't really have to, Clarice explained so clearly — finding herself loving surrendering to a woman's voice, feeling blessedly without ego, without the drive to excel or the fear of making mistakes. In any case, it turned out that beginners required a lot of correction, and that involved a woman touching you gently at the shoulders or laying her hands on your lower back, at the kidneys.

But as she lay on her face with her legs open behind her like a frog's, and knelt on all fours with her butt and chin in the air and her pelvis and stomach dropped, Anna's face burned at the thought of being seen by the person behind her, or by Clarice. After class she crouched against the hall wall putting on her sandals, grateful to be coiled forward. Clarice was chatting with people as she organized the register and checks and money she'd collected. Lithe and well-heeled, they wanted to tell her about some injury they had that made a particular pose problematic, about the minutiae of their bodily response, about their *shakra* or their *prahna*. People seemed to imprint upon their yoga teachers, Anna noticed.

She gave a quick sheepish thanks to Clarice, who called out "Nice to meet you, Anna and Monica," and walked out with Monica. They looked at each other expectantly, and laughed.

"Not the manliest postures I've ever found myself in," Monica said.

Anna snorted so hard it hurt. "Are we even *meant* to open up our hips?"

"I don't think so," Monica laughed again. "I think we're meant to keep them tight. And unswaying."

"There weren't a whole lot of hairy legs in there either, I'll tell you that."

Monica nodded. "But I liked some of the poses, the more muscular ones" — she made her voice comically gruff and masculine — "like the warrior poses."

"Yeah, me too."

"So whaddya say, champ, you gonna go again?"

"Well you *know* she thinks we're lovers," Anna said. "And now she's going to be all respectful of our partnership. But hey. It's free, at least for a while."

She went to another class, thinking she'd use up the eight free ones and then decide whether she wanted to continue. As Clarice opened by having them build a sitting posture, she started saying things that astonished Anna, that she felt she had been longing to hear her whole life. *Lift your heart. Release your belly.*

Who on earth ever told you to release your belly?

She learned how to do sun salutes, and how to spread her toes to root herself in the earth, and how to find her breath, and how to stand on her head, which brought her pleasantly back to her childhood. When Clarice asked them to say a kind word to their hearts, Anna silently addressed hers as an old comrade, for it had been bruised and battered and could still be made to stir and flower. Clarice told them that the key to balancing was not giving a damn whether you fell. She told them that one part of their back is where we used to have our dinosaur's wings, and, in an afterthought, her voice thickening with mirth, reassured them that it was okay if they didn't remember back then, that that was why it was called the *practice* of yoga. She told them to lengthen and soften. She told them to bring the nape of their neck back as though they were kittens being lifted by their mother. She invited them to feel their organs slosh against each other like water against a boat.

In Anna's fourth class, she put them in a pose that made Anna's face burn: arched back and lying supine over a bolster, the soles of her feet touching and strapped in, her knees splayed open. Clarice strolled around the room adjusting people and making them more comfortable. "You should feel like a king or queen in this pose," she announced. Anna heard the brush of her bare feet on the floor and felt her presence hover over her. "Do you feel like a queen?" Clarice asked in a light smiling voice.

Anna peeked over at Monica, who was splayed clumsily over a bolster and shooting her a merry glance. She had no idea how to begin to answer. "Uh...," she said, and nodded.

"Uh...," Monica mocked her after class, her face loosening into stupid bewilderment. "Let's see, do I feel like a queen?"

Anna punched her on the arm. "Well what would you say?" They trotted down the stairs, laughing, and stepped out into the sunny commotion of the street.

Anna began doing sun salutations at home, facing the big courtyard windows, and she began alternating yoga classes and running. She craved running now; the contrast to yoga was a kind of relief, the impact and pounding and power, the driving from the thighs, the sheer *crisis* of her body when running, and her capacity to calm and manage it.

As she lengthened and softened, her worry about her mother's health receded; so far the doctors had found nothing wrong with her, so Anna was off the hook till the next crisis. There arrived the last two weeks of class, and there too she felt her heart lifting, her belly releasing. They were working full-time on their final stories. Chris never showed up again, and Anna tried to make her peace with that. She got used to her small raggedy band of remaining soldiers, their boots worn and rations dwindling, but their spirits battle toughened and their rapport reasonable. One morning she shocked them all by bringing in a blueberry coffee cake and a gallon of milk. "Did you make this?" Vanessa asked, tickled.

"Yup," Anna said. "It's my mother's recipe."

They ate it with care, forkful by fastidious forkful. Warm weather had finally divested them of their winter layers, and Anna enjoyed the sight of the bare brown skin of their arms and wrists, which made them look younger and more vulnerable.

Some days they dictated to Anna, and some days she had them write on their own or in pairs. Antwan was writing about his mother's death. Memories surfaced about the hospital and the doctors; there had been a fight about some procedure that Antwan now thought had probably been deemed too expensive, and once the kids had had to sit waiting in the emergency room for nine hours when she had fallen into an insulin coma. Anna looked up and said incredulously, "Nine hours?" and Antwan found himself rattled, then enraged, by the realization that his mother had gotten bad medical care. Like he didn't know that already, he thought: why did it come as a surprise every time?

Robert wrote, as Anna had expected, about Reggie Jr.'s death. But the story took a strange turn. By the time he heard, Robert told Anna, he was back home. And a few weeks later he was in a bar on Halsted, and ran into the door gunner of the chopper that had lifted him out of the jungle for good. They got to talking and one thing led to another till Robert realized he'd been on the same chopper as Junior's body, but had been too stoned to notice.

Anna frowned over the implausible coincidence. "How could you notice? Weren't the bodies in body bags?"

"No, by that time there wasn't none left." Robert sighed. How could he explain this story? He'd rested his legs, his dirty boots, on top of some dead cat's legs.

Anna looked at his craggy iguana face, the twitch of his eyes as he struggled to reveal or conceal. How, she wondered — assuming that the gunner was in fact the same one who'd been with Robert in that helicopter, and could recognize him in a completely different context — had he known that Junior had been in that very helicopter, not to mention remembering it vividly enough to recount it much later? She had to think that Robert's story was garbled by some combination of heroin and the years passing by. "So what was the turning point here, Robert?"

Robert brushed his knuckles against his nose. He didn't have the words to say what that meant to him, his oblivious keeping-company with his dead cousin. He could have kissed him, or wiped his face. He looked at Anna's expectant and doubtful face, and fell back on the tried and true. "I guess it was Junior who got me wanting to read. Because he was always excited about reading Malcolm and such."

Anna sighed. It sounded an awful lot like what he might imagine she wanted to hear. "Are you sure?" she asked.

Sure about what? Robert felt a mild, sick faintness in the place he imagined his soul was. "Yes," he said.

"Okay," Anna said. "Let's write that down."

Had Robert in fact accomplished a lot this year? She watched him hunch down, clutching his pen with dolorous fingers. She thought he had, although she had to think about it. He was still flummoxed by certain letter patterns, and still read aloud woodenly, word by word, having to go over each sentence several times to get the meaning.

She went over to Cheryl and glanced over her shoulder at her paper, which was covered in sentences in slanting block letters, about half of them ending in exclamation marks. Cheryl would jump right to pre-GED, she was that good. She had gone through many drafts of her essay, which was a surprisingly romantic account of her relationship with Germaine, her drug-dealer boyfriend who had died. "Y'all want to hear about niggas and homies and dawgs," her essay began. "But to bad! LEAVE ME ALONE." When Anna told Monica about that opening, Monica drawled, "I see that Cheryl is no stranger to the Foucaultian notion of incitement to discourse," which made Anna laugh. Cheryl's essay went on to talk about how much Germaine had loved her, how he liked to tease her about being a bad-ass, how he called her "a whole lotta smart with too little to do." Anna, taking dictation for her one day to let her associate freely, mused, "It sounds like your parents thought you could only come back to school after he died, but you're saying that it was Germaine himself who gave you the confidence to do it."

Cheryl's eyes flashed. "Write that down," she demanded.

On the last day of school, Cheryl came into class a few minutes late with a large picture in a frame, wrapped in brown paper. When everybody had arrived, she marched to the front of the class. "We made this," she announced to Anna, handing it to her. Anna tore off the paper and held it away so she could see it. Set in a black plastic frame was a drawing that Anna immediately recognized as a depiction of the corner of Lawrence and Winthrop, the havoc-prone corner outside their classroom window. "Wow," she said. It overwhelmed the eye, there were so many small, deft details. Two cars had collided in the intersection, and their drivers were standing outside gesticulating. A woman was behind the wheel at the one stop sign at the intersection, with her turn signal on. On the building wall at the back end of the parking lot a young man was spraying graffiti, the words from their stories rendered as a graffiti collage. The graffiti was the only part of the drawing Cheryl had colored in, in lurid yellow-green crayon. It read:

Which way to turn?
They told me he died.
They came out and said "your mother passed."
My sister, who died.
Cat got greased he told me.
That's how all the stories start.

The moon

     his boots

         that school

              my heart

It was signed, by Cheryl, Robert, Antwan and Vanessa, each in their own handwriting.

Vanessa peeked over Anna's shoulder, and breathed, "That came out good!" Anna noticed the lower right corner: the sign for Pathways on an open door, tiny, smaller than scale, heartbreakingly incidental; and someone just disappearing into the building, only the bottom half of one leg still visible outside.

"My God, you guys, this is fantastic," Anna said.

Cheryl shrugged. It had started with a doodle the other night, her parents asleep and that whack-job Dr. Laura on TV. Dr. Laura was screaming at her callers till they were speechless, and Cheryl wondered for the millionth time, Why do they even call in? Do they think they the one person she ain't gonna go off on? But she loved the violence, too, loved seeing this skinny white bitch play the dozens. Meanwhile, her hand skimmed over the page till the picture grew too large in conception for the scrap of note paper she was doodling on. She groaned with impatience: she was going to have to start all over again. She went into her room, found her stash of good stiff drawing paper, and brought a sheet back into the living room. She heard her father cough in the bedroom. She went into the kitchen and spilled a handful of chocolate chips from an open bag into her hand. She ate them while staring at the TV, then licked her hand to get off the remaining chocolate and wiped it on her pants leg. She sat cross-legged on the floor, sighed at the prospect of blank paper. Dr. Laura was incensed. People weren't taking personal responsibility. Cheryl bent over the paper and began to draw. It didn't occur to her that the drawing would become a gift. Only the next morning, when Vanessa summoned her and Antwan in the hall and asked if they thought they should get Ms. Singer something, did she think of it. She demanded their turning points and three dollars from each student, and they handed them over without question. They left the execution of the picture entirely in her hands, and, like the most competent person in the workplace, she was both glad she'd be able to do it right, and infuriated by their passivity.

Now she gave Anna an aggravated look and said, "I couldn't put your turning point, because you didn't give me none."

"Why didn't you want to write for us?" Vanessa demanded.

Anna shrugged, then shrugged again. She had tried to write about her father's death, thinking that she should share something important about herself with her students, giving back what they'd given, being as brave as she asked them to be every day. On the other hand, the idea of dramatically pulling the curtain away to reveal her own suffering, at the end of their time together, mortified her. It felt like a big song and dance. And writing in a language they could read: she worried about writing something much richer than their stiff and ritualized accounts, but also felt strange about simplifying it, as though that would be condescending. How could she concoct a style in front of them? Or a self, for that matter? — she couldn't tell if she wanted that self to be intelligible or unintelligible to her students. In the end, she just hadn't gotten around to it.

The traffic made a racket through the open windows, and a quick wind ripped through, ruffling papers. Anna handed out their stories with a ceremonial flourish; they had been desktop-published into an attractive booklet that contained short pieces from the students in the other classes as well. She had them go around the class reading their own, and then she read a few of the pieces from other students, at levels both below and above their own, stories about adversity, failure and triumph. Their favorite was a story someone had written about a puppy his neighbor kept chained up, and which grew till its collar embedded into its neck; it was a crudely funny account of the dog's fantasies about the adventures it'd have when it broke free, which included humping all the neighborhood bitches, stealing steaks from people's tables, and attacking its negligent owner. Reading it, Anna had to pause several times till their laughter subsided and they were wiping their eyes with their sleeves. She herself felt a great antagonism toward the story, unable to tell whether it was utterly frivolous or incredibly deep. When she got to the end, Cheryl complained, "Why do ours got to be so serious?"

Anna looked at her, blinking. Had she forgotten, in her drive to get at what her students cared about most, the whole imaginative and playful aspect of writing? It was a question that would haunt her for weeks.

At the end of class she gave them each a gift-wrapped and inscribed copy of *Bastard out of Carolina*. The idea was that they'd finish the last third or so on their own; she knew that was highly unlikely, but she wanted to be the one to give them their first book. She ended the class without speeches. "You guys," she said, and put her hand on her heart. "Good work. Keep going. See you in September."

Cheryl was gone in a flash, leaving her booklet behind, but the others lingered, Antwan last of all.

"Where you headed?" Anna asked, and he shrugged. The warm air outside Pathways seemed to him full of promise and malice.

On an impulse, Anna came up and gave him a hug. Pulled up on her tiptoes, she could feel his breath on her ear, his hand patting her back. When she landed back down on her heels, she looked up into Antwan's flushed face, which was full of such sweet shyness it broke her heart. "Good luck, man," she said.

"Thanks," he said.

On the way out she stopped at Renée's office, and sank into a chair. Renée was decked out in a festive flowered blouse and bright red lipstick; she swiveled toward Anna and folded her hands behind her head, in an uncharacteristic gesture of feline laziness. "You're all done!" she said, then added shrewdly, "Does it leave you just a little empty inside?"

Then she sat forward, all business again. "Listen, I got a call from the Chicago Parks District. They're looking for someone to work in Jackson Park over the summer, tutoring kids who are in a summer arts program. I think it pays pretty well. They're also looking for someone to coordinate the tutoring component of the summer arts program, but I don't know if that's something you want to get into or if you'd like more of your summer free."

She was stripping a piece of paper off a pad and handing it to Anna. Anna looked at the name and number, folded it and put it in her back pocket. She was getting the feeling that she might be able to piece together a living at this godforsaken profession. It was so much easier for women like Renée and the others who taught here; their work was their families' second job, the husbands bringing in the big bucks and the benefits. Still, between teaching, administration, maybe a little grant writing, who knew? Renée would continue throwing opportunities her way; she was a good friend that way. Anna stood and grinned, remembering Sidney Poitier finally getting his engineering job, but deciding to remain a teacher after all. "I'm starting to feel like Sir at the end of *To Sir With Love*."

Renée looked at her with a frown, then remembered the movie and shocked Anna by singing, in a spot-on imitation of Lulu, "But what do I give someone, who has taken me from crayons to perfume? What can I give you in return?"

Anna laughed and applauded. "I don't think I've ever seen this side of you," she marveled. "And hey, what's up with those lyrics, anyway?"

"I don't know," Renée said, a look of comic perplexity coming over her face. "As an educational philosophy, it sure is some weird shit."

Anna's departure left Chris with an emptiness that she attributed to boredom and the state of limbo she was in. Maybe she *should* have gone back with her, she thought; she was going to have to get on with her life, whatever it came to look like.

That night, after Gladys had gone to sleep, Chris took the phone out to the back steps, fished a slip of paper with a phone number on it out of her pocket, and called Dennis. "Chris," he said, his voice husky. "Hey buddy."

"Hey." She lit a cigarette and blew into the yard, which was illuminated by street lights.

"Where are you? I tried you at home, but Kathleen was all hush-

hush about your whereabouts."

"I'm staying with a friend down in Cal City for a while."

There was a pause. "No more class?" he asked. "There's only a few more."

"Not right now, Dennis."

He was silent.

She cleared her throat. "How are you doin'?"

"Not so great. My mother passed away last week."

"Aw man, I knew it." Her heart drummed with the desire to assuage his misery, but she couldn't find the words. They hung mutely on the phone. Finally Dennis said, "Listen buddy, I'm sorry I was away these weeks, I'm sorry I let you down."

"Dennis," she said, pained. He'd loved his mother, an old firebrand who still got riled up over a good injustice, and when he talked about her, Chris got a fresh and salty whiff of a world where people talked and argued about important things. "Did your students cut you a break at least?"

He laughed faintly. "They're teenagers, and it's May — nothing gets past their radar except for their hormones and their music and the end of school."

"Creeps," Chris said.

"Listen, buddy, I'd sure like to spend the summer working together."

The screen door of the house next door swung shut, and after a few moments Chris smelled a freshly-lit cigar. She bent over the phone and lowered her voice. "That's how you want to spend your summer?"

"Well," Dennis said. "What else are we gonna do with ourselves?"

In bed that night, cool air ruffling her cheek as the fan rotated, Chris found herself thinking about *Stone Butch Blues*. She thought about how all the butches in the book believed they had something special wrong with them that even the other butches couldn't understand. She didn't know why she had that thought, but it made her feel as though the whole breed was kind of cockeyed. Even Jack probably felt that way, which was probably why she was such a son-ofabitch in the first place.

She turned onto her side. It was time to go home. But first, she would get Gladys in good shape; it was the least she could do for her. And when the time came, she suddenly knew, she would move Gladys in with her, whether she was living with Kathleen or not.

Over the next few days Chris fixed the faucet in the kitchen sink, repaired the bathroom fan and scrubbed off the mold that had formed on the ceiling, and cleaned the gutters, which were still choked with leaves from the previous fall. One morning, as Gladys sat at the table drinking her coffee, Chris stood in the kitchen with her hands on her hips taking a mental measurement of the floor. "I can do it for under $300," she said. That day she and Gladys went to the Home Depot to look at new kitchen flooring. Gladys took forever to choose a linoleum, and paid for it with cash, rolling off fifties with slow fingers. When they returned, Chris tore up the old kitchen floor and prepared to lay the new one. For the next few days, as she worked, Gladys fed her well, cooking steaks and chicken on the grill while her kitchen was out of commission. Each night, without having showered, Chris sat in a plastic chair on the tiny backyard deck after Gladys had gone to bed, listening to the neighborhood dogs calling to each other and to air conditioner units thrumming on and off, drinking heavily as the evening cooled into some semblance of May.

She went home on a Saturday morning, taking the bus to the Greyhound station and the El to Belmont from downtown. She splurged on a cab from the El station, since she had her suitcase with her. The moment the cab pulled up in front of her house, she could see that the lawn was torn to shreds. What asshole had driven over her lawn? But her indignation subsided as quickly as it had come. The truth was, this house had left her cold from the start, the sense of dread and obligation too heavy on her heart. She thought of the pleasure she'd had fixing things around Gladys's house; she'd never felt that way about her own. With a house you owned, you were never finished fixing the things that needed to be fixed; there was always something more, and it came out of your own hide.

If she left Kathleen, would she forfeit this house? Kathleen had paid the down payment after all, and this year, most of the mortgage payments. Could Chris stand to lose everything? At her age, with her liabilities?

She fumbled for her keys, and at the sound of them Rufus stopped barking. The moment she entered the darkened house he thrust his muzzle into her palm, his tail thwacking the table in the hall. "Hey buddy," she said, stroking his head and stooping to kiss him between the eyes. "Where's Kathleen?"

She froze at the sound of something coming from the backyard, a thud so profound it seemed to raise dust deep inside her. She walked back to the kitchen and looked out the door. Outside, the little yard was despoiled by huge piles of stone. Chris blinked, trying to decipher what she was seeing; she had the odd sensation of looking at rubble from a bombed-out building. She noticed Kathleen and Keith standing at the corner of the gouged yard, in work clothes and gardening gloves, their hands on their hips. Kathleen was wearing one of Chris's work shirts; her face was scarlet from exertion. There were a few neat piles, Chris was noticing, stones chosen for their likeness in shape to one another. And a work table. They were building; they were building Kathleen's retaining wall.

CHAPTER TWENTY-FOUR

The stone is delivered in great quantities bundled by wire. The truck gores your front lawn on its way to the backyard, strips of lawn peeling off its giant treads and giving off an earthy stench, and you wonder what in heavens you've gotten yourself into. You've never done a project like this in your life. The next morning, making coffee, you steal a glance out the back window and your stomach takes a nosedive.

And yet, you've thought about this from the moment you moved into this house. You were poring over the pictures of prehistoric implements and memorizing their names while your butch was memorizing all the new streets and the El stops to school. (Belmont, Addison, Irving Park, Montrose, Wilson, Lawrence. She rattled them off in a careless slur — not even really trying to remember, just trying to show it was easy to do, she was as smart as anyone.) You have been collecting tools over the past year: a chisel here, a mattock — it said in the book that you could find a mattock at a flea market, and what do you know, one Sunday morning you did just that. You've collected small stones and shims, surprised at how much stone you can find on a normal day in the city just walking down the street with your eyes open. They sit in a bucket by the back door.

The two of you unpacked the house, discovering all the hidden things that needed repair. Each one enraged her — the dripping shower, the rotted-out shelf under the kitchen sink, the window that leaked when it rained. She thought she should have seen it coming. She started to demand your help. Once upon a time she had been reluctant to show she needed you so much. Now she had a demanding tone, calling you to come into the room she was in to help her read something instead of getting off her fanny and coming to you. You came to hate the sound of your name in her mouth, your name suddenly shortened by half so there would be no waste to the demand. They're always saying people should express their needs, but with her, you're sorry, it was downright unattractive. You liked it when her need was shy and nervous and you had to find it yourself. Half the joy was sensing it and coaxing it out, unfurling her defensive body like a map, or a flag. Funny to say, you often felt that in bed, you were having orgasms more for her than for yourself. Coming for two, the way the way they say pregnant women eat for two. You saw how your pleasure made her feel, and felt in your conscience that if you could do that for somebody, you would be selfish not to.

You have a theory about the way she changed. She was testing you to see if you really wanted to be with her now that you owned a house bought with a down payment you had provided. Look at the bed you made, living with an illiterate: now go lie in it! She was daring you to make a peep about it.

Well you're making a peep. You broke right into the settlement money to buy this stone. You feel like Lucy Ricardo: you've really done it now!

Over the next week you do some reading. You take the stonescaping book into bed with you, and fall asleep with it in your arms. In your dreams, you draw designs, crazy things with benches and turrets. Once you dream a crow crashes into your head and flaps wildly in your hair, then grabs the design right out of your hands with its huge bony beak. Once you're a finalist for a national contest on stone wall design, and spend the whole dream trying not to get your hopes up. When you awaken, you have to peel the book's warm pages off your chest, and they leave a faint ink smudge slanted on the insides of your breasts that takes days to scrub off.

You take your coffee out to the backyard and stand in shorts and flip-flops just looking at the stone. Finally, one Saturday morning you

think: this wall isn't going to build itself! You set your coffee on the
back steps, put on a pair of thick gloves and begin to sort, undecid-
ed whether you've officially started working on it or whether you're
just doing a little straightening up in preparation for work. When
you have the sense to notice that you're still wearing flip-flops and
could crush a toe, you go back into the house to find socks and work
boots. When they are on, and you are stooping to touch rock, you
suppose you have begun.

You move like stones into piles, laying out the capstones so
you'll get to know them just by being around them every day. You
stretch before setting down to work, and plunge your knees down to
the ground before lifting; you learn to lay the wheelbarrow on its
side right next to the stone, shove the stone in, then pull the wheelbarrow towards you till it's upright. The next day your breasts and
armpits are studded with pain. You stand under the shower using up
all the hot water, and lie diagonally on the bed, your body red and
steaming, your arms dead weights at your sides. You're not going to
be able to do this project by yourself; that has become clear. What
on earth made you imagine you could?

The dog lays his big head on the edge of the bed and lets out a sigh.
You turn your head and contemplate his concerned eyes, the black
lower lip shiny between his jowls. The day you brought him home from
the shelter Chris curled around him on the bedroom floor, tucking his
nose into her neck so he could breathe in her smell. She called it his
nozzle, and then sulked when you laughed and cried "Muzzle!"
Eventually they both fell asleep that way, Chris snoring, the puppy
twitching in his dreams. Now she's abandoned him, too.

Your ex-husband stops by one Saturday. The sound of his truck
brakes squealing brings relief streaming through you. He sets thick
gloves and safety goggles on the kitchen table and fusses over your
drawing, scratching his chin and worrying that you've conceived this
project too grandly since you've never built a wall before. Do you have
to make it curve — wouldn't it be easier to build three sides of a square?

He keeps suggesting ways to make the wall simpler and, in your opinion, less special. Maybe you could put plants in between the courses so they'll grow out nice and wild, like he's seen before. The thought appalls you: you want a fresh, neat-looking wall. *No,* you say, and: *yeah, but still.* He says he doesn't want you to be disappointed and you give him a look. A little late for that, isn't it?

But he helps you make the cut in the berm, and, experienced at eyeballing measurements, shows you a clever way to keep track of the batter. Together, you rake out the gravel bed and choose two corner stones, and he helps you lay the first course. Working with him, digging in the gravel and the ground to set the stones at the right height, optimism rises and bobs within you. Then the next Saturday morning he fails to show and to your surprise, his older daughter comes in his place, wearing baggy bell-bottoms, a t-shirt that reveals her belly button, and inappropriate shoes. Taking care to sound pleased to see her, for fear she'll think you don't want her here, you ask what she's doing here, wondering what use she'll be to you. She shrugs and says they made her. She says they thought if she was left to her own devices, she'd be riding motorcycles with gangbangers on drugs without wearing a helmet, and then having unprotected sex with them.

You know that for her, it's Chris who's the glamorous one, the one who has mysteriously and tragically vanished — even though Chris never did a thing for her except take credit for the gifts you bought. Your butch is an outlaw to a girl like her. You? — you're just an aunt with a double chin and candies in a bowl. C'mon, you say to her, let's show them how two broads can lift these stones. She rolls her eyes: Is this, like, a wall, she drawls, or some kind of feminist statement?

But she turns out to have a wonderful eye: standing back and eyeing the stone, she picks the exact right one, helps you settle it down in a way so subtle you barely need to use a shim. And after a few weekends she attracts a neighborhood teenager. You don't think they've ever spoken; he just got a whiff and drifted over like a goose gliding on southern winds. He is a silent boy by the name of Smoky.

One cloudy Sunday they're all there, and you're looking for a good corner stone for the next course. Your ex is staring at the stone with his hands on his hips, and his daughter is redoing her ponytail; the boy squats on the ground picking at his chin. Paper cups with limp root beer in them litter the tiny patio. What do you know, you think; it takes a village. A tentative sense of well-being taps at your door like a shy neighbor. The feeling vanishes as quickly as it came. As a person, what do you have to offer, really? You're not funny or fun to be around; you're not a good cook. You don't know the right things to say at the right moment, and you don't have the knack of making people feel good about themselves. You don't know how to keep them with you without some trick up your sleeve. They will leave the moment this project ends. It's not you who draws them, not you at all.

You're in a North Side pub with friends after seeing a drag show. It must be 1972, because it's not long after you got together. You all piled into a car and drove to Chicago, and watched the queens preen and sing while the boys in the audience fiercely assessed their beauty. Now you feel daring and sophisticated, out in the big city. Especially you — why, just five minutes ago you were a housewife fixing supper for your hubby!

Chris is joking about how much this one queen could float her boat. She buries her face behind the laminated menu, then peeks over it at you, her eyes bright. *What're you having, darlin'?* she asks, thrilling you to your toes.

A smile drifts over your face. You're not sure yet, you say, and name some of her favorites.

How perfect you wanted to be at it! You could brook no criticism. It was your art, helping her in ways nobody but she could see. *Let's see,* you'd say in later years, later restaurants, I'm deciding between the pork chops and the sirloin. What do you think? Or more daringly, daring her to lean on your expertise and trust this more sophisticated ruse: Do you know what *you're* having? Because surely she was allowed not to be sure yet; all she had to say was *I'm not sure,* because plenty of literate people are unsure about what they want from the menu. All she had to do was say it, and it would look as though she was intelligently pondering the menu; all she had to do was ask what you're having; and when you completed the conversation by putting some options out there — food that she liked — her handicap would be hidden even more deeply, even more naturally.

Couldn't she see how perfect that would be, to let the secret float the way a body floats, if you'll only let go and trust the water? She could if she wanted, it's just that she just refused to see it. Nobody was ever as stubborn as she was. You'd ask her in front of people if she'd read that story in the *Tribune* yet. Read it *yet*, that's what you'd say, because surely plenty of literate people haven't gotten around to reading the paper yet today. And here you were suggesting that at some future moment you and she would have read and discussed a newspaper story together. You gave her a smoldering look as you spoke, remembering that day in Chicago, when she invited you to dance this dance.

And what would you get? A look of rage and panic that made her look wildly illiterate in front of others, and that made you feel that she was just a stupid person. She couldn't trust that you had something in mind; she thought you were trying to expose her. She demanded why you had to be so cute; she said this wasn't about how clever you are.

What was so wrong with being clever? You really want to know.

God knows the other was no secret at all. That one was like a dark wine birthmark right on your face. Alone in the straight world you were just fine, an ordinary human being to whom people said *Thank you* and *Excuse me*. But at the side of your hairy rugged beast of a butch: if looks could kill, you'd have been moldering in your grave long ago. They knew instantly what you were, and that's all you were, nothing else. Why, during those last years of Vietnam, as far as you're concerned it might have been your own neighborhood that was booby trapped. When the country's not at war, it's hard to remember what it felt like when it was, the way women are supposed to forget the pain of childbirth. But you remember. You plastered American flag stickers all over your car bumper, because back then the very sight of your butch seemed to make men want to ram their cars right into you. One glance, that's all it took in those days, and they puffed up like adders. Secretly, you understood their rage. It seemed as though every living soul in your neighborhood had lost a friend or brother or father, and here your butch was, living another day to screw her girlfriend. You saw the ones who returned on crutches or in wheelchairs in the hardware store, and they'd get a gander at the two of you and their faces would twist with a bitterness that seemed to make your own tongue shrivel in your mouth. They were thinking: *For this?* You felt ashamed. You wondered: What kind of selfishness made you insist that *this* was what you wanted, as though you were so special? In wartime, things get stripped to basics. Do your job, love your country, drop in on a neighbor, pick your kids up from school. That's what everybody was doing while you opened your legs to a grunting he-she wearing a strap-on.

And yet, can you really say you didn't like it? — didn't like being the center of the universe, blown up by this butch who left huge craters in you, the air whistling in?

At work, you've seen a lot of illiterates; you're probably the only one who even recognizes them. You've slid in and made their lives a little easier. *Here, let me fill that out, it'll be quicker, I do it all the time* — all business, not even saying "let me fill that out *for you*," not even looking up to see the relief fly across their faces. You have a gift and it makes you feel good about yourself. You're the only one in your office who can offer that to a patient.

Now, a nicely-dressed Hispanic lady about your age is looking up helplessly from the form and telling you she's forgotten her glasses. And suddenly you believe she thinks you're an idiot and is feeding you a line. You roll your eyes and snatch it from her so you can read it aloud for her and fill in the answers yourself, and then hate yourself as she becomes very very small in the chair across from you, the lines around her mouth showing as she purses her mouth.

You are becoming a loose cannon. The irony is not lost on you: while Chris was in the picture you held it as a secret that wasn't a secret, and things were fine and dandy as long as you didn't push the point. Once in a while somebody would say carefully, Will you be spending the holiday with your friend? Now that she's gone, and the ground around your house is torn up, you look at the slow-moving women around you and want to push their complacent noses in it! Oh you know they've gone through their own trials and tribulations; one's husband has prostate cancer, another has a son who's been in and out of rehab. But sitting at your computer, your aching arms lifted to the keyboard, you are boiling. Who do they think they are?

One day when it's almost quitting time, an old bulldagger comes in to make an appointment. She's hard of hearing and doesn't catch on so quick, and the receptionist speaks sharply to her — a loud bossy "ma'am!" You find yourself bolting out of your chair and snapping *Hey!* — you don't look at her as you knife your shoulder in between her and the computer, calling loudly, your face tilted up so the bull can see your lips, *Let's see what we got here, darlin'.* You take your sweet time with her, making sure the time is written down and handed to her on a card, and that she's picked a butterscotch out of the candy jar. When she's gone, you saunter back to your computer, through silence so absolute it makes your ears pop.

Chris could always see right through their bullshit. She used to say, *Nobody's meaner than a secretary* — and then she'd stagger around, gasping, eyes rolling, trying to reach back for the imaginary knife stuck in her back.

Ha ha, you'd say. *Very funny.*

Your face and shoulders burn in the sun, and you start wearing sunscreen and a floppy gardening hat when you're working. You forget to eat all day, and then make burgers or chops at night, taking cold meat that numbs your fingers, and tossing it into a frying pan. You don't have it in you to bake a potato, or make a salad, so you've been buying apples by the half peck, and that's your dinner: meat and an apple. If you want to add a starch, you eat a piece of bread.

One Monday morning, dressed for work, you're rummaging in

her tool box for the tape measure, which isn't in any of the usual draw-ers. Moving aside a plastic box full of loose screws, you see something strange inside it. You open the box; inside, among the screws, glistens a scattering of gel capsules. The St. John's Wort you bought for her when she was going through withdrawal. You stare at them till they blur into a gummy mass. Blood pounds into your face. How she must have laughed at you! What a fool you were, shopping for them with such a glad and excited heart, getting the gel caps instead of the capsules because they'd be easier to swallow. You handed them to her yourself every morning, with a glass of orange juice; she must have hidden them in her cheek, like a character in a movie about an insane asylum.

You pick up the phone and call in sick. You throw off your work clothes, making a run in your stockings in your haste; you violently ball them up and stuff them in the bathroom wastebasket. You spend the morning in bed watching the morning shows, your nightgown twisting stickily around you, kicking off the covers so your feet can breathe.

You hate her for making a patsy of you, hate yourself for your own bovine steadiness. Everybody has always counted on you, even when you were a child. You know that if you think about all the pain in the world, all the hunger and violence, being called upon to run an orderly home after your mother died hardly measures up. Nobody killed her, so you didn't have to think the world was evil; nobody hit you, or did the unspeakable things that are done to girls every day. And yet, the whole thing put you off family the way that if you get sick from eating some kind of food, you can never eat that food again. Your memories are dreary the way dusk is dreary when it's drizzled all day. In the kitchen of the farmhouse, the morning dim outside the windows, the wet sounds of the dogs wolfing down their food in the mud room, their tags clinking against the bowls. The crackle of gravel as your father pulled away in the pickup while your brother and sister squabbled, and you scrubbed egg yolk off the breakfast dishes, looking out at the bar-ren tree line at the edge of the fields and thinking about the school day to come, where no teacher would think to take an interest in you because you weren't a genius and you weren't a troublemaker.

After school, before homework, you squeezed lemons into lemon-
ade for the farmhands who would come shuffling to the screen door to
say your father said they could have some. The sting of the lemons was
brutal on your fingers because you bit your nails. You'd close your eyes
and imagine you were being tortured, but never let out a sound. Your
captors released you out of sheer respect. Now that you think about it,
those daydreams were a huge feature of your youth, scattered across the
gloomy afternoons like a system of secret caves. In church on Sundays,
where the folks lay their heavy pitying hands on your shoulder and
praised you for being a good girl, you felt the bones of your butt press
into the pew and imagined being flayed. You were captured by many
evil people, and not once did you make a peep. It was as close as you
came to play.

One day you can't find a single stone that fits, and you notice that
you've got the beginnings of a running joint. Standing glumly over the
pile of misfit stone, you resign yourself to start cutting. Your ex says to
let him try it. While you fill in the backfill with a trowel, he sets up a
worktable and lines up stone along the edges, outlines and scores and
chips with consummate patience and care. You watch him with gratitude and admiration. He's a man who knows how to do a job right. The
problem with him was that you came to look like each other, like dogs and
their owners, much too fast. Both tall and thick, with the same color hair
and the same mild expressions on your freckled faces. And here you were,
only in your twenties! He thought he wanted you, but it turns out that what
he wanted was a woman he'd have to walk on eggshells with, one who would
make him bend toward her so she could whisper her commands into his
hungry ear.

And what does it turn out you wanted?

To cry out. To be fucked and goaded and cradled till a cry lurched out
of your throat like a creature from a lagoon.

The truth is, that isn't what you want anymore; in fact, it seems a little silly. At this point in your life, a nice pat on the shoulder as you fall

asleep will do just fine. But Chris still loves to crank up the drama, to show she still can. That's why she storms out, and why she pushes the envelope.

The sky is bright blue today instead of white, a child's crayon drawing of a sky. He's got his transistor out here in the yard, and they're playing a Springsteen ballad. You sink back on your heels listening to the song's regretful chords.

Keith stops chipping and steps back. You rise to take a look, and the two of you stand with your hands on your hips staring at the space he's trying to fit the stone in. You take off the gardening hat, gather your damp hair in one hand and sweep it back. Just then, a motion by the house steals your attention, and you see her face peering out the back door. She is squinting, or scowling. She opens the door and steps out, her figure darkened by a shadow passing over the house. The change of light brings a memory: Chris hearing The Boss on the radio for the first time, at the kitchen table back in the Clyde Ave. house, her hand freezing as she brought a beer bottle to her lips. You forget which song it was, but you remember that stilled hand, and her eyes growing round as saucers. And you remember thinking, for the first time but not the last, how pleasure always came to her as a surprise.

The dog slips past her and trots over to the bushes. You toss the trowel to the ground and peel the gloves off your sweaty fingers. Keith turns and notices her, nods a sober hello. She comes down the steps and stands beside you scrutinizing the work you've been doing, as you scan for signs of displeasure or drug use. Her hair is shaggy, her face unreadable.

You reach up to her neck to smooth a crinkle from her collar. *Hello stranger, you say.*

416

ACKNOWLEDGMENTS

My warmest thanks to:

Elizabeth Tocci at The Patch, Calumet City, and Beth Hook from Integrity Builders, Amherst, MA, for generous and informative conversation.

Literacy Volunteers of America, Illinois, for training me, and Rhonda Storball, for inspiring me in more ways than one.

The Astraea Foundation, for timely financial support.

Karen Oosterhous, for her enthusiasm for the novel, and for helping to make it more disciplined.

Emily Shelton, for the conversations, over Greek food, that got me started; Michèle Barale, Lisa Beskin, Anston Bosman, Paula David, Tom DiPiero, Fred Errington, Marjorie Frank, Tony Frank, Deborah Gewertz, Daniel Hall, Jennifer Higgins, Suvir Kaul, Rebecca Leopold, Roland Merullo, Claire Messud, Catherine Newman, Andrew Parker, Cindy Patton, Paul Statt, Susan Stinson, and Melissa Zeiger, for diverse and wonderful forms of encouragement along the way.

Amy Kaplan, Mary Renda, Karen Sánchez-Eppler, and Elizabeth Young, for bringing to earlier drafts their imaginative sympathy and prodigious critical skill.

Leslie Feinberg, for writing *Stone Butch Blues.*

And finally, Elizabeth Garland, who — in fiction and in life — looks at clumsy, rudimentary first drafts, and imagines with me their ideal form.

READER'S GUIDE:
QUESTIONS FOR DISCUSSION

1) What is the significance of the title? Who do you think the crybaby butch is? In what sense is this a novel about crying? What things are mourned by the characters in the novel?

2) Why does Anna react so strongly to the sight of Chris in her bedroom, in detox? And to Monica, when she says, after Anna has related the story about almost being swept out to sea as a child, "I would have saved you"? How does this novel, which opens with two characters watching *Rescue 911*, raise questions about people's capacity to save others?

3) The opening epigraph, by Chang-Rae Lee, concludes "There is something universally chilling about a new plot." What does Lee mean? How does that idea relate to the act of reading in *Crybaby Butch*? Does it agree with your experience of reading a story or novel for the first time? What elements of reading that experienced readers take for granted are brought out by the novel?

4) Is Anna a good teacher? What are her strengths and weaknesses? Why does Chris feel Dennis to be an effective teacher, while she has trouble tolerating Anna? Does the novel portray something about the experience of teaching that you hadn't thought of before?

5) One of the central actions of the novel is Anna's giving Chris a copy of *Stone Butch Blues*. What is the importance of Leslie Feinberg's novel

in *Crybaby Butch*? How does Judith Frank use it to engage with the history of butch/femme in the U.S.? What do you think Anna is trying to tell Chris by giving it to her? What are some of the ways Chris responds to the novel — as a new reader, a student, a butch? Why does Chris respond in the ways she does?

6) At one point in the novel, thinking about how embarrassed she feels when Star calls her a woman, Anna wonders uncomfortably "whether all butches were as misogynist as she was." And Chris, ruminating on her past with Gladys, thinks, "Gladys had just been what?—a dingbat femme who wanted to paint the ceiling of the bar black with the solar system on it, or have Heavy Petting Night, where everybody would bring their pets, and they'd dress them up and give them prizes." The butches in Chris' first bar shock her by calling her first girlfriend "Killer pussy." What do you think of the denigration of femmes, or women, by these butch characters? Is it compatible with a feminist worldview?

7) What do you make of Star's accusation, when Anna breaks up with her, that sex with Anna was like rape? What does Anna hear in that accusation, and how does it echo the line in Chapter 1: "If you weren't an awfully lucky butch you might be a criminal?" Do you think that Star's accusation is true? What are the connections in this novel between power and pleasure, and between power and violence?

8) In a novel about the possibilities of upward mobility, Chris Rinaldi is a character who has refused to benefit from her family's rise to the middle class. What investment does she have in her working-class status? Why might she be ambivalent about the upward mobility that literacy might bring? How is her allegiance to her class status connected to her gender identity?